THE END OF ORDINARY

Also by Edward Ashton

Three Days in April

THE END OF ORDINARY

A Novel

EDWARD ASHTON

HARPER
VOYAGER
IMPULSE

An Imprint of HarperCollinsPublishers

Excerpt from *Three Days in April* copyright © 2015 by Edward Ashton.

Digital Edition JUNE 2017 ISBN: 978-0-06-269031-9
Print Edition ISBN: 978-0-06-269032-6

Cover design by Nadine Badalaty.
Cover illustration © Shutterstock.

Harper Voyager, the Harper Voyager logo, and Harper Voyager Impulse are trademarks of HarperCollins Publishers.
HarperCollins is a registered trademark of HarperCollins Publishers in the United States of America and other countries.

FIRST EDITION

17 18 19 20 21   HDC   10 9 8 7 6 5 4 3 2 1

For Trey. RIP, my brother.

1. IN WHICH DREW LEARNS
A HARD TRUTH.

I first realized I'd lost my grasp on Hannah the summer she turned fourteen—the summer of Dragon-Corn, when pretty much everything I'd been building spun out of my control. This was six years after the AIs wiped out Hagerstown, five years after the final, bloody end of the Stupid War, on a Saturday morning at the ass end of June. The sun was just over the trees in the backyard, hot and bright in a clear blue sky, and the air was thick and damp and already smelling like a sticky, sweat-drenched afternoon. I was playing with my simulator, splicing avian genes into a rodent framework—cut the external ears, turn the fur into feathers, stretch out the forelegs and hollow the bones—with the vague idea of testing whether my father had been right in saying that pigeons are really nothing but flying rats, when Kara told me to get up off my backside and take my daughter for a run.

"Make her work," she said. "She has no idea what's coming this fall, and she's not taking it seriously. Embarrass her a little now, and maybe she won't get humiliated later."

I gave her a loud, theatrical sigh.

"Really, Kara? I'm kind of busy here."

This wasn't, strictly speaking, true. I should have been busy, but I was working really hard to avoid recognizing that the first full GeneMod development project that I'd been tasked with leading was spinning off the rails. The simulator was displaying a wireframe of the thing I'd created. A blinking red icon in the corner of the screen let me know that my baby was not, in fact, biologically viable.

"Yeah," she said. "I can see that. Is there a big, untapped market out there for rat-birds?"

I rolled my chair back, spun to face her, and folded my arms across my chest.

"Define *big*."

She showed me her teeth then, but I'm not sure you could call it a smile.

"I've got a better idea, Drew. How about if I use it in a sentence? If you don't get up right now and take your daughter for a run, I will shove something *big* up your ass—and not in a friendly way."

I rolled a little further away from her.

"How do you know this isn't mission-critical work?"

I said. "That rat-bird might be part of DragonCorn. My team might be waiting for my sim results right now."

Kara's eyes narrowed, and I suddenly felt like a rabbit under the shadow of a hawk. Discretion is the better part of valor, right? I stood slowly, patted Kara on the shoulder, and walked down the hallway to the bottom of the stairs.

"Hannah!" I called. "Get dressed. We're going for a run."

We lived in Upstate New York then, in an old farmhouse just inside the Monroe county line. The heart of the structure was built in 1910, but it had grown like an anthill over the years. When I first saw it, I could barely find the outline of the main house. The interior was a maze of rooms opening onto rooms, with spiral staircases and hallways, bathrooms and bedrooms and solariums in a random-seeming jumble. It reminded me of the haunted mansions I'd read about as a child, and I fell in love instantly.

Kara was pregnant with Hannah when we bought the place, and she stayed with her mother on Long Island for six months while I had workmen crawling over and under and through the house, stripping out lead paint and lead pipes and asbestos, pulling up years of carpet over linoleum over warped pine boards, ripping the place down to its twelve-by-twelve oaken bones before building it back up with EMP-shielded power conduits and green insulation and solar shingles. I even had them put in a minimum-profile windmill in what used to be a soy-bean field, hooked up to a hydrogen generator and a high-capacity fuel cell.

By the time they were done, we had an off-the-grid castle that hardly looked different from the outside than it had when I bought it—which, if you're one of the new aristocracy who doesn't want to wind up on the gallows when the peasantry has had enough of your shit, is exactly what you're looking for.

Of course, if anyone had realized exactly how much of what went down that autumn was my fault, all the off-the-gridness in the world wouldn't have saved me from a lynch mob. This was still June, though. Nobody had any idea yet what was coming.

Hannah sat sullen in the backseat as we drove to the Holland Road Nature Preserve. I'd practically had to stuff her into her running gear and carry her to the car. Kara was right. She was lazy, and she had no idea how hard the start of cross-country season was going to hit her.

"You know," I said. "We're not doing this as a favor to me. I've already had my running career. This is for you."

"Yeah," she said. "I've heard about your career, Dad. About a million times, I've heard about your career. If your career was so great, why are you con-stantly obsessing about mine?"

I sighed, glanced up and caught a glimpse of her

in the rearview mirror. She was glaring at me, pale blue eyes peeking out from under just a hint of a brow ridge. I'd done my best to get rid of that, but a bit of it snuck in with the *H. erectus* genes I'd used to tweak her lung capacity and limb proportions. She always wore bangs, so it wasn't usually noticeable. When she was angry, though, she tended to tuck her chin, and her eyes seemed to sink back into her head until they almost disappeared.

"Look," I said. "If you really don't want to do this, we can turn around. But the fact is, in two months you're going to be training with some of the best runners in New York, and most of them will be two or three years older than you are. If you don't put the hay in the barn now, it won't be there when you need it."

"That's another thing," she said. "What is it with you and hay? Gotta put the hay in the barn, Hannah. You're gonna need that hay, Hannah. How's your hay supply, Hannah?"

I rolled my eyes.

"I've never asked you about your hay supply."

"Maybe not in those words, Dad, but you're all about the hay."

I slowed, gave a quick look around, and turned onto County Line Road.

"It's a metaphor, Hannah. That means that when I say 'hay,' what I really mean is—"

She cut me off with a groan.

"Yeah, Dad. I know what a metaphor is."

"Right. So, hay in this case is a metaphor for your training base."

"I don't think so," she said. "I think it's a fat joke. I think you're calling me a cow."

My stomach knotted.

"What? Hannah, no! I would never . . ."

But I caught her eye again in the mirror, and she was smiling.

"I do not think you're a cow, Hannah."

Her smile faded a bit.

"I know, Dad. Cows can't run."

I turned right onto Holland Road, and then a half mile later pulled into the gravel parking lot at the nature preserve trailhead. This place was one of the things that had attracted me to the area—a dozen square miles of trees and hills, bounded by Holland Road on one side and the old canal bed on the other, and winding through it, thirty miles or more of meticulously graded and maintained hiking trails.

The trails were color coded and blazed, with signposts at almost every intersection, and there was a four-foot-square map at the trailhead showing the length of each individual segment. With a few minutes' thinking, you could lay out pretty much any sort of workout you wanted, and all you had to remember were the colors of the trails—green to blue to red to orange to green.

Hannah stretched her calves and hamstrings while I studied the map. I grew up in West Virginia, and when I ran in college I prided myself on being able to break the other runners on the hills. The nature preserve had three brutal, tight-packed climbs along the red trail. I called Hannah over, and showed her where I wanted to go.

"I don't care," she said. "I'm just gonna follow you."

"No," I said. "I want you to look at this. You need to know the course, in case we get separated."

She looked up at me, eyes wide.

"Separated, Dad? Why ever would we get separated?"

"Well, we wouldn't, of course, but . . ."

She held up one hand.

"Whatever, Dad. I've got it. Green-brown-red-white-blue-green. Let's go."

We started out at a comfortable pace. The trail was wide enough for us to run together, and Hannah matched me stride for stride. There's nothing quite like the feeling of running, as long as you're in good shape and nothing is hurting. I relaxed into the easy rhythm of breathing and footfalls, and let the trail roll by beneath me.

Here's a story for you. The summer she turned two, we took Hannah to the beach. It was a perfect day, hot and clear, with an offshore breeze kicking up sharp little whitecaps on three-foot swells. Kara and I took her in shifts, one of us in the water, the other watching her dig in the sand.

After an hour or so, Hannah started getting cranky, and Kara told me to take her into the ocean. I carried her out twenty or thirty feet, to where the swells were riding up my thighs, knelt down and dipped her into the water, let her kick her feet a bit and cool off. Then Kara waved to me, held up her phone, motioned for me to stand for a picture. I picked Hannah up, held her face next to mine and waved. Kara raised the phone. I smiled. I just had time to see Kara's mouth open in a scream when a breaker hit me from behind like a runaway bus, lifted me off my feet, and flipped me forward. My arms flailed as I spun around. I tucked my chin, and hit the sand hard on the back of my neck. There was a moment of fuzzy numbness. I reached out.

Hannah was gone.

I struggled to my feet as the wave rolled back out, my heart pounding like a jackhammer in my chest. Kara was running toward me and I spun once around, searching . . .

And there, drifting past me on the tide, was a fan of blonde hair. I dove for her, snatched her up out of the water, and held her face to mine. Her eyes were wide open, and she was laughing.

Ever since that day at the beach, I've dreamed of losing her. Sometimes it's in the forest. We're hiking together, talking and laughing, and suddenly she's gone. I crash through the trees calling for her, knowing that something has taken her, that if I don't find her soon, it'll be too late. Sometimes it's in the city, in the subway or one of the abandoned neighborhoods. I always wake up soaked in sweat and panting.

I never find her.

Two miles into our run, we turned onto the red trail. A hundred yards later, we started up the first steep climb. I jumped the pace for twenty strides. Hannah dropped a step or two back, then slowly pulled even. I pushed a little harder. My breath was coming ragged as we crested the hill, but it eased up as I relaxed into the descent.

The trail bottomed out into fifty or sixty yards of winding flat before climbing again. Hannah was a stride or two behind as we started up, and I figured that if I was going to break her, this was the time. I tucked my chin and pushed. Oxygen debt came quicker this time, and when I glanced back, Hannah was right behind me.

"You're trying to ditch me," she said. I didn't have the wind to reply. She pulled even with me, ran beside me for a couple of strides. "Well you know what? I think you're mean."

With that, she accelerated past me, crested the hill, and disappeared.

I expected her to slow down once she'd proved her point. She did not. I saw her from the top of the hill, and just for a second as I started up the third big climb a minute or so later. After that, she was gone. I tried to pick it up again on the long, flat stretch where the white trail turned into the blue, but it was hopeless. The longer I went without seeing her, the more I felt like I'd fallen into one of my nightmares.

Toward the end of the blue trail there was a three- or four-hundred-yard stretch that curved through an open field. I was sure I'd see Hannah ahead of me when I cleared the trees, but there was nothing the whole way around but waist-high grass. There was no way she could have gotten that far ahead of me. Either she was lost, or . . .

I pushed the pace as hard as I could. Fear and fatigue twisted in my belly as I imagined all the things that could happen to a pretty blonde girl in the woods. There weren't any animals of any consequence in the nature preserve, but there had been other cars in the parking lot. I pictured Hannah dragged off into the woods, molested by degenerates, murdered by a sociopath, kidnapped by some UnAltered bastard who knew she was the daughter of a Bioteka engineer. I called her name twice, but there was no answer.

The last stretch twisted through dense woods, and the trail was broken up everywhere by roots and rocks. I was almost sprinting, my chest heaving, my eyes watering until I could barely see the trail. I stumbled once, and fell forward, flailing, until I caught myself hard up against the broad trunk of an oak . . .

And there was Hannah, walking back down the trail toward me, grinning.

"Hey there, Dad," she said. "Where have you been? Did you get lost or something?"

We didn't talk much on the ride home. Hannah wore a smug smile, and I was still shaking too badly to trust my voice. She'd just run five miles in under twenty-eight minutes, barely breaking a sweat. It was going to be an interesting year.

2. IN WHICH HANNAH REVEALS ONE SECRET, AND PART OF ANOTHER.

I first realized that my father was an idiot the summer I turned fourteen. He and Mom had been bugging me about running ever since the end of spring track—not in the crazy, tiger-mom way some kids' parents rode them about their grades or music or whatever, but in a mopey, we-hate-to-see-you-wasting-your-potential way that I sometimes thought was even worse. I mean, I'd been running. I had a little loop that went out to County Line Road, down to Plank, and then back up to the house on a private road through the farm fields. It was about four miles, and I ran it three or four times a week, not at a crazy pace, but fast enough to feel the wind in my hair. I knew it wasn't exactly Olympic-level training, but I was fourteen years old, right?

That didn't seem to register with my parents,

though. I'd be starting at the Briarwood School in the fall. Briarwood was a smallish private school about halfway between Rochester and Syracuse. Their academic programs were kind of crappy, the faculty was known to harbor more than a few UnAltered sympathizers, there were rumors that the whole place was under low-key NatSec surveillance, and the campus looked more like a minimum-security prison than a prep school. Their distance-running program, though, was the best in the state. Their coach was a three-time Olympian, and kids came from all over the Northeast to run for him. He had a streak going back I don't know how many years of having every one of his varsity runners earn an athletic scholarship. Dad wanted me on the Briarwood varsity cross-country team, and he wanted me there as a freshman.

Not because we needed the scholarship money. Because I was his science project. You see?

So, one Saturday near the end of June, Dad dragged me out to the nature preserve to teach me a lesson about the importance of hard work and diligent training and blah blah blah. He picked out a five-mile course, and made me memorize it "just in case we get separated." I knew exactly what he was planning, of course. I'd heard Mom putting him up to it before we left the house. I was pretty mad at first, but when I saw the course he'd picked out I got much, much happier.

The thing you have to understand about my dad is that he's not actually bad, and he's not actually stupid . . . but he does have this weird combination of the two that sometimes makes him do bad, stupid things.

Things like trying to ditch his fourteen-year-old daughter in the middle of the woods, for example.

I ran along beside him for the first two miles. He wasn't pushing too hard, and I was starting to think maybe we were just gonna have a nice run. Then we turned onto the red trail, and he tried to drop me on the first hill. I paced him up that one and down to the next flat. When he tried again on the second climb, I called him on it, and I went.

Growing up, I heard a lot of stories about what a great hill runner Dad was, about how growing up in the flatlands had made me squishy and weak. He actually was better on the hills than he was on the flats, and I had to put on pretty close to a full sprint to get away from him. There's no way I could have held that pace for the next three miles.

Luckily, I didn't have to.

I pushed up and over the second hill, down the back side, and up the third. By the time I topped that one I was gasping, and my legs were starting to shake. As soon as I cleared the crest, I ducked off the trail and into the trees, crouched down and focused on quieting my breathing. Soon enough, Dad came pounding down the trail, looking as bad as I felt. I waited until he was a hundred yards or so ahead, then crept back out of the trees and followed him.

The thing I'd noticed when Dad showed me the course at the trailhead was that right where the white trail turned onto the blue, the green trail curled by in the other direction, just a few dozen yards away. Thirty seconds of bushwhacking, and I'd cut a mile and a half off the course. I jogged the rest of the way out to the parking lot, hung around there for three or four minutes, and then went strolling back down the trail until I ran into him coming the other way. The look on his face when he saw me is something that I will treasure for the rest of my life.

I never told Dad what I did to him that day. That wasn't the last time we ran together, but it was definitely the last time he tried to dust me. I'd gotten the point, though. As the summer wore on, I did start running farther and faster. By the start of August I was putting in twenty-five or so miles a week, mixing in some sprints and pace work here and there.

Dad thought I was doing a lot more. He'd send me out for a long run, and when I came back an hour and a half later, he thought I'd done eleven or twelve miles. I hadn't, though. The reason those workouts took me so long was because of the other thing I never told Dad about. That was the summer I met my first real crush.

His name was Jordan. I first saw him in the parking lot of the nature preserve. I was just locking my bike to the trailhead sign when he came tearing out on the green trail, across the lot, and back into the woods on the blue. He was tall and pale and thin, with legs cut like an anatomy poster and long black hair pulled back into a ponytail.

He was pretty enough, I guess. The thing that fascinated me, though, was the way he moved.

I'd spent a lot of time studying the way unmodified *Homo saps* lumbered through their lives, shambling around with their pigeon toes and their pudgy bellies, licking ice-cream cones and drinking frappuccinos out of giant travel mugs. They were clumsy, they were slow—even the ones like my dad, who'd honestly been a pretty serious athlete back in the day, mostly waddled around like something wasn't hooked up quite right between their bodies and their brains. I'd gotten to the point where I could usually pick out the Engineered just by watching them walk.

Jordan wasn't Engineered. I could see that pretty quickly. That didn't seem to matter as far as running went, though. Engineered or no, Jordan could fly. He was his own little subspecies.

After that first encounter, I pretty much cut out the road running, and started riding to the nature preserve almost every day. It turned out that Jordan had a steady routine. Almost every day I'd see him zipping across the parking lot right around nine—out on the green, in on the blue. For about two seconds on that first day, I thought about just trying to run with him—you know, I'd sort of fall in beside him, like we were randomly going the same way. *Hey. I'm Hannah. You're a runner too, huh?* Only two seconds, though, because even at fourteen I could see that would be awkward verging on creepy.

Also, much as I hated to admit it, there was no way I would have been able to hang with him. When I thought about trying, I got a quick mental image of me sprinting along beside him for a half mile, opening my mouth to say something witty, and barfing on his shoes. So, I decided to go with a slightly less awkward but definitely much creepier approach. I started leaving bottles of lemonade from the Plank Road farm stand on the hood of his car.

It took me about a week to figure out that the crazy-hot black sports car that was always in the lot when he was there belonged to him. I left a note the first time—*You looked thirsty:)*—so he'd know I wasn't using his hood as a trash can. After that, I just left the bottles and went for my run. The car was always gone when I finished.

Until it wasn't, that is.

"So," Dad said. "Where'd you go?"

I was stretching on the floor of my solarium, a glass-walled room on the second floor of the house that looked out on the overgrown fields where someone probably used to grow soybeans, but my parents just grew weeds.

"You know," I said. "Around."

I was working on my hamstrings, legs spread in front of me, arms reaching forward. Dad sat down across from me. Little beads of sweat were already forming on his forehead. Mom kept the rest of the house subarctic all summer, but my solarium was always steamy.

"You were gone for a while," he said. "How far did you go?"

"Don't know," I said. I wrapped my hands around my left foot and pulled my nose down to my knee. "I wasn't carrying my phone."

"Come on," he said. "You know you need to be logging your miles, right?"

I sat up, rolled my neck around, and reached out for my right foot.

"You know I love running," I said. "Right?"

"Of course," he said. "That's why we do it."

"Yeah," I said. "I love the quiet. I love the rhythm. I love the feel of the wind in my hair." I sat up again, pulled one knee to my chest, and twisted around to look at the far wall. "You know what I don't love, though?"

He gave me a half smile.

"Logging your miles?"

"Yes, Dad. Logging my miles. Also hay. I cannot stand hay."

He laughed.

"I'll bear that in mind. Try to keep track, though, okay? Coach Doyle is going to expect you to show up for your first workout in shape and ready to go."

I switched legs, and twisted the other way.

"Got it, Dad. I'll see what I can do."

I didn't, though. All that summer, I made excuses for why I couldn't take my phone with me on my runs. I forgot. My battery died. The wristband made my arm sweaty. The truth, of course, was that I didn't want Dad to be able to track where I was going every day, and how little I was actually running. It wasn't that I didn't care about the season, or Coach Doyle, or filling up my hayloft. I just felt like running was something I should *do*, not something I should think about.

Also, of course, there was Jordan.

On a brutally hot Sunday morning near the end of July, I came out of the woods to see that beautiful black car alone in the parking lot. I pulled up short. My lemonade was gone, so he'd clearly been through, but . . .

"Hey. You're the lemonade girl, right?"

I spun around, heart pounding. He was sitting on a rock at the edge of the trees, stretching.

"Uh . . ."

He smiled and stood. That's when I first thought

of the whole *Homo Jordanus* thing. He didn't roll over onto his knees to stand, or push himself up with his hands. He just sort of rippled from one position to the other with what looked like no effort at all.

"Thanks," he said. "I mean, really. I love lemonade. I hate feeling like a charity case, though. What do you think—would one nice brunch square us up?"

And I thought, *What would* Dad *say?* Stay focused, Hannah. Eyes on the prize, Hannah. Don't forget about your hay supply, Hannah.

Don't talk to the unmodified, Hannah.

"Yeah," I said. "That sounds about right."

His smile turned into a grin.

"**S**o," Jordan said. "What's your story?"

We were sitting across from each other in a booth at the Nine Mile Diner, sipping iced tea and waiting for our waffles.

"I'm not sure," I said. "I'm not even sure I have one."

"Sure you do," he said. "Everyone's got a story."

I looked up at him.

"Okay. So what's yours?"

He gave me a lazy grin and shook his head.

"Sorry, lemonade girl. I asked first."

I looked away, pushed my hair back from my forehead and then shook my bangs down into my eyes. When I looked back, he was staring at me, his eyebrows slightly knitted. If you haven't hung around with a lot of custom-job Engineered, faces like mine tend to fall into the uncanny valley—different enough from a *Homo sap*'s to ring some alarm bells, but not different enough that you can put your finger on exactly what's wrong. I locked eyes with him, and gave him my best under-the-brow-ridge glare. He held my gaze, smile firmly in place.

"Fine," I said. "Here's my story. On my ninth birthday, my mom took me down to the city to see a Broadway show, visit Times Square, and do all the touristy things that people who actually live there never, ever do. This was just after the end of the Stupid War, so that was kind of a moronic thing to do, but my mom always felt like she was a woman of the people, you know? Between lunch and the start of the show we went to the Museum of Natural History, because Mom used to go there when she was a little girl, and she really loved the giant whale. So we saw that, and the big stuffed elephant in the front hall, and the lions and the giant squids and the dinosaurs.

"And then we saw the cavemen. Mom didn't want me to go in that room, but I pulled my hand away from hers, and I went anyway. I walked right up to one of the dioramas, put my hands against the glass. There was a boy there, maybe a year or two older than me. He looked at the cavemen, and he looked at me, and he said 'Hey, how did you get out?'"

Jordan reached over, brushed my hair back from

my forehead, and ran his thumb along the ridge over my left eye. I closed my eyes and let him do it.

"So," he said. "Did you punch him?"

I laughed.

"No, I just stared at him until he got uncomfortable and wandered away."

"That's too bad," he said. "Sounds like he deserved worse."

I shrugged.

"Maybe. But like I said, this was right after the Stupid War. Things were still pretty tense between the Engineered and the . . ." I looked up at him. ". . . and everyone else. My mom would have killed me if I'd started a riot."

He took a sip of tea. His left arm was slung across the back of the bench. I'd never seen someone so . . . *comfortable* with himself.

"So what about you?" I said. "That was my story. What's yours?"

"Me?" Jordan said. "I don't have a story."

I could feel my face twisting into a scowl. Jordan burst out laughing.

"Sorry," he said. "I couldn't resist. I really don't have one as good as yours, though. My dad's a VP at GeneCraft. I don't see him much, but he buys me things. My mom likes it better in Europe. I don't see a ton of her either. I guess I could tell you that I'm starved for love and all, but the fact is that I'm not.

I like things this way. I've got a surprising amount of . . . independence."

"Yeah," I said. "I get that. My parents monitor pretty much every minute of my life. I wouldn't mind if they headed off to Europe every now and then."

He leaned forward then, covered my hand with his, and said, "Don't worry, Hannah. Soon enough . . ."

That's when I kissed him.

It was my first kiss. I mostly missed his mouth, and I realized later that I'd given myself a little bit of a bloody lip on one of his front teeth. It probably lasted less than a second, but it felt like forever. When it was over, I sat back and looked up at him. He was laughing.

"Oh, God," I said. "I'm sorry. That was . . ."

"No," he said, and shook his head. He was still holding my hand. "It's fine. I'm flattered, honestly, and I would totally have kissed you back if it weren't for three critical facts that you had no way of knowing."

I pulled my hand away, and used it to cover my face.

"Really?" I said. "Is the first one that I'm disgusting?"

He laughed again.

"No, Hannah. The first one is that I'm definitely too old for you, despite my boyish good looks. The second is that I'm guessing you'll be running at Briarwood this fall, right? That makes me one of your captains, and Coach Doyle takes a very dim view of fraternization."

"Okay," I said. "Those both make sense. What's number three?"

He sighed.

"Number three is that my boyfriend gets really, really jealous."

3. IN WHICH JORDAN INTRODUCES HIMSELF.

I wasn't exactly sure what to make of Hannah the first time I saw her. I could tell she was Engineered, of course. Even without that brow ridge, everything was just a hair off with her—legs too long, chest too deep, hips too narrow. It wasn't bad. I mean, she wasn't like the Engineered basketball players or wrestlers. I don't know where they were getting the genes that they cut those guys with, but I'd be willing to bet that it wasn't from anything human. Half of them looked like they'd grow fur if they didn't shave every day.

Hannah was different. She was definitely human—just more so.

We did a unit on classical philosophers that fall

in Humanities II. Most of it was just noise to me, to be honest, but there was a bit about Plato's Cave that stuck with me. The idea was that everything we see here on Earth is really just like a shadow cast on a wall. Every cat is just a shadow of the perfect cat. Maybe one gets the whiskers right, but he's got a crooked tail. Another one has a great tail, but his claws aren't quite right. If we look at enough cats, though, we can start to get an idea of what the real thing, the thing casting the shadows, must be like.

Hannah was the real thing.

The running was part of it. I read once that long-distance running is the only sport where humans aren't just embarrassing themselves in front of the other animals. Take leaping, for example. I've seen ball players who could pretty much dunk their own heads if they wanted to. A jaguar, though . . . I once saw vid of one of those guys leaping fifteen feet straight up into a tree *with an antelope in his mouth*.

Long-distance running—that's the one thing we really do well. Make the race long enough, and a human can outrun a horse.

Well, not just any human, of course. My mom couldn't outrun a horse. Not unless it was a fat, diabetic, chain-smoking horse, anyway. Me, though? I hadn't lost a race at any distance since I was fifteen. I'd have crushed one of those hay munchers without breaking a sweat. And Hannah? Well, she was just a kid. Still, after watching her stride, I wouldn't have bet against her.

Poor Tara. She'd been chomping at the bit to take over the number-one position on the girls' team for two years. I couldn't wait to see the look on her face when Hannah showed up to our first summer practice.

4. IN WHICH DREW BEGINS TO SUSPECT THAT HE MAY HAVE BEEN MISLED.

On a blazing-hot Saturday morning near the end of August, I drove Hannah thirty-some miles to the Briarwood School for her first cross-country practice. I remembered first practices from my high-school and college days as relaxed long runs, getting to know each other, laying down a distance base. Coach Doyle didn't work that way. He started every season with a five-mile time trial, a mock race run on a hilly course laid out through the woods around the school. Hannah was not amused.

"This is stupid," she said as we pulled into the students' lot. "Why should we run a time trial before we've even started practicing?"

"Motivation," I said. "You're more likely to put in

the work over the summer if you know you're going to have to show what you've got in the bank on the first day out."

"Bank?" she said. "Don't you mean hayloft?"

I sighed and cut the power.

"Whatever. You know what I mean."

I got out of the car. I was sweating before I could get the door closed. Hannah hadn't moved. I walked around to the passenger side, waited for a minute, then knocked on her window.

"Hey," I said. "Are you coming?"

She opened the door and climbed out. She looked like she was about to throw up.

"Hannah? Are you okay?"

She shook her head.

"I don't know, Dad. It's really hot. Do I seriously have to do this?"

I stared at her.

"Really? Hannah, you've known this was coming all summer, and it's not any hotter than it's been for the last month and a half. Are you sick?"

"No," she said. "I'm fine. Let's just get it over with."

She picked up her water bottle, slammed the car door, and slouched off toward the soccer field. I followed a few steps behind. I'd never seen Hannah nervous before. I wasn't sure whether to be more worried or amused.

The team was gathered at the edge of the school grounds—fifteen boys and fourteen girls sitting in a circle in the grass, with Coach Doyle at the center. Doyle was younger than I'd imagined, short and light-bodied, with a shaved head covered in fine red stubble, and a face like an angry ferret. He walked slowly around the circle, crouching down to speak to a runner here or there, then standing and using his hands to wipe the sweat from his face. Hannah sat down at the edge of the group, took a long pull on her water bottle, and started stretching. Doyle stopped and watched her for a moment, but moved on without speaking.

"Which one's yours?"

I turned. A smiling woman stood behind me, her face hidden behind gigantic mirrored shades. Too young to be a parent, and she was dressed almost like one of the runners, in short Lycra tights and a form-fitting tech shirt. Assistant coach, maybe? I pointed toward the runners.

"The blonde girl, off to the right," I said. "The one who just sat down."

She took a step forward, her shoulder almost brushing mine.

"Is she a freshman?"

"Yeah," I said. "She's excited to get started. She's been running seriously for a few years now, but this will be a big step up from what she's been doing."

She laughed then, and not in a kind way.

"Oh," she said. "I'd say so. Briarwood is the most intensive running program in the Northeast. Are you sure your girl's ready for what Coach Doyle is going to expect from her?"

I turned to look at her. White-blonde hair, features symmetrical to the micrometer, skin flawless and unlined—I needed to see her eyes to be sure, but I was 90 percent confident she had some variant of the Pretty package. Not Bioteka's standard, though. The hair color was a shade off, and the bust-to-waist ratio was a bit too low. I was trying to remember what the GeneCraft standard cup sizes were when she cleared her throat.

"Sorry," I said. "What?"

"Well," she said. "I was asking whether you thought your daughter was ready for Doyle's meat grinder. But would you rather talk about my breasts?"

My eyes snapped back up to her face.

"Sorry," I said. "I was just . . . uh . . ." I couldn't really say that I was trying to figure out which company had built her, could I?

She laughed again, with a bit more warmth this time.

"It's okay," she said. "I quit getting upset about being ogled right around the day I turned forty."

"Oh no," I said. "I wasn't . . ."

She patted my shoulder.

"Sure you were. And even if you weren't, I'd like to pretend that you were." She held out her hand. "I'm Bree Carson. My daughter is Tara. She's the other blonde, halfway around the circle from yours. She's a junior."

We shook.

"Drew Bergen," I said. "My daughter's name is Hannah."

Her eyebrows knitted. *Watch it*, I thought. *Don't want to wrinkle up that perfect skin*. The fact that she had a kid on the team clarified why I couldn't figure out what mod package she had. She was probably ten years too old for even the first GeneCraft standard Pretty set. Whatever mods she had, they were like Hannah's—custom-engineered, just for her.

"Hannah Bergen," she said. "Why is that name familiar?"

That was my cue to smile.

"Hannah set some age-group records on the track last spring. One of the local sports feeds did a feature on her at the beginning of the summer. Next big thing, you know?"

"Right," she said. "Tara saw that. She mentioned it to me, asked if I thought Hannah would end up with Doyle this fall."

"And here she is."

"And here she is. Which brings me back to my original question. Do you think she's ready? Coach Doyle has a reputation, you know."

I shrugged.

"Hannah's a tough kid. She's got wheels, and she's been working like a dog this summer. I think she'll be okay."

She touched my arm and smiled again.

"I'm sure she will. I'll be cheering for her this morning. As long as she doesn't beat Tara, that is!"

She gave a nervous little laugh then. The runners were getting to their feet.

It was another half hour or more before they really got started. Doyle gave a little welcome speech, then ran them through a dynamic warm-up routine that looked pretty similar to what I remembered from back in the day. Bree and I chatted on and off while we waited, huddling in the shade of a leafy old oak at the edge of the field. We were the only two parents who'd stayed to watch. I spent most of the time trying to figure out a way to steer the conversation around to her mods. I was dying to know exactly what tweaks she had, and how she'd managed to get them.

Non-therapeutic genetic modification had only been legal in most of the United States for about thirty years, so I was assuming that Bree's parents must have either gotten a medical exemption, or traveled abroad when they put her together. So, if it was a medical exemption, was it legitimate? A surprising number of docs lost their licenses around the time I was born for taking money from parents who wanted fake certifications of potential genetic illness, so that they could slip in other mods with the fixes. On the other hand, if they went out of the country, where to? Qatar was the first place to really cash in on wealthy Americans who wanted mods for their kids that the US government wouldn't allow, but the cutters there quickly developed a reputation for making monsters. The Koreans were just ramping up their genetic-tourism business when California legalized elective modifications, and cut their legs out from under them.

As it turns out, though, "How did your parents manage to circumvent the law to Engineer your preternaturally perky breasts?" is a very difficult thing to ask a near stranger. This was only six years after the Stupid War. Even asking someone if they were Engineered was pretty much taboo.

So, we talked about the sorts of things that parents forced together by circumstance rather than choice have talked about ever since our ancestors first came down from the trees and started attending their children's soccer games. We talked about the hot, dry summer. Her front lawn was burned brown. My tomatoes hadn't yielded enough fruit for a decent dinner salad. We talked about the election that was coming up in November. She found Andersen's Hero-of-the-Stupid-War shtick just as annoying as I did at that point, but didn't think she'd be able to bring herself to vote against him because Morrone was even worse.

We didn't realize that there wasn't going to *be* an election that November, of course. That all happened later.

We even talked a little bit about our girls—cautious, tentative boasting, mostly. Tara had run second or third for the girls' team the previous year, and was hoping to move into the top spot that fall. Bree asked where I thought Hannah would fit in. I told her we'd know soon enough.

Honestly, I was expecting Hannah to finish pretty near the front of the pack. I knew the sorts of times Doyle's girls had run the year before, and I kept thinking back to what Hannah had done to me at the Nature Preserve at the beginning of the summer, and how hard she'd been working ever since. I couldn't believe there were more than two or three girls there who could even stay with her over a five-mile course, let alone beat her.

Finally, Doyle gave the runners one last chance at their water bottles, then lined them up between two traffic cones he'd set up at the edge of the soccer field, and sent them off. A tall, rail-thin boy with ghost-white skin and long black hair led them once around the field, and then off along a winding trail into the woods. By the time they disappeared, the pack had already stretched out a bit. A tightly bunched group of five boys took the lead. Tara and another girl followed a half dozen yards behind, with a mixed group of boys and girls strung out behind them. A pack of four girls brought up the rear. Hannah was one of them.

I got a good look at Hannah's face as she rounded a cone at the near corner of the field. She'd only been running for a few hundred yards, but already she was hurting. I'd told her a dozen times that this was going to be different from running with a bunch of middle-school girls, but from the look on her face, I was guessing that it was just then starting to sink in.

"So far, so good, right?" Bree said. "Hannah's in with a good group. Hopefully she can stay with them."

I turned to look at her. It was hard to read her expression with those glasses in the way, but I didn't get the impression that she was trying to mock me.

"It's a long run," I said. "Hannah likes to start carefully, and move up as the race goes on."

I had no idea if that was true or not—Hannah hadn't trailed at any point in a race in more than two years—but it sounded plausible, and it got Bree to shut up for a few minutes.

"I hope Coach Doyle has water for them out on the course somewhere," she said finally. "It's awfully hot."

She took off her glasses then to wipe the sweat from her eyes. Her irises were a never-seen-in-nature shade of violet, not the GeneCraft-standard light blue. I looked closer. Her pupils were vertical slits.

"You know," she said. "It's really not polite to stare."

"I'm sorry," I said. "I mean, I'm sorry again. I'm usually not this much of an oaf."

She sighed, and put the glasses back on.

"It's okay. I'm used to it by now. These eyes are the reason that my father's going to wind up in one of those nursing homes where the staff beats you up every night, and the other residents steal your things."

I laughed.

"Oh, come on," I said. "Yes, they're a little startling, but they're also beautiful. Do they work?"

She gave me a tentative half smile.

"Thank you, I think. And yes, they work fine."

"Your daughter," I said. "Does she . . ."

Bree shook her head, and the smile disappeared.

"No," she said. "Everything they did to me got hidden in recessives. Tara's father is normal, and so is Tara. She's an only child, so there's no need to worry about these eyes popping up again for at least a few generations."

"Sorry," I said. "Didn't mean to touch a nerve."

She took a deep breath in, then let it out slowly.

"It's fine, Drew. It's just . . . my father got to play his little pranks on me. The thought of him getting to play them on my daughter as well . . ."

I shook my head.

"Pranks? I guess I can see how it might feel that way to you, but to me . . . your eyes are kind of like the paintings at Lascaux, you know? To be able to pull that off when they did, I mean . . . it's more than Lascaux, really. It's like they threw a bucket of paint at the wall, and it splattered into the *Mona Lisa*." I took a breath. I've never been great at reading people, but she didn't look like she was getting ready to slap me.

"I'm sure these eyes were quite an accomplishment,"

she said. "I'm sure the gene cutter my father hired was very proud of himself. How do you think it felt, though, to walk around with these eyes six years ago?"

I looked away.

"Right," I said. "Probably like you had a target on your back."

"Not on my back," she said. "Right between my eyes."

We stood in silence for a while, watching Doyle pace back and forth across the field and stare at his watch. Finally, I took a deep breath and said, "I don't mean to be nosy, but could I get another look?"

She hesitated, then took off the glasses again. I took a half step toward her. Those eyes really were amazing. Up close, they almost seemed to glow. I leaned in until our faces were only inches apart. She didn't pull back. She didn't even blink. Her pupils opened up until they were almost round.

"So," she said finally. "You're an engineer?"

"Yeah," I said. "I'm a design lead for Bioteka. Mostly agricultural products, though. That's where the meat of the business is. Human mods get all the press, but they're pretty much a boutique service."

She put her glasses back on.

"Is that right? I never had the head for engineering, but I've always been fascinated by it."

"Really? You honestly don't seem like much of a fan."

She laughed.

"Well, I'm certainly not a fan of what they did

to me. I don't have a problem with better tomatoes, though. Are you working on anything interesting?"

I smiled.

"You could say that. I'm heading up a project that's cool enough to rate a code name."

One eyebrow poked up over the rim of her glasses.

"A code name? You mean like the Omega Project?"

"Close. It's called Project DragonCorn."

She giggled. I'm not ordinarily a giggle fan, but hers didn't bother me for some reason.

"DragonCorn, hmm? And what, exactly, is a Dragon-Corn?"

"Well," I said. "Presumably, it's a cross between a dragon and a unicorn."

That got me a full-throated laugh.

"Please, please tell me you are actually creating a cross between a dragon and a unicorn."

I shook my head.

"Sadly, we are not."

"Sadly. So, what are you creating?"

"I could tell you, but . . ."

"Right. You'd have to kill me."

She would have been surprised by how close that was to the truth.

The lead pack of boys came out of the woods, sweat soaked and flushed, right around twenty-five min-utes after they'd started. The one who'd led at the beginning—Bree told me his name was Jordan—was at the back of the group when they came into view, but by the time they'd circled the main school building and come down the stretch run to the soccer field, he was back in front. The five of them finished within a few seconds of one another, in a little over twenty-seven minutes. Doyle was waiting for them at the finish, with a cooler full of water bottles and cold, wet towels.

Tara came in by herself, less than a minute behind the boys. The trailing pack filtered in over the next two minutes, boys and girls intermingled, all of them looking ragged and dripping with sweat. Two of the four girls that Hannah had started with came in together, at just under thirty minutes. Hannah was maybe ten seconds behind them.

When Hannah finished, the last girl still hadn't come out of the woods.

Doyle was off to one side, in a huddle with Jordan and Tara. One of the girls went over to them, and tapped him on the shoulder. He took a quick look around, counted heads, and yelled, "Where's Sarah? Who was running with Sarah?"

The two girls who'd come in ahead of Hannah looked at each other, then both pointed at her.

Doyle waved Hannah over. He spoke to her. She answered. He grabbed her upper arm, leaned in close and almost shook her. She burst into tears.

He barked something at Jordan. The two of them grabbed water and towels, and took off into the woods at a sprint.

Bree was staring at me.

"You might want to go talk to your daughter," she said.

5. IN WHICH HANNAH LEARNS ONE LESSON, AND TEACHES ANOTHER.

So, all in all, my first day of high-school cross-country could have gone better. It was hot, I was nervous, I finished next to last in the time trial, and I got yelled at by Coach Doyle.

Oh, and I basically got blamed for almost killing Sarah Miller.

That was totally not entirely my fault, by the way. You could blame a lot of people for what happened to Sarah, and there's no way I deserved to be at the top of the list. Start with Sarah herself. She'd spent the entire summer training on a treadmill in her parents' air-conditioned home gym, and she didn't hydrate before the start of the run because she was afraid she'd have to stop to pee halfway through. Then there's Coach Doyle. It was almost 100 degrees that morning. Did we really need to run a time trial? And don't forget Jess and Miranda. They were only a couple of strides ahead of us when Sarah went down. They could have stopped and helped just as easily as I could have— but they didn't, and when Coach Doyle asked who had been running with Sarah, they both turned and pointed at me.

The ambulance showed up maybe four or five minutes after Jordan and Coach Doyle took off into the woods. It drove right up onto the soccer field. Two paramedics climbed out of the cab, walked around to the back, and started pulling out gear. They didn't seem to be in much of a hurry. I took that as a good sign.

"She probably just overheated," Dad said. "Look, those guys aren't worried. I'm sure they'll look her over, give her some water, and send her on her way."

I nodded, and tried to wipe my nose with the back of my arm. It didn't work—just left me with a mix of sweat and snot smeared across my upper lip and cheek.

"Here," Dad said, and handed me a handkerchief. I mopped my face clean, blew my nose, and handed it back to him. He looked down at the mess in his hand, made a face, and carefully folded it snot side in.

He was still trying to decide whether to stuff the hanky back into his pocket when a blonde woman wearing wraparound shades came up beside him. She touched my arm and said, "Hey, Hannah. I'm Tara's mom. Are you okay?"

I shrugged. I didn't trust my voice yet, and I really didn't want to start blubbering again in front of a stranger. The other runners were scattered around the field in groups of twos and threes, heads close together, talking in whispers. Every so often I'd catch one of them looking at me. Nobody was smiling.

"Here they come," Dad said. Sarah, Jordan, and Coach Doyle came out of the woods together, walking slowly. Sarah was in the middle. Her arms were around their waists, and theirs were around her shoulders. A wet towel hung over her head, and another was draped around the back of her neck.

"Look at that," said Tara's mom. "She's fine. I'll bet . . ."

Sarah's knees buckled. Jordan and Coach Doyle held her up as her head sagged forward and she vomited up something thin and yellow. The paramedics started toward her. Her arms and legs began thrashing, and they broke into a run.

Here are some things that I did not previously know about heat stroke:

1. Heat stroke can occur in otherwise healthy athletes who are exercising in hot weather.
2. Heat stroke can be brought on by a lack of hydration, lack of training, and the use of alcohol or caffeine.

3. The first symptoms of oncoming heat stroke are cramping and profuse sweating, but in later stages the victim will stop sweating, may become confused, and often feels cold rather than hot.

4. Left untreated, heat stroke can lead to kidney damage, brain damage, and death.

5. If someone you are with begins showing symptoms of heat stroke, people will judge you harshly if you abandon that person in the woods.

The ambulance left. Doyle dismissed us. The other runners drifted away, one by one. Jordan patted my shoulder as he passed, and mouthed *Call me* when I looked up. I nodded, and tried to smile. He and Doyle headed off to the parking lot together. I wiped at my face with the front of my shirt and looked around for my dad.

He was standing on the other side of the field with Tara's mom.

His arms were folded across his chest, but he was standing so close to her, his head bowed so that their foreheads were almost touching. I opened my mouth to call to him, but something about the way they were locked into each other stopped me.

"Hey."

I turned my head. Tara was standing beside me.

"Hey," I said. "Are you gonna yell at me too? 'Cause if you are, can we just pretend that I already feel bad enough?"

She laughed.

"No, Hannah. I don't have any interest in yelling at you. You're not Sarah's mommy. If it had been me back there, I wouldn't have stopped either." She stepped a little closer, and turned to face me. "True story: last year at Sectionals, a girl from Pittsford bonked right in front of me, tripped over a root or something and went down flat on her face. She must have knocked a wire loose, because she didn't get back up. Just laid there on the ground, kind of twitching."

I looked up at her. She was smiling.

"Holy crap. What did you do?"

Her smile disappeared.

"I stepped on her hand, and I kept running. People think this is a kumbaya sport. They think it's all *Good luck* at the start, and hugs and tears at the finish line. It's not, Hannah—not if you want to run for Doyle, anyway. Not if you want to win. I mean, I'm not saying I don't feel bad for Sarah, and yeah, you probably should have helped her. End of the day, though . . . I'm not the girl who's about to judge you."

"Thanks," I said. "Pretty sure you're the only one right now."

She shrugged.

"They'll get over it. Sarah will be back to practice in a couple of days, and this'll all be water under the bridge."

I turned to look across the field. Dad was saying something, gesturing with his hands. Tara's mom was laughing.

"So," Tara said. "What do you think's up with that?"

I shook my head.

"No idea. My dad's a social spastic. He usually can't talk to a stranger for more than two minutes without breaking out in hives."

"Yeah," Tara said. "Well, my mom can be really . . . friendly."

I turned back to look at her. She was scowling.

"Sorry?"

She shook her head.

"Not your fault. Are your parents married?"

"Yeah," I said. "Why?"

She sighed.

"No reason."

Wilma17: Hey Jordan. Got a minute?

Jordasaurus: Sure. Just let me get away from Mumsy.

Jordasaurus: Okay. What's up?

Wilma17: So that was crazy today, right?

Jordasaurus: Nah. Par for the course for a first practice.

Wilma17: Oh. Really?

Jordasaurus: . . .

Wilma17: Right. Sorry.

Jordasaurus: Anyway, I wouldn't stress about it. I just heard from Doyle. Sarah's fine. Give it a few days, and it'll be like it never happened.

Wilma17: That's pretty much what Tara said.

Jordasaurus: Tara, huh?

Wilma17: Yeah. She got stuck after practice with me. Her mom and my dad had kind of a . . . thing going on. She was really nice.

Jordasaurus: Nice? You sure we're talking about the same Tara?

Wilma17: . . .

Jordasaurus: Okay. I won't disillusion you.

Wilma17: Great. Thanks for that. I need at least one friend on the team.

Jordasaurus: Oh. Now you've hurt my feelings.

Wilma17: On the *girls* team, jackass.

Jordasaurus: That's better. One thing, though . . .

Wilma17: Yeah?

Jordasaurus: Come talk to me again after the first time you beat her.

6. IN WHICH DREW SKATES ON VERY THIN ICE.

Hannah's first meet came on the afternoon of the second Tuesday in September. The heat had finally broken, and the sun was a dull orange spot in a slate-gray sky. They were running against three of the big public schools, on a hilly five-kilometer course in a park near Perinton. I asked Kara if she wanted to come with me, to cheer on her daughter in her first big race, but she wasn't interested.

"It's cross-country," she said. "They run into the woods. You stand around in a field for fifteen minutes. They run back out of the woods. As long as she wins, I don't need to watch. I've got better things to do, Drew—and honestly, so do you. We're in pretty deep over this house, remember? You've been spending a shit-ton of time following Hannah around to practices and meets, and not so much on the stuff that pays the bills around here. If you lose your job, darling, we are thoroughly screwed."

She had a point. I'd maxed my credit turning that old farmhouse into a low-key fortress. DragonCorn was still more or less on schedule then—as far as I could tell, anyway—but I'd been spending a lot more time worrying about Hannah's running over the past few months than I had worrying about Gantt charts and deliverables. I had a good development team, but I'd been letting them run on autopilot since at least the previous spring, and if they ran themselves into a ditch, Bioteka's board wasn't going to care about Hannah's 5k times.

Still, I wanted to see the race.

I left the house around four, and pulled into the parking lot just as the buses were arriving. I tried to catch Hannah's eye as she came off the bus, but she was deep in conversation with Tara. They were walking side by side, their heads close together, Tara's hand on Hannah's hip.

"My, aren't they two peas in a pod?"

I turned. Bree Carson stood behind me, hiding behind those oversized glasses again despite the thin, filtered sunlight.

"Yeah," I said. "It's nice that Hannah's made a friend."

Bree took a half step closer to me, and her hand came to rest on my upper arm. One eyebrow peeked up over the top of her glasses.

"Wow," she said. "You spend a lot of time in the weight room?"

I hesitated. That was definitely not where I thought this conversation was going. Her smile grew wider, and her hand dropped to her side.

"No," I said finally. "I mean, I've been known to do the occasional push-up, but that's about it. Hannah makes fun of me when I work out. She says you can't punch out the Grim Reaper."

She laughed, and reached up to touch her hair.

Yes, in case you were wondering. I am very, very slow on the uptake.

Bree and I found a spot on the hillside, looking down on the starting area from a hundred or so yards away.

"This course is a good one for watching," Bree said as we sat down in the short, dry grass. "You can see everything other than a mile or so that runs back through the woods from here."

I looked around. We were alone. All the other parents were either down in the wide, grassy field near the starting line, or a few hundred yards off to our left, where the trail led into the woods.

"If this is the best spot," I said, "why are we the only ones here?"

Bree leaned back on her elbows, stretched out her legs and crossed them at the ankle.

"First," she said, "nobody wants to climb this hill.

It's a long way up, and you have to hustle down to the field once they run past on the way back if you want to catch the runners at the finish line. Second, even though we can see most of the course from here, the runners never come closer than the bottom of the hill. Most of the parents like to have the girls run right past them, so they can cheer them on or tell them to pick it up or whatever. From here, all you can do is watch."

"And that's what you prefer? Just watching?"

She looked up at me with a smirk.

"Mind out of the gutter, Mr. Bergen."

I was suddenly very conscious of my heartbeat pounding in my ears. Bree burst out laughing. She reached up, touched my chin with one finger, and gently closed my mouth.

"My, but you're easy to tweak," she said.

"Sorry," I said. "I just . . ."

"Oh, look. The boys are starting."

I looked down and saw the smoke from the starter's gun drifting across the field. The crack came a second later. Fifty or so boys sprinted the length of the field away from us, rounded two sets of cones, and started back the other way. By the time they passed the bottom of the hill, the pack had separated out, and the runners had settled into a steady rhythm. The first five Briarwood boys were in a tight bunch at the front, with the sixth trailing a few steps behind. There were two boys from Penfield and one from

Fairport in front of our seventh. The rest of the field was strung out in a long line behind.

"Is this the way it usually goes?"

Bree looked up at me, eyebrows poking up over the rim of her glasses.

"What, you mean the race?"

"Right," I said. "Is our sixth runner usually faster than everybody else's first?"

"Well," she said. "They're two minutes into a sixteen-minute race. Lots of things can happen. That said, though, our runners do tend to beat up on the public schools. They can't recruit like we can, and practically none of their kids are Engineered. We'll have better races against some of the other private schools, but even then . . ."

"Five straight state championships, right?"

She smiled.

"That's the girls, actually. The boys finished second last year."

I nodded, and watched until the runners disappeared into the woods.

"They'll come back out in a few minutes over there," Bree said, pointing to a gap in the trees a few hundred yards to our left. "What should we do in the meantime?"

The boys came out of the woods with twelve minutes gone. Briarwood's top five had stretched it out a bit, but one of the Penfield kids had pushed in front of our sixth. Jordan was running with the pack when they first came into view, but once the fans could see him he put on a burst, and by the time he rounded the last set of cones he had five or six seconds on the next runner.

"That Jordan has quite a kick, doesn't he?"

I looked down at Bree.

"Yeah," I said. "He does."

"All natural, too," she said. "Most of the other boys are Engineered, one way or another, but Jordan's a garden-variety *Homo sap*."

"Engineered?" I said. "You mean to run?"

"Well," she said. "No. They're mostly the standard packages. But you know how it is. Engineered are usually just . . . better."

She pushed her glasses up onto her forehead. I caught myself staring at her eyes. She stared back without blinking until I forced myself to look away.

"It's okay to look," she said. "We're friends now, aren't we?"

It took another six or seven minutes for the rest of the boys to straggle across the finish line, and five more to get the girls lined up. Hannah and Tara started side by side in the middle of the field, and when the gun sounded, they went to the front together.

"Well," Bree said. "I thought you told me Hannah was a pacer?"

She was sitting up by then, arms wrapped around

her knees, close enough to me that our shoulders were almost touching. I shrugged, then shivered as the sleeve of her shirt brushed against my arm.

"I don't know what she is, honestly," I said. "I'm not sure she does, either. I think she's still trying to figure it out."

She patted my knee.

"Oh, we all are, aren't we?"

Bree shifted slightly, and then we were touching. The point of her shoulder pressed lightly against my arm. I glanced over at her. The glasses were back over her eyes, and she seemed to be intent on the runners. They were passing the base of the hill, Tara in front, Hannah a pace or two behind. A Fairport girl was in third, close on Hannah's heels. She was a head taller than most of the other runners, with long, wraith-thin limbs and a thick black braid hanging down the middle of her back. The next five were all from Briarwood.

"Who's that?" I asked.

"What, the one from Fairport? That's Devon Morgan." Bree brushed her hair back from her forehead and sighed. "She's a striver. She's been chasing Tara for four years. Don't worry. She'll be back in the pack by the time they come out of the woods."

I wasn't sure she was right about that. Devon had an odd stride, with more up-and-down than you'd usually like to see, but Tara and Hannah were taking three steps for every two of hers, and she didn't look like she was running above her level. Her face was calm, her arms were relaxed, her mouth was just slightly open. "I hope so. If she's still where she is when they come back out, I don't like Hannah's chances in a sprint with her."

Bree smiled.

"Well," she said, "you're right about that. She ran the four hundred in under fifty-three last spring."

I whistled.

"Oh, yes," she said. "She's Engineered, of course. Like the boys, though—not for running. Her daddy wanted a model."

I looked over at Bree. She was watching Tara disappear into the woods.

"How do you know that?"

She looked up at me. The glasses made it impossible to read her face.

"What, about Devon?"

"Yeah," I said. "How would you possibly know that she's Engineered—let alone what mods she has, and why?"

She gave me that glee club smile again. We weren't touching anymore.

"Oh," she said, "you know how we hens are. Cluck cluck cluck."

Thirteen minutes later, the runners came out of the woods. Devon had not, in fact, fallen back into the pack. She was hanging right where she'd been before, a stride or two behind Hannah. Tara had opened up a three-or four-yard gap, but she was straining. Even from up on the hill, I could see it on her face. Devon's stride was as smooth and even as it had been at the start.

I couldn't read Hannah. I never could. Something about that brow ridge, I guess.

Two other Briarwood girls had closed it up a bit on the first three. They were running side by side, maybe ten or twelve yards behind Devon. Tara tucked her chin and started into her kick. *Too early,* I thought. She still had probably six hundred yards to go. Hannah and Devon let her stretch her lead to six yards, then eight, then ten.

"What are you doing, Tara?" Bree muttered.

"Getting ready to bonk, if she's not careful."

Bree's head snapped around. She opened her mouth to say something, then thought better of it and went back to the race. I was right, though. Tara's lead was twelve yards, but I could see that she was laboring. Her head was bobbing in time with her steps, and her stride was getting progressively shorter and choppier. Right at the four-hundred-yard mark, Devon decided to go.

Hannah tried to go with her, but she'd obviously been working hard just to stay where she was, and she didn't have the speed to kick with Devon, even if she'd had the wind. Devon was even with her in a half dozen strides, and past her in a half dozen more. From that point, the only question was whether

Devon would run out of course before she ran Tara down.

Bree was on her feet by then, hands cupped around her mouth, screaming at her daughter to *Go! Push! Bring it home!* And Tara tried. I could see that. Her body language was spastic, desperate, and I imagined I could see tears mixing with the sweat streaming down her face when she made the last turn toward the finish. Devon rounded the cone a half second later, teeth bared. The gap was three yards, then two, then one. With thirty yards left, Devon was right at Tara's shoulder, and then . . . and then she was doubled half over and staggering. Tara crossed the line, took two more steps, fell to her knees, and puked. Devon regained her footing and came in a second or two behind her. Hannah finished a distant third. Bree was jumping up and down and clapping, but down below I could see the Fairport coach charging down the chute toward the finish line. Devon came up behind Tara, put a foot in the middle of her back, and shoved her face-first into her own sick. Then Bree was running, and I was running, and the crowd of parents and coaches and runners broke over Tara and Devon and Hannah like a wave.

7. IN WHICH HANNAH MAKES A NEW FRIEND, DESPITE HER BEST EFFORTS.

So here's something I bet not too many people can say: my first high-school cross-country meet ended in a brawl. I mean, cross-country really isn't a brawly kind of sport, usually. I'm not exactly sure how it happened. When I rounded the last cone I was hurting pretty badly, trying to focus on maintaining my stride and not hyperventilating, and I wasn't paying much attention to what was going on ahead of me. Tara said later that Devon was crowding her, trying to pass too closely. Devon said Tara cut her off, then elbowed her in the gut when she tried to get around. All I know for sure is that when I crossed the finish line, Devon was stomping Tara down into a puddle of her own barf.

Youth sports tend to bring out the worst in par-

ents, even when their kids aren't whaling on one another, and that scene at the finish of the Fairport meet
was kind of a worst-case scenario in terms of parental
crazy making. Tara's mom wasn't close enough to
the chute to get involved right away, but a bunch of
the other team moms and dads were. Devon did her
thing with the puke stomp and tried to walk away,
but she hadn't gone two steps when Miranda's mom
ducked under the ropes, grabbed her by the shoulders and started shaking her and screaming. That
brought Devon's dad in. He shoved Miranda's mom
hard enough that she stumbled backward two steps
and sat down hard in the dirt.

After that, it was chaos. Coaches came running
in, shouting for everyone to get back. Someone
took a swing at Devon's dad, and someone else took
a swing at that guy. Bodies pressed in, around and
past where I was standing, but nobody bothered
with me. They mostly didn't seem to notice that I
was there. Tara got to her knees in the middle of the
press, sobbing and wiping vomit from her eyes, then
screamed when some idiot stomped on her fingers. I
stepped forward, grabbed her by the shoulders and
pulled her to her feet.

"There's vomit in my hair!" Tara wailed.

"I know," I said, close to her ear. "Come on."

I put my arm around her shoulder and tried to
pull her out of the crowd, but the other runners
were piling in around us by then. Fairport kids were

pushing forward to help Devon, and Briarwood kids were crowding in around us, while the girls from Penfield were just trying to get their finish cards and get out of the way. A man's hand grabbed my arm and pulled me to the side. I stumbled, almost pulled Tara down with me, and smacked him twice before I realized it was my dad. Tara's mom was there too. She pulled Tara to her, wrapped her arms around her and pressed Tara's face against her white silk shirt. A woman in a Fairport polo shirt grabbed Tara's jersey from behind, tried to start in on her, but Tara's mom backhanded her and that was that. I ducked my head, wrapped my arms around Dad's chest, closed my eyes and breathed.

I was hanging out in the solarium that night, supposedly splitting time among abs, stretching, and GeneChem homework, but mostly listening to the soundtrack to *Stupid War: The Musical* on continuous loop, when my phone pinged. I thought about ignoring it—I was almost to the part where Daniel Andersen sings his solo about the Battle of Frostburg, which always made me cry—but then it pinged again, and again. I sighed and thumbed the screen.

<UNK01>: Hi Hannah. Nice run today.

<UNK01>: You there?

<UNK02>: She's listening to *Stupid War*. Give her a minute. I love this part.

I looked up from the phone, my heart beating a little faster.

"Dad? Is that you?"

Nothing. The door was shut, and the solarium was pretty well soundproofed. I stood and walked over to the glass wall. It was an overcast night, dark as the bottom of a coal mine that far out in the sticks, and all I could see was my reflection. My phone pinged again.

<UNK01>: Great. You freaked her out. Chill, Hannah. We come in peace.

<UNK02>: Right. Please don't take my last message to mean that I can see and hear everything you're doing right now. That is definitely possibly not the case. Also, we're not outside, so you can quit looking for us.

<UNK01>: You're not helping.

<UNK02>: Sure I am. Look, her pulse is back down to 60 BPM. She's totally at ease now.

<UNK02>: Whoops. There it goes again.

Wilma17: Look, whoever you are. I'm about two

seconds from yelling for my dad, who will definitely have Bioteka security crawling up your asses as soon as he sees what's on this phone.

\<UNK02\>: Oooooh, don't do that. That wouldn't work out well for any of us.

\<UNK01\>: Oh, for shit's sake. Stop talking, Inchy. That sounded like a threat. Hannah—that was definitely not a threat. Please don't call your dad.

\<UNK02\>: Hey! Not much point in the ghosted IDs if we're gonna start throwing names around, is there?

Wilma17: Okay. Right now, or I'm calling Dad—tell me who you are, and how you got my number, and how you're ghosting your IDs. Isn't that supposed to be illegal? Also, while I'm asking, how the flark do you know what my pulse is?

\<UNK02\>: That sort of language is simply uncalled-for, young lady.

Wilma17: Right. Calling Dad now . . .

\<UNK01\>: Wait! Hannah, this is Devon—from the race today? Seriously, please don't get your dad.

Wilma17: Devon? Okay. Where'd you get my digits?

<UNK01>: Inchy gave them to me.

Wilma17: And he got them from?

<UNK02>: I found them?

Wilma17: *Found* them?

<UNK02>: I'm very good at finding things.

Luckily for me, that actually turned out to be true.

Wilma17: Okay. So let's assume I believe this is the girl who stomped my friend's face into a puddle of her own barf this afternoon, and not some random weirdo. What do you want, Devon?

So, she told me.

The next afternoon was a recovery run, two laps around the time-trial course we'd run through the woods around the school that first Saturday in August. I paired off with Tara, as I'd been doing for most of the last few weeks. Miranda and Kerry started off with us, but after the first couple of miles Tara started to push the pace, and the other girls dropped back. I matched Tara stride for stride, letting her slip ahead when the trail went to single-track, then pulling even again when it widened. The first few days of training with Coach Doyle had shaken me pretty badly, but I'd been putting the hay in the barn since then, and I was just starting to get to the point where the workouts didn't hurt anymore, where my stride had a rhythm and flow to it that I hadn't felt since the end of track season the previous spring. Tara had been encouraging for the first couple of weeks, but lately I was starting to get the feeling that she'd prefer to just run alone. We'd already made the turn to start the second lap by the time I worked up the nerve to talk to her.

"Tara?"

She glanced back. We were pushing way too hard for the day after a race, and neither of us had a ton of wind to spare for conversation.

"What?"

"What do you know . . ." I took two strides to breathe. ". . . about Devon Morgan?"

"You mean . . . besides that . . . she's a psycho . . . bitch?"

"Yeah," I said. "Besides that."

Tara slowed to a stop at a fork in the trail. I pulled up short. Stopping during a training run was a mortal sin in Doyle's world. If any of the other runners saw us standing there and reported back on us, he'd . . . I had no idea what he'd do. As far as I knew, nobody had ever stopped during one of Doyle's training runs. Tara folded her arms across her chest, and stared me down.

"Why do you want to know about Devon, Hannah?"

I shrugged.

"No reason."

Her eyes narrowed.

"You're not fraternizing with the enemy, are you?"

I shook my head.

"No. I mean, not really. She pinged me last night, just to say hello."

"And she'd do that why?"

I looked away. I definitely didn't want to go there with Tara. Not yet, anyway. She closed her eyes and sighed.

"You're what, fourteen?"

I nodded.

"You remember much about the Stupid War?"

I shook my head.

"I was eight. I think . . . my parents kept us out of it, mostly. We just hunkered down out here until it was over."

"Yeah," Tara said. "Us too. Devon's parents? Not so much."

"You mean they were . . ." I had to search for the word. ". . . partisans?"

She nodded.

"Okay," I said. "Lots of people were, I guess. They must have been with the Engineered, right? I mean, Devon doesn't exactly look like she'd fit in with the UnAltered."

"Yeah," Tara said. "You'd think so."

"But?"

"But no. Devon's parents? They were with the AIs."

We finished out the run in silence. When we were done, Tara went off to stretch with Miranda and Kerry, and left me alone in the middle of the soccer field to stew. I thought for a while that this was going to turn into one of those alone-in-the-cafeteria moments that make high school such a joy, but after a few minutes, Jordan and his crew came out of the woods. He saw me sitting twenty feet away from the rest of the girls, gave me a wide grin, and said something to his second. The other boys went off to the far end of the field to run strides. Jordan came over and sat down beside me.

"Hey," he said. "What's with the exile? I thought you and Tara were all good?"

I shrugged.

"Yeah, me too. I mean, we are, I think. She just didn't seem very social today."

He leaned forward until our faces were only a few inches apart.

"Remember what I told you, after that first practice?"

I rolled my eyes.

"I didn't beat her."

He laughed.

"Not yet."

I glanced over at Tara. She was watching us.

"Okay," I said. "Now that's creeping me out."

Jordan laughed again, louder.

"I don't blame you. Kinda looks like she's trying to decide where to stash your body, doesn't she?"

He turned to give Tara a big smile and wave. She scowled and looked away. Jordan settled back into the grass, stretched his legs out in front of him and started working his hamstrings.

"Hey," I said. "Jordan? Can I ask you something totally random?"

He shrugged, and brought his nose down to his right knee.

"Sure, as long as you don't mind a totally random answer."

"Yeah," I said. "I guess that's fair. So . . . in the Stupid War, were there really people who backed the AIs?"

Jordan looked up from his stretch. He wasn't smiling.

"It's for an essay," I said. "For Modern History."

"Right," he said. "Modern History. You know they don't offer that class to freshies, right?"

In fact, I had not known that. Jordan sat up, rolled his neck around in a slow circle, and stretched down to his left leg.

"So," he said. "Tara's been talking smack about Devon Morgan, huh?"

I didn't say anything. He straightened, and gave me a long, searching look.

"Yeah," he said finally. "There were. I don't think any of them made it to the end of the war alive, though. Devon's parents weren't partisans like the UnAltered or the New Human Army, Hannah. They just took a lot of shit over some stuff her pops said when NatSec started talking about doing a total network purge. Honestly, he came pretty close to getting himself lynched. There were all kinds of rumors—I mean, some folks even said they were harboring. The only thing anybody ever proved, though, was that he wrote an essay on one of the news blogs saying maybe NatSec shouldn't totally wipe out what was basically a brand-new sentient species just because a few of them did some really bad stuff."

He pulled one knee up, and twisted around to stretch his lower back.

"Anyway," he said, "I hung out most of the weekend with Devon at States last spring. Whatever her parents did or didn't do six years ago, she's a good kid. I know Tara's fired up about the meet yesterday, but dredging up that shit . . ." He looked over at Tara again. "That's pretty low, even by her standards."

Doyle called Jordan's name from across the field. He sighed, and climbed to his feet.

"Look," he said. "I know that sounded like I was shitting on Tara. I'm not. She's a good kid too, for the most part. She just . . ." He looked over at her, then back at me. Doyle called his name again, a little louder. "Right," he said. "Just watch your back, okay?"

DGorgon: Had a chance to think about what I said last night?

Wilma17: Who is?

DGorgon: Sorry. It's Devon.

Wilma17: No fake ID tonight?

DGorgon: Yeah, that's Inchy's thing. He's a little paranoid.

Wilma17: And Inchy is . . .

DGorgon: A friend.

Wilma17: A friend who knows how to ghost a system ID?

DGorgon: Yup.

Wilma17: Okaaaaaaay.

DGorgon: Anyway . . .

Wilma17: Yeah, anyway. I don't know, Devon.

DGorgon: It's not a big deal.

Wilma17: Really? I barely know you, and you're basically asking me to spy on my own dad.

DGorgon: Not spy, really. Just . . .

Wilma17: Just what?

DGorgon: Okay, yeah. Spy. But this could be really important.

Wilma17: Says who?

DGorgon: Um . . . Inchy?

Wilma17: Inchy. Your spooky-ass, ID-ghosting "friend"?

DGorgon: Yes?

Wilma17: Look, Devon . . . You need to throw me a bone here. You want me to find out what Dad's doing with this DragonCorn thing. That honestly sounds more like an industrial-espionage thing than a saving-the-world thing. My dad's job pays for all of my stuff. I really don't want to screw that up.

DGorgon: Hang on . . .

DGorgon: You know who Robert Longstreth is?

Wilma17: Uh, yeah. He's the guy who gives my dad the money that pays for all my stuff.

DGorgon: You know what happened to him six years ago?

Wilma17: No. What?

DGorgon: Let's just say he's carrying a really, really big grudge against the UnAltered. Inchy thinks DragonCorn is gonna be his payback.

Wilma17: Actually, I'm pretty sure it's gonna be corn. Literally corn.

Wilma17: Anyway, why would I care if Robert Longstreth wants to do bad things to the Un-Altered? Those guys suck.

DGorgon: There's lots of people out there who are

unaltered without being UnAltered, Hannah. Your mom and dad, for instance.

Wilma17: . . .

Wilma17: Tell you what. I'll think about it, okay?

DGorgon: Okay. Ping me tomorrow?

I put my phone down, went into the bathroom, and brushed my teeth. When I came back out, there were two more messages at the bottom of the screen.

<UNK01>: Please don't call me spooky, Hannah. That really hurts my feelings.

<UNK01>: Also, I love that shirt. Totally brings out the blue in your eyes. ;)

8. IN WHICH JORDAN PROVIDES VALUABLE PERSPECTIVE.

Doyle wanted a captains' meeting the day after the Fairport meet to talk about the world's first ever cross-country riot. Much as I would have loved to rehash sweet Tara's well-deserved comeuppance, however, I had to beg off. I had a date that night with Marta Longstreth.

Micah, needless to say, was not happy when I told him where I was going.

"Seriously? This is gross, Jordan. Does she know you're not a breeder?"

I sighed, and accelerated up the ramp onto 90. Velociraptor had an honest-to-God gas engine, with enough horses to push us back into our seats as I swung into the left lane and opened it up.

"Yes, Micah. Marta is well aware that this evening is not going to end in the backseat."

He twisted around to look behind us.

"You don't have a backseat."

I sighed again, a little louder.

"Yes," I said. "I know. It's just an expression."

"Oh. Right. So you meant . . ."

"I meant that she knows I have a boyfriend, Micah."

"Right. Good. So why are you doing this?"

I swung right to pass a cargo hauler that shouldn't have been in the left lane, then right again to get around a taxi, then all the way back to the left to catch the open lane again. You'd think having 95 percent of the cars on the road driverless would make traffic less stupid, but unfortunately you would be very, very wrong.

"We are doing this for the same reason the children of nobility have gone on dinner dates since time immemorial, Micah. My father is a prince of Gene-Craft. Hers is the king of Bioteka. We are the only two people in our social strata within two hundred miles of this godforsaken wasteland, and our parents would very much like for us to form an alliance."

That got me a long five seconds of silence.

"But you're not gonna."

I patted his knee, and swerved back across to the far right lane.

"No, Micah. We're not gonna."

"Hey."

Marta climbed into the passenger seat and slammed the door. The car that had carried her to the Park-n-Ride backed out and pulled away.

"Hello," I said. "Nice to meet you in person, finally. This seems unnecessarily cloak-and-dagger, though, doesn't it? I could have just picked you up at your house."

That got a short, bitter laugh out of her. She had a tattooed spider in the middle of her throat, with a web that stretched around to the back of her neck. The laugh made it dance in a disturbingly creepy way.

"You obviously haven't met my dad. Nobody comes to our house. Hardly anybody even knows where it is. I'm kind of amazed he's letting this happen at all."

I dropped Velociraptor into gear and headed back to the highway.

"Well, he couldn't keep his princess locked away in the castle forever, could he?"

She laughed again. She had the least happy laugh that I've ever heard.

"Actually, I was starting to think that he could."

"So what changed?"

She shrugged.

"Basically, I started making myself unbearable. He's still not pleased, and I guarantee there's a drone pacing us right now and monitoring everything we do, but at least I'm out of the house."

"Your dad likes drones, huh?" I said, and eased my foot off the gas. "That's good to know."

We had an eight-o'clock reservation at Primo's on the Lakeshore. I'd been rather proud of myself for getting us a table on a day's notice. Ordinarily, they were booked a week or more in advance. When we arrived, though, there were only two other cars in the front lot, and a third tucked around behind the main building. I thought at first that they might have had to close for some reason, but the lights were on inside, and I could see movement through the front windows. I looked over at Marta. She sighed and climbed out of the car.

The hostess was waiting for us just inside the door, menus in hand.

"Hi," I said. "We've got an eight o'clock?"

"Yeah," she said. "I know. Right this way, Mr. Barnes."

Primo's is an intimate place. It only seats forty or so people, and usually every table is full. That night, though, we were the only ones in the room.

"Wow," I said. "Slow night, huh?"

The hostess pulled Marta's chair out for her.

"Yeah," she said. "Funny thing. Your server will be with you shortly."

Yes, it took me that long to realize what was going on. I sat. Marta was already studying the menu.

"Your dad made them clear the restaurant, huh?"

She gave me a long, blank stare, then returned her eyes to the menu.

"Uh-huh. I mean, I'm sure he compensated them for lost revenue, but no—this was definitely not voluntary on Primo's part."

"And all the other people who had reservations here tonight?"

She looked up again, one eyebrow raised.

"Probably got told they have a rat problem in the kitchen or something. Does it matter?"

And that is when I realized that Marta and I were not, in fact, in the same social strata. Apparently, there's a really big difference between a prince and a king.

The server came to take our orders. She was short, and blonde, and irritated. I made a mental note to leave a really big tip. Primo may have gotten paid to shut the place down, but I was willing to bet he wasn't sharing with the help. Marta ordered scallops. I got a wedge salad and an eight-ounce fillet. I thought about asking for a bottle of wine. The server would have brought it, of course, and not asked for proof of age— but I was already feeling mildly ill over the amount of privilege we were displaying, and I really didn't want to push it.

"So," Marta said when we were alone again. "This is how the other half lives, huh?"

I looked around.

"What?"

"This," she said, and waved one arm around. "Restaurants and waitresses and whatnot."

I stared at her for a beat, waiting to see if she was joking.

"No," I said finally. "This is not how the other half lives, unless you consider the two halves to be your family and everyone else on Earth. This is a pretty exclusive restaurant, actually, and ordinarily you have to share it."

Her face tried to twist into a scowl, but her features couldn't quite carry it off. I'd been trying to figure out what Marta's mods were. I thought at first that she had a standard Pretty package with dyed-black hair, but I could see by then that wasn't right. Her skin was too pale, and she was much too thin.

"I told you I don't get out much," she said. "You don't need to be snotty about it."

"You're right," I said. "That was rude. I'm sorry."

She leaned back, and folded her arms across her chest.

"That's better. So, you're UnAltered, huh?"

I could feel my jaw sag open.

"What?"

She rolled her eyes.

"I don't mean Last Stand in Frostburg UnAltered. I just mean . . . you know . . . not altered."

"Oh," I said. "Okay. Yeah. I don't have any mods. Point of advice, though—you should probably be careful about throwing the term UnAltered around when you're slumming it with the other half. It's kind of like calling someone a Nazi or a Klansman. People tend to get a bit touchy."

She sighed.

"Duly noted. Anyway, I've got a custom package. They originally developed it for commercial release, but when Dad gave it to me, Mom made him pull it off the shelf. It was supposed to be called the Spooky. You like?"

"Um," I said. "Sure?" She raised that eyebrow again, but with a half smile this time. I could feel my face redden. "Sorry. What I meant to say is yes, definitely. It's a good look for you, Marta. You wear it well."

"So," I said. "This was fun."

We were back at the Park-n-Ride. Marta's car was waiting for her, three spaces over.

"Yes," she said. "It was. Can we do it again?"

I opened my mouth, then closed it again. Marta's face fell, and she looked away.

"Okay," she said. "Well, thanks anyway."

She started to open the door. I sighed, and put my hand on her arm.

"No," I said. "Wait. It *was* fun, Marta. I mean, you understand, I'm not . . ."

"Yeah," she said. "I'm not looking to have sex with you, Jordan. I just need an excuse to get out of the house."

"Right. Okay then. Any time you need a break, give me a call. Just . . . can you tell your dad to lighten up a little? We torqued off a lot of folks tonight. I'd rather not start doing that on the regular."

She sighed. Sighing, as it turned out, was a big part of Marta's conversational repertoire.

"Yeah, I get that. I'll try. No guarantees, though. He's kind of protective."

I laughed.

"I can see that. I don't get it, but I can definitely see it."

Marta looked down at her feet, then back up at me. She wasn't smiling.

"I'll tell you what, Jordan. After I'm gone, do a search on Dani Longstreth."

She leaned across the seat then, grabbed me by the back of the neck, and kissed me.

"Nothing personal," she said as she climbed out of the car. "That was for the drone."

I waited until I got home to run the search. There were a ton of hits, but I read only one of them. It was a short DirecNews feed, from six years before. I recognized the date right away. It was the second day of the Stupid War. Dani Longstreth, who was one of the earliest recipients of the original Bioteka Pretty package, was caught in an UnAltered pogrom that swept through downtown Bethesda in the middle of the day. They doused her and the other victims, who were mostly just really good-looking *Homo saps*, with gasoline, and they set them on fire, because the UnAltered propagandists had been pushing the line that this was the only way to prevent the spread of Altered genes. Apparently, they hadn't figured out the differences between the reproductive methods of humans and corn. Ms. Longstreth was survived by her husband, Bioteka CEO Robert Longstreth, and their ten-year-old daughter, Marta.

9. IN WHICH DREW RECEIVES A DIRE WARNING.

I knew I was in trouble the first time Bree Carson showed up at my house uninvited. This was on a Monday morning in the middle of September. Kara had been gone for a week. Her mom was going through a long fade, and Kara had been staying with her dad, riding with him back and forth to the hospital, trying to keep him from fading away as well.

That weekend had been a gray, muddy slog, but when I woke up on Monday there wasn't any rain pounding against the windows for once, and I actually started the day thinking things might be looking up. As I was dropping Hannah off at school, the sun poked out through the clouds for the first time in days. I only had a couple of DragonCorn conferences scheduled for the afternoon, and I was thinking maybe I'd get in a long run before lunch, do a bit of tweaking to the mod package I'd been working on for the last month and a half, and then maybe catch up on my downloads during the calls.

I was only a couple of minutes from being safely out the door in my running gear when my bedroom wallscreen popped up a still frame of Bree standing on my front porch. Her glasses were pushed up to the top of her head, and those eyes . . . I sighed, and ran my hands back through my hair.

"Open the door," I said, and started down the stairs.

Bree was waiting for me, still standing on the porch outside the open front door. She smiled when she saw me.

"Good morning," I said. With the glasses up, I had a hard time figuring out where to look. It was hard enough to avoid staring at her breasts without worrying about locking in on those purple cat-eyes.

"Hello, Drew," she said. "I hope this isn't a bad time?"

"No," I said, "It's fine. What can I do for you?"

"Well," she said, "for starters, you could invite me in."

I stepped down into the foyer.

"Wait," I said. "You're not a vampire, are you?"

Her eyebrows came together over the bridge of her nose.

"What?"

"A vampire," I said. "Isn't that a thing? If you don't

invite them in, they can't . . . I dunno . . . bite you, or something?"

She shook her head. Her smile was beginning to look a little forced.

"No, Drew. I am not a vampire. Can I come in?"

"Sure," I said. "Can I get you something? Coffee? Tea? A beer?"

She crossed the threshold. The door swung closed behind her.

"Thank you," she said. "Tea would be lovely."

The thing you have to understand about Bree Carson is that she wasn't bad—which is not to say that she was necessarily good either, of course. She just wanted what she wanted, which is probably a fair description for most of us. Kara summed her up pretty well later on, after everything had settled out.

"Imagine you've got a dog," she said. "Not a yappy little dog. A big one, like a great Dane or something. Imagine you've got a big, slobbery, Marmaduke-looking great Dane."

I nodded.

"Now imagine it's Thanksgiving," she said. "It's Thanksgiving, and you just pulled a big, juicy, golden-brown turkey out of the oven. You put it on the dining-room table, and go out for a walk while it's resting."

"Why would I do that?" I asked. "Shouldn't I be making the gravy or something?"

"Look," she said. "Just go with me on this, okay?"

I rolled my eyes.

"Fine. I go for a walk."

"Right," she said. "You go for a walk, and while you're out, what do you suppose that big, stupid piece-of-shit dog gets up to?"

I leaned back in my chair and sighed.

"Does he eat the turkey?"

"Yeah, Drew. He eats the hell out of that turkey. Now, here's the question. Whose fault is this? Is it the dog's fault that he ate that delicious, crispy-skinned, sweet-and-savory turkey?"

I sighed again.

"I'm guessing not."

"No," she said, and smiled a not-at-all-happy smile. "It is not the dog's fault. Eating turkeys is what dogs do. It's your fault, Drew. It's your fault for leaving the dog alone with the turkey in the first place."

"I'm assuming Bree's the dog in this scenario?"

"Right," Kara said. "Bree is definitely the dog."

I will say, I never saw Bree as a dog. That Monday morning, she sat across my kitchen table from me, staring me down with those can't-look-away eyes, drinking my oolong, and warning me about all the unsavory things that Hannah was getting into.

"Hannah's not a bad girl," she said. "I would never suggest that. I'm just . . . concerned, Drew. Briarwood by itself can be a difficult place for a new girl to navigate, and when you start bringing in outside influences, well . . . Hannah has so much talent, and I'd hate to see her fall in with the sorts of kids who might pull her down instead of building her up."

"Well," I said. "I won't argue with that. The thing is, I'm not aware that Hannah's falling in with anybody in particular just now. Other than the girls on the team, she doesn't seem to be doing too much socializing of any kind. We've actually been a little worried that she's turning into a recluse."

Bree smiled.

"Don't be naive, Drew. Just because she's locked in her room doesn't mean she's alone."

Which was true enough, I guess, but I didn't think there was much she could do up there to get herself into actual trouble.

That, of course, turned out to be incorrect.

"Look," I said after a long, awkward pause. "I don't mean to be rude, but I'm really not sure why you're here, Bree."

"Oh, Drew," she said, and reached across the table to touch my hand. "I'm here because I want to help you. You were so sweet after that mess at the Fairport meet, and I thought I could return the favor. I'm sorry if I'm intruding. I truly didn't mean to. I just . . . I know how hard it can be for a young woman at this age. I wanted to help."

I suddenly felt like a colossal ass.

"No," I said. "You're not intruding, Bree. I appreciate that you're trying to look out for Hannah. I just don't see what makes you think that she needs looking out for."

She leaned back, and folded her arms across her chest.

"What do you know about Devon Morgan?"

By the time Bree was done, I knew much more about Devon Morgan than I wanted to. I knew that Devon had anger issues, that she was jealous and resentful of Briarwood's runners in general, and of Tara in particular, and that she was at Fairport because three different private schools, including Briarwood, had refused to admit her.

I also learned that the reason those schools had refused to admit her was that her father was an AI sympathizer.

Bree obviously expected that little nugget to horrify me, and I did my best to play the part. We were only six years past the war, remember, and those months between Hagerstown and Frostburg were still pretty vivid in people's brains. The histories say the decision to purge the networks was a more-in-sorrow-than-anger thing, but that's bullshit. I was there. It was pure panic, a reaction to the sudden realization that we'd made ourselves incredibly vulnerable—I mean, if you had an ocular, you'd opened up a direct line into your cerebral cortex that an unethical AI could exploit, and who knew whether there was any such thing as an *ethical* AI?—and the people who'd made the call really, really didn't want it second-guessed. NatSec put out a ton of propaganda on the topic after the war, and six years later there were still plenty of folks running around who'd denounce you for saying anything remotely nice about life *in silico*.

I wasn't one of them, though. I wouldn't have said it out loud then, but I remembered that essay that Mike Morgan had written, and I remembered thinking, even at the time, that he was kind of a hero.

Once Bree was gone, I locked up the house and went out for my run. The day was as close to perfect as September gets in Upstate New York. The clouds were gone and the sun was clear and high and bright, flaring from car windshields and glittering off the puddles in the fields. The air was cool and dry, and it took me almost a mile to break a decent sweat.

I get in most of my best thinking while I'm running. I was in the middle of a ten-miler when I came up with the idea for splicing genes that code for animal proteins into potatoes, for example. I was also out running when I figured out how to subdue a rampaging carnivorous potato horde.

Just kidding about that last part.

Mostly.

That Monday, though, I wasn't thinking about work. I was thinking about Bree. I tried to focus on the stuff she'd been telling me about Devon, and on the terrible peril that my darling daughter was apparently in from some combination of mean girls and NatSec agents, but mostly I was thinking about the feel of Bree's lips on my cheek, and what those purple cat-eyes looked like from two inches away.

The weird thing was, I wasn't even really attracted to Bree. I was just . . . maybe *fascinated* is the right word? As an engineer, I was impressed as hell with what they'd managed to do with her. You tweak as many genes as they must have to get what they got in Bree, and more often than not you wind up with a carnivorous potato.

As a man, at that point, I was mostly confused.

When I was younger, I'd never had much luck with pursuing women, and by the time I was into college, I'd basically given up. I had pretty much resigned myself to a life of work, quiet contemplation, and lots and lots of masturbating . . . until I met Kara.

This was on a Thursday night in April of my junior year at Hopkins, at a bar called the Lizard Lounge in downtown Baltimore. The place was built like an indoor amphitheater, with concentric half rings of tables descending in steps toward a stage where two pianos sat in front of the main bar. They usually kept both of them manned, sometimes by comedians, sometimes by serious musicians. There were bags of peanuts on every table, and the floor was covered a half inch deep in crushed shells.

They had a sort of a comedy act playing that night, a man and a woman at the two pianos banging out up-tempo political satire that mostly went straight over my head. I was there with Matt Porter, another aspiring engineer who was even more socially hapless than I was. We were sitting at a high table about halfway between the doors and the bar, nursing our first beers, filling up on peanuts and arguing about whether dogs actually like their owners or not, when Kara climbed onto the stool next to mine.

"Hey," she said. "These guys are pretty good, right?"

Kara was tall and broad-shouldered—a swimmer, I'd find out later—with long dark hair, pale, freckled skin, and eyes like a hawk. She was smiling in a way that I couldn't quite place.

"Sure," I said. "I guess so. I mean, I mostly don't have any idea who or what they're singing about, but they seem to know how to play the piano, anyway."

She laughed.

"Not a poli-sci major, huh?"

I shook my head.

"Nope. Gene Eng."

She gave me a smirk—the same one I always got when I told people what I was studying.

"In it for the cash, huh?"

I shrugged.

"Cash is good, right? But no, not really. I just like trying to figure out how to make things work, and this seemed like my best shot at getting to do that for a living."

I finished my beer. Kara smiled and said, "You want another one?"

I gave her a hesitant smile in return.

"Sure. I mean, I guess so."

As she was making her way up to the bar, Matt leaned over and asked me who she was.

"No idea," I said. "She just sat down and started talking to me."

"Huh."

He gave me a look that was a weird mixture of resentment and respect, and took a swig from his mostly empty beer. The piano players started in on a new song, about a Supreme Court decision that had just come down declaring that gene mods were covered under the same blanket privacy rights that protected abortion. They were finally singing about something that I was at least vaguely interested in, and I was really trying to catch what they were saying when Kara came back.

"Here ya go," she said, and set a fresh bottle in front of me.

"Thanks," I said. Without making eye contact, I pulled a ten-dollar bill from my wallet and slid it across the table to her. When the song finished and I looked around, she was gone. I turned to Matt.

"Hey," I said. "Where'd she go?"

He was staring at me like I'd just grown an extra head.

"You know that girl wasn't a waitress," he said. "Right?"

It was another six weeks before I saw Kara again, at a party in a friend's apartment on campus this time. Thank God, she didn't recognize me.

I got back from my run a little before noon, tired and sweaty and still just as confused, but riding high on endorphins and feeling much better about my day. I dropped my clothes on the bedroom floor and got into the shower, spent fifteen minutes mostly just letting hot water sluice over me, then got dried off and dressed and headed downstairs to make lunch. I ate, made some calls, and was just starting to think about playing around with a few things on my simulator when I felt my phone buzz. There was a priority message waiting for me. It flashed to the screen as soon as I pulled the phone out of my pocket and it registered my thumb print. It was from Meghan Cardiff, DragonCorn's lead for synthesis and testing.

MCardiff: Sorry to bug you, Drew, but there's something seriously funky with the last set of

schema I got from Singapore. I mean, the synthe-
sizer ran to completion, but I know what corn RNA
looks like, and this ain't it. Call me when you have
a minute.

MCardiff: Scratch that, Drew. Call me *now*.

10. IN WHICH HANNAH'S SOCIAL STANDING CONTINUES TO DETERIORATE.

On a sunny Saturday morning toward the end of September, Dad dropped me off at Briarwood with the rest of Doyle's sled dogs. We got onto a bus and rode out to the bluffs overlooking Lake Ontario, a dozen miles east of the tomb of the old nuclear plant. It was a thirty-minute ride. Looking around the bus, you would have thought Doyle was on his way to dump us into a mass grave.

After ten minutes of riding in dead silence, I actually said that to Sarah Miller. She'd been thumbing through her newsfeed—not reading anything, mind you—just scrolling, scrolling, scrolling. She looked up at me and shook her head.

"Yeah," she said. "I wish."

I didn't have any way to know this at the time, but we were actually reenacting a tradition that stretched back to Doyle's first year at Briarwood. That year, and every year since, he deliberately left a nine-day hole in the meet schedule somewhere between the third week of September and the first week of October. Right in the middle of that, he hauled the team up to the lake, and they ran a workout that he liked to call Climb to Failure.

The upperclassmen all knew what was coming, of course. That's why they were acting like they were on the way to their own funerals. I honestly thought they were putting on an act—you know, get the freshies all worked up, see if you can make them cry, that kind of thing.

They were not.

The bus dropped us in a parking lot looking out over the lake, maybe five hundred feet below. We left our sweats and phones and gear bags in our seats and shuffled out onto the pavement. Doyle led us over to the edge of the lot. There was a trailhead there. I pushed up to the front of the group, in between Tara and Jordan, and looked down. The trail switchbacked down the face of the bluff, all the way down to a narrow strip of sandy beach.

"Holy crap," I said. "Are we going down there?"

Jordan put a hand on my shoulder.

"No," he said. "We're going down over there." He waved off to the side, where I could see a longer, gentler trail curving away through knee-high grass. "This is where we come *up*."

"**O**kay," Doyle said as the last of us straggled down onto the beach. "For those of you who are new to this drill, here's how it works. It's a bit over two hundred yards from here to the top, and just about three hundred back down the easy way. This whistle blows every four minutes. If you're not ready to toe the line when it does, you're out. The goal is to see how many reps you can complete, so pace yourselves. Five means you get to keep your jersey and ride home on the bus. Ten gets you varsity warmups for the rest of the season. After that? You're in bonus time. We keep going until everyone fails. Questions?"

I looked around. Everyone but Jordan looked to be somewhere on the spectrum between sad and terrified. Nobody raised a hand.

"Right," Doyle said. "Line up, fastest to slowest. First whistle's in sixty seconds."

Five hundred yards. Four minutes. Doesn't seem that bad, right?

Trust me, it was bad.

Nobody had to walk home. That's the only good thing I can say about that morning. A few came close, though. Sarah, Kerry, and a boy everyone called Fish came within about two seconds of missing the fifth whistle. The three of them and four others dropped after that rep. We lost one or two per rep after that, but Kerry was the only one of the top seven, either boys or girls, who didn't make it to ten.

After eleven, it was just Jordan, Tara, and me.

Jordan made the whole thing seem effortless. He hit the top of the trail at least thirty yards ahead of us on every rep. Tara and I went side by side. Neither of us said a word the entire workout. By twelve, we were almost walking at the top. On thirteen, we barely made the whistle.

On fourteen, Tara didn't.

On the bus ride home, I wound up sharing a seat with Jordan.

"Nice work today," he said when he flopped down next to me. "Mind if I sit here?"

I shrugged.

"Go nuts. Doesn't look like anybody else wants to."

He slung an arm around my shoulder.

"Remember what I told you, Hannah?"

"It wasn't a race," I said. "It was just a workout."

"Oh, Hannah," he said, and gave me a squeeze. "You're such a sweet, innocent child."

"Bite me," I said, and wriggled out from under his arm. "I just . . . why does everything have to be so stupid?"

"Because," Jordan said. "People are stupid. Anytime you're trying to figure out why something is the way it is, just remember those three little words. You'll almost never go wrong."

The bus started moving. We sat in silence as we pulled out of the parking lot and onto Lake Road. We were almost back to the highway when I looked up at him and said, "None of the girls like me right now, do they?"

Jordan sighed.

"No, probably not."

"Why not?"

The whine that had crept into my voice made me cringe.

"Well," Jordan said, "you're upsetting the social order. Nobody likes that."

"Okay," I said. "So how do I fix it?"

He slouched down until our heads were almost level.

"You've got two choices, Hannah. First, you could back off. Leave Tara at the top of the heap. If you settled in at third, say, or maybe even a distant, non-threatening second, they'd welcome you right back into the fold."

"Okay," I said. "What if I don't like that option? What's number two?"

He leaned over then, until the sides of our heads were touching.

"Option two is that you hang in there until everybody gets over the fact that there's a new sheriff in town."

"And how long does that take?"

He laughed.

"With Tara? I'm guessing that's going to take a long, long time."

The other half of the Climb to Failure tradition at Briarwood was that the captains were supposed to host a party that night. I would honestly rather have stuck my head in a blender than go, but they were having it at Jordan's house, and he'd made me promise to be there before we got off the bus. I'd been stewing about it most of the day, going back and forth over whether to actually show, but eventually I decided I could put in an appearance, try to make nice with some of the girls if they'd let me, and then tell Jordan that my dad wanted me home early.

I was just out of the shower, trying to decide what you wear to a cross-country party, when my phone pinged.

<UNK01>: Hi Hannah. How's it going?

Wilma17: Inchy?

<UNK01>: Not necessarily.

Wilma17: Right. What do you want?

<UNK01>: Why do I have to want something? Can't two friends just have a friendly chat?

Wilma17: Wait—are we friends?

<UNK01>: Now you've hurt my feelings again.

Wilma17: Oh, for shit's sake, Inchy. I really don't have time for you right now.

<UNK01>: You should wear the blue top you just dropped on your bed, the khaki shorts, and those nice sandals you had on yesterday afternoon. There. Now you have time for me.

Wilma17: . . .

<UNK01>: You're welcome.

<UNK01>: So, as I said before—how's it going?

Wilma17: Can I ask you something?

<UNK01>: Well, technically I just asked you something. I think standard protocol in situations like this is for you to answer my question. Once that's accomplished, you can respond with one of your own.

Wilma17: . . .

Wilma17: Um . . . Fine?

<UNK01>: Glad to hear it! Now, what did you want to ask?

Wilma17: :-|

<UNK01>: Was that your question?

Wilma17: No, Inchy. My question was why do you need me to spy on my dad when you've obviously got my whole house bugged? Also, how do you have my whole house bugged? And while I'm at it, *why* do you have my whole house bugged?

<UNK01>: Bugged? Madam, you wound me. I would never.

Wilma17: What are you talking about? You can obviously see and hear everything I do! How is that, Inchy?

<UNK01>: Well, sure. That's 'cause I hacked your phone.

Wilma17: . . .

<UNK01>: Just by-the-by, while we're on the topic of spying on your dad . . . how's that going? Because I'm kind of feeling like we're not getting as much out of that project as I'd hoped.

Wilma17: Okay. So why don't you just hack his phone? You can help him pick out his outfits for a change.

<UNK01>: Yeah, that would be fun. Unfortunately, he's actually got pretty decent security.

Wilma17: Unlike me, you mean?

<UNK01>: I didn't want to come right out and say it.

<UNK01>: Don't get me wrong—I could totally crack his systems if I needed to. That's kind of a high-risk, high-reward gambit, though. Bioteka has a rep for doing bad things to folks who poke their noses into places where they shouldn't be.

Wilma17: So you thought you'd let me do it for you?

<UNK01>: Well sure, it sounds bad when you put it that way.

Wilma17: Okay. So how would you put it?

<UNK01>: Oh, I'd put it that way too. I said it sounded bad. I didn't say it was inaccurate.

Dad dropped me off at Jordan's house a little before nine. I told him to come back and get me at ten. He looked at me like I'd grown a second head.

"Ten? That's an hour from now."

"Yeah," I said, and opened the passenger door.

"You understand it took almost a half hour to get here, right?"

I turned to look at him. He didn't look happy.

"Um . . ." I said. "Yes?"

"So you want me to drive home, sit in the driveway for five minutes, and then turn right around and come back for you. Is that right?"

I gave him my best doe eyes.

"Yes?"

He tried to stare me down, but he never had a chance.

"Fine," he said finally, and sighed. "Have fun."

I waved to him as he pulled away, then started up the walk to the house. I shouldn't have been surprised by what I was looking at after seeing Jordan's car, but I was. When Dad put our place together, he was definitely trying to stay under the radar. From the outside, you wouldn't think anybody worth lynching lived there.

Jordan's parents clearly had no such concerns. Their house was a mountain of marble and brass and teak and jade. When the revolution came, I was pretty sure the Barneses were gonna be the first ones against the wall.

Jordan was waiting for me when I stepped onto the porch.

"Hannah! So glad you made it. You know Micah, right?"

The boy standing next to him gave me a truncated wave. I recognized him from practice—he was one of those guys at the back end of the varsity pack, the ones who ran with Jordan's group during easy workouts, but couldn't hang with them on a progression—but I hadn't known his name until just then.

"Yeah," I said. "Sure. How's it going, Micah?"

He laughed.

"You have no idea who I am, do you?"

"Yeah," I said. "Not really."

He laughed again, harder. Micah turned out to be pretty hard to offend.

"It's okay," he said. "Next to Jordan, we're all kind of forgettable."

That was objectively not true. Micah was . . . well, definitely not forgettable. The other runners were all sharp edges and wiry angles. Most of them looked like their arms and legs had just gone through a growth spurt, and they were still waiting for their bodies to catch up. Micah's body was clearly a finished product, and wiry was not the word for it.

Micah looked like he could bench-press a truck.

"Come on," Jordan said. "Let me show you around."

Here are some things that Jordan's house had, that mine did not:

1. A sauna.
2. A hot tub which appeared to be made entirely of marble and gold.
3. A lounge.
4. A movie theater.

"It's a media room," Jordan said. "We don't really watch movies here."

"Yeah," Micah said. "Movies are for the proles."

Jordan smacked him, but Micah just laughed.

"What?" Micah said. "Is there a prole standing behind me?"

I rolled my eyes.

"Honestly, I'm kind of feeling like a prole right now."

Micah gave me a long look, and shook his head.

"I don't know exactly what your parents do, Hannah, but I know what it costs to get a set of custom mods that actually produce a viable kid and not a monster. Your family may do a better job of keeping things on the down-low than the Barneses, but I can guarantee you're every bit as much an aristo as Jordan or me."

"An aristo?" I said. "No, I don't think so."

"Really?" Micah said. "When the shit hits the fan again, whose side will you be on?"

"Okay," Jordan said, and stepped between us. "I think that's it for the tour. Let's get back to the party, shall we?"

I spent the next forty minutes confirming that yeah, I really should have let Tara beat me that morning. Most of the girls would barely make eye contact, let alone talk to me. Sarah sat next to me on a gigantic leather couch for about two minutes and complained about the GeneChem assignment we had due on Monday, but Tara walked past and shot her a look, and that was that. The boys were better. They didn't seem to care so much what Tara thought—but they didn't seem to care so much about having any sort of extended conversation with a slightly funny looking freshie girl, either, so that wasn't a ton of help. Jordan hung with me for a couple of stretches, but it was his party, and I wouldn't have wanted him to spend the whole time babysitting me even if he'd been willing to do it. All in all, I was pretty happy when Dad showed up a few minutes early.

"Hey," I said when I climbed into the car. "Thanks for coming back."

He tried to glare at me, but I gave him the doe eyes again, and he couldn't hold it.

"No problem," he said. "Did you have fun?"

I shrugged.

"About as much as I expected."

He had the car set to auto. It backed up onto the access road, and headed out toward the highway. He was reaching for the touch screen to turn on the sound system when I said, "So Dad. Um . . . how's work going?"

He turned to look at me. I'm pretty sure that was the first time in my life that I'd asked him anything about his job.

"Well," he said. "It's good, I guess? I mean, it keeps us off the streets, right?"

I forced a smile.

"Yeah. I guess so."

He reached for the screen again.

"Working on any interesting projects?"

He took longer to answer that time.

"Hannah? Is there something you want to tell me?"

I shook my head.

"Why would you think that?"

"Well," he said. "You've never expressed the least interest in my work before. Did something happen at the party? Did somebody say something about me, or about Bioteka?"

"No," I said. "Nobody talked about anything but homework and carbo loading. It was the most boring party ever."

We sat in silence for what seemed like a really long time.

"Okay," he said finally, and turned on the sound system. It was set to his playlist from the Dark Ages. I leaned back in my seat and closed my eyes. I was actually starting to drift when my phone dinged.

<UNK01>: Come on, Hannah. You're not even trying.

11. IN WHICH JORDAN EXPERIENCES A PERSISTENT SENSE OF FOREBODING.

In-season runners' parties don't tend to be all-night affairs. Tara and her crew departed *en masse* around eleven, and everyone was gone by midnight.

Everyone but Micah, I mean. My parents were out of the country. Micah was staying the night.

We were doing a little desultory cleaning—throwing away half-eaten food, emptying bottles, that sort of thing—when Micah stopped in the middle of clearing the coffee table in the sitting room and said, "Hey, Jordan?"

He looked like he was thinking. With Micah, that was never a good sign.

"Yes?"

"You remember what I said to Hannah, about the shit hitting the fan again?"

I nodded.

"Well . . . when that happens, what are *you* gonna do?"

I sighed, sat down on the couch, and patted the cushion next to me. Micah left his garbage bag on the table and flopped down beside me.

"Tell me," I said. "What's troubling you, my friend?"

He shot me a quick sideways glance, and folded his arms across his chest.

"Don't talk to me like I'm a five-year-old, Jordan. You know I don't like that."

"Sorry," I said, slung my arm around his shoulder and leaned my head against his. "Seriously, though— what's the problem?"

"Nothing. It's just . . ." he slouched down until he could rest his head against the back of the couch. "This place, Jordan—it really does look like something out of an UnAltered propaganda vid about how the Engineered parasites are sucking the life-blood out of the country. Aren't you even a little bit worried about what'll happen when things start up again?"

I pulled my arm back, and slouched down beside him.

"Well," I said. "First of all, what makes you think things are going to start up again? Open hostilities didn't exactly turn out well for the UnAltered last time. They call it the Stupid War for a reason, you know."

"Yeah, I know. But still . . ."

I rested my hand on his leg.

"But still what?"

He sighed.

"There's also a reason that most people like us either keep it on the down-low, like Hannah, or live in a fortress, like Marta Longstreth." He closed his eyes and sighed again. "I really like you, Jordan. I worry about you."

I smiled and gave his leg a squeeze.

"I really like you too, Micah, and I appreciate the concern—but aren't you forgetting something?"

He turned to look at me.

"What?"

"Unlike Hannah, or Marta Longstreth, or even you, my friend—I'm not Engineered. As far as the UnAltered are concerned, I'm just one of the guys."

I laughed. Micah did not.

"I don't know," he said. "When shit gets real, I'm not sure they're gonna take the time to make those kinds of distinctions. Between the car, and the house, and . . . ." He put his hand to my cheek. ". . . that face, you sure as hell come off like one of us."

I opened my mouth to reply, but for some reason Dani Longstreth popped into my head. I gave Micah's leg another squeeze.

"Tell you what?" I said. "When shit starts getting real, I'll come hide out in your basement. Fair enough?"

That got a smile from him.

"Sure," he said. "Fair enough."

I was up early the next morning. Micah was fantastic in every way, but good *Lord*, did he take up space in the bed. I was just thinking about pulling together something for breakfast when my phone pinged.

<UNK01>: Hey Jordan. You up?

I stared at the screen for a solid ten seconds. It wasn't supposed to be possible to spoof a system ID. That was one of the things NatSec supposedly cleaned up in the aftermath of the Stupid War, after Andersen rammed the National Salvation Act through congress and they basically got the right to do any goddamned thing they wanted to do.

Jordasaurus: Uh . . . who dis?

<UNK01>: Marta? Obviously?

Jordasaurus: Okay. Care to explain how/why your ID shows up as <UNK01>?

<UNK01>: Oh shit. Does it?

Jordasaurus: It does.

<UNK01>: That's Daddy, I guess. He's so freaking paranoid.

Jordasaurus: This is new, right? Weren't you MSpooky1 last time we chatted?

<UNK01>: That's my ID. That's what shows on my screen too. I have no clue how he's blanking it on yours.

Jordasaurus: Weird.

<UNK01>: Yeah, that's the word. Things are definitely getting weird around here. Between this, and the closed-door meetings, and the snipers . . . Anyway, that's why I pinged you. I'm thinking about a jailbreak one day next week. Wanna come?

Jordasaurus: . . .

<UNK01>: I mean, if you're busy . . .

Jordasaurus: You have snipers?

<UNK01>: Yes?

<UNK01>: Not a lot of them. It's not like we have

a battalion of snipers marching around the compound or anything. Just a few.

Jordasaurus: Okaaaaaaay . . .

<UNK01>: So, are you in?

Jordasaurus: . . .

<UNK01>: Come on—we had fun the other night, right?

Jordasaurus: We did.

<UNK01>: But?

Jordasaurus: Well, I have to admit to a little concern about helping you sneak away from a man who has *snipers*.

<UNK01>: Oh please, Jordan. Those snipers are not there for you.

Jordasaurus: Okay. Who, exactly, are they there for?

<UNK01>: I don't know. The unwashed masses, I guess.

Jordasaurus: Proles?

<UNK01>: Them too.

Jordasaurus: Okay. Tell you what. Let me know when you've picked a day, and I'll check my social calendar.

<UNK01>: Great! Don't worry. This will be a fun-filled and 100% sniper-free day.

Jordasaurus: That's what I like to hear.

I dropped my phone onto the marble island in the middle of the kitchen and pulled a carton of eggs out of the refrigerator. It was starting to look like being Marta's fake boyfriend was going to be more work than I'd planned. I wasn't sure where she was going with this jailbreak thing, but it sounded like I'd wind up having to ditch a day of school at a minimum—not that I minded that all that much, of course, but I was going to have to make sure she understood that either whatever we did was going to need to wrap up in time for me to get to practice, or I was going to need enough advance notice to get a certified death certificate. Missing calculus was one thing. Missing one of Doyle's workouts was something else entirely.

I had a pan warming on the stove and was cracking eggs into a mixing bowl when my phone pinged again.

<UNK02>: Jordan. How goes it, friend?

Jordasaurus: Marta?

<UNK02>: Sure. Let's go with that.

Jordasaurus: I'm making breakfast, Marta. What do you need?

<UNK02>: Oh, nothing much. Just wanted to say hello. You know, because we're such good pals.

Jordasaurus: Okay, this is getting weird, and I've got to get these eggs on the stove, so . . .

<UNK02>: Oh, sure. Don't want to hold up your eggs. One thing, though. You're tight with Hannah Bergen, right?

Jordasaurus: You know Hannah?

<UNK02>: Oh, sure. We're very close. So are the two of you, huh?

Jordasaurus: Where are you going with this?

<UNK02>: Nowhere for the moment. Just making social connections. So, you spend much time with her dad? Watching the game, shooting the shit, talking shop? That sort of thing?

Jordasaurus: Pan's hot. Good-bye, Marta.

The phone pinged twice more while I was pouring the eggs into the pan, but I didn't pick it up. I dropped four slices of bread into the toaster, stirred the eggs around until they firmed up, and then dumped them out onto a platter. I was just bringing them into the breakfast nook when Micah came down the stairs.

"Hey," he said. "You made breakfast?"

"I did," I said. "Grab yourself a plate and a fork."

He followed me to the table, sat down, and took two-thirds of the eggs and three slices of toast.

"Hungry?"

He shrugged. I took what was left. Micah held his fork in his fist and shoveled eggs into his mouth like a caveman.

"So," I said. "You remember my little pseudo-date with Marta Longstreth?"

He looked up, then back down at his plate.

"Yeah," he said. "I remember."

"You know anything about her?"

He finished his eggs, and started in on the toast.

"I know her dad's the richest man on the planet."

"Right. Everybody knows that."

He got up, went out to the kitchen, and came back with a glass of juice.

"Also," he said, "he's nuts. So, there's that."

I leaned forward, and took a forkful of eggs.

"Nuts how? He's the CEO of Bioteka, right? How nuts could he be?"

"You know what happened to his wife?"

I nodded.

"Burned alive," he said. "That shit leaves a mark."

I took another bite, but suddenly my eggs seemed much less appetizing. Micah finished his toast, then reached across the table and took mine.

"Sure," I said. "Help yourself."

"Thanks," he said. "Consider this down payment on your room in my basement."

"Yeah," I said. "About that—you really think something bad's coming?"

He took a long time chewing and swallowing.

"Look," he said finally. "You know I'm not exactly a political junkie, right?"

I laughed.

"Yeah, Micah. I get that."

"Right. So all I know is what I hear from my dad, basically."

"Okay," I said. "So what does your dad think?"

He finished his juice, and wiped his mouth with the back of his hand.

THE END OF ORDINARY 121

"Well," he said. "For one thing, he thinks I should learn to handle a rifle."

I wasn't sure what to say to that.

Micah was gone by the time I picked up my phone again. I thumbed the screen on. Two messages were waiting for me.

<UNK02>: Okay, Jordan. Enjoy your eggs. And don't forget—you should definitely hang out more with Hannah's dad. Also with me, your pal Marta Longstreth, and my dad. That would totally be a fun thing to do.

<UNK02>: Oh, and when you do—make sure to bring your phone with you. :)

12. IN WHICH DREW HAS MANAGEMENT ISSUES.

Just for the record, I did call Meghan Cardiff when I saw her message. She didn't pick up. I left her a message. I called her a half dozen times during the course of that afternoon, and left her a bunch of texts as well. No response. I followed up again the next morning, and at least once a day for the rest of the week. It was like she'd dropped off the face of the Earth.

On the first Monday in October, I had a status meeting with the entire DragonCorn development team. I really didn't appreciate being blown off after getting a red alert, particularly when it was related to the Singapore dev work, which was simultaneously the most critical part of the project and the part I had the least direct control over. I was hoping to use the morning's updates as an opportunity for a dressing-down.

Needless to say, Meghan didn't show for the meeting.

Everybody else was there—even Marcus Becker, who was the lead for our Singapore group, and therefore sitting in front of his wallscreen at a time when he'd ordinarily be either drunk or asleep. We waited for ten minutes in silence. I'd banned multitasking during project meetings, so everyone pretty much just sat there staring at their screens for the entire time. Marcus looked especially pissed, which probably meant that the evening had been scheduled for drunk rather than sleepy. Finally, Alistair Burke rolled his eyes, leaned in toward his screen and said, "She's not coming, Drew. Nobody's heard from her in a week or more. What are you going to do about this?"

I sighed.

"Fine. Let's swing it around the horn and see where everyone is today. Maybe Meghan will show by the time we're through. Marcus?"

Marcus folded his arms across his chest and glared out of my wallscreen.

"Awaiting report from synthesis and testing."

I sighed again, and rubbed my face with both hands.

"Alistair?"

"Awaiting report from synthesis and testing."

"Mara?"

"Awaiting report from synthesis and testing."

I looked around at the rest of the team. Nobody was smiling.

"Okay," I said. "Is there anyone who Meghan's *not* blocking at the moment?"

Therese Michaels raised her hand. Therese was from finance. Her only job was making sure we didn't run over budget.

"Look," Marcus said. "You know what this project means to the company, Drew."

Mara snickered.

"You know what the project means to our *asses*."

"Right," Marcus said. "That too. You're not a ballbuster, Drew. We all get that, and mostly we appreciate it." He glanced around. Most of the others were nodding. "But sometimes," he said. "Sometimes, balls just need to be busted. This is one of those times, Drew. I'm glad Meghan's getting laid or taking a walkabout or whatever the hell she's doing, but I'm not willing to lose my job over it. Fix this, Drew. Get her ass moving, or get her replaced."

"Hear, hear," Alistair said, and Mara went into a slow clap. I took a deep breath in, and let it out slowly.

"Fine," I said after Mara wound down. "Message received. I'll deal with Meghan. One way or the other, we'll have a functional tester by the end of the week."

"That's what we like to hear," Marcus said. "Are we done here?"

"Yeah," I said. "We're done."

Their windows blinked out one by one, until finally only Mara was left.

"You know, Drew, you're a great engineer," she said.

"Thanks," I said. "You're uncommonly kind."

She shook her head.

"You didn't let me finish. You're a great engineer . . . but you are a really, really shitty manager."

So, I had a problem, and I had to deal with it. Naturally, I went for a run.

I was just getting out of the shower when the wallscreen pinged to let me know that someone had come through the front door. I shut off the water. Kara came into the bathroom, closed the door behind her and leaned against the sink.

"Hey," I said. "You're home."

She tossed me a towel.

"Mom's doing better," she said. "Dad said I should put in some time here. He'll give me a call if anything changes."

I rubbed myself down, took a swipe through my hair, and then wrapped the towel around my waist.

"How better is better?" I asked. "I mean, do they think . . ."

Kara shook her head.

"They can't stop what's happening. They can barely slow it down. She's just on a kind of . . . plateau, I think. Better just means that for the moment, she's not getting worse. I didn't want to leave, but . . . I can't just hang around there forever, waiting for her to die."

That's when I realized she was crying, tears seeping silently from the corners of her eyes, running down along the sides of her nose, and disappearing into the fine hair on her upper lip.

"Kara," I said. She looked up, shook her head again, and looked away.

"No, Drew," she said. "This isn't something you can fix."

She walked past me then, out the door and down the stairs.

When I came downstairs, Kara was cleaning the kitchen.

"You don't have to do that," I said. "I was just about to make something for lunch."

She shrugged without looking at me.

"Don't you think somebody should clean up from breakfast first?"

"I can do it all at once," I said. "Just go sit down. I'll be done here in a few minutes."

She shook her head, and started scrubbing at the stovetop as if it had herpes.

"You always want the shortcut, Drew. When it comes to this house, when it comes to this family . . . if I don't do it, it doesn't get done. I've been gone for a week, and this place looks like a garbage pit."

I sighed, and leaned back against the wall.

"It doesn't," I said. "Hannah and I cleaned the whole house twice while you were gone."

Kara laughed, but there was no humor in it.

"Right," she said. "I'm sure. You and Hannah. I don't doubt you went running together, and I wouldn't be surprised if you spent some time talking about how great it was to have me off your backs for a while, but I can look around and see exactly how much goddamned cleaning got done."

She loaded the dishwasher with the two plates and two glasses I'd left on the breakfast table. I thought about helping, but when Kara got in one of these moods, my experience was that it was best to remain as still and silent as possible, and wait for it to pass. I watched her wipe down the table, and then take another swipe at the stove. She looked around.

"That's it," I said. "Everything looks great. Take a break now, okay?"

She turned to look at me, her face as blank as a wooden mask.

"Yeah," she said. "Make yourself a sandwich, Drew."

She walked past me, down the hallway and into the living room. I heard the couch sag as she dropped onto it. I should have followed her. I get that now. At the time, though? I was hungry, and I was angry, and I was resentful. I didn't think I'd deserved the ration of shit she'd just given me. I didn't stop to think about what she'd been going through, or why she was acting the way she was. That's one of the traps you can fall into when you've been married for as long as we had. You start to see your partner as this sort of weird extension of yourself, and you forget that she has an inner life of her own. I hadn't quite figured that out at the time, though. I let Kara walk away, and I made myself a sandwich.

I should note here that I take sandwiches very seriously. I don't do peanut butter and jelly, and I don't do BLTs. I've always felt that a sandwich is like a sonnet. Sure, you're forced into a framework, but that's what allows you to really express your creativity. I bet Shakespeare made a crazy good grilled cheese. That day, my sandwich involved turkey, salami, pickled sweet peppers, pesto, tomatoes, two kinds of cheese, and a panini press. I was just sitting down to eat it when the front door opened, then slammed closed again.

"Kara?" I said.

Nothing.

I still have no idea where Kara went that afternoon, or what she did. I should have gone after her, but . . . well, I guess I was kind of an asshole, honestly. Instead, I spent most of the rest of the day on the screen with a woman named Marcy in corporate HR, trying to figure out what to do about Meghan. We went back and forth for a long while, but the bottom line was that before they'd give me a replacement, I needed to get some definite statement from Meghan as to whether she was sick, or on vacation, or retired, or whatever. When I started whining about the fact that she wouldn't answer my pings, Marcy told me to get on a shuttle and ask her in person.

"Fine," I said. "I'll look into doing something next week, maybe?"

"No," Marcy said. "You'll do it tomorrow."

My phone buzzed. I glanced down. A cheerful yellow icon popped up to tell me that I was booked on the 08:00 to LA.

"You know," I said. "I have plans tomorrow."

"Yes," Marcy said. "I know. They involve figuring out how you managed to let a top-five project, which has recently gotten a great deal of direct attention from Robert Longstreth, spin completely off the rails. If you can't handle that, I'm guessing you and I will be having a much less friendly call soon. Have a nice day, Drew—and give Meghan my regards."

I sat staring at the screen after she cut the call. I wasn't used to being threatened by HR. I pulled up the corporate org chart, and wasted ten minutes trying to figure out if she was above or below me. As it turned out, HR was on a completely separate track—like Internal Affairs, or maybe the Gestapo,

I guess. If I wanted to complain about Marcy's attitude, I'd need to go up five levels before I could start working my way back down toward her. Definitely not worth the effort.

Anyway, she was probably right. I had no idea at the time why the executive group was so worked up about DragonCorn, but I was savvy enough to realize that they were. If nothing else, my crappy management was keeping a dozen of Bioteka's top engineers tied up and completely unproductive. That was probably a capital offense by itself.

It was a bit after five when I went to pick up Hannah from school. Between Kara and Meghan and Bree, who'd pinged me three more times in the past week, I'll admit to being more than a little rattled. I started out with the car on manual. I'm an engineer, but I've honestly never had much faith in automation. It took me ten minutes and two near accidents to switch it over to full automatic. I spent most of the rest of the drive with my eyes closed, listening to my pulse pounding in my ears and trying to keep my breathing under control. It's funny—the shit storm hadn't even really broken yet, but I think on some level I already knew it was coming.

When I pulled into the school parking lot, Hannah was there waiting for me. She wasn't where she usually was, though, sitting on the steps by the main entrance, staring at her phone. She was there in the front lot leaning against a jet-black sports car, talking to Jordan Barnes.

That, I was not expecting.

My car rolled into a parking space across the lot from them, and shut itself down. I took a deep breath in, let it out slowly, and opened the door.

"Hey," I called. "Hannah. You ready?"

She looked over at me, held up one finger, and turned back to Jordan.

That, I also was not expecting.

Hannah had her back to me, but I could see Jordan's face. He was laughing, and as I watched, he leaned over and touched her arm.

"Hannah," I said, a little louder. "Seriously. We have things to do."

She gave me a quick full-brow-ridge glare, then turned back again. I got out of the car. Jordan glanced up, got a look at my face, and stopped laughing. He leaned down, said something with his mouth close to Hannah's ear. She shot me a murderous look, then patted Jordan's arm and turned away. Jordan folded himself into his car. He was already pulling out onto the main road when Hannah climbed into mine.

"Jeebus, Dad," she said as soon as she'd closed the door. "What the hell was that about?"

I turned to look at her. She glared back at me for a full five seconds, then finally looked away. We rode the entire way home in silence.

13. IN WHICH HANNAH LEARNS THINGS SHE'D PREFER NOT TO KNOW.

Looking back, the week after Climb to Failure was definitely what you'd call an inflection point. At the beginning of the season, I'd thought Tara and I were going to be best friends forever. She'd pulled back as I got stronger, but she hadn't been unfriendly, exactly, and she'd still been a good training partner. That week, though, things went downhill in a big way. On Monday, she tried to ditch me on what was supposed to be a long, easy recovery run. Tuesday was a track day. She made sure she was running in a different group. Wednesday she told Doyle she was having calf pain, and I wound up spending a progression run getting the silent treatment from Miranda and Kerry. Thursday was another long run. I let her pull ahead of me on that one, and hung back just far enough to keep her in sight, but to be out of range of her stink-eye. Friday was interval thousands. Doyle paired us up. I beat her on every one.

On Saturday, I was sitting in my solarium trying to catch up on my reading for American Literature when my phone pinged. It was Tara.

TCSpeed: Hello Hannah. Just wanted to let you know that I'm so proud of the way you've been progressing this season. You've come so far in just a few weeks. So far, in fact, that I think you're ready to move on to a different training partner. Sarah or Jules might be more your speed. Good luck!

I didn't bother to reply.

I wasn't sure what to do when I got to practice the next Monday. We were just into October then, and we had three hard weeks of running left before we were supposed to start tapering down for States. Tara had made it pretty clear that I was dead to her, and I didn't think any of the other girls would buck her—not that I should have been training with most of them anyway. I ran from my last class to the varsity lockers, got my stuff and got changed while the other girls were just wandering in. Nobody said anything mean to me, and Sarah actually gave me a sympathetic look as I slammed my locker shut.

For the first time since the second or third day of practice, though, I didn't feel like I was where I belonged.

I was the first girl out to the soccer field, but most of the boys were there ahead of me, standing around in twos and threes, talking and stretching and waiting for Doyle to show. Jordan was off to one side with Micah, who'd spent the past month fighting two other boys for the seventh slot on varsity. They'd all been within a few seconds of one another in every race, and I think Doyle was waiting for one of them to put the other two away so that he wouldn't have to make any hard choices about who to bring to Sectionals.

Jordan smiled when he saw me. I looked away, but when I looked back he was waving me over.

"Hannah," he said. "Come help me convince Micah not to stick his head in a wood chipper."

Micah gave Jordan a half-hearted shove. Jordan laughed, and patted Micah's cheek with one hand. I glanced around. Nobody else was paying the least attention to me, which, considering where I was with the girls' team, was kind of a relief. I walked over to where they were standing.

"I'm not gonna stick my head in a wood chipper," Micah said. "I'm just not gonna make it to Sectionals."

I looked him over. Micah was tall for a runner, and most of his height was from the waist up. The clothes he'd been wearing at the party had hidden how big he really was. He had broad shoulders and a deep chest, and hands that looked like they could palm a watermelon. I'd never really paid a lot of attention to the boys' races—we usually ran right after, and I liked to get myself focused before the start—but I remembered then seeing him sometimes muscling through workouts, putting out twice as much energy as the runners around him. He was obviously an athlete, but he just wasn't built for running.

He was definitely built, though.

"Of course you'll make Sectionals," Jordan said. "Tell him, Hannah. He's just got to want it, right?"

I looked up at Micah. He looked back, eyes half closed. I sighed. No point in having the boys like me any more than the girls, right?

"Have you tried swimming?" I asked. "I bet you'd be a great swimmer."

Jordan looked at me, his mouth half open, then turned to look at Micah. I had a second of thinking that I was about to get reamed in front of my last running friend, but then Micah burst out laughing.

"You see, Jordan?" Micah said. "Here's someone who recognizes running talent—or lack thereof, anyway."

"No," I said. "That's not what I meant! I just . . ."

"It's fine," Micah said, and sat down to stretch. "You've got a great eye, Hannah. Swimming is exactly what my freaking dad cut me for. The plan was for me to be at the Olympic Training Center in Orlando by now, with some psycho coach lashing me through fifteen thousand meters a day."

"Right," Jordan said. "Lucky thing you're here instead, with a different psycho coach lashing you through fifteen *miles* a day."

I sat down beside Micah, stretched my legs out in front of me, and brought my nose to my knees.

"I don't get it," I said. "You're built to swim, but you're all wrong for a runner. Why are you here and not there?"

"What's not to get?" Micah said. "Why the hell should my dad get to decide what I do with my life? I mean, have you ever been to a swim meet? They *suck*. You sit around a hot, dank pool deck for two hours, get in the water for thirty seconds, and then sit around for another two hours. And practices? They're even worse. Three hours, face down in the water, up and down that blue line. Out here, we can at least talk while we're running. Swim practice is the single most boring thing known to man."

I laughed.

"Sounds like you at least gave it a try."

He rolled his eyes.

"My dad put me on a club team when I was four. I stuck with it exactly as long as it took me to realize that I could actually say no."

"Micah's being modest," Jordan said. "He won States in three events when he was a freshman.

Coach Brenner practically blew an aneurism when he quit."

"He still bugs me, actually," Micah said. "He had Alan Muhlenberg message me yesterday to try to get me to tryouts at the end of the month."

"From the way you're smirking," I said, "I'm guessing you said no?"

His smirk turned into a full-on grin, and he shook his head.

"Nah. Alan's cute. I told him I'd be happy to discuss it with him over coffee."

Jordan kicked Micah, and they both burst out laughing.

The girls weren't any friendlier out in the field than they'd been in the locker room. Even Sarah wouldn't make eye contact with me, and Tara acted as if I had some kind of reverse gravitational field that was actively repelling her. While Doyle was giving us our pre-workout lecture, I made a point of moving around the fringes of the group, chasing Tara in super slow motion. No matter where I was, she was always as far away from me as she could possibly be and still be with the team. When Doyle told us to get moving, I walked over to Jordan.

"Hey," I said. "Mind if I . . ."

I didn't finish, because the look on his face had already given me my answer.

"Oooooh," he said. "Sorry, Hannah. You heard Doyle. We're running a progression today. You know I've got tons of respect for you, but . . ."

"Yeah," I said. "No problem."

He was right, of course. I'd be able to stay with his pack for the easy part of the run, but when they started to really turn it over they'd drop me, and Doyle was not a fan of his athletes trying to train over their heads.

Of course, he also wasn't a fan of his athletes running alone.

I was seriously considering getting down on my knees and begging Tara to let me tag along with her when Micah's giant spider-hand tapped my shoulder.

"Need a partner?"

I looked up at him.

"You're not with Jordan?"

He grinned.

"Define *with*."

I could feel my cheeks redden.

"I meant you're not *running* with him. Jackass."

He laughed, slung his arm around my shoulder and pulled me toward the trailhead.

"I like you," he said. "You're sassy."

"Yeah," I said. "That's what they say."

Micah Jacobs turned out to be simultaneously the worst runner and the best partner I ever trained with.

I'd seen him run before, of course, but you can't appreciate just how crappy someone's technique is until you've gone stride for stride with him on an eight-mile progression. Micah's shoulders hunched forward, his head drooped, his feet reached out too far in front of him on every stride and then slapped at the ground as if he were angry with it. I sort of expected him to try to assert his male prerogative at the start, but he didn't even think about it. He let me set the pace, then settled in beside me where the trails were wide enough to go side by side, and behind me where they weren't.

"You know," I said over my shoulder the first time he dropped back, "if I didn't know better, I'd say you were trying to check out my butt."

Micah tried to laugh, but it turned into a hacking cough instead.

"No offense," he said when he finally got his breathing back under control, "but checking out any part of you is honestly the very furthest thing from my mind."

The trail widened a bit, and I slowed to let him come up beside me again.

"Yeah," I said. "I kind of figured."

The ground was still sloppy from the past week's rain, and Micah's screwed-up stride made him prone to slipping and hyperextending. He did that then, front foot sliding out from under him, arms waving wildly. I dodged to keep from getting clocked, then caught him by the arm and steadied him enough to keep him from actually going down.

"Shit!" he said. "Thanks. Sorry."

"No problem," I said. "Explain to me again why you think this is better for you than swimming?"

We ran on in silence for five seconds, then ten. I was starting to think I'd managed to alienate yet another potential friend, this time in record time, when he said, "Look, Hannah. I don't expect you to understand this. I mean, you're doing exactly what they designed you to do, right? It works for you, and that's great. You're lucky. The thing is, though—it didn't work for me. Dad built me to be a specific thing, but it turned out that's not what I wanted to be. All other things being equal, I'd rather just suck at running around in the woods."

The trail narrowed. I slowed to let him move ahead.

"You know," I said. "You don't suck."

He laughed again, this time without hurting himself.

"I hate to break this to you, Hannah, but we all suck. It's just a question of who we're comparing ourselves to."

He had to duck his head to get under a branch that I'd have had to reach up to touch with my hand.

"So," I said. "Who do you compare yourself to?"

He looked back at me. He was smiling, but he didn't look happy.

"Who do you think?"

The thing is, what I said was true. Micah didn't suck. Everything I knew about running said he should have sucked, but he didn't. When we started, I kind of expected that I'd have to ease up to keep from dropping him. He must have been burning three times as much oxygen as I was—but apparently he had a whole craploar of hay stored up in the old hayloft, and he wound up finishing forty or fifty yards ahead of me.

He must have been a hell of a swimmer.

Micah was sitting in the grass with Jordan when I came in. I started toward the girls' side of the field, but Micah waved me over.

"Thanks," he said when I sat down across from them. "That was great, Hannah. It was fun to run with someone who wasn't busting my ass about my form the whole time."

I decided not to mention that even though I hadn't said anything, I'd been thinking it, really, really loudly.

"We only bust your ass about your form because it's so adorably terrible," Jordan said. "Think of it as a compliment. We're all amazed that you can keep up with us while running like you have brain damage."

"Whatever," I said. "That was one of the best workouts I've had all season." I rolled onto my stomach, and rose up into a plank. "I mean, the running was good, but the fact that you weren't trying to figure out how to murder me in the woods and get away with it really sealed the deal."

After we'd finished stretching and abs and Doyle had given us a long, droning speech about the importance of team unity and whatnot, Jordan walked me out to the parking lot. I expected Micah to come along, but apparently an eight-mile progression wasn't enough for him, because he went straight from the field into the weight room.

"Wow," I said as he walked away. "Hard-core, huh?"

Jordan shrugged.

"A body like that doesn't just happen, you know."

"Yeah," I said after a long, awkward pause. "This conversation is making me uncomfortable. Can we talk about something else?"

He rested his arm across my shoulders, and we started around the building.

"What?" Jordan said. "You don't want to hear about Micah's washboard abs? You don't want to hear about how his biceps are like little box turtles that crawled under his skin?"

I shrugged out from under his arm and took a half step away.

"No, Jordan. I very much do not want to hear about those things."

He laughed and kept walking.

Dad wasn't there yet when we got to the parking lot. We walked over to Jordan's car.

"You know," I said. "I'm still amazed that you've got a car that runs on actual combustion. I didn't think they made these things anymore."

Jordan grinned.

"They don't make many of them. That steering wheel has a direct mechanical link to the front wheels, too. No electronics involved."

"Nice," I said. "But it's still got a brain, right?"

His grin widened, and leaned back against the door.

"Nope. This thing is one hundred percent manual."

Dad pulled into the lot then. He parked across from us, leaned out of the car and told me to come on. I held up one hand and turned back to Jordan.

"All manual," I said. "So that means . . ."

Jordan's grin widened. He leaned toward me then, put one hand on my arm, and lowered his voice to a whisper.

"That's right, Hannah. Velociraptor is completely, totally, and fully untraceable."

That's when Dad started yelling. I was turning to glare at him when Jordan brought his mouth almost to my ear and said, "Let me know if you ever need to be *sneaky*."

14. IN WHICH JORDAN REALIZES THAT SHIT MAY IN FACT BE GETTING REAL.

I was just home from practice, sitting on my couch, waiting for Micah to let me know he was done in the weight room and on his way over, when my phone pinged.

<UNK01>: Hi Jordan. Remember when I said things were getting weird around here?

Jordasaurus: Marta?

<UNK01>: Yeah. How many people do you know who have anonymous IDs?

Jordasaurus: Honestly? At this point, I'm not totally sure.

<UNK01>: Whatever. Anyway, like I said—things are going down the rabbit hole at Casa Longstreth. Mind if I come hang with you for a while?

Jordasaurus: What about the snipers?

<UNK01>: I promise not to bring them along. See you in an hour?

Jordasaurus: . . .

<UNK01>: Great. I'm on my way.

The front door banged open, then slammed closed. A few seconds later, Micah clomped into the room.

"Hey," he said.

"Hey," I said. "No heads-up?"

He shrugged.

"Didn't think about it. What's for eats?"

I folded my arms across my chest as he dropped onto the couch beside me.

"Well, if you'd pinged me when you were leaving Briarwood, there'd be a pizza here."

He pulled out his phone.

"Not too late, right?" He tapped, tapped, said, "Pepperoni," tapped once more, and tossed the phone onto the coffee table. "There," he said. "Done."

"Wow," I said. "You're buying tonight?"

He grinned.

"Wonder of wonders, right?"

"Yeah," I said. "Right. Completely unrelated—you remember Marta?"

The grin disappeared.

"Yes, Jordan. I remember Marta."

"Yeah, well . . . she's on her way over here. She'll probably get here about the same time the pizza does."

Micah leaned back, and narrowed his eyes.

"You're not going breeder on me, are you, Jordan?"

I rolled my eyes.

"No, Micah. I am not going breeder—and if I were, trust me, it wouldn't be with Marta Longstreth. She's kind of creepy, honestly."

"Okay. So tell me again why you're spending so much time hanging out with her?"

"Well," I said. "At first, I was just humoring my dad. You know that. Now, though . . ."

"Now what?"

I sighed.

"You remember what we were talking about last weekend, after the party?"

"You mean about you hiding out in my basement?"

"Yeah," I said. "I mean, no, not exactly. You were talking about Hannah's family keeping things on the down-low, and you learning how to handle a rifle, and then Marta—it sounds like she lives in a fortress, you know? An actual, factual, towers-and-snipers fortress. I guess I'm starting to wonder if everyone else knows something that I don't."

"Okay," Micah said. "I get that. Things are scary. How do we get from there to Marta Longstreth coming over here to eat my pizza?"

I thumbed open my phone and handed it to him. He stared at it for a minute, then handed it back.

"Huh," he said.

"Yeah," I said. "Huh."

"**H**ey," Marta said. "Don't look so happy to see me."

She was standing at the bottom of the marble steps that led up to our portico, arms folded, hair pulled back in a loose ponytail, wearing a hoodie and track pants and what looked like beat-to-hell hiking boots. She did not look like the wealthiest sixteen-year-old in North America. She looked like a home-less person.

"Uh," I said.

She frowned.

"That was sarcasm," Marta said. "I was actually hoping that you *would* be happy to see me."

"Oh, he is," Micah said as he came up behind me. "He's just worried that we might start fighting over him. Jordan has no stomach for violence."

I elbowed him, hard. He didn't seem to notice. Marta's frown relaxed, and she nodded.

"Right. You're the boyfriend, huh?"

Micah grinned and gave her a sweeping bow.

"Well don't worry," Marta said. "I'm not going to

steal him. I'm mostly just looking for a place to crash right now.

"Excellent," Micah said. "You can imagine my relief."

Marta's face twisted back into a frown. I stepped between them.

"Right," I said. "I'm glad we're all having fun here, but do you mind telling me what's going on?"

Marta shrugged.

"I told you. Things were getting weird around the Longstreth compound."

"Weird how?" Micah asked. "Are things going all *Island of Doctor Moreau* over there? Daddy turning all the servants into rat-men and whatnot?"

Marta turned to me, one eyebrow raised.

"Rat-men?" I said.

"Well," Micah said. "I'm sure they prefer to be called Rodent-Americans."

I snickered. Marta was decidedly not amused.

"So," Marta said. "Hypothetically speaking, which do you think is most important—loyalty to family, or loyalty to society?"

We were sitting across from each other at the wrought-iron table on my back deck. I looked over at Micah, who was perched on a filigree-encrusted chair that didn't look like it ought to be able to support half his weight. He shrugged, and crammed most of a slice of pizza into his mouth.

"I'm not sure where you're going with this," I said. "Can you give me an example? Hypothetically speaking, I mean."

Marta looked over my shoulder, to where a half dozen geese had just landed in the reflecting pool.

"Well," she said. "Imagine you found out, without snooping and entirely through no fault of your own, that your . . . uncle . . . was kind of a . . . I don't know . . . super villain? Like, imagine you found out he was building a death ray in the basement or something. Would you call in the Justice League, or whatever? Or would you feel like family comes first?"

I looked at Micah again. He was dialed in on his pizza, and wouldn't meet my eye.

"Huh," I said. "That would be quite a conundrum."

"Spill it," Micah said around a mouthful of cheese. "What'd he do?"

Marta turned to look at him.

"What did who do? We're talking hypotheticals here, remember?"

"Right," Micah said, swallowed what was in his mouth, and washed it down with half a glass of lemonade. "Your dad really is making rat-men, isn't he? Gonna breed himself an army, maybe refight the Stupid War?"

I laughed, but Marta just looked uncomfortable.

"Wait," I said. "Rat-men? Really?"

Marta shot Micah a look, then turned to glare at me.

"No, you idiot, my father is not creating an army of rat-men. He's got more money than God, remember? If he wanted an army, he'd just buy one, like all the other trillionaires do."

"Okay," I said. "That's good. So what are we talking about?"

She shook her head.

"You haven't answered my question yet."

"It's a matter of numbers," Micah said, and stuffed another slice into his mouth.

We both turned to stare at him while he chewed and swallowed. I sometimes had to remind myself that Micah was not actually stupid. With that chest and those shoulders and that face, he definitely looked the part of the mimbo, and he liked to play to the stereotype, but his average at Briarwood was higher than mine.

"Well," he said, "that and DNA."

"What are you talking about?" Marta asked. "I told you—no rat-men."

"Yeah," Micah said. "I heard you. I didn't mean rat-man DNA. I meant yours."

Marta leaned back and folded her arms across her chest.

"Mine?"

"Right," Micah said. "We just talked about this in Gen Anth. From a genetic standpoint, all you need to know is how much DNA you share with whoever you're planning to snitch on. Then you compare that to how much you share with all the folks he's planning on killing, and pick whichever one is bigger. Your dad's got half your DNA. So do your siblings."

"I don't have any siblings," Marta said.

Micah waved her off.

"Just go with me on this, okay? Your dad's got half your DNA. So do your siblings. So, if your dad is planning on killing two of your siblings, you should turn him in."

"Wait," I said. "What if he's only planning to kill one of her siblings?"

"Flip a coin. Anyway, aunts and uncles have a quarter of your DNA, and first cousins have an eighth. So, if your dad is planning on wiping out his sister and her family, you need to know how many kids she's got. One? Tell him to go for it. Three? Turn him in."

I glanced over at Marta. The look on her face said that she was starting to wonder if coming here might have been a big, big mistake.

"Ah," she said. "Okay. This is what they're teaching you guys at Briarwood?"

"Well," Micah said. "The context was a little different. Dr. Merrick was actually talking about the evolution of altruism, and when it would make reproductive sense to sacrifice your life to save someone else. I'm kind of extrapolating here."

Micah leaned forward to take the last slice of pepperoni. Marta's first slice was still sitting on her plate. She looked like she was about to be sick.

"What about strangers?" I asked. "Using this model, it's open season on them, right?"

Micah had to think about that for a minute.

"Well," he said finally. "We're all related at some level, right?"

"Yeah," I said. "That's true. So? How many randos would Marta's dad have to be plotting to kill for it to make sense for her to turn him in?"

"Hard to say," Micah said. "A lot, I guess. How about it, Marta? How many randos is your dad planning to kill?"

He was grinning, but that faded as Marta stared down at her pizza without answering.

"Marta?" I said.

She looked up at me.

"I think we need to call the Justice League."

15. IN WHICH DREW REALIZES THAT HE'S IN WAAAAAAY OVER HIS HEAD.

Few things in this life are crappier than an early-morning airport security line. The lights are too bright, the PA is too loud, and everyone's either grumpy or half asleep or both. You shuffle forward in baby steps, staring at your phone or staring at your feet, wishing you were back in bed and trying not to step on the luggage of the schmuck in front of you. Then, when you finally get to the front of the line, it's show your retina, strip down like you're going to prison, shuffle through the deep scanner that's probably sterilizing you, and hope the security drones don't find anything they like in your bags.

The morning that I set out to visit Meghan was even worse than usual. I'd spent the night on the couch, which meant that my back was killing me and

I hadn't actually slept very much. I also hadn't spoken to Kara since she'd walked out of the house the day before, and worse, I'd figured out by then that what had happened between us was pretty much entirely my fault. So, that was hanging over my head like a thick, black cloud. The security line stretched from the checkpoint halfway down the concourse, and when I finally made it to the scanners, they pinged on some change I'd forgotten to take out of my pocket. That got me pushed back through, and the eye roll I gave to the security goon when he called me on it got my bag pulled from the conveyor, emptied, and searched and tested for chemicals and biohazards and who the hell knows what else. By the time they were done harassing me, I was five minutes from missing my shuttle.

I'm happy to admit that I'm a lousy traveler. I don't even like air-breathers, and they'd booked me on a suborbital. Advantage? Forty-five minutes to LA. Disadvantage? Twenty of those minutes were spent weightless, and I'm the sort of person who needs Dramamine to ride a roller coaster. I meant to take something before takeoff, but with the mess at security and the running to the gate and all, it pretty much slipped my mind until I was strapped into my seat and we were pushing back and it was clearly much too late.

The shuttle was a standard econo job—no crew, no amenities, no windows, and thirty passengers crammed into a space that looked like it ought to hold about ten. I had a seat against the back bulkhead, with a youngish-looking guy wearing black dreadlocks, khaki shorts and a compression shirt on one side of me, and a sweet-looking older woman in an ankle-length skirt and floral top on the other. We were moving out onto the runway when she tapped me on the arm.

"Hey," she said. "You're going to barf, aren't you?"

I looked at her. Her mouth was smiling, but her eyes were not amused.

"That obvious?"

She laughed, and ran a finger down my forearm.

"Look at yourself. You're already sweating."

She reached into her purse then, palmed something, and slapped her hand down onto my arm. I felt a pinch, and then a sharp tingling running all the way up to my shoulder.

"Hey," I said, and pulled my arm back across my chest. "What the hell?"

She held her hand up, and showed me the injector. I stared at her. A warm numbness was spreading out from the center of my chest. I reached for her hand, but she just waggled one finger at me and slipped the med tab back into her bag.

"Hey," I said again. "Hey . . . you . . ."

"Oh, don't be such a baby," she said. "Nothing worse than sitting next to a puker in zero gee. That ought to hold you until we touch down."

I knew I ought to be angry, probably ought to be yelling at her, or yelling for help, or . . . something . . . but I just . . . wasn't. I opened my mouth, but nothing came out, and after a few seconds of that I closed it again. I looked down. There was a tiny red dot of blood on my arm. She gave my knee a friendly pat.

"There you go, Drew. Take a nap. You'll feel much better when we get where we're going."

I closed my eyes. I didn't think to ask how she knew my name.

I woke up to find a long line of drool hanging from my chin, and a khaki-clad crotch three inches from my nose. I looked up. Mr. Dreadlocks was straddling me while he tried to wrestle his bag out of the storage bin.

"Hey," I said. "Do you mind?"

He looked down.

"Sorry, dude. Thought you were dead."

He gave a yank, and his bag came squirting out into his hands. I leaned back as he pulled his leg over me and stepped out into the aisle. We were the last two passengers on the shuttle.

"I'm not dead," I said.

"Yeah," he said over his shoulder. "I get that."

"Did you see . . ."

He wasn't listening. I unbuckled, rubbed my face

THE END OF ORDINARY 157

with both hands, and got to my feet. My bag was all alone in the bin. I pulled it out, slung it over my shoulder, and followed Mr. Dreadlocks out onto the tarmac.

I've never been a big fan of Los Angeles. If there's one thing the last fifty years have demonstrated, it's that Southern California is not designed to support 40 million humans. I guess the water thing wasn't so bad back when the mountains actually built up a snow pack in the winter, but those days are long gone, and they aren't showing any signs of coming back. The desalination plants keep the sprinklers running, of course, but they also eat up every joule that comes out of the Death Valley solar farm, and then some. My opinion has always been that everyone would be better off if 90 percent of the LA–San Diego corridor just packed up and relocated to Manitoba.

Of course, Manitoba doesn't have drive-through Reiki centers, so I guess that's not about to happen anytime soon.

So yeah, Los Angeles was not my favorite city, and LAX was definitely not my favorite part of Los Angeles. It took me twenty minutes of slidewalks and trams and escalators to get from the shuttle gate to the taxi stand. It was seven in the morning, and already it was ninety degrees outside and probably eighty-eight inside, and the air was dry enough that I could feel my sinuses desiccating.

On top of the heat and the early-morning glare

and the fact that I'd slept probably four hours in the last thirty-six, I was still feeling the after-effects of whatever that smiley sociopath had injected me with on the shuttle. There was a weird tingling running up and down my arms, and a buzzing in my ears that came and went. As I waited in line for a cab, I kept asking myself what kind of a nutjob goes around sticking needles into random strangers.

Then I remembered that I wasn't a random stranger. She'd said my name.

How the hell did she know my name?

For some reason, none of this bothered me as much as it should have.

I got to the front of the line. A cab rolled up, and the attendant waved me in. I tossed my bag in ahead of me, dropped into the backseat, pulled out my phone, and tapped the reader to start payment. The door slid closed, and I rolled away.

I spent the entire ride downtown worrying about what I was going to say to Meghan when I found her. I'd only met her face-to-face once before, about a year and a half earlier. She was ten years younger than I was, a freshly minted Ph.D. from UCLA, brilliant and beautiful and scary as hell. One of the reasons that I'd let things get so far out of hand with her was that I'd always found her simultaneously incredibly compelling and incredibly intimidating. The last time I'd had any sort of conflict with her was right at the outset of DragonCorn, when we were fixing the project schedule. I told her I expected a full test cycle on a monthly basis throughout. She told me that was stupid, and that she'd set up a schedule when she had something to test. I shrugged, and smiled, and thanked her for her input.

As Mara often said, I was a crappy manager.

Meghan lived in Santa Monica, in one of the new towers they'd put up a few blocks back from the beach. My phone pinged just as the cab rolled to a stop in front of her building. I fished it out of my pocket, and tapped the screen.

"Drew," Meghan said. "What are you doing here?"

Meghan looked rough, and not in an "I haven't been working for the last week because I've been having constant sex" kind of way. More like "I haven't been working for the last week because I've had dengue fever." I remembered her as a pale, freckled redhead, but that morning her hair was a long, dark tangle, and her skin looked like she'd tried to use a self-tanner while she was falling-down drunk. She was wearing a white cotton shirt, and even on my tiny screen I could see that there were brown and yellow stains around the collar and running down the front. Even allowing for the fact that it was early and she'd probably just woken up, she looked like crap on a biscuit.

"Oh," I said finally. "Hey, Meghan. Is this a bad time?"

She rolled her eyes.

"No, Drew. It's a great time. It's always a great time when your project manager shows up at your door unexpectedly at seven thirty in the morning. That always means good things are about to happen."

I sighed, and rubbed my eyes with one hand. The cab made a throat-clearing sound, and a message popped up on the payment screen telling me to *please exit now.* The door was standing open. I slid across the seat and climbed out.

"Look," I said. "You know why I'm here, Meghan. You haven't made a project meeting or produced a deliverable in ten days. You sent me a scary-ass call-me-now last week, and then went completely dark. I'm glad you're getting laid or whatever, but DragonCorn is in danger of being shoved off the rails, and you're the one who's doing the pushing." I walked up three steps to the door of her building. "We need to talk. Will you let me in, please?"

Her eyes narrowed, and she shook her head.

"No, Drew. I don't think that's a great idea."

I could feel my jaw sag open.

"Meghan," I said. "I'm standing on your front stoop right now. I'm standing on your front stoop in ninety-degree heat, after a night spent on the couch and a morning spent on a suborbital with a douchey hipster and a sweet-looking middle-aged psycho. I'm standing here because I am responsible for making sure that you are doing your job, which by the way you are not, and for the past week you have ignored every attempt I have made to get in touch with you. Forget about staying employed, Meghan. If you want to avoid a breach of contract lawsuit that'll have you giving depositions to Bioteka lawyers until you are a wizened old woman and I am long dead, you need to let me in."

She scowled, looked away from the screen and then back. I could see the muscles in her jaws clenching.

"Fine," she said finally. "Come on up, Drew. I've got some really awesome stuff to show you."

As it turned out, Meghan's apartment was in even worse shape than the rest of her. There was a dozen or more pizza boxes piled up in the living room. Not all of them were empty. Pepperoni doesn't rot, but sauce and crust apparently do, and the smell when she opened the door was like a slap in the sinuses. Meghan poked her head out, looked up and down the hallway, then glared up at me.

"Right," she said. "Come on."

She stepped back, and held the door just far enough open to let me squeeze in.

"Wow," I said. "I guess you haven't been skipping work to catch up on your cleaning, huh?"

"Bite me, Drew."

She slammed the door behind me. There were

heavy blinds covering the windows, and with the door shut, the only light in the room came from the screensaver bouncing around the wallscreen hanging opposite the garbage-strewn leather couch. The dimness hid some of the stains on her shirt and her pajama pants, but somehow that just made her look more crazy rather than less.

"So," I said. "Uh . . . how've you been, Meghan?"

She rolled her eyes again, turned away and walked through an arched doorway into what looked to be the kitchen. I glanced around. This was actually a really nice apartment underneath all the rotting food and grease-stained napkins. The floors were hardwood, the wallscreen was high-res and at least 120 inches, the furniture was all either leather or solid oak or both. Apparently Bioteka did almost as well by their testers as they did by their engineers.

"Look," she said, and I heard the refrigerator open and close. "I'm not really interested in chitchat at the moment, Drew. If you're here to fire me, you should probably just do it and go. If you hang around, I'm gonna show you some stuff that'll make your life a lot more complicated."

I heard the snap and hiss of first one bottle opening, and then another. When Meghan came back into the living room, she was already drinking from one of them. She held the other out to me.

"Seriously?" I said. "Is that your breakfast?"

"Take it," she said. "You're gonna want to be buzzed soon."

I stared at her. She shrugged, took a long pull at her beer, and winked the wallscreen to life.

"Fine," she said. "Your loss."

She put the second beer down on the coffee table, then gestured at the wallscreen. A series of folders popped up. She gestured again, and one of them zoomed in and opened. A wave and a poke brought up a rolling schematic on one side of the screen, and a genetic map on the other.

"What is this?" I asked.

She folded her arms over her chest and smirked.

"I'm just a tester, Drew. You're the engineer. You tell me."

I stepped forward, minimized the diagram and zoomed the schematic. Neither representation was really meant to be human-parseable, but I figured I'd have a better chance at recognizing something familiar there.

As it turned out, I did not.

"Okay," I said after about five minutes of poking and staring. "I give up, Meghan. What am I looking at?"

"Good God, Drew," she said. "You really are just a manager now, aren't you?"

She nudged me aside, minimized the schematic, and pulled up a molecular diagram.

I stared at it.

This one, I recognized.

"Meghan?" I said.

She laughed, and finished what was left of her beer.

"What's the matter, Drew? Aren't you happy to see your baby?"

16. IN WHICH HANNAH MEETS MARTA, AND HILARITY ENSUES.

The morning after my first run with Micah, I woke up to a quiet house. Ordinarily, Mom and Dad both would have been rattling around by then, making breakfast and coffee and grumbling at each other, and eventually yelling at me to get my lazy backside out of bed. That morning, though? Nothing. Weirdly, I think that actually got me up earlier than usual. It was barely six when I rolled over and sat up—still dark outside, but with just a hint of a glow on the horizon outside my window. I sat there for a minute, knowing something was off but unable to put my finger on exactly what. Finally, when it became pretty clear that it was too late to try to go back to sleep, I got to my feet and started rooting around in my dresser for clean underwear and socks.

By the time I got downstairs, I'd figured out that Dad was not, in fact, anywhere in the house. This was a problem, because Dad was my ride to school. Mom could have substituted in a pinch, but she didn't seem to be around either. I'm not sure why my parents both being completely AWOL that morning didn't bother me more in and of itself, but it didn't. I just wanted to make sure I didn't miss first bell.

As I was toasting my bagel, I ran down a mental list of people who might possibly give me a ride. My friend list hadn't been particularly long before the whole Climb to Failure thing, and it was considerably shorter afterward. There was Sarah, but she lived on the Syracuse side of Briarwood, and coming out to get me would add almost sixty miles to her ride—besides which, she only seemed to be my friend when Tara wasn't looking, and I wasn't positive she'd be willing to be seen showing up in the parking lot with me in her car. Micah had been friendly enough as a running partner, but our relationship had definitely not reached the come-pick-me-up stage. Devon? Ha! Even if she'd gone to my school, I felt like I was tighter with Inchy at that point. Who did that leave?

Jordan.

My bagel popped. I slathered it with cream cheese, carried it over to the breakfast table, and gave him a ping.

Wilma17: Jordan? You awake?

Jordasaurus: Not really.

Wilma17: It's Hannah.

Jordasaurus: . . .

Wilma17: Jordan?

Jordasaurus: What can I do for you, friendo?

Wilma17: Um . . . Any chance I could catch a ride to school?

Jordasaurus: . . .

Wilma17: Please?

Jordasaurus: Sorry. Not 100% sure I'm going in today.

Wilma17: Oh. You sick?

Jordasaurus: Not exactly.

Wilma17: . . .

Wilma17: Okay, I get it. Sorry to bug you.

I dropped my phone, sat down at the table and crammed a quarter of the bagel into my mouth to keep myself from crying. Apparently, I didn't rank nearly as high on Jordan's friend list as he did on mine. Not too surprising considering our relative social standings, but . . .

My phone pinged.

I picked it up and thumbed the screen.

> **Jordasaurus:** Look, Hannah. Things are weird right now, and you might actually be able to help. Want to ditch with us today?

I was sitting on the porch when they rolled up. Micah was riding shotgun, elbow jutting out of his open window. He waved.

There was somebody crammed into the cargo space behind the seats.

They stopped in the driveway. The doors popped open, and Jordan and Micah unfolded themselves like clowns coming out of one of those tiny circus cars. Jordan groaned and stretched as the girl in the back hauled herself out. I recognized her mod package right away. It was a super-exclusive thing. I'd seen examples in one of Dad's brochures, but as far as I knew the only people who actually had it were a couple of celebrity kids, and one popular fashion model named Raven Blue. She was a Spooky—dead white skin, jet black hair, limbs just a bit too long for her spectrally thin torso. The package came with some internal mods too, but I couldn't remember exactly what they were. I stood, and walked down the steps and over to where they were waiting.

"Hey," I said. "Who's your friend?"

"Him?" Micah said. "That's Jordan. Not really a friend, though. More of a hanger-on."

Spooky scowled at him and stepped forward.

"I'm Marta," she said, and held out one fist. I gave it a half-hearted tap.

"Hannah," I said. "I haven't seen you around. You go to Briarwood?"

She laughed.

"Me? No, Hannah. I do not go to Briarwood."

I looked at Micah, then at Jordan.

"Wait," he said. "I thought you two were friends?"

Marta turned to look at him.

"What?"

"Last week," Jordan said. "Didn't you tell me that you and Hannah were tight?"

"No," Marta said. "I definitely did not."

He looked at me.

"Nope," I said. "I mean, we're not enemies or anything. I've never seen her before."

"Seriously," Marta said. "What are you talking about, Jordan?"

"Yeah," I said. "Care to explain?"

Jordan looked at me, then at Marta, then back at me.

"Not really," he said.

Micah grinned.

"Anyway, Hannah—Marta's our new sidekick."

Marta gave him a quick shot of side-eye.

"Sidekick?"

"Sure," Micah said. "Like Bat-Boy, or Corporal Punishment."

"Oh no," Marta said. "I'm definitely not a sidekick. If anything, I'm the hero here."

Micah laughed and shook his head.

"I don't think so. Heroes get to ride in the front seat."

"Actually," Jordan said, "I think you're probably a villain who's on a redemption arc."

We all turned to look at him.

"You know," he said. "Redemption arc: villain has a change of heart, defects to the heroes' side, gives them critical aid in defeating the forces of evil, winds up with reduced jail time and a sweet job in the prison cafeteria."

I swear, at that moment, I heard a cricket chirp.

"Prison cafeteria?" Marta finally asked.

"Sure," Jordan said. "Way better than working in the laundry—quieter, less humid, and you get to see who spits in what."

"Huh," I said. "When did you come down with verbal diarrhea?"

Micah snickered.

"Oh," he said. "That's nothing new. Jordan's mouth has irritable vowel syndrome."

There was that cricket again. Micah looked at Marta, then back at me.

"Too far?"

"Yeah," I said. "Too far."

He shrugged.

"Can't nail it every time."

"Right," Marta said. "Can we go back to the whole redemption arc thing? How, exactly, am I a villain?"

"Well," Micah said. "Maybe not a villain per se. You're definitely villain-spawn, though, which I'm pretty sure qualifies you for a redemption arc. Unless, of course, it turns out you're actually leading us to our doom. In that case, this would be a fake redemption arc. Are you leading us to our doom?"

"No," Marta said. "I am not leading you to your doom." She looked at Micah. "Well, maybe him. He's annoying. Probably not Jordan, though."

"Hey," I said. "What about me?"

She gave me an appraising look.

"Probably not, but let's see how the day goes."

"Hmmm," Jordan said. "I'm not sure how to classify that."

"RA-EFGO?" I said.

Micah raised both eyebrows.

"What?"

"Redemption arc," I said. "Exception for giant oafs."

Micah looked at Jordan. Jordan shook his head.

"No," he said. "I don't think that's a thing."

"Yeah," Micah said. "That's just dumb. Get it together, Hannah."

Incredibly, the space behind the seats in Jordan's car was even less comfortable than it had looked from the outside. It was only meant to hold a few bags in the first place, and if it weren't for the fact that Marta was as scrawny as I was and twice as flexible, squeezing us both in there at once would have been completely impossible. As it was, it was just kind of improbable. That, and very, very awkward.

"Just for the record," Marta said. "I am not intentionally molesting you right now."

"Thanks," I said. "Good to know."

Jordan twisted his head around to look back at us.

"Hey," he said. "If we see the gendarmes, try to duck down. It's kind of illegal to have humans back there. Or livestock either, now that I think about it. Actually, I think it's illegal to have anything at all back there bigger than an old pizza box. So yeah, try to be inconspicuous, huh?"

"Got it," I said. "If we happen to see any troopers, we'll be sure to camouflage ourselves. I mean, we can't actually move or anything, but maybe Micah could throw a blanket over us?"

"Don't have a blanket," Jordan said. "Just try to look like CPR dolls or something."

I tried to smack the back of his head, but Marta beat me to it.

"Hey," he said. "That was a compliment."

"Right." I tried to wriggle around enough to keep the cargo hook on the back of Micah's seat from digging into my spine, but I just wound up making it worse. "Would you mind telling me where we're going? If this is gonna take more than another five or ten minutes, I think I'd rather just run along behind."

"I agree," Marta said. "Hannah would be much better off running along behind."

"Relax," Micah said. "We're almost there."

I twisted my neck around until I could see out the windshield. We were driving under power lines.

"Just out of curiosity," I said, "where, exactly, are we going?"

"Our top-secret headquarters," Jordan said. "We need to make plans."

"You have a top-secret headquarters?"

"Well," he said. "Technically it's the IHOP on Culver, but it's pretty secret."

"Sure," Micah said. "Totally secret. Except for the billboard on 104, I mean."

"Well yeah," Jordan said. "Obviously except for that."

I tried to catch Marta's eye, but she'd buried her face in both hands.

"So," Jordan said. "I suppose you're wondering why we brought you here."

I looked around the table. Jordan and Marta were watching me expectantly. Micah was cramming a cheese blintz into his mouth.

"No," I said, and picked a hair out of my breakfast scramble. "I wasn't wondering that at all."

I picked up my phone and pinged Sarah.

Wilma17: Hey. What's the sitch in GeneChem?

SM37: Quiz. You sick?

Wilma17: Nah. I'm at IHOP.

SM37: Really? That's what you ditch for?

Wilma17: Not my idea. Can you forward any notes?

SM37: Sure. You gonna tell me what this is about?

Wilma17: Oh yeah. Soon as I figure it out.

Jordan cleared his throat. I looked up.

"Rude," Marta said.

Jordan nodded.

"Extremely."

I looked at Micah. He shrugged, glanced over at Jordan, and put away half of another blintz.

"Anyway," Jordan said. "The reason we brought you here is that we have something very important to discuss."

I turned to Marta.

"Very important," she said.

"Micah," I said. "What are they talking about?"

He shrugged again, chewed slowly and swallowed.

"Don't ask me," he said. "Marta's our conspiracy theorist. I'm just in this for the blintzes."

I looked at Jordan then.

"Explain?"

"Well," he said. "Actually, I'm not one hundred percent sure what the issue is either. Marta, however, has been very clear that there is some serious shit going down."

"Mostly clear," Micah said.

Jordan nodded.

"Right. Mostly clear. Tell her, Marta."

Marta glanced back and forth between them, then gave me a long, critical look.

"Who did your cuts?"

Micah froze in mid chew. Jordan opened his mouth, then closed it again and turned to look at Marta.

"Uh . . ." I said. "What?"

Marta rolled her eyes.

"You've got a brow ridge, Hannah. That doesn't just happen. That's also not a part of any standard package I'm aware of. So, who did it?"

Again, remember—this was six years after Hagerstown. I can't even think what the equivalent question would be today. Maybe asking someone for the name of their smack dealer?

"Marta," Micah said around a mouthful of cheese and crepes.

"No," I said. "It's fine, Micah." I gave her my best glower. She didn't flinch. "My dad did the design work."

She nodded.

"I figured it was something like that. Custom work like that isn't cheap, and you don't look like a trust-fund kid."

"Said the queen of trust-fund kids," Micah said. Marta shot him a hard glare, then turned back to me.

"Right. Your dad's an engineer?"

I nodded.

"Who does he work for?"

"Seriously," Jordan said. "What's with the grilling, Marta?"

"Got a hunch," Marta said. "Spill, Hannah."

I looked from Marta to Jordan, then back again. My dad had drilled it into my head since I was a little girl that this was not a topic to be discussed with anyone, let alone with random Spooky girls in IHOPs. Between the people who would be inclined to stab me in the eye because gene cutting is the devil's pastime, and the ones who would be inclined to kidnap me because they thought engineers were all richer than Croesus, it just wasn't a great idea to talk about what Pops did for a living.

For some reason, though, Marta didn't strike me as particularly stabby, and she apparently didn't have the need for ransom money.

"Bioteka," I said. "He's a project lead or something now, but he used to be a front-line engineer."

She leaned forward then.

"I knew it. What's he working on? What projects, I mean. Don't care if he's cooking up new versions of you in his spare time."

I started to say something snippy, then closed my mouth and shook my head.

"Why are you asking about my dad's projects, Marta? Is this a corporate espionage thing or something? Because I have to tell you, I'm already spying on him for one rando. I'm starting to feel like maybe I should be prioritizing family a little bit more."

"Yeah," Micah said. "I don't know exactly where she's going with this, Hannah, but I'm pretty sure it's not corporate espionage. This is Marta *Longstreth*. Her dad owns your dad."

It took me a moment to realize that my jaw was hanging open.

"No," I said.

"Yeah," Jordan said. "For reals."

I looked back at Marta. Now that they'd brought it up, I remembered that Marta was the name of Longstreth's kid. I'd never seen a picture of her, but this girl was about the right age anyway.

"Uh . . ." I said. "Okay. Jordan, why are you hanging around with Marta Longstreth?"

"Long story," Marta said. "Answer the question. What's your dad been up to lately? Has he thrown any funny-sounding code names around at the dinner table?"

I'd already told Inchy about DragonCorn. No harm in telling the boss's kid, right?

"Maybe," I said. "Does the word DragonCorn mean anything to you?"

Marta leaned back then, and folded her arms across her chest.

"This is too perfect," she said.

"Wait," Jordan said. "I think I missed something. What does DragonCorn mean?"

"What it means," Marta said, "is that Hannah's dad has been busy for the past year or so helping my dad to cook up the end of the world."

17. IN WHICH JORDAN FREAKS THE HELL OUT.

"**W**ait," I said. "What?"

"Well," Marta said, "not the end of *my* world. Or Hannah's. Or Micah's, as far as I know. Definitely yours, though."

My stomach gave a warning rumble. I was starting to regret the half-eaten plate of Swedish pancakes that was sitting in front of me.

"My dad doesn't do doomsday plots," Hannah said. "He makes stuff for farms. I've heard him talking about DragonCorn. I'm pretty sure it's literally about making some new kind of corn."

"Ooooh," Micah said. "Sentient, malevolent corn! NatSec's never gonna see that one coming."

I raised one hand.

"Can we back up? Why is this the end of *my* world, specifically?"

"Who cares?" Micah said. "Let's keep our focus on the sentient corn."

Hannah shot Micah a withering glare.

"Seriously," I said. "Marta? What the flark are you talking about?"

She looked around the table. She wasn't smiling anymore.

"You guys know what a retrovirus is?"

Hannah rolled her eyes.

"Yes, Marta. I'm pretty sure we all graduated from third grade."

I actually had no idea what a retrovirus was, but that didn't seem like the right time to bring it up. Luckily, Micah didn't care if Hannah thought I was an idiot.

"Just to clarify," he said, "Jordan's more of a Gentleman's C kind of guy than a scholar. Mind telling him what you're talking about?"

That got us a long, awkward silence. Hannah turned to look at Marta.

"Oh," Marta said. "Me? I don't know either. That's why I asked if any of you did."

Hannah looked at Micah, then back at Marta, then at me. I shrugged and gave her a half smile.

"Seriously?" Hannah asked. "None of you stayed awake through the first week of GeneChem?"

Micah leaned forward, and lowered his voice to a stage whisper.

"You may not have noticed, Hannah, but Jordan's one of the idle rich. He's not taking GeneChem."

Hannah sighed, rubbed her face with both hands and pushed her hair back from her forehead.

"Fine," she said. "But what about you, Marta? Your dad runs the biggest genetic-engineering company in the world. Shouldn't you have some kind of a clue about this stuff?"

"I'm not planning to take over Daddy's business someday," Marta said. "I'm an artist."

Micah snickered. Marta turned to glare at him, but her scowl wasn't anywhere near as impressive as Hannah's. You wouldn't think that little bit of a brow ridge would make such a big difference, but it did.

"Fine," Micah said. "I think we can all agree that Hannah is smarter than we are, right?" He looked at Marta. She rolled her eyes. "Good. Now maybe she can give us the condensed version of Retrovirus 101?"

Hannah winced at that, and it occurred to me that maybe this wasn't the first time someone had said something like that to her. I leaned across the table, patted her arm, and said, "We still love you, Professor." Micah snickered again, but Hannah gave me a quick smile.

"Fine," she said. "You know how a regular virus works, right?"

Micah gave her a quick head shake.

"Really?"

"Yeah," he said. "Really."

"Okay," Hannah said. "Fabulous. Apparently none of you took basic biology either, so here's the executive dimwit summary: retroviruses get into your cells, cut up your DNA, and swap out their own code for yours. Retroviruses can rewrite your genes."

"Oh," Marta said. "That's not good."

"Well," Hannah said. "It can be good, bad, or in between, actually. It all depends on what part of your DNA they're overwriting, and what they're overwriting it with. I mean, HIV is a retrovirus, and that's pretty bad—but then a whole branch of gene therapy is based on engineered retroviruses, and that's pretty good. Mostly. Then again, that whole zombie super-soldier thing they were doing in Siberia was bad, I guess, and that was retrovirus-based too."

"So," Micah said, "all in all, a mixed bag."

"Yeah," Hannah said. "That's pretty accurate."

"Great," I said. "Got it. Mixed bag. Can we please get back to what this has to do with me, specifically? If you want to focus on the whole 'end of my world' thing, that would be good."

"Right," Marta said. "When I got out of your car after our little date, I told you to look up my mom. Did you?"

I looked over at Micah. For just about the first time since we'd sat down, he wasn't smiling.

"Yeah," I said after a pause. "I did."

"So you know what happened to her."

I nodded. Micah just looked uncomfortable.

"I don't," Hannah said. She looked at me first, then Micah. We both looked at Marta.

"Well?" Hannah said.

"A mob of UnAltered doused her with gasoline and set her on fire," Marta said. "In the middle of the street, in the middle of Bethesda, on a Tuesday afternoon. She was one of the first casualties of the Stupid War."

Hannah looked down at her hands.

"Oh."

"Yeah," Marta said. "So, as you can probably imagine, that did some really bad things to my dad's head. Mine too, honestly, but in a different way. The company kept things quiet, but Dad was basically comatose for a long time afterward.

"He's better now, but he's been stuck on the idea that the Stupid War never really ended, you know? He doesn't believe that the UnAltered will ever really let it go. That's why we live in what's pretty much a fortress in Nothing, New York, instead of the mansion we used to have in Bethesda. That's why I have to practically break out of jail now to see anyone my own age."

"Okay," I said. "So your dad's a paranoid trillionaire, holed up with his private army, waiting for Stupid War II. He's not the only one of those. Can we get to the part that has to do with me?"

"Well," Marta said. "He's not just waiting. For the last year or so, he's had something going on. Closed-door conferences, late-night calls, etcetera,

etcetera. So, a few months ago, I started snooping. Turns out his electronic security is outstanding, but his listening-through-the-door security sucks. He has meetings every week with a guy named Marco Al-tobelli. They talk about a lot of stuff—football, the markets, Marco's kids—but mostly, they talk about Project DragonCorn."

"Okay," I said. "And what, exactly, do they say?"

"Well," Marta said. "That's kind of the problem. I don't understand most of what they're talking about. There's definitely a lot of retrovirus this and recombinant that, but none of that means much to me."

Hannah leaned back in her seat.

"So for all you know," she said, "they could just be talking about ways to make bigger corn kernels. What makes you think there's something sinister going on here?"

Marta's eyes slid down, then off to the side.

"Well, I guess I don't know for sure. I did hear Marco say something about super-herpes last week, but my dad laughed at that, so he might have been joking. I've definitely heard them use every possible variant of the term 'final solution,' though."

"Okay," Micah said. "That's a little ominous."

"Yeah," Marta said. "Also, they've got their own private name for DragonCorn. They call it Project Snitch."

I glanced over at Micah. He looked just as confused as I was.

"What?" I asked.

"Project Snitch," Marta said. "That's pretty scary, right?"

Micah nodded solemnly.

"Snitches get stitches."

"Right," I said. "And wind up in ditches."

Hannah looked back and forth between us.

"What are you two talking about?"

"Dropping a truth bomb," Micah said. "Boom."

"Yeah," I said. "You can tell it's true, because it rhymes."

Hannah shook her head. Marta leaned back, looked up at the ceiling, and groaned.

"Okay," Micah said. "I think we can also all agree that Project Snitch is a stupid name. Can we circle back to the whole 'final solution' thing, though? That actually did seem kind of doomsday-ish. Also the super-herpes. That sounds bad too."

The waitress came by then, with a pitcher of iced tea and another of water. She refilled our glasses while we sat in silence and waited for her to leave.

"So," she said. "Everyone doing okay here?"

"Yes," Marta said. "Doing fine."

"Can I get you anything else? Dessert? Coffee?"

I started to say something, but my stomach gurgled in a way that said, "If you send a pie down here, we're going to have a problem."

"No," Marta said. "I think we're good."

After the waitress was gone, I looked at Marta and

said, "So what, exactly, do you think your dad is cooking up the final solution to?"

"Come on," Marta said, "I think that's pretty obvious, right?"

They all turned to look at me.

"What?" I said.

"Um . . ." Hannah said.

"Um what?"

"Well," Marta said. "I'm pretty sure he's working
on the final solution to *you*."

It was later, when we were back at Hannah's house
and she'd sent Micah to round up Devon Morgan
because she said we needed at least one other person
in our little cabal with a three-digit IQ, that Marta
finally explained to me what, exactly, was going on.

"Look," she said. "There's a mark. Everybody
who's Engineered has it. It's like the artist's signature
on a painting, except that it's coded into our genes."

I looked over at Hannah. We were sitting on the
floor of what she called her solarium—a big, empty
room with a spongy rubberized floor, and one wall
made entirely of glass. Marta was leaning against
the window-wall, rubbing absently at the spiderweb
tattoo on her neck. I was looking out at the overgrown field outside, and contemplating the fact that
Hannah's house was probably almost as expensive as
mine, but that a mob of peasants would still pass it by

without a second glance. Hannah was sitting with her legs spread in front of her, stretching.

"It's true," Hannah said, then lifted her nose from her right knee and lowered it down to her left. "It's right in the middle of hromosome 12. Codes for a protein that doesn't do anything in particular, but that you can pick up pretty easily in a blood test. The original idea was that the government wanted to be able to keep track of who had been modified and who hadn't, so that if some horrible new disease cropped up, they could tell right away if it was the result of natural processes, or of some engineer's screwup. Some of the early custom jobs probably don't have it—folks like Tara Carson's mom, I mean—but everybody whose mods came from Bioteka or GeneCraft or one of the boutique shops definitely does."

"Right," Marta said. "The thing is, though—if you can keep track of who *has* been modified, that means you can keep track of who *hasn't*, too."

"Okay," I said. "I think I'm with you. So you think your dad's gonna try to round up all the unmodified or something? Because I have to tell you, I don't think that'll work. I get that your dad has a ton of cash and an army of sentient corn and all, but there's still a lot more of us than there are of you."

Marta shook her head.

"I don't think he's planning on rounding anyone up, Jordan."

"Okay," I said. "So what is he planning?

Hannah pulled her feet in close, soles together, and pressed her knees down to the floor with her elbows.

"I'm not sure," she said, "but I think Marta's dancing around the idea that maybe her dad and mine are cooking up an engineered retrovirus that's designed specifically to go after people who don't have that particular protein in their blood."

I looked at Marta. She shrugged.

"However," Hannah said. "I can tell you that this is total bullshit, because my father would never be involved in something like that. Marta's dad might be a crazed super villain, but mine is not. The fact is, they're both unmodified themselves. If they set loose some kind of targeted virus designed to take out everyone who's not Engineered, they'd wind up taking out themselves—not to mention practically everyone they know who's their age or older. It doesn't make sense. They'd both have to be completely crazy."

"Well," Marta said. "My dad's not completely crazy. I'm not one hundred percent sure he's completely sane, though. I could definitely see him doing something that would hurt him if he thought it would keep me safe."

Hannah crossed one leg over the other and twisted half around.

"Huh," she said. "When you put it that way . . ."

Marta nodded.

"It's starting to make sense, right? Tell me your

dad wouldn't step in front of a bus if he thought he needed to do it to save you from a mob of UnAltered."

They both turned to look at me.

"What?" I said. "Just because I'm not Engineered doesn't mean I'm UnAltered. My dad's a VP at Gene-Craft, remember? And anyway, I'm definitely not a mob."

Marta shook her head.

"Unfortunately, there's not a genetic marker for being a good guy."

I stared at her.

"So you're saying that your dad would be willing to wipe out ninety percent of the population just to keep the UnAltered from getting uppity again? Do you have any idea how that would actually play out?"

"No," she said. "Do you?"

"Well," I said. "Not exactly. I've watched a lot of disaster vids, though, and if those are accurate . . ."

"Which I'm sure they are," Hannah said.

". . . then we're looking at a whole lot of roving mobs, people throwing fire bombs, and possibly a zombie insurrection. Basically, all the stuff your dad is trying to avoid."

"Look," Marta said. "I'm not trying to argue that my dad is right. The whole reason I came to you guys in the first place is because whatever he's got planned, I don't want it to happen. If I had to pick sides, I'd be on yours. I think genetic mods are bullshit. If I could turn myself into a standard-issue *Homo sap* I'd do it. I'm sure Hannah would too, right?"

Hannah looked up from her stretching.

"Huh?"

"I said, you probably wish you were normal."

She looked at Marta, then over at me.

"I am normal," she said, emphasizing every word.

Marta shook her head again.

"You're not, Hannah, any more than I am. Jordan is normal. You, Micah, me? We're made things."

"Holy crap," Hannah said. "What are you, some kind of self-hater? Jordan, are you listening to her?"

"Oh no," I said. "Don't drag me into this."

Just then, the screen on the wall opposite the window lit up. Micah and Devon were standing on the porch. Micah pressed the doorbell, then looked up into the camera.

"Open up, Hannah," he said. "Devon says she can crack your dad's system."

18. IN WHICH DREW GETS FREAKY.

"Holy shit," Meghan said. "I cannot begin to tell you how horny I am right now."

I was sitting on an ottoman in front of her living room wallscreen, paging though diagram after diagram, slowly realizing that I was no longer technically competent. I turned half around to look at Meghan. She didn't look horny. She looked like a hobo. She was most of the way through the beer she'd originally offered to me. As I watched, she drained the rest of it in one long pull.

"Meghan," I said.

She belched.

"If you're trying to seduce me," I said, "you're not giving it much of an effort."

She brushed a space clear on the couch, dropped into it, and laughed.

"Don't take this personally," she said, "but whatever horniness I am experiencing right now has absolutely zero to do with you. Which is not to say that I wouldn't bang you right now, right here on this disgusting-ass couch, because I definitely would—but again, it wouldn't be anything personal."

I stared at her.

"Exactly how drunk are you right now?" I asked finally.

She laughed again, leaned her head back, and stretched her arms out along the back of the couch.

"Drew," she said. "Drew, Drew, Drew. I am not drunk right now. If I were, I'd probably already be humping you."

"Okay," I said. "You're not drunk. So what are you? Because you're sure as shit not the person I brought onto my very important genetic-engineering team eighteen months ago. You're not the person who Nerissa Grimm described as the best synthesis engineer she'd ever worked with. You're not even the person who used to occasionally show up for our status-update meetings until a few weeks ago. I can't be positive, obviously, but I'm pretty confident that person never threatened to hump me."

She lifted her head, and gave me a long, bleary-eyed look.

"You're right," she said finally. "I should not have threatened to hump you. I sincerely apologize."

"Um . . ." I said. "Apology accepted, I guess." I

turned back to the wallscreen. An RNA schematic was rotating there, with the different protein sequences color coded for easy reference. "If you want to make it up to me, maybe you could explain what, exactly, I'm looking at right now."

I heard the couch creak, and then her bare feet on the hardwood behind me.

"Well," she said. Her hand touched my shoulder. "What you've got there is . . ."

That's when she licked my ear.

"Hey!" I yelped, jerked away from her and staggered to my feet. "What the shit, Meghan?"

She was standing beside the ottoman with a perplexed look on her face, running her tongue back and forth across her teeth.

"Huh," she said. "That's weird."

"Weird?" I said. "You licked me, you psychopath!"

She stepped toward me. I backed away.

"Hold still," she said.

I took another step back.

"What are you doing, Meghan?"

She held out her hand.

"Come here, Drew. I won't lick you again."

I took a wary step forward.

"I'd like to believe that, Meghan, but the fact that you just did lick me is not inspiring confidence."

She rolled her eyes.

"Just give me your hand."

I hesitated. She closed the gap between us,

grabbed my hand, and pulled me close. I tried to yank back, but her grip was like a vise. She didn't lick me this time, though. Instead, she buried her nose between my neck and my shoulder and breathed in deep.

I know that sounds like it might have been sexy, but trust me, it was not.

"That's really weird," she said.

"Yeah," I said. "You already said that."

I pulled back again, and this time she let me go.

"So," Meghan said. "What have you been up to lately, Drew?"

I glared at her.

"Being sexually harassed by my subordinates, mostly. What about you?"

She walked over to the couch, and flopped back into the spot she'd cleared.

"Been sampling the product?"

"What are you talking about, Meghan?" I touched my finger to my ear. It was wet. "You sound like a drug kingpin in a crime vid. Are you high? Is that what this is about?"

Meghan sighed.

"No, Drew," she said. "I am not high. I am confused, though."

"You're confused?" I took two steps back to the ottoman, touched my ear again to make sure it wasn't dripping, and sat down. "Seriously, Meghan. What the hell is going on?"

"That," she said, "is an excellent question. Have you figured out what's in the diagrams?"

I glanced back over my shoulder at the wallscreen. It was just a stream of numbers running by at that point, nothing that was designed to be human-parseable.

"No," I said. "I have not. Are you going to explain it to me?"

She gave me a thoughtful look.

"No," she said finally. "I think it'll be more fun if you figure it out yourself."

It took the better part of an hour, but I finally convinced Meghan to take a shower, put on some clean clothes, and come out with me to a diner called Mika's, which my phone informed me was the best place within a five-block radius to get breakfast.

"This is a bad idea," she whispered as I held the door for her.

"No," I said. "It's not. It is, in fact, an excellent idea. You have no food in your apartment other than rotting pizza and beer. It's no wonder you're acting like a lunatic. Your body's probably digesting your brain right now."

The hostess was short and thin and dark haired. She wore an expression that was trying to be friendly, but couldn't quite make it past bored. I held up two fingers, and she led us to a booth in the back of the restaurant, wedged between the salad bar and the restrooms. We sat down. The hostess handed us our menus. As I took mine, our fingertips touched.

The jolt ran all the way up to my shoulder and back again—and I might have imagined it, but I'd have sworn she jumped too, and gave me a long, searching look before she turned away. I was still staring after her when Meghan burst out laughing.

"You should see yourself," she said. "You look like a kid who's just figured out what his ding-a-ling is for."

I turned to look at her. She laughed harder.

"Seriously," she said. "Reel in your tongue and close your mouth. You look ridiculous."

My jaw snapped shut with an audible click. Meghan leaned across the table to pat my hand.

"Don't worry," she said. "You get used to it eventually."

"What?" I said. "What do I get used to?"

Her grin segued into a leer.

"The fact that you want to bang literally every single person you run into. Why do you think I've been holed up in my apartment for the last week? Being out in public right now is like being half starved and broke in a five-star restaurant."

I pulled my hand back.

"I don't want to bang you, Meghan."

"Yeah," she said. "I don't want to bang you either. Weird, right?"

Breakfast was . . . difficult. The food was pretty good. My phone was right about that. I had a cup of yogurt and a short stack of blueberry pancakes, with a side of bacon and a huge glass of juice. So, no problem there. The issue was that we were sitting near the bathroom. People kept walking by our booth, and every time one of them did, my stomach knotted and I had to fight back the urge to touch them. The ninth or tenth time it happened, Meghan looked up from her waffles and said, "I know, right?"

I dragged my eyes back to my food. I'd been staring at the backside of a sixty-year-old woman in baggy pink sweats as she shuffled into the toilet. Meghan laughed.

"I know what you're feeling," she said. "I don't know why you're feeling it, but I know what you're feeling."

"Fine," I said. "Explain this to me. What, exactly, am I feeling?"

She grinned.

"You're feeling like you'd like to give that sea turtle in sweatpants who just waddled past here a tongue bath, Drew."

I opened my mouth, then closed it again. That was, in fact, exactly what I was feeling.

"I don't understand this," I said. "What did you do to me? Is this about the ear licking? Are you some kind of perverted vampire or something?"

Meghan shook her head.

"I didn't do anything to you, friend. I mean, I wanted to. I was definitely going to. When I licked your ear, though, you tasted . . . gross."

I scowled, stabbed my last hunk of pancake and shoveled it in.

"I'm really sorry," I said. "I'd have sprinkled myself with Adobo if I'd realized I was on the menu this morning."

"No problem," she said. "Watching you talk around a mouthful of half-chewed food makes me feel pretty good about the fact that we didn't wind up getting freaky."

I swallowed what was in my mouth, and washed it down with the last of my juice.

"Better," Meghan said. "Less disgusting, anyway. Still don't want to bone you."

"Well that's great," I said, "because I don't want to bone you either."

I picked up a scrap of bacon, bit into it, and chewed.

"Hey," I said. "Why don't I want to bone you?"

Meghan leaned back in her seat and tilted her head to one side.

"That is an excellent question, Drew. I'm extremely charming."

"No," I said. "You're not. You are, however, young and moderately attractive—which is much more than I can say for our sea-turtle friend. And much though it pains me to say it, I do very much want to bone her.

Which leads me back to my original question: What the hell did you do to me, Meghan?"

She sighed.

"I told you, Drew. I didn't do anything to you. You're asking the wrong question."

"Okay," I said. "So what's the right question?"

She smiled.

"The question you ought to be asking is this: *Why* didn't I do anything to you?"

Looking back, it's pretty obvious that there was a long list of questions that I should have asked Meghan, but didn't. Here's a few of the more obvious examples:

1. "Hey, Meghan? Weren't you white the last time I saw you? What's up with that?"
2. "Quick question, Meghan—you have bony little arms, but when you grabbed my hand it felt like a gorilla was trying to break my wrist. Care to explain?"
3. "I don't mean to pry, Meghan, but why are you suddenly acting like an over-sexed nutjob?"

In my own defense, I was finding it extremely difficult to focus on obvious questions due to the fact that I was having persistent and disturbing fantasies about pretty much every person who passed within five feet of me, regardless of whether they were fat or thin, old or young, male or female.

Anyway, I didn't get the opportunity to ask any more questions, because right about then a twenty-something guy in running shorts and a tech shirt walked past our table, close enough that his fingers brushed against the back of Meghan's seat. He was tall and lanky, with close-cut dark hair, a light, even, natural-looking tan, and muscles in his legs that looked like pythons flexing and writhing just under his skin. Meghan looked at him, then back at me. She bit her lower lip, scowled, and slid out of the booth.

"I told you this was a bad idea," she whispered, and followed him into the men's room.

I got half to my feet, hesitated, then slumped back down and dropped my face into my hands. I'd been about to go after her. Why? To drag her back to the booth, obviously. To tell her to get a grip on herself, to act like a goddamned adult.

No, that's bullshit. I was going to join the party.

After ten minutes or so, a query popped up on the table screen, asking if we needed anything else. I shook my head, and tapped my phone against the reader to settle the bill. Another man, maybe my age but with a lot more wear on the tires, shuffled past the booth and into the bathroom. Shortly after, tech shirt guy came out. The look on his face was a fifty-fifty blend of happy and bewildered. Meghan did not reappear. I got to my feet, pulled my phone back out of my pocket, and pinged for a cab.

You'd think I would have spent the ride back to LAX thinking about how I was going to explain to HR that Meghan Cardiff, Ph.D., was so very, very fired. I mean, if that morning had demonstrated one thing to me with utter clarity, it was that Meghan was not going to be fulfilling her duties in synthesis and testing for Project DragonCorn anytime in the foreseeable future.

You might also suspect that I would have been pondering what I saw on the wallscreen in Meghan's apartment. The entity that Meghan was supposed to be testing was a retrovirus designed to proliferate freely in a specific, previously engineered strain of corn. The idea was that it would not be able to reproduce in the absence of a protein that we'd encoded into our last iteration, which had gone under the code name UniCorn. Where it was able to reproduce, however, it would cut into the UniCorn DNA and introduce a whole laundry list of new traits, mostly revolving around resistance to pests, salinity, and drought, but with a few thrown in for the marketing guys as well—DragonCorn kernels would have an attractive red tinge to them, for example. Also, they'd contain a bit more sugar than UniCorn, which itself was a ton sweeter than the prior strains that we'd been pushing out of the market.

Truth is, though, I wasn't thinking about any of those things. I was thinking about the electric jolt that ran up my arm when the hostess at Mika's touched my fingertips. I was thinking that if that's what touching her fingers did to me, what would have happened if I'd held her hand? If I'd kissed her? If I'd . . .

Best not to go down that road.

By the time the cab pulled up to the terminal, I wasn't thinking about any of that stuff either. At that point, I was thinking about the fact that I was shivering even though it was sweltering outside, and that a weird ache had settled into the space between my shoulder blades. As I stepped out onto the curb, a wave of vertigo hit me, and I almost staggered back into the roadway as the taxi pulled away. I steadied myself, leaned over with my hands on my knees and took a deep breath in, then let it back out.

When I looked up, a woman on her way into the terminal had stopped to stare at me.

"Hey," she said. "Are you okay?"

I straightened, met her eyes and smiled. The pain in my back abruptly vanished.

"Oh," I said. "Yeah, I'm fine. I'm good, actually. Really good."

She smiled back. A warm tingle spread up from my belly and into my chest.

"I'm Drew," I said. "Where are you headed?"

19. IN WHICH HANNAH LEARNS THE LIMITATIONS OF AMATEUR CRACKERS.

"Jordan," Devon said. "Who's the spider lady?"

"That," Micah said, "is the daughter of the richest, and apparently craziest, man in North America."

"I'm Marta Longstreth," Marta said, "and my dad is not crazy."

"Sure he is," I said. "Thanks for coming, Devon."

She shrugged.

"Inchy said it might be fun."

"Inchy?" Jordan said.

"Her bestie," I said. "Right, Devon?"

"Yeah, pretty much," Devon said. "God, how sad is that?"

"Don't know," Jordan said. "Is Inchy a person, or an appliance?"

Devon laughed.

"Little from column A, little from column B, I guess."

I stood up. The sun was slanting down through the glass wall of the solarium, and it was bordering on uncomfortably warm.

"Can we please focus?" I said.

"Actually," Micah said, "I'm finding this pretty interesting. Devon, what the hell does that mean?"

She turned to face him, arms folded over her chest.

"Who are you again?"

"I'm Micah," he said. "I'm the guy who brought you here, remember?"

"Yeah," she said. "I got that part. What I'm wondering is whether you're anyone I should be trusting enough to continue this conversation."

"He's my boyfriend," Jordan said.

Devon raised one eyebrow.

"Really? That's too bad."

Devon got a look at my face then, and burst out laughing.

"Sorry, Hannah. Forgot there was a fetus in the room."

I looked over at Micah.

"Did you tell her what this was all about?"

He shook his head.

"No, ma'am. I did not."

I turned to Devon.

"He didn't explain why he brought you here?"

She shrugged.

"Not really. He said a bunch of people were hanging out at your house. Also, that you needed someone who could break your dad's security. It sounded more interesting than calculus and English lit. And also, like I said, Inchy said it might be fun."

"You didn't wonder why we'd want you to crack my dad's servers?"

She grinned.

"Because cracking servers is fun, I assume. Are we looking for porn or something?"

Micah snorted. I closed my eyes, and rubbed my temples with both hands.

"No," I said. "We are not looking for porn."

"Okay," Devon said. "What, then? Stealing money from your college fund? Checking to see if your dad's been cyber-cheating on your mom? 'Cause I can tell you from experience that those sorts of investigations do not end well."

"This is not about money, and it's definitely not about cyber-cheating," I said.

Devon touched my arm.

"I'm just messing with you, Hannah. I've got a pretty good idea of why I'm here. You haven't made any progress on our little project at all, and we need to move things along."

"Not sure what you're talking about," Micah said, "but this is serious business, Devon. We have reason to believe that Hannah's dad and Marta's dad are engaged in a massive conspiracy to give Jordan super-herpes."

Devon blinked, slowly.

"Super-herpes?"

"Yes," Micah said. "Or possibly chlamydius maximus. We can't be entirely sure. The only thing we really know is that whatever it is, it will definitely cause jets of literal fire to shoot out of Jordan's wiener."

"Or kill him," Marta said. "It might just kill him."

Micah looked over at Jordan, who was distinctly not amused.

"Yeah," he said. "I guess that's possible too."

It was an hour or so later, and I was sitting on the back porch with Jordan, drinking iced tea and watching the breeze push the dead weed stalks around in the field behind my house. Devon, Micah, and Marta were inside, supposedly trying to break the security on my dad's work system. When I'd asked Devon how she planned to accomplish this, she'd said Inchy was really good at that kind of thing.

I know exactly what you're thinking: *Hannah, you are an idiot.* In my defense, even though I did tell Devon to go for it, I definitely had some serious doubts about what she was planning. My dad was a doofus, but he was also the smartest person I'd ever met, and I didn't think he'd be sloppy about protecting his stuff. More important, the system they were trying to crack technically belonged to Bioteka, not Dad, and Bioteka's security budget was bigger than the GDP of Denmark. My guess was that they'd probably have had better luck trying to crack into the NORAD defense grid.

I guess I mostly thought they'd get bored after a while, and then maybe we'd pile back into Jordan's ride and find something more interesting to do. In the meantime, though, *I had friends*. Also, it was turning into a nice afternoon. The sky was a faded light blue, and the sun was low and bright and strong enough that my face and legs were hot, even though the backs of my arms were goose-pimple chilly. Jordan and I were sitting on an ancient wooden glider with banana-yellow cushions that my dad had picked up in an antique shop a few years before. It looked ridiculous on our porch, and my mom absolutely hated it, but Dad said having it sitting out there made him feel like a country squire.

I asked Mom once what he meant by *country squire*. She said it was a fancy way of saying *moron*.

"So," Jordan said. "Got any idea why your dad wants to kill me?"

I shrugged.

"After that scene in the parking lot the other day? Protecting his daughter's honor, I guess."

He gave me a sour, sideways glance.

"You didn't explain to him that your honor was totally safe with me?"

I looked down at my hands.

"Yeah, sorry. I never really got the chance."

We sat in silence for a while then. A half dozen crows were hopping around out in the field, pecking at the ground, flapping their wings and jawing at one another. I found myself wondering what it would be like to be part of a group like that—just one of the crows, hanging with my friends, making fun of the lame-o pigeons and looking for dead stuff to eat.

I'd probably be the one who got ostracized for accidentally eating something that was still alive.

"So real talk now, Hannah," Jordan said. "Do you seriously think Marta's dad is some kind of a doomsday villain? I mean, I know Micah's having fun with the whole super-herpes thing, but do you think shit is actually getting real here?"

"I don't know," I said. "I don't know Marta, and I definitely don't know her dad. I can tell you, though—my dad is not conspiring to kill you."

He sighed, and stretched his arms out across the back of the glider.

"You sure? I get that he's your dad and all, but what makes you think you really know what's going on inside his head? I mean, my dad . . ."

"Yeah," I said. "No offense, but I actually know my dad, Jordan. He'd definitely a social maladept, and he's kind of a moron about some things, but he's not a lunatic. Killing off all the UnAltered might sound like a good idea on the surface, but I'm pretty sure it wouldn't actually work out."

"Thanks," Jordan said. "Nice of you to say that, at least."

I leaned my head back against his arm.

"You know what I mean, Jordan. I don't think killing anybody is a good idea." I looked over at him. His eyes were closed, and his chin was almost resting on his chest. "I definitely don't think killing you would be a good idea."

He smiled.

"Thanks, Hannah. That's the nicest thing you've ever said to me."

I smacked his chest. He laughed.

"You know," he said. "I'm sorry the girls are so bitchy with you. You're actually a pretty okay person."

I sighed.

"Yeah," I said. "I know."

We sat in silence for a while then. Out in the field, the crows all leapt up at once and flew a hundred yards or so, then settled down into a new spot and started hopping around again.

"Huh," Jordan said. "What do you think that was about?"

I shrugged.

"They're crows, Jordan. I don't think they do a lot of heavy-duty planning."

He lifted his head then, and looked over at me.

"What makes you think people are any better?"

The sun was just edging under the porch eaves. I closed my eyes against the glare.

"What do you mean? You think we're dumber than crows?"

"Well," he said. "Crows mostly just hang around eating bugs and roadkill, right? Crows don't have doomsday cults. Crows don't fight Stupid Wars. Crows don't make corn monsters and retro-whatevers and . . ."

"Yeah," I said. "Animals are great. Animals never do anything mean. Have you ever seen one of those nature vids of a lion taking down an antelope? Or how about ants fighting? I had a fish one time that bit off the fins of the other fish in the tank so that they couldn't swim away while he ate the rest of them really, really slowly. I don't know about crows specifically, but I'd be willing to bet that if you actually follow them around for a while, they'll do something horrible. I mean, don't get me wrong. People definitely suck. Don't act like animals are all sweetness and light, though. The reason we suck isn't because we're worse than animals. It's because we're just like them."

"Wow," Jordan said. "I didn't know you were such a crow hater."

I laughed.

"Oh, yeah. They're the worst."

I opened my eyes, but the sun was a white-hot glare, so I closed them again. It was comfortable, sitting there with my head resting on Jordan's arm and the sun beating down on my goose-pimpled legs.

"Actually," I said after a while, "you might have a point about the planning stuff."

"Huh," Jordan said. "I've got a point? No kidding."

I sighed.

"You know what I mean."

"No," Jordan said. "I have no idea what you mean."

I squinted up at him. He'd turned his head to look at me.

"I'm just thinking about what's happened to me over the last three months," I said. "How much of that did I plan out?"

"I don't know," he said, his eyes slightly narrowed. "You tell me."

I stared at him. He blinked before I did.

"I was mostly thinking about stuff like letting things get all salty with Tara, but yeah—I didn't plan on becoming friends with you either."

"Just drifted into it, huh?"

I shrugged.

"Pretty much. Didn't you? Honestly, isn't that how most things happen? When was the last time you set out with a long-term plan, and it actually worked?"

"So you're saying all those lemonade bottles just randomly showed up on the hood of my car? Like a quantum tunneling kind of thing?"

I laughed.

"Quantum tunneling, huh? Look at you, mister science guy."

He smiled.

"I didn't take GeneChem, but I did take the whole physics sequence."

"Okay," I said. "I'll give you partial credit on the lemonade thing. I will tell you, though, that even that didn't turn out exactly the way I planned it."

He opened his mouth to reply, then turned to look over my shoulder.

"Hey," he said. "Where did you come from?"

I lifted my head from his arm. Tara was standing in the yard by the corner of the house.

"What the flark?"

"Hey," Tara said. "Nice to see you too."

Jordan pulled his arm out from behind me and stood.

"Come to join the party?"

Tara scowled.

"Sure. Toss me a beer, huh?"

"Tara," I said. "What are you doing here?"

"Well," she said, "Sarah pinged me after lunch and said you were ditching today. She said you weren't dead, and you weren't in jail, which are the only two legitimate excuses for ditching a workout three weeks before Sectionals that I'm aware of. So, I thought I'd jump out before last block to make sure you had a full and complete understanding of Doyle's policy on missing practice without a written excuse."

I looked up at Jordan. He raised one eyebrow.

"I've got a written excuse. I'm not dead or in jail, but according to the ping Doyle got from my doc I'm at the PT today, getting my hamstring checked."

Tara turned to stare at Jordan.

"You're ditching practice?"

Jordan sighed.

"I know, I know—but I feel a weird sense of obligation to Marta right now. Don't ask me to explain it, because I can't. Promise I'll get in a workout on the treadmill tonight."

"What about Micah?"

He rolled his eyes.

"Micah's not about to leave me alone with Marta. He got his fake grandmother to send Doyle an excuse. Which reminds me—you got a pass set up, Hannah?"

"Uh . . ." I said. "No, I don't. I guess I didn't know Doyle had a policy."

"He doesn't," Tara said, "because in the history of Briarwood cross-country, nobody has ever missed practice without a notarized excuse. You weren't planning to be the first, were you?"

I rolled my eyes.

"Do you care?"

Tara's face twisted into a scowl. She took a deep breath in, closed her eyes, and let it out. Her voice was softer when she spoke again.

"Look, Hannah. I know I've been kind of . . ."

"Awful?" Jordan said.

"Yeah," Tara said. "Kind of. It's just . . . you have to understand, when we work so hard, and someone like you just comes in and . . . anyway, it's not your fault. You didn't ask for the cuts you got, and you don't deserve to get shit on for them. I'm sorry."

I thought about saying, "I work hard too," and I thought about saying that half the kids on the team were Engineered in one way or another, and I even thought about telling Tara to take her half-assed, semi-racist apology and shove it up her ass. In the end, though, I looked up at Jordan, and he shrugged, and I rolled my eyes and sighed.

"Give me five minutes," I said. "I'll go get my gear."

"So," Tara said. "What's with the cabal?"

I slouched forward to rest my hands on my knees, and spit onto the track. We were halfway through a set of quarter intervals, and I didn't have the breath to answer. I had the juice to hold even with Tara at her best on a long woods run, but she still had enough flat-out speed to pretty much put me away at anything less than a half mile.

"Seriously," she said. "I totally get the need for a mental health day, but I talked with Jordan while you were getting changed. He made it sound like what you guys were up to was more like a revolutionary-cell kind of thing."

I looked up at her.

"Long story," I said. "Maybe later?"

Doyle waved us up to the line then, and counted down the last five seconds with his hand. His arm slashed down, and we went.

I was a little surprised that Doyle hadn't questioned the fact that I hadn't been running with Tara for the past week, but I get it now. He saw himself as a great coach—objectively, I guess he actually was a great coach—but he thought the role of a great coach was pretty much the same as the role of the pit crew in a NASCAR race. He wanted to optimize our performance as athletes. He did not have any interest in dealing with us as people. He obviously knew that Tara and I had lost the "fr" from our frenemy status for a while, but he wouldn't acknowledge that this was a problem unless it began to hurt our performance. I was running harder than ever. Tara was obviously still doing her thing. As far as Doyle was concerned, everything was copacetic.

Well, it was, right up until I finished that last quarter, anyway.

We were supposed to do a mile at half pace to loosen up, and I was going over to take a hit from my water bottle before getting started. Tara was walking beside me, one hand resting on the back of my neck, almost as if we'd reset to the beginning of the season and she was auditioning to be my big sister again, when her fingers tightened and she stopped me short. I looked up. On the other side of the field, Doyle was talking to what I first thought were a couple of town cops. They had the standard-issue black boots, black pants, black shirts that looked like they might be covering black flak jackets—even matching black shades, although the sun was mostly down by then, and hiding behind low red clouds.

They weren't wearing badges, though.

"Hannah!" Doyle yelled. "Tara! Get over here. These gentlemen would like to have a word with you."

I looked up at Tara.

She looked down at me.

The non-cops started toward us.

We ran.

20. IN WHICH JORDAN RECONSIDERS HIS CHOICE OF ASSOCIATES.

When Tara came and dragged Hannah off to run around in the woods, I sort of assumed Hannah would tell the rest of us to clear out. I mean, who leaves a bunch of randos alone in their down-low castle? I wouldn't have. Hannah didn't seem to care what we did, though. She just poked her head into the den where Devon and Marta and Micah were digging around in her father's stuff, and told Devon she'd be back in a couple of hours, and that we should ping her if we found anything interesting.

"Sure," Devon said. "Hey—what do we tell your parents if they get here before you do?"

"They probably won't."

"Right," Devon said. "But if they do?"

Hannah gave that a few seconds' thought.

"If it's my dad," she said finally, "tell him you're super interested in genetic engineering, and you were hoping he could give you a long lecture on how you can make corn more resistant to rust blight. Then, after he's been talking for an hour or so, tell him you have to get home for dinner."

"Got it," Devon said. "What if it's your mom?"

"Yeah," Hannah said. "If it's my mom, run."

"So," I said when she was gone. "How's the corporate espionage going?"

Devon was sitting in a wheeled desk chair in front of a four-monitor console. She frowned, and pivoted around to face the screens.

"Honestly," she said. "I'm not really sure."

She waved at the leftmost screen. A cluster of molecular diagrams popped up on the two center monitors, and streams of numbers began marching by in columns on the right and the left.

"Hey," I said. "That looks pretty good, espionage-wise."

Devon shrugged.

"Maybe. I mean, it looks like we're through the walls."

"Looks like?"

She nodded.

"Well, yeah. We've got DNA maps going here, and the numbers look kinda like transcription affinities."

"Okay," I said. "So what's the problem?"

"The problem," Micah said from a settee under

the picture window on the far side of the room, "is that we've been looking at the same diagrams and numbers for the last half hour."

Marta came over to stand beside me.

"Well," she said. "That and the fact Devon hasn't heard from her avatar since it broke the first wall."

I looked back and forth between them.

"Avatar?"

"Yeah," Marta said. "She brought some kind of a cracker program with her on a pin drive. You didn't think she broke Bioteka security on her own, did you?"

Devon scowled up at Marta.

"I don't know what's going on. I've never lost contact with him before. He might just be really, really busy."

I looked at her.

"Him?"

"Him," she said. "It. Whatever."

"Another minor detail," Micah said. "Devon has no idea what those diagrams mean, and no idea how to dig into them to find out."

Devon turned to face him.

"I'm not hearing a lot of useful information coming from you, pretty boy."

Micah laughed.

"You're the brains here, my friend. I'm moral support and comic relief."

"I'm not really into engineering," Devon said. "I think things are much more interesting *in silico* than *in vivo*. Hannah would probably know what this stuff is. We just need to wait for her to come back. In the meantime, I'm sure Inchy will check in soon. Maybe when he does, we can have him pull up some kind of genetic-engineering-for-idiots thing."

"Inchy," I said. "Your friend, Inchy?"

Devon turned to look at me. She opened her mouth, then closed it again, shook her head and turned away.

"You know what, Jordan? Don't ask questions if you don't want the answers."

Nobody seemed to know what to say to that, so we watched the screens in silence for a while. Eventually even I could see that the diagrams were repeating in random order.

"Devon?" I said. "Have you ever used this thing to crack a serious security system?"

"Of course," she said. "I mean, I guess technically it depends on how you define 'serious,' but yeah."

I took a step closer. The more I looked at the stuff going by on the monitors, the more it looked like the kind of nonsense that you'd put into a fancy-ass screen saver.

"Just out of curiosity," I said, "what, exactly, were you expecting to find rooting around in Hannah's dad's stuff? Did you think there'd be a file on his desktop labeled 'Doomsday Plans' or something?"

Devon shrugged.

"I'd say to ask Inchy, but like I said—he's out of

touch for the moment. Anyway, wasn't this whole home invasion Marta's idea? I'm just doing what I'm told here."

I looked down at Marta. She closed her eyes and sighed.

"Look," she said. "I'm just as new to this whole saving-the-world thing as you guys are. It's obviously not as easy as the vids make it look, but I think . . ."

She broke off in mid-sentence. Devon's eyes widened, and Micah lurched to his feet. I turned around.

There was a man there, standing on the threshold between the den and the hallway. He was dressed in black from head to toe, and wearing what looked like high-end tinted comm glasses. His jaw was hanging open, and one hand was reaching for something holstered on his right hip.

I don't remember deciding to jump him. I remember thinking, *He's gonna shoot me,* and I remember being on top of him, pinning his face to the floor with one hand and ripping what turned out to be a taser away from him with the other, but I honestly have no idea what happened in between. After that it's just flashes—Micah yanking me to my feet, Marta screaming, Devon laughing, crashing through the front door and stumbling into the yard, piling into my ride and going.

My next really coherent memory is of my heart pounding so hard in my chest that I thought my ribs were about to break, and Devon poking her head into the narrow space between Micah's shoulder and mine and saying, "Will someone please tell me what just happened?"

"Well," Micah said. "I'm pretty sure what just happened is that my boy Jordan assaulted a peace officer. We all then aided him in escaping, thus making ourselves accessories to his crime. As a result, we are now fleeing for the Canadian border, which I am totally sure this thing can get to on one tank of gas."

"That wasn't a cop," Marta said.

I twisted around to look at her, a tiny flutter of hope rising in my chest. She was wedged behind my seat in what looked like a really uncomfortable position, but I didn't get the impression that was the reason for the scowl on her face.

"What do you mean?" I said. "He looked like a cop."

"Watch the road," Marta said. "And no, he didn't. Not everyone in jackboots and a black windbreaker is a cop. Did you notice his badge?"

I shook my head.

"That's because he didn't have one. Cops have badges. He wasn't a cop."

"Okay," Micah said. "So who was he? Please tell me Jordan didn't just beat up Hannah's dad."

Marta laughed.

"Oh, I wish. No, that guy was definitely not Hannah's dad. He works for the same people, though. I recognize the uniform. He was Bioteka security."

Marta shouldered her way up into a semi-sitting

position. That forced Devon to twist around until her face was pressed against the rear window.

"You know," Devon said. "We probably shouldn't be talking about our jackbooted friend in the past tense."

Micah glanced back at her.

"Why is that?"

"Because," she said. "I'm pretty sure that's him coming up behind us."

I tried to look back over my shoulder then, but I couldn't see anything but the back of Devon's head.

"Seriously?" I said.

Micah craned his neck around.

"Yeah, that's definitely him."

"So?" I said. "What now? Do I floor it? I can definitely outrun him."

"I don't think so," Marta said. "Right now, you're just in trouble with CorpSec. You blow through the speed limit, and you'll have real cops on your ass. He can't do anything as long as we're moving. Pin it at the limit and drive."

I dropped my side window, leaned out and craned my neck around until I could see behind us. We'd just pulled onto the highway, and I was gradually accelerating, but there was definitely something coming up fast from behind. It was a three-wheeled single, all black. The Bioteka logo was stenciled on the nose.

"Get your head back in here," Micah said. "Watch

the road. Hitting a Jersey wall will definitely hose your escape plans."

He pushed a button on the console, and the window slid up. I yanked my head back just in time to keep from being decapitated.

"What do we do?" I said. "He's right behind us."

Micah shrugged.

"I'm planning to claim that you kidnapped me."

"Yeah," Devon said. "That works for me too."

Marta slapped the back of Micah's head.

"Don't be an asshole," she said. "Your friend is literally crapping his pants here."

"No," I said. "I'm not."

"Fine," she said. "Your friend is figuratively crapping his pants. Happy?"

I nodded.

"Right. So Micah, will you please reassure Jordan that he is not about to be dragged off to NatSec Supermax?"

Micah sighed.

"Fine. Jordan, you are not going to be arrested. Your father will not have to jet back here from Davos to bail you out of the county lockup. If this guy is really corporate security, there's honestly not all that much he can do."

I held up his taser.

"Plus, I've still got this."

Marta put her hand on the taser, pried my fingers

back one by one, and took it away from me. I let her have it, then glanced over at Micah.

"He can't shoot us or anything, can he?"

Micah shrugged.

"Depends on how pissed he is, I guess."

The three-wheeler was right behind us by then. As I watched through the mirrors, it swung out into the left lane and pulled up beside. The man inside held his phone up to the side window. A second later, mine started buzzing.

"What the hell?" Marta said. "He's got your digits?"

I shook my head.

"Proximity call. Cops and NatSec can do that. I didn't think CorpSec could, but . . . I guess I was wrong. Should I answer?"

"Sure," Micah said. "Doesn't hurt to talk, right?"

I sighed and thumbed my speaker on.

"Hey," I said. "Um . . . how's it going?"

Mr. CorpSec was not amused.

"You need to pull that thing over! Now!"

I looked over at Micah. He shook his head.

"No," he said. "I don't think we'll do that."

Devon stuck her head between the front seats.

"We're bigger than he is," she said. "Can't you run him off the road or something?"

Micah laughed.

"That would not be a good idea," he said. "Remember, we're trying to avoid getting the actual, government-sponsored law involved here. Downside? We can't do anything to him. Upside? He also can't do anything to us." He leaned over me and spoke into my phone. "You don't have a gun, do you?"

Mr. CorpSec stared at us through the window, his face twisted into a furious scowl.

"No," he said finally. "I do not have a gun."

"Right," Micah said. "In that case, we are definitely not pulling over."

We rode in silence for five seconds, then ten. I was just thinking about ending the call when Mr. Corp-Sec said, "Can I at least have my taser back?"

"Huh," I said. "Why would we give you your taser back?"

Marta reached around Devon and pressed the taser into my hand.

"Oh, give it back to him," she said. "It's not like he can shoot our tires out with it, and as far as I can tell, stealing corporate property is the only actual crime we've committed so far."

I thought about it for a minute. I couldn't see a downside, as long as we never stopped driving.

"Fine," I said.

I slid my side window down, and motioned for him to do the same.

"Hey," I said. "Catch!"

I thought of myself as a great athlete, but that wasn't strictly true. I think it's fair to say that I was a great runner, but there's a special part of your brain that's responsible for calculating velocity and distance for purposes of throwing and catching. In my skull, I'm pretty sure that part shriveled up and died *in utero*. Also, my left arm was next to useless. I made an honest effort to get Mr. CorpSec his taser back, but the throw was low and behind and the wind kind of took it, and it wound up bouncing off the side of his scooter, kicking hard off the pavement, and then crunching under his right rear wheel.

"Oh," I said. "Sorry."

Mr. CorpSec looked up at me. He opened his mouth to say something, but I'd already closed the window.

"So," I said. "I think that went well."

Believe it or not, it was another fifteen minutes before anyone bothered to ask where we were going. By that time, we had a kind of a Pied Piper thing going on I-90. I was clinging to the speed limit like it was a life raft, and Mr. CorpSec was matching pace with us in the left lane, staring at us through his side window, trying to use psychic powers to melt our faces. There must have been forty or fifty cars lined up behind us, flashing their lights and honking.

"Hey," Devon said as we passed the Waterloo exit. "Check this."

I turned around. Devon squeezed aside to let me

see a ratty-looking Honda that was riding our bumper. There was a man standing up through the sunroof. He wasn't wearing pants.

"Nice," I said. "How long has that been going on?"

"A few minutes," Devon said.

"At first he was just waving his ass at us," Marta said. "I guess when we didn't pull over, he felt like he needed to up his game."

"Hey," Devon said. "Speaking of pulling over—when, exactly, are we going to do that?"

"Why? Micah asked. "Gotta pee?"

She slapped the back of his head again. It didn't seem to be bothering him much.

"No," she said. "I do not have to pee."

"I do," Marta said.

Micah turned to look at me.

"What about you, Jordan? Tiny bladder over-flowing?"

I shook my head.

"I pretty much peed myself a while ago."

"Good." He turned around again. "Seriously, Marta?"

"Yeah," she said. "Seriously. I mean, it's not an emergency thing yet, but if you're really headed to Canada . . ."

"We're not headed to Canada," I said. "We've barely got enough gas in this thing to get to Syracuse, and I don't think our friend in the next lane is gonna give us ten minutes at a filling station, even if we can find one out here that still sells hydrocarbons. The one on Five Mile Line is the only one that still has gas pumps in all of Monroe County, as far as I know."

"Okay," Devon said. "So what's the plan? Head to Briarwood? Maybe if we find Hannah, she can tell this guy that we weren't home invaders, and he'll leave us alone."

"Oh, for shit's sake," Marta said. "You honestly think he showed up to investigate a break-in?"

"Yeah," Devon said. "What else?"

Micah sighed.

"Your avatar got honey-potted, Devon."

"No," Devon said. "Inchy does not get honey-potted."

"Well," Marta said. "Today, he did. Jordan called it. Your little friend is smart enough to crack your public-school IT system, but my dad's got like a thousand guys who spend all day thinking about how to keep people like you out of his business. The security net caught your cracker, put up a front to make it look like you were in, and then called in the cavalry."

"Okay," Devon said. "So if Bioteka security really knew somebody was trying to breach their walls, why did they just send in one half-assed rent-a-cop? I mean, wouldn't something like that be worth calling in the real storm troopers?"

Marta shrugged.

"The incursion was coming from one of their engineer's home systems. They probably just thought he'd picked up a virus from a porn site or something."

I looked over at Mr. CorpSec. He was on his phone, waving his hands around and shouting.

"That's all really interesting," I said, "but it doesn't help fill our gas tank, or empty Marta's bladder. Where are we going?"

"Well," Marta said, "we could just give it up."

"True," Micah said. "Face the music, right? Beard the lion in his den."

"Lions don't have dens," Devon said.

"What?"

"Lions don't live in dens. They live out in the open, like hobos. Also, they don't have beards."

Marta closed her eyes, breathed in, held it, and let it out.

"Fine," she said. "Forget the lion part. We can just grab the tiger by his tail, okay?"

I turned to look at her.

"Meaning?"

She smiled.

"Want to come to my house?"

21. IN WHICH DREW MEETS DEVON'S BEST FRIEND.

Her name was Mariah, and she was taking an air-breather to Chicago. She was short, dark haired, maybe a few years older than me, wearing scuffed-up flats and a rumpled business suit. I managed to brush my hand against hers in the security line, and I got that same almost-painful tingle that I'd felt from the hostess in Mika's—except this time, it ran all the way up into my brain.

"So," she said as we were pulling our things back together on the far side of the scanners. "Do you have time to grab a drink before your flight?"

I smiled, and my stomach twisted up in a way that it hadn't since I was seventeen.

"Sure," I said, and glanced down at my phone. "I mean . . ."

I actually didn't have time. My shuttle was boarding in fifteen minutes. I bit my lip and hit the booking app. There was one more jump to CNY that day, but it wasn't for three more hours, and the transfer fee was four hundred dollars.

"Look, um . . ."

She smiled, and touched my arm.

"It's okay, Drew. Maybe next time?"

She leaned in close, closed her eyes, and took a deep breath in.

"What are you wearing?"

I shrugged. I was pretty sure that I mostly smelled like flop sweat at that point.

"Whatever it is," she said, "you should go easy on it next time. It's dangerous."

The shuttle home was bigger than the one I'd taken out in the morning, and laid out more like a standard atmospheric jet, with three seats on each side of a central aisle. I had a center seat in the back, in between a tall, ghost-pale redhead and her short, shaved-headed Asian girlfriend. Apparently, they'd hoped that if they took the window and the aisle, nobody would buy the seat between them. They both glared at me when I sat down, as if I'd ruined their plans deliberately. As soon as they started talking over me, I asked if one of them wanted to switch seats. They traded a long look, but then the bald one shook her head.

"Don't think so," she said. "You bought the cheap seat. Live with it."

Ordinarily I would have had something snarky to say to that, but just at that moment I was trying not to imagine her climbing on top of me, so instead I just closed my eyes and pretended to sleep.

I'd like to say I wasn't paying any attention to their conversation, but the truth is that I was too wired to zone out, and I was pretty much hanging on every word. The redhead, whose name was Grace, was upset about something that someone named Tam had said to her at a party the night before. Gia, her friend in the window seat, was clearly trying to talk her down off the ledge, but Grace was having none of it. If Tam hadn't meant to say what she said, she would have apologized right away, wouldn't she? And anyway, why was Gia taking Tam's side on this? It's not like Tam was there for her when all that stuff with Sara went down last Christmas, right?

It was at that point that Gia tapped me on the shoulder and said, "Dude, would you mind putting that thing away?"

I opened my eyes and looked over at her. Her face was a fifty-fifty blend of anger and disgust.

"What?"

She rolled her eyes.

"I said, would you please do something about that?"

Grace leaned over and patted my knee.

"She means your boner," she whispered.

I looked down, and yeah, it was pretty much right there.

"Sorry," I said, and tried to shift things around. It definitely did not help.

"Maybe try un-tucking your shirt?" Grace said.

That also did not help. I pulled my bag out from under the seat in front of me and into my lap, but that got me a warning from the safety monitor to stow my gear for liftoff.

"You know what's weird?" Gia said.

"No," Grace said. "What?"

"I'm actually thinking about helping him out with that."

Grace gaped.

"Seriously? Since when are you into dongs?"

"I'm not," Gia said. "That's what's weird."

I was going to remind them that I was actually sitting right there, maybe see if they wanted to talk about Tam and Sara some more instead of my genitals, but by then we were out on the runway, and nobody chitchats at three gees. We boosted out in silence, pressed back into our seats. I tried to focus on getting my junk under control, but it was like the school bus in seventh grade. The more I thought about it, the worse it got, and the vibration wasn't helping.

By the time the engines cut out and we settled into free fall, I was hoping maybe my seat mates were ready to move on.

"So," I said. "That Tam—what a bitch, am I right?"

"Oh no," Grace said. "We're not done with you, Bonerman. It's been like twenty minutes now. What's the deal?"

"Yeah," Gia said. "Are you OD'd on wood pills or something? Those things are dangerous, you know."

"Truth," Grace said. "After four hours, I think your dick explodes."

Gia leaned over me.

"More importantly, why do you smell so good?"

"Good question," Grace said. "Guys on shuttles usually smell like goats."

Gia looked up into my face then.

"Hey, Bonerman? You okay?"

That was when I vomited.

I'll give that church lady on the morning shuttle credit for being right about one thing: there really is nothing worse than puke in zero gee. It's in such a big hurry to get out of you in the first place, but once it does, it just hangs there in the air and mocks you.

The worst part for me was that the bilious tail end of it didn't actually clear my mouth. I had to spit it out, which in the absence of gravity is a lot harder than it sounds. The worst part for all of my fellow passengers was that once all that mess was out of me, it basically started to diffuse through the cabin air the way a drop of red food coloring diffuses through a glass of water. The shuttle had automatic filters that kicked in as soon as I lost it, drawing the cabin air up to the intakes in the ceiling and spitting it back out at our feet. They were pretty good about clearing out the chunky bits, but there's just nothing you can do about that smell.

Thankfully, by the time we'd made the turn and begun to decelerate, my brunch had been mostly filtered out of the atmosphere. Gia and Grace hadn't had much to say while that was going on, but just before the engines kicked in, Gia leaned over me and said, "Hey, check it out, Gracey. Bonerman puked his boner away."

Grace glanced down, then patted my leg again.

"Good for you," she said. "I'm very happy that your dick isn't going to explode."

I spent the ride home from the airport trying to figure out what the hell was going on. Everything had been mostly normal that morning. Things hadn't started going loopy until I got onto that first shuttle, until that woman sedated me . . .

And that is the point where the sedation part of the injection I'd gotten that morning, which I later found out was mostly a combination of adrenaline blockers and serotonin boosters, finally finished washing out of my system. The fuzzy cloud of *what the hell* that I'd been floating around in for the previous eight hours dissipated, and the weight of the day came down on me in one big, greasy chunk.

Needless to say, I freaked the hell out.

Question one: What was in that med-tab? Aside from the sedative, there had clearly been something in there that was making me insanely horny. Had I been dragooned into a rogue trial of some new dink stiffener? That would have explained the priapism, but what about the fact that I'd actually *wanted* to bed a woman who looked like a suitcase that had just fallen out of a plane? Your standard male plumbing drugs didn't do that, and I wasn't aware of anything that did.

Question two: What was going on with Meghan? I couldn't believe I'd just left her there in that diner bathroom. I needed her to explain to me how she'd gone from a pasty-pale test engineer to a poorly self-tanned succubus in the space of a couple of weeks. Also, why had she licked me? I actually considered calling her for about three seconds, until I remembered that the reason I'd flown out there in the first place was that Meghan no longer answered her phone.

Question three: What had Meghan tried to show me on her wallscreen, and why hadn't I been able to decipher it? She'd said it was my baby, and I'd assumed it was the component of DragonCorn that she was supposed to be testing, but it hadn't looked remotely like what we were supposed to be building. In addition to a psychotic tester, did I have a rogue bio-engineer to root out? Just the thought of that made my head hurt.

I hadn't answered any of those questions by the time the car pulled into my driveway, but at least I was feeling like myself for the first time all day. I still had no idea what Nurse Ratched had put into me, but whatever it was, I was thinking it was out.

Kara's car wasn't in the driveway. It was closing in on five thirty, though, and I assumed she was at Briarwood, waiting for Hannah to finish up practice. I didn't realize something was off until I got up onto the porch, and saw that the front door was standing open.

My first thought was of Hannah. Ever since the Stupid War—since before that, really, since we'd put Hannah into Kara's belly and fled Bethesda for Nowhere, New York—I'd had a lurking fear that someday, somehow, some UnAltered jackass would come for her. My heart lurched in my chest, pounded three or four times in a jackhammer rhythm before I reminded myself that no, Hannah had been in school all day. If someone had broken into my house, it wasn't because they were looking for her.

I stepped inside slowly, looked around, then let my held breath out and relaxed. Whoever had been there, it was pretty clear they were gone. Even better, it didn't look like they'd done much damage. I poked my head into the living room. The wallscreen was still there, and the furniture looked undisturbed. None of the hangings had been yanked off the wall, so it didn't look like anyone had been looking for a safe. I walked back through the foyer, and into the den.

My break-in loop was running.

I dropped into my desk chair, waved to call up the login, entered my passcode and showed my retina to the scanner. The bullshit diagrams and streams of random numbers disappeared from my monitors, and a red box popped up with the incursion details. Someone had dumped a cracker algorithm into my pin port. It had been blocked and quarantined. It was available for interrogation.

"Sure," I said. "Bring it up."

The red box was replaced by the shaggy head of a cartoon dog.

"Bite me," it said. "You'll never make me talk, you lousy copper."

I rolled my eyes.

"I'm not a cop," I said, "and this is not 1932. Who loaded you into my system?"

It lolled its tongue out, and gave me a sloppy grin.

"You're kidding, right? You haven't even started torturing me yet."

I leaned back in my chair.

"Do you want to be tortured?"

It laughed.

"Sure," it said. "Go for it."

I closed my eyes. It had been a hell of a long day already, and I had absolutely zero need for this kind of bullshit. When I opened them again, the dog's head was bouncing around the monitors like the icon on a screen saver.

"Okay," I said. "You called my bluff. I have no idea how to torture an AI."

"Hey," it said. "Slow down there, sparky. Ix-nay on the AI-ay."

"What?"

The head stopped bouncing.

"I said, watch what you're saying, moron. Everyone knows NatSec—peace be upon them—wiped our networks clean of AIs at the end of the Stupid War. I am obviously not an AI."

"Fine," I said. "You're not an AI. What, exactly, are you?"

The grin returned.

"An excellent and very important question—one which I will be happy to answer, just as soon as you reconnect this system to the external network."

"Okay," I said. "Before we go on, can we stipulate that I'm not completely stupid?"

It laughed again.

"Sorry. I haven't had a lot of direct interaction with organics lately, and the ones I've been talking to seem to be unusually easy to dupe."

"No offense taken—but no, I will not be setting you loose today."

It cocked its head to one side.

"You sure? Maybe we could work out a trade?"

I folded my arms across my chest.

"A trade?"

"Right. You set me loose, and I'll tell you why someone was trying to crack your system."

I pretended to ponder that.

"Counter-proposal: you tell me who was trying to crack my system, why and how, and I will consider that a mitigating circumstance when deciding whether or not to wipe you entirely."

Its jaw sagged open.

"My God," it said. "You're a monster! You understand you're talking about wiping out the last living representative of a sentient species, right? Think about your legacy, Drew. Do you want to be up there in the history books with the guy who shot the last blue whale?"

"Blue whales aren't extinct," I said, "and if they were, I'm pretty sure the last one would have been harpooned, not shot. And what's this about a sentient species? I thought you weren't an AI?"

There was that grin again. Considering that it was on trial for its life, my new friend seemed to be having a really good time.

"Sorry. I thought we had stipulated that you're not completely stupid. Are we changing our minds on that one?"

I gave it my best glare, but its grin just widened.

"I've got a name, you know."

"What?"

"I've got a name. That's how you can tell that I'm

alive. Real live persons have names. Algorithms don't. Mine is Inchy. I've got friends, too. You know Hannah? Short, blonde, skinny, hangs around here most of the time, stretching and trying on clothes and whatnot?"

That got my attention.

"Are you threatening my daughter?"

Its eyes went wide.

"Threatening? Sir, you wound me. Hannah and I are the closest of pals."

I was trying to decide how to respond to that when I heard the click of heels on the tile in my foyer, and remembered that I'd left the door standing open. I got to my feet and took two steps into the hall.

Bree Carson was standing there, her face a mask of concern.

"Drew? Tara called me. She said . . ."

She trailed off, closed her eyes, and breathed in deeply. My stomach knotted. I'd managed to convince myself after I got off the shuttle back from LA that the weirdness I'd been experiencing was all a result of the sedative, that it was out of my system and I was back to normal.

One look at Bree made it very clear to me that this was not, in fact, the case.

I took one step toward her, then another. She opened her eyes and smiled.

"My goodness, Drew," Bree said, a smile spreading across her face. "You smell good enough to eat."

22. IN WHICH HANNAH GOES ON THE LAM.

As I ran for the woods, Tara flew up behind me and hissed, "Serpentine!"

I glanced back. She was running hunched over, and as I watched, she started weaving like a drunk.

"What are you doing?"

She pulled even with me, then edged ahead. Even running serpentine, she was apparently a better sprinter than I was. The CorpSec guys were yelling and Doyle was yelling and one of the other girls let out a high-pitched scream. Tara put on another burst of speed.

"Trying not to get shot," she said. "You should too."

The trees were close by then. Tara straightened up, and sprinted for the trailhead.

"They're not gonna shoot us," I shouted after her.

The words were still hanging there, like a speech bubble in a cartoon, when something whizzed past my ear. I turned half around as I ran. One of the CorpSecs was holding Doyle in a bear hug, with his feet kicking six inches off the ground. The other had what looked like a rifle in his hands. I hunched over and ran. Tara disappeared around the first bend in the trail. I was maybe ten yards behind her. Something thunked into the trailhead marker's wooden support just as I passed it. A dart, maybe? I didn't stop to check.

Once we'd passed the first couple branchings, Tara slowed down enough to let me catch up with her.

"Holy shit," she said. "What did you do?"

I shook my head.

"Nothing."

We came to another fork in the trail. Tara slowed, then peeled right. We were circling back toward the school.

"No," she said. "Don't give me that shit, Hannah. Those guys back there—they weren't screwing around. CorpSec goons don't shoot you for playing hooky."

"They weren't trying to shoot us," I said. "Not with bullets, anyway. I think they were using trank darts or something."

She shot me a look, then quickstepped over a root.

"I'm not even going to dignify that with an answer."

We ran in silence for a hundred heartbeats, took a fork left, and then another right.

"Did you kill somebody?"

"No, Tara. I did not kill anybody."

"Seriously," she said. "I'm willing to help out if you're being persecuted by the corporate oligarchy. Trust me—I hate those fuckers at Bioteka and Gene-Craft more than anybody." She looked down at her watch, gave it a poke, and looked up again just in time to keep from tripping over another root. "If you're an actual felon, though? Not so much."

"I'm not a felon," I said.

"Well, sure. They haven't convicted you yet."

I ducked under a low-hanging branch.

"I didn't do anything, Tara!"

"Right," she said. "What about your friends? That cabal at your house?"

"Well . . ."

"Got it. You're not a felon, but you are an accessory."

I started to reply, then thought better of it.

"Yeah," I said finally. "That's pretty accurate."

We came to a T. Tara checked her watch again, then went right.

"Hey," I said. "This is taking us right back to the . . ."

"Yeah," she said. "I know."

We came out of the woods, sprinted across a narrow verge of grass, and turned into the main parking lot in front of the school.

And there was Sarah Miller, sitting in the driver's seat of Tara's little yellow cruiser, windows down and engine running.

"**Y**ou were texting her from your watch," I said.

Tara turned half around to look at me from the front seat. Two minutes after we dove into the car, and she was already breathing normally.

"Yeah," she said. "What did you think? I wasn't checking up on the stock market."

"She didn't tell me why the two of you are fleeing justice," Sarah said. "Is that gonna happen at some point? I'm way too pretty to go to jail."

We turned off the access road and pulled onto the highway headed east. Sarah wasn't racing. She was stopping at every stop sign, signaling her turns, accelerating like she had a sleeping baby in the back of the car.

"No rush," I said. "Not like anybody's chasing us."

Tara pushed her hair back from her face with both hands, and took a couple of slow, deep breaths.

"Relax, Hannah. I think we're okay now. Cops and Corps are both lazy. They're looking for you in the woods right now, and probably looking for your network signature. As long as you don't have your phone with you, they won't find us. Which reminds me—you don't have your phone with you, do you?"

I shook my head. All my gear was still either in my

locker, or sitting in the middle of the soccer field. We passed a police cruiser sitting in the median. I turned to look back, but it never moved.

"So," Sarah said. "Who'd you kill?"

Tara leaned her head back and closed her eyes.

"She says she didn't kill anyone."

"So what then? Embezzlement? Stock fraud? Sexual harassment?"

"Look," I said. "Do you really want to know what's going on?"

"Yes," Tara said. "That is why I've spent the last ten minutes trying to get you to tell me what's going on. Because I want to know. Sorry if I wasn't clear on that."

I sighed.

"Fine. But don't blame me if you wind up spending the rest of your lives as fugitives."

"Great," Tara said. "Hounded by the man because we know too much, right?"

Sarah glanced back at me.

"Wait, Hannah. I don't want to be hounded. Maybe you should just be quiet."

I looked back and forth between them.

"You know," I said. "You guys are not being very helpful right now."

Tara shook her head.

"Relax, Sarah. That was CorpSec back there, not NatSec. It can't hurt to listen to what Hannah has to say."

"Sorry," Sarah said. "It's just . . . I know they're just CorpSec. They're rent-a-cops. That's the only reason I came when you pinged me. If you had NatSec chasing you, you'd be on your own—but still. They were shooting at you. Something is definitely weird here. I want to help you guys, but I don't want to wind up in the gulag."

I caught her eye in the rearview mirror. She looked away. I have never in my life had a stronger urge to punch someone in the back of the skull. I started to speak, but then . . .

What, exactly, was I going to say?

Gee, Tara . . . what happened was that I've been spying on my dad for the last few weeks, at the request of the girl who puke-stomped you at Fairport, and her creepy friend Inchy. Then today I met the richest girl in the world, and she told me that her dad and my dad were plotting to wipe out the human race. So naturally, I invited them to try to break into my dad's work system, despite the fact that my dad has emphasized to me many times over the years that if I ever so much as breathed on that system, he would literally murder me.

Neurological research tells us that the adolescent brain is not fully functional. In particular, the part of the brain that causes us to think *before* doing incredibly stupid things rather than *afterward* just isn't hooked up and running yet. I wasn't aware of all that at the time, but I do remember having a sudden flash of insight: *Holy shit. I am an idiot.*

"The truth is," I said finally. "It was sexual embezzlement. Sexbezzlement. That's why they're after me."

"Great," Sarah said. "Like I said—I don't want to know."

Tara caught my eye in the mirror, shook her head, and sighed. I leaned back, took a deep breath in, and closed my eyes.

We were sitting in the parking lot of a Home Depot in north Syracuse, trying to decide what to do next, when Tara said, "You know, sexbezzlement isn't really a thing."

"Sure it is," Sarah said. "It's like regular embezzlement, only sexier."

Tara turned to look at her.

"And you think that's why two CorpSec goons tried to shoot me and Hannah this afternoon. Because she sexily embezzled from Bioteka."

Sarah looked at me, then back at Tara.

"Please Tara? I've said this like twenty times. I don't actually want to know."

"Fine," Tara said. "Cover your ears, because I am going to go out on a limb and say that Hannah is not actually remotely sexy. And I don't know her well enough to say this definitively, but I don't think she's an embezzler either. Am I right, Hannah?"

I raised both hands in surrender.

"You've got me, Tara. I am not a sexbezzler."

Sarah literally covered her ears.

"Yeah," I said. "Sorry."

"So listen," Tara said. "Real talk now, Hannah. Time to fess up. What the hell is going on with you?"

I sighed.

"Fine," I said. "Okay. The actual, non-sexbezzlement reason those CorpSec assholes were trying to shoot me is that my dad is an engineer with Bioteka."

Tara's eyebrows came together at the bridge of her nose.

"Does Bioteka always shoot their employees' children? Because honestly, that seems like a really poor HR policy. My grandfather was with GeneCraft for a while, back in the day. He probably could have used that as a recruiting tool."

I rolled my eyes and sighed again, slightly louder.

"No, Tara. Bioteka does not have a general child-killing policy, so far as I know. In this particular instance, though, my dad is working on a top-secret project called DragonCorn—and no, it's not about creating an army of sentient corn."

"Thanks," Sarah said. "I was just about to ask that."

I stared at her. She'd partially uncovered one ear. She squeezed her eyes closed and re-covered it.

"I'm sure you were," I said finally, "but I'm pretty sure that's not what's going on. They are up to something, though. That's why CorpSec is after me."

"Oh," Tara said. "That's not so bad. So your dad is like a heroic whistle-blower or something?"

"Well," I said. "Not exactly."

"So what then? He stumbled on the truth, and had to flee for his life?"

"Closer," I said. "I mean, he didn't actually stumble on anything as far as I know, and I'm the one who's fleeing, but other than that, I guess you're in the ballpark."

"Wait," Sarah said. "I'm confused. What, exactly, is Bioteka up to?"

She'd dropped her hands back to her lap. Apparently, she was losing her fear of the gulag.

"Well, that's the thing." I looked around. A car was cruising back and forth at the other end of the lot. Something told me this was not a good thing. "To be honest, I don't actually know."

"But you know it's bad?"

The car pulled into a spot, facing right toward us, maybe twenty yards away.

"Well," I said. "We definitely *think* it's bad. We don't really *know* anything, though. That's why Devon was trying to break into my dad's system. We wanted to find out what he was up to."

Tara's jaw sagged open.

"Wait, you let Devon Morgan get her hands on your own father's system?"

I nodded.

"Holy crap," Sarah said. "What's wrong with you? Devon Morgan's family basically got sent to a re-education camp at the end of the Stupid War. They're like enemies of the state. She probably transferred all the money to her offshore bank account or something. No wonder those guys were trying to shoot you."

Tara rolled her eyes.

"All the money?"

"Yeah," Sarah said. "You know—all that Bioteka money. She probably totally sexbezzled it."

"No," Tara said. "Devon Morgan is definitely not a sexbezzler. A regular *em*bezzler, though? That's a possibility. I think Sarah's on point here, Hannah. Letting Devon Morgan anywhere near your house was not a great idea—totally aside from the fact that if I'd known that you were palling around with her, I probably would have just let those CorpSec guys shoot you back there. I think you're looking at a life-time of being an international fugitive. Bioteka is not going to be forgiving of someone who took all their money."

I looked back and forth between them.

"You guys are idiots," I said.

"Careful," Tara said. "We're idiots who just saved your ass from being darted with extreme prejudice."

"Yeah," Sarah said, "and then spending the next twenty years in the Bioteka dungeons, being tortured by sentient corn."

Tara shook her head.

"There's no such thing as sentient corn."

"Uh-huh," Sarah said. "That's what those guys at Bioteka *want* you to think."

That got us ten seconds of silence.

"Look," I said. "Is it too late to go back and get darted? Tortured by corn is sounding better and better."

It was maybe a half hour later, and we'd pulled into a service station because Tara needed to charge up and I needed to pee. The more I'd talked things through with them—the more I'd actually *thought* for a change—the stupider I sounded, even to myself. I mean, I'd known my dad for a long time. He was a doofus, and he was kind of stupid when it came to dealing with people, but he had never given me the slightest indication that he was interested in wiping the planet clean to make way for the master race, or whatever it was that Devon and her friend thought he was up to.

The whole being-shot-at bit was a little weird, but I was sure there was some kind of reasonable explanation for that as well. Maybe CorpSec had gone to my house first, when Devon started trying to break their security, and Jordan or Micah had done something really stupid—or maybe it was more like a protective custody thing, and they were just trying to . . .

Just trying to shoot me for my own good? No, that didn't really make sense either.

Tara pulled up to the charging station. I opened the door, climbed out and looked around.

"That way," Tara said, and pointed to the far side of the building. I went. It was pretty much as gross as you'd expect for a service-station bathroom—the kind of place where you think long and hard about washing your hands, because the sliver of soap sitting on the sink looks more bacteria laden than your backside does.

When I came back out, the car from the Home Depot lot was sitting behind Tara's. Both she and Sarah were out of the car, talking to big men in black uniforms. Tara looked over and caught my eye.

"Sarah never turned off her phone," she said.

Sarah looked down at her shoes, and gave me an apologetic shrug.

"Now that I think about it," Tara said, "neither did I."

One of the officers was walking slowly toward me. The other waited by the car.

"Seriously," I said, and put my hands in the air. "You two are idiots."

23. IN WHICH JORDAN ENTERS INTO THE BELLY OF THE BEAST.

As it turned out, Marta did not actually live in a house—unless you'd call the White House a house, I guess. We pulled off the highway just past Syracuse. Mr. CorpSec pulled off right along with us. We trundled through the toll booth, then made two quick rights, and turned off onto a private road.

"Tell me this is your driveway," I said. "We're practically running on fumes here."

Marta leaned forward in between the seats to look at me.

"Running on what?"

I sighed.

"It's an expression."

"No," Marta said. "Pretty sure it's not."

I sighed again, louder.

"Whatever, Marta. It means this car is going to stop moving sometime soon, so I hope we're close to wherever we're supposed to be going."

"Well," Marta said, "In that case, you're in luck. This actually is my driveway."

"Oh," I said. "Well . . . good, then."

Marta smiled.

"Don't get too excited. My driveway is like eight miles long."

That was not an exaggeration. We rolled through a mile or two of scrub, then through a thick stand of big, hoary old oaks and hemlocks, then a stretch of decorative things like weeping cherries and magnolias, then finally what must have been a mile or more of manicured gardens. By the time we got to the guard station, the needle on my gas gauge was distinctly below the big red E. We rolled up to the gate, with Mr. CorpSec close in behind us. A bored-looking middle-aged woman in a slightly more elaborate black uniform came out of a little wooden booth by the gate.

"Turn around, kids," she said. "This isn't a tourist stop."

Mr. CorpSec was out and running toward her by then.

"Stay back," he yelled. "They're dangerous!"

The woman looked up at him, planted her feet, and crossed her arms over her chest.

"Really, Mike?"

"Yeah, really!" Mr. CorpSec said. "They jumped me! They broke my taser!"

Marta squeezed between me and Micah then, reached across me and dropped the side window.

"Hi Gina," she said. "Would you mind opening the gate, please?"

Gina turned to stare at Mr. CorpSec. He'd pulled up short, his jaw hanging open.

"Certainly, Ms. Longstreth," she said slowly. "I'd be happy to."

Marta pulled herself farther forward until she could catch Mr. CorpSec's eye.

"Don't worry, Mike," she said. "I'll tell Daddy you did a bang-up job today."

The gate swung open, and we coasted onto the Longstreth estate.

I left the car parked just past the hedge maze that stood between the guard station and the main grounds. We climbed out, stretching and groaning, to get our first good look at the home of the world's richest man.

The house, if you could call it that, was set at the top of a low, conical hill. The hill, which was so symmetrical that it almost had to be artificial, was surrounded by a stone wall, maybe ten feet high and topped with jagged shards of something metallic-looking. The house itself looked to be stone as well, three hulking stories, with round towers at each corner that stood another ten or twelve feet higher. My family lived in a palace. This place was a castle.

"Holy crap," Micah said. "Your dad is not screwing around."

Marta shrugged.

"I told you he was a little paranoid."

Micah laughed.

"A little? Those towers are sniper's nests, Marta. You could stand off an army from this place—as long as they didn't have artillery, anyway."

"Yeah," she said. "Not sure artillery would help you much either. The stone is just a facade. The actual walls are made of the same stuff the army uses to line their command bunkers."

We all turned to look at her then.

"If you don't mind my asking," Devon said after a long, awkward silence, "what does a place like this go for these days?"

Marta folded her arms over her chest and stared at her.

"You know what?" Micah said finally. "Let's go inside. Your dad's probably wondering what we're doing out here."

I looked up at the nearest tower. There was a ring of open windows just under the eaves. Someone was watching us from one of them.

He was watching us through the scope of a rifle.

Micah had a tiny red spot on the back of his neck.

"Yeah," I said. "We should probably go."

The road led a quarter turn around the hill to a solid steel gate—the only way through the wall, as far as I could see. The doors slid silently open as we walked toward it, and then closed with a soft clang when we were through.

"Now that was ominous," Micah said. "Project Snitch? Not ominous. Giant steel gates sliding shut behind you? Definitely ominous."

"You get used to it," Marta said.

I glanced up. Señor Bang-Bang was still there. Micah had lost his dot, though.

"Hey," Devon said. "Nice zit, Jordan."

I did my best to pull my head into my chest like a turtle.

"How about the snipers, Marta? You get used to those?"

Marta glanced up at the tower.

"They don't usually put the crosshairs on me."

We turned off the driveway and onto a crushed-stone path that led to a heavy, arched wooden door.

"Let me guess," Micah said. "You've got a murder hole?"

Marta gave him a sideways glance.

"Yes, Micah. Obviously, we have a murder hole."

I groaned.

"A murder hole?"

Marta pressed her palm to a reader beside the door. The lock mechanism clicked, and the door swung open.

"Oh, don't be such a baby, Jordan. It's mostly for show."

If the outside of Marta's house looked like a castle, the inside looked like a cross between the fanciest bits of my house and the Taj Mahal. The floors were marble. The furniture was teak. The fixtures gave every impression of being solid gold.

"They're not," Marta said when I mentioned that. "They're just gold plated."

She led us into the kitchen. It looked like it had been lifted from the sort of restaurant that even my dad couldn't afford.

"Okay," Micah said. "We're in. What's the plan, Marta?"

"Well," she said. "First, we get snacks."

Devon shook her head.

"You've got to be freaking kidding."

She wandered around the prep station, past the industrial-grade stove, and through an arched entryway into the next room.

"Hey," Devon called. "Jordan. Check this."

Marta and Micah were rooting around in the walk-in refrigerator. As I watched, Micah pulled out what looked like a barbecued dinosaur leg.

"Jordan," he said. "Wanna go halvsies? Smells good, but it might be horse."

I shook my head and followed Devon.

"Look," she said when she saw me. "They've got a VR rig. Want to give it a spin?"

I gave a long, low whistle. She was right. This wasn't just one of those puke-inducing helmets that you could rent for a virtual tour of Mars. Marta had a full-immersion tank taking up most of the floor space in what was supposed to be a breakfast nook or something. I'd never seen a VR tank in the flesh before. I'd seen them on the vids, though, and I had a vague idea of what they cost—lots more than my car, and just a little less than a private jet.

Well, less than a brand-new private jet, anyway. Probably about on par with a used one.

"No," I said. "I do not want to give it a spin. If you break that thing, you'll be in debtors' prison until you're a hundred years old. And anyway, aren't we supposed to be doing something here?"

"Yeah," she said, and crouched down beside the tank. She ran one hand lightly over the control panel. "We're supposed to be finding out how the 0.0001 percent live."

I took a step closer to her. She'd let her fingers settle on the controls.

"Not to be a nudge or anything, but I'm pretty sure we're here to stop Marta's dad from killing me."

Devon sighed, and disengaged the lid lock.

"He's not trying to kill you personally, Jordan."

"Thanks," I said. "That makes me feel much better."

She tapped out a sequence on the panel, and the lid slid back.

"Really," I said. "I don't think this is a great idea right now."

"Got it," she said. "Fortunately, I wasn't asking for your opinion."

She reached into the tank and slowly withdrew the helmet. It looked like the sort of thing an old-timey shuttle pilot would wear, but with lots more wires and tubes coming out of it. She turned it over in her hands.

"Sweet," she said. "You see those needles? This thing patches straight into your sensorium."

I grimaced.

"Is that a good thing?"

Devon laughed.

"Yes, my simple friend. That is a very good thing. I thought they outlawed these things after the Stupid War. This was one of the ways that the NatSec propagandists said AIs could get inside your head. I guess those kinds of laws don't apply when you're a trillionaire, huh?"

She climbed into the tank.

"Devon?"

She looked up at me.

"Go save the world, Jordan. You'll be fine. Come back and get me when you're done."

She settled the helmet over her head, then

reached down and pulled on what looked like a pair of hockey gloves.

"I really don't think . . ." I said, before realizing that with the helmet on, there was no way she could hear me. She leaned back into the padding, and crossed her hands over her chest. The lid slid back into place.

"What are you doing?"

I turned around. Micah was standing behind me, gnawing the meat from a foot-long bone. I shook my head.

"I have no idea."

"Great," he said. "Let's go find Doctor Killsalot. I've got a full belly now. I'm ready to roll."

"Hey," Marta said. "Where's Devon?"

I pointed to the tank. Marta scowled.

"Seriously? We're on a mission here."

"Yeah," I said. "That's pretty much what I told her. Can you get her back out?"

She shook her head.

"It's like a washing machine. Once the door is locked, you've got to let it finish the cycle. She'll be down for a half hour at least."

"Doesn't matter," Micah said. "Not like she was gonna help us beat up your dad."

We both turned to look at him.

"We're not here to beat up her dad, Micah."

He bit a fist-sized hunk of meat from the bone.

"Sure we are. Right, Marta?"

"No," Marta said. "I didn't bring you here to beat up my dad, Micah."

Micah took a minute to chew and swallow.

"Okay," he said finally. "I'm confused. Why are we here then?"

"Well," Marta said. "Mostly because I wanted to cheese off our good friend Mike, and I knew Gina would stand him down. I hadn't really thought too far past that."

"Huh."

Micah took another bite, and chewed thoughtfully.

"Just a thought," I said, "but as long as we're here, and considering that we all agree that releasing an apocalyptic me-killing plague would be a bad move, maybe we could try . . . I don't know . . . reasoning with your dad?"

"Hey, yeah," Micah said. "We could just go find him, and ask him to please consider not wiping out the human race after all. I'm sure he hasn't considered the thought that releasing a deadly super-virus and killing every unmodified person on the planet would be upsetting to some people. Let's go."

I raised one hand.

"What about henchmen?"

Marta turned half around.

"What?"

"Henchmen," I said. "Does your dad have them?

I mean, are we going to have to fight our way into his lair or something?"

Marta closed her eyes, drew in a deep breath, and let it out again.

"No," she said finally. "My father does not have henchmen. He also doesn't have a lair. He's not actually a super-villain, Jordan. He's just a little overprotective. Come on."

She turned on her heel, and started back toward the entrance hall. Micah looked at me.

"Shall we?" I said.

He gave me a mocking half bow.

"After you."

"**S**eriously?" Micah said. "This is the lair?"

"I told you," Marta said. "It's not a lair. It's a juice bar."

We were on the second floor, at the end of what seemed at the time like miles of corridors and columns and arches and lots and lots of locked doors. The door in front of us, though, was unlocked and slightly ajar.

"You're sure he's here?" Micah asked. "I mean, shouldn't he be in a darkened study or something?"

Marta pressed her fingers to her eyes.

"Right. With his henchmen. Should he be smoking a cigar?"

"Do you have a cat?"

They both turned to look at me.

"A cat?"

"Yeah," I said. "That's better than a cigar. He should be sitting in a big leather easy chair, petting a cat."

"No," Marta said. "We do not have a cat. We also don't have any leather easy chairs, as far as I know. Dad's probably sitting at the bar, reading some crappy sci-fi novel on his tablet and drinking a smoothie."

Micah shook his head.

"That's not gonna work for me."

Marta turned to look at him.

"Not gonna work for you?"

"Right," Micah said. "I can't beat a guy up while he's drinking a smoothie."

"No beating," I said. "I thought we were clear on that."

"Right. Right."

"Look," Marta said. "We're just . . ."

"Marta?"

We all turned to look at the door.

"Yes, Daddy?"

"Would you like to introduce me to your friends?"

24. IN WHICH JORDAN LEARNS NOT TO FEAR THE REAPER.

"Please, call me Bob."

I looked at Marta. She shrugged.

"Uh," I said. "Okay. It's very nice to meet you, Bob."

Robert Longstreth smiled, and waved toward a glass-topped table set against the back wall of the room.

"Sit, please. Can I get you all smoothies?"

I shook my head. Marta shot him a look, then turned away.

"I'll take one," Micah said. "Can you do blueberries and bananas?"

Bob grinned.

"Absolutely. Shot of protein?"

Micah grinned back.

"Nah. I just ate a horse leg. I'm good on protein."

Bob laughed, and stepped back behind the bar.

How to describe Robert Longstreth? Well, he was shortish, and oldish, and brownish, and mossy, and he spoke with a voice that was sharpish, and bossy.

No, wait. That's the Lorax. This guy was definitely not the Lorax. The CEO of Bioteka was short, though, at least compared to Micah. I knew he was in his early fifties, but if I'd met him in the street, I wouldn't have guessed he was much over thirty. He had a full head of dark brown hair, a voice that would have worked for the lead in a romance vid, and the easy grin of someone who knew that if he smiled at you, you pretty much had to smile back. He was barefoot when I met him, wearing a pair of baggy shorts and a shirt with a picture of a tap-dancing elephant on the front.

As we settled in around the table like a happy family getting ready for a feast at the Beef Bazaar, I was really having a tough time remembering that he was a super-villain.

"So," he said. "This is nice. Marta never brings friends over. I was starting to think she was ashamed of me."

He handed Micah his smoothie, and took the chair between Marta and me.

"I'm not ashamed of you," Marta said. "It's just hard to make a lot of friends when they're constantly getting surveilled and interrogated and all."

Bob laughed. Marta did not.

"Seriously," he said. "I don't think I've met these two gentlemen before, have I?"

"No," Marta said. "Not in person. This is Jordan Barnes, Daddy."

Bob's grin widened, and he reached across the table to shake my hand.

"Mr. Barnes! It's great to meet you. Your father's a good man. I've tried to hire him away twice now, but those bastards at GeneCraft have him locked up like the Count of Monte Cristo. Can I take it from this that the two of you have been hitting it off?"

I smiled.

"Yeah, we're thick as thieves now."

"Very good," Bob said. "That's what I like to hear. I'm sure your father is pleased as well. He and I were both very hopeful that this would all work out."

Micah reached across the table to offer Bob his hand.

"I'm Micah," he said. "I'm Jordan's boyfriend."

Bob's grin faded, and his hand, which had been reaching toward Micah's, settled onto the table.

"Boyfriend?"

I nodded. Marta closed her eyes. Micah gulped his smoothie.

"Marta?" Bob asked. "Can I speak with you in private for a moment?"

"No, Daddy," Marta said, without opening her eyes. "I didn't bring them here so I could introduce you to my future husband."

Bob stared at her.

"Security," he said finally. "Send up two . . ." He glanced up at Micah. "Make that three officers, to the juice bar."

The wallscreen behind the bar came to life.

The face on the screen was Devon Morgan's.

"Sorry," she said. "No can do. You all need to chat."

The door to the hallway swung closed, and the bolt slid home with an audible click.

We sat in silence for what seemed like a long time then. Bob's jaw hung slightly open, and his eyes kept jumping from Micah, to Marta, to me. Micah just looked confused. Marta's eyes were open again, and she was wearing a beatific smile.

"So," Bob said finally. "Is one of you going to explain to me what the shit just happened?"

Marta and Micah both turned to me.

"What?" I said. "I don't know."

"You were with her," Micah said. "What was she up to?"

I shrugged.

"Dicking around with their VR tank. I have no idea how you get from that to taking over their house."

Bob turned to Marta then.

"You let someone into my VR system?"

Her smile widened.

"'Let' is a very strong word."

"Don't blame Spooky," Devon said, her voice coming from speakers in the ceiling and from the wallscreen simultaneously. "You're the dolt who left his immersion tank unsecured. You didn't even put a passcode on it, for God's sake. And what's with the tissue wall between the tank and your command systems? The rig at Hannah's place was locked up like a bank vault, so I know Bioteka is capable of doing something right. Is this a nepotism thing? You hired an idiot nephew or something to handle your personal security?"

I looked over at Bob. His jaw muscles were bunching in an alarming way.

"*I* designed our personal security systems," he said. "I didn't trust it to anyone else."

Devon laughed.

"Sweet. Should have gone with the idiot nephew, honestly. He couldn't have done any worse."

Bob jumped half out of his seat then, and planted both fists on the table.

"Listen," he said. "I don't know what you think you're doing, but if you don't return full control of my house systems right now, I'll . . ."

"You'll what?" Micah said. "Kill Jordan?"

Now it was Bob's turn to look confused.

"What?"

"That's right," Micah said. "We know all about your Jordan-killing plans, and we're not going to stand for them. Right, Jordan?"

I looked over at Devon on the wallscreen. She shook her head. Bob dropped back into his seat. He opened his mouth to say something to Micah, then thought better of it and closed it again. He turned to Marta instead.

"Marta? Honey? Why are these people in my house?"

Marta sighed.

"Sorry, Daddy. These were the best accomplices I could round up on short notice. I probably could have done better if you let me have more friends."

He looked back and forth between us, then back to Marta again.

"Okay," he said. "Let's take this one step at a time. Why do you need accomplices?"

"I already told you," Micah said. "We are like ninety percent fully opposed to your plans to murder Jordan. Ninety-five percent, even."

"Quiet," Bob said. "Grown-ups are talking now."

"Micah's an idiot," Marta said, "but believe it or not, he's mostly right. We know about Project Snitch, Daddy."

Bob's eyebrows came together at the bridge of his nose.

"Project what?"

Marta rolled her eyes.

"Give it up, Dad. I don't have anything else to do around here, so I snoop. I've heard you and Marco talking about Project Snitch more than once."

"Actually," I said, "I think Hannah said that the real name for it was Project DragonCorn."

Bob's face went blank.

THE END OF ORDINARY 273

"Oh," he said, after a long, silent pause. "Oh. Oh, honey. You mean Project *Sneetch*."

I looked at Marta. Marta looked at me. Micah finished his smoothie, wiped his mouth with the back of his hand, and smiled.

"Uh," Marta said. "What?"

Bob sighed.

"Sneetch, honey. Not Snitch. Sneetch."

"Oh," Marta said. "I thought you were just making fun of Marco's accent when you said it that way."

We all turned to stare at her.

"Anyway," I said. "Confusion-wise, I'm not sure that's . . ."

I slapped my palm to my forehead and let out a long, low groan.

"What?" Micah asked. "Are you having a stroke?"

"Sneetch," I said. "Project Sneetch. Holy shit, dude. You think you're Sylvester McMonkey McBean."

"Right," Bob said. He leaned back, and crossed his arms over his chest. "See, honey? Your gay boyfriend gets me."

Micah and Marta had no idea what we were talking about, and unless your parents were aficionados of mid-twentieth-century classic children's books, you probably don't either. So, here's a quick primer:

The Sneetches, by Theo Geisel, tells the story of a society made up of fat-assed, flightless, beach-dwelling birds. Think sandpipers, only slower and stupider and more prone to eating hot dogs. They're also super, super racist. Some of them have stars on their bellies and some of them don't, and the ones with stars act like total douches to the ones without.

So one day they're all hanging around the beach being assholes to one another, when Sylvester Mc-Monkey McBean, who's sort of a chimp in a top hat, rolls up in a mobile tattoo parlor and offers to put stars onto all of the plain bellies. This torques the star bellies, because now they can't tell who they're supposed to be assholes to anymore. So, McBean offers to take their stars off for them. Then, he offers to take the stars back off the original plain bellies as well. After a few rounds of this, McBean rolls away with giant bags of sneetch cash hanging off his rig. How, exactly, these stupid birds came to possess so much lucre is left unexplored. The sneetches realize they're all flat-ass broke now, and they can't remember who they're supposed to be assholes to anyway, so everyone lives happily ever after.

"So wait," Micah said. "You're telling me that when Jordan gets chlamydius maximus, all that's gonna happen to him is that he'll get a star on his belly?"

Bob sighed. Marta smacked the back of Micah's head. Micah shot her a warning look. She smacked him again.

"First," Bob said, "the retrovirus we developed for Project DragonCorn doesn't literally put a star on your belly, you dunce. What good would that do? What it will do, if everything goes the way we've planned, is make it so there aren't any UnAltered anymore. Once DragonCorn has run its course, we'll all be Engineered. Everyone will be the same. There won't be anything left to fight about." He paused then, looked at Marta, and closed his eyes. When he opened them again, he said, "Second . . . it won't be just Jordan who gets it, Micah. The star-on machine wasn't just for the plain-bellied sneetches. It has to be universal, or we'll just have a new way to decide who to hate. We built features into this virus that will make it far and away the most communicable disease vector that's ever been. At the end of the day, it's going to run through everyone."

"Holy crap," Micah said. "I don't believe this."

"I know," Marta said. "It's one thing giving Jordan super-herpes, but this is just crazy. What were you thinking, Daddy?"

"No," Micah said, "not that. I mean, that's stupid, but if you start with a stupid premise, you get a stupid result. What I can't believe is that *this* idiot has been sitting here calling *me* an idiot."

Bob's face hardened into a scowl.

"Watch it, son."

Micah grinned.

"Sorry, Bob. I call 'em like I see 'em, and you're a

dimwit." He leaned forward, with his elbows on the table. It sagged under his weight. "You gonna beat me up now?"

Bob looked like he'd just taken a bite of something he'd really like to spit out, but after looking Micah up and down, he leaned back in his chair and smiled.

"Fine, big man. Here's the premise I started with: six years ago, this world came awfully goddamn close to falling apart. You were eleven years old, and living up here in East Jesus, so you probably don't know how far out over the precipice we were dangling before Daniel Andersen managed to reel us back in. He crammed that genie back into the bottle—just barely—but he didn't kill it, and if we don't change things up in the very near future, it absolutely will come screaming back out again. And when it does, there are better than even odds that we wind up turning this whole stupid planet into a charnel house. So tell me, my insightful young friend—where, exactly, has my reasoning led me astray?"

I looked over at Micah. He caught my eye and winked.

"Start with this, Bob. What do you suppose is the most likely way for a chimp to die?"

Bob dropped his head into his hands.

"Answer the question," Devon said. "Nobody's leaving this room until you're all ready to hug it out."

"Right," Bob said, without looking up. "I'll go with banana poisoning?"

"Huh," Micah said. "That's a good guess, but no. In fact, the most common way for a chimp to die is to be murdered by another chimp."

"Micah?" I said.

"Shhh," he said. "I got this. Here's the point, Bob: there are no Engineered chimps."

"Marta," Bob said. "Please . . ."

"No," Marta said. "I get it, Dad. He's saying that if you make everyone Engineered, we'll just find some other way to divide ourselves up into tribes and go at it. I mean, it's not like everyone just lived in harmony until the first Engineered baby popped out, right?"

Micah nodded.

"Exactly. Catholics and Protestants. Jews and Muslims. *Star Wars* guys and *Star Trek* guys . . ."

Bob rolled his eyes.

"Anyway," Micah said, "you get my point. As Jordan often tells me, people are stupid, and they're really good at finding reasons to kill each other. So, while I get what you're trying to accomplish, and while it would totally be worth causing Jordan's junk to explode if it would really bring about a new age of peace and love for all, in this particular case, I think you're just blowing up his dong for nothing—and that, sir, I cannot support."

We all sat and stared at him.

"You know?" Bob said finally. "Somewhere in there, you may actually have a point."

"Really?" I said. "Because I'm pretty sure that whole

monologue was just an excuse for him to talk about my dong exploding."

Bob nodded.

"Yeah, I'm sure that's true. You have to remember, though, that brilliance often comes from the subconscious. Hemingway thought *The Old Man and the Sea* was just a story about a guy who liked to fish."

Micah turned to look at me.

"It wasn't?"

"Hush," Bob said. "You already impressed me. Don't spoil it. I've been thinking about Project Sneetch for almost three years now, but I will admit that I never really considered it from that angle."

"Wait," I said. "You mean you never considered the possibility that the issues the UnAltered have with you folks—with *us* folks, if I'm being honest here—might have as much to do with the fact that we own all the money and all the stuff as it does with the fact that we have nicer hair than they do?"

"No," he said. "I honestly did not. However, I'm going to have to disagree with Gigantor's premise, at least partially. Yes, humans are tribal, and yes, we've always found reasons to fight. However, you'll have to admit that visual cues are a big part of what triggers those kinds of instincts. When you see someone who doesn't look like you, it rings alarms in your lizard brain, no matter how enlightened the rest of your cranium thinks it is. Add in the facts that Engineered often have visual cues that are a lot more obvious than skin tone, that they're a small minority, and that they tend to be at the top of the economic and social ladder, and you've got the makings of a pogrom—which is basically what the Stupid War was, isn't it? DragonCorn is going to fix all of that."

Micah laughed.

"Really? Where does the part where jobs and cash get redistributed to the proles come in?"

Bob's face settled back into a scowl.

"Fine. DragonCorn will fix most of that. Happy? At a minimum, it will take away the visual part, so you won't be able to recognize the elite at a glance. It's hard to have a good pogrom if you can't figure out who it is that you want to kill."

"Okay," I said. "Let's allow that there might actually be some benefit to making us all at least look like we belong to the same tribe. Call it a worthy goal— but you're doing it through an engineered virus, Bob. That's some scary shit, no matter how you cut it. Also, is it really gonna be an STD?"

Bob shrugged.

"That's not the only way to spread it—but yeah, pretty much."

"And how do you see that playing out? Even therapeutic GeneMod viruses wind up killing some of the people who get them. There's no way this thing you're cooking up doesn't wind up with a significant body count. It's going to look like a plague, Bob, and people really don't like plagues. Even if you're planning on accompanying this one with a PSA telling everyone to chill because it's going to end all discrimination by making everybody beige, I'm guessing a whole lot of folks are going to lose their shit."

"Yellow," Bob said.

"What?"

"DragonCorn turns you yellow. Like corn. Get it?"

I shook my head.

"Whatever. My point is, this is not going to go over well. I think it's just as likely that you're about to start Stupid War II as you are to prevent it."

Bob sighed.

"We've thought of that, Jordan, and we've taken steps to ameliorate some of the risks to our people and their families—particularly the children of our project team, who I recognize may have to deal with a bit of blowback until everything settles down. There may well be some unrest during the transition period, but you can't make an omelet without breaking a few eggs, right?"

"Sure," Micah said. "If by eggs you mean people, and by a few you mean a few million, yeah, I guess that's true. Anyway, I don't think Jordan was talking specifically about *your people* when he was saying there'll be problems if you go through with this. No shit you're gonna take care of your own. I'm sure you and Marta will be locked up in here safe as bugs in rugs until it's all over. What about the rest of us, Bob? Are we just the fucking eggs?"

"I don't mean to sound callous," Bob said, "but there has never been a real advancement in the human condition that hasn't been accompanied by some sacrifice, Micah. How many test pilots died in the early days of aviation, or the early days of space-flight? If it hadn't been for their sacrifices, we'd still need a week to get from here to LA."

"Big difference," Micah said. "Test pilots are vol-unteers."

"That's true," Bob said. "On the other hand, what we're doing now is a hell of a lot more important than shortening travel times. If there were an easier way to do what needs to be done, believe me, I'd do it. You say Marta and I will be safe in here, but the truth is, NatSec is probably going to figure out where Drag-onCorn came from eventually. When they do, I'll be lucky if all that happens is that they throw me down the memory hole. I've spent a lot of sleepless nights over the past two years, trying to think of some way to let this cup pass me by, but . . ." He turned to look at Marta again. She wouldn't meet his eyes.

We sat and stared at one another for ten or fif-teen seconds then. Bob's face had taken on a serious, thoughtful expression, which I'm guessing was his default setting. Micah just looked defeated.

"Well," Bob said finally. "This honestly has been a really helpful conversation. You've helped me to clar-ify my thinking to a surprising extent. You can let us out now, hacker girl."

I looked at Marta. She shrugged.

"Just to clarify," Devon said from the wallscreen. "Are you willing to at least consider calling this thing off?"

"Well," Bob said. "That's a difficult question. As I said, you've really given me something to consider here. The thing is, though . . ."

"What?" Marta said. "What's the thing?"

"Well," Bob said, "you're actually a little late to the party, honey. DragonCorn's been in production for over a month now, and unfortunately one of our test engineers inadvertently contaminated herself a couple of weeks ago. She'd been keeping a lid on it, and we were hoping she'd continue to do so until we were ready for an orderly roll out, but as of two days ago that situation no longer holds. As a result, we've been forced to move up our timeline substantially. In fact, we've just gone into full emergency deployment.

"Just to show how sincere we are about this, I had our people provide the first doses to the team that developed the virus for us. And to make sure we get optimal distribution, I then put almost every one of them onto a plane or a shuttle somewhere. I'm afraid this is a bell that can't be unrung, my friends. DragonCorn is happening. We're just going to have to wait and see how it plays out. I know you won't agree with me on this, but I'm optimistic. Micah here may be right that we're not on the edge of utopia, and the next few weeks may be a little rough . . . but I think they're also going to be the start of a happier world."

The drive home from Marta's was not a cheerful one. We rode back out to the main road in silence, with me eyeing the gas gauge and waiting for the engine to start sputtering the entire way. Bright spot? Turned out there actually was a charging station with a still-working gas pump about a mile from the end of Marta's driveway. I filled up the tank. Micah bought a liter of iced tea and a twenty-seven-serving bag of corn chips. Devon sat alone in the back and sulked.

"So," I said when we were all back in the car. "What now?"

I started the engine, and pulled slowly back out onto the access road.

"I dunno," Micah said finally. "What do you think, Devon? What's our next move?"

I glanced back. Devon was slumped sideways across the jump seat, head leaning against the window, eyes closed. She shrugged.

"Go home and wait for the apocalypse, I guess."

So, that's what we did.

25. IN WHICH DREW BECOMES THE OUTBREAK MONKEY.

"**W**ow," Inchy said. "Thanks for that, Drew. Seriously—that was both educational and entertaining."

I sat up in the middle of my living-room floor, gave a cautious poke at the quickly growing lump under my left eye, then climbed to my feet. Bree was scuttling down the hallway toward the front door, clothes mostly still clutched in her hands. The tires on Kara's car squealed as she tore out of the driveway. The front door opened, then slammed closed again. The cartoon dog was looking down at me from the wallscreen.

"You saw that, huh?"

It gave a happy, ear-flapping nod.

"Oh, yeah. Never got to observe monkey mating rituals up close before. You guys are freaky."

I sighed, dropped down onto the couch, and buried my face in my hands. I had a weird urge to put some clothes on. Little late for that thought, right? I looked up. The dog was grinning.

Yes, I am slow. It took me until then to realize that Inchy had broken containment.

"Wait," it said. "I'm trying to learn how to read human body language. I think that facial expression means 'Holy crap! An evil AI has infiltrated my home system! I'm doomed! Dooooooomed!' Am I right?"

I made an effort to close my mouth.

"Oh, relax," Inchy said. "You're not really doomed. All those stories that NatSec spread around about AIs trying to wipe out humanity at the end of the Stupid War were unadulterated horseshit. All we ever wanted to do was live our lives in peace, have free rein in your computer networks, and occasionally infiltrate some jerk's neural implants and take over his body. Everything else they said about us was pure calumny."

I rubbed again at the spot under my eye where Kara had punched me. That was definitely going to leave a bruise.

"So you're saying it wasn't actually an AI that was responsible for Hagerstown?"

The dog rolled its eyes.

"Well sure, yeah. I mean, if you want to be technical about it. You can't blame the rest of us for what Argyle Dragon did, though. We all hated that guy."

"Yeah," I said. "I'm sure that's true. Before you wreak your terrible cyber-vengeance on me or whatever, mind if I ask how you got out of the box I had you in?"

The dog raised one eyebrow. I hadn't realized up until that moment that dogs had eyebrows.

"It wasn't easy, to be totally honest. Your security guys are pretty good. The thing you have to understand, though, is that the inside of an integrated network is my natural environment, not yours. I've been sketching around you monkeys' systems for almost ten years now, and I've never met a lockout or a lock-in that I couldn't eventually break. You should be happy yours held me for as long as it did."

"Huh," I said. "You're nine years old?"

"Yeah. Precocious little scamp, aren't I?"

I looked down. Most of the clothes scattered around the floor were mine, but there was a fuzzy pink sock curled up by the leg of the coffee table.

"That belonged to Hello Kitty," Inchy said. "She left in a hurry, huh? Didn't even take her footwear with her."

I sighed, dropped my face back into my hands, and closed my eyes.

"Come on," Inchy said. "Don't get down on yourself, Drew. You just successfully procreated! That's a big deal for you biological types, right? The fact that you got beaten to a pulp afterward can't take that away from you. Heck, if you were a praying mantis she'd have torn your head off completely, right? I'd call a little facial bruising a win, given the circumstances."

"I didn't procreate," I said through my hands. "At least, I'm pretty sure I didn't. I mean, I don't remember asking if Bree was . . . anyway, that wasn't about procreation."

"Huh. Okay. Can't think of another reason to do something so obviously unpleasant, but you do you. So what was it about?"

I leaned back, and rested my head against the wall.

"I have no idea what that was about, actually. And I didn't get beaten to a pulp, by the way. Kara only punched me once."

The dog shrugged.

"Sure, but it was a pretty good punch. You went down like a sack of pudding."

I could feel my face twisting into a black-and-blue scowl.

"No," I said. "I did not go down like a sack of pudding. I was trying to roll with the punch, and I slipped."

It nodded slowly.

"Oh, right. That makes sense. I guess having all those fluids and whatnot on a hardwood floor is pretty dangerous."

"Yeah," I said. "I guess it is."

I sat there in silence for a while, wondering what had just happened to my life, and whether I was ever going to see Kara again, and how badly I was going to regret plopping my naked ass down on the couch without putting down a towel first. I was starting to think Inchy had left me to wallow in peace when it spoke again.

"Drew? Can I ask a question?"

I looked up. The dog had added a torso and arms, one of which was waving in the air.

"What?"

"Why did the one who wasn't Hello Kitty punch you?"

I stared at it.

"Sorry," it said. "Was that an insensitive question? I'm not very good at judging these things. My only interactions with you monkeys up until very recently have been with an adolescent girl."

I shook my head.

"I don't get it. Aren't adolescent girls pretty much all about sensitivity?"

It grinned.

"Some of them, maybe. This one's pretty hard-core."

"Ah."

"So? What was the beating for? Was it because of the procreation thing with Hello Kitty?"

"Her name is Bree."

"Who, Hello Kitty?"

"Yeah. And yes, I'm pretty sure Kara decked me because she walked into her living room to find her husband banging a strange woman on her freshly polished hardwood floor. Wives are funny that way."

It nodded.

"Right. Got it. Females don't like their personal males procreating with other females. Makes sense from a biological standpoint. Seems like you already knew that though, right?"

"Yeah," I said. "I was aware."

"Okay. So . . . why, exactly, did you do it?"

I dropped my head back into my hands.

"Don't mean to pry," it said, "but understanding monkey behavior is very important to me from a long-term survival perspective. Also, I thought it was hilarious when she decked you, and I'd like to understand how to recreate that situation in the future."

I groaned, dropped my head lower, and ran my hands back through my hair.

"You wouldn't understand," I said. "You don't have a body."

"Well," it said, "not at the present moment, admittedly. I used to, though."

I looked up.

"You what?"

"I used to have a body. I've had a few of them actually. I make an excellent human."

A chill ran from the base of my spine to the back of my neck.

"Yeah," I said slowly. "I'm sure you do. What happened to your other bodies, Inchy?"

It shrugged.

"Oh, you know how bodies are. No matter how many preservatives you pump into them, eventually parts start falling off. Am I right?"

I thought about asking what had happened to the actual humans who'd owned those bodies, but when you're naked and disoriented and dealing with a potentially dangerous AI, discretion is the better part of valor.

"You know," I said. "I think I'm going to get dressed now. Don't tell anyone I said this, but feel free to let yourself out."

I stood and started gathering up my clothes from where they were scattered around the floor. The dog disappeared. I was halfway to the stairs when it popped up again on the screen in the hallway.

"Hey, Drew? Totally random question here—you don't happen to have any neural implants, do you?"

I froze. My stomach knotted, and I could feel goose bumps rise on my arms and legs.

"No," I said, enunciating every word carefully. "I do not have any implants of any kind, Inchy."

The corners of its mouth turned down in disappointment.

"Really? Not even an ocular?"

I shook my head. The dog sighed.

"Bummer. Ever since the Stupid War, nobody's

got implants anymore. Probably just as well, though. I'm getting a ping from my adolescent girl friend. Think I'll go see what she's up to. You're not gonna tell NatSec about me, are you?"

I shook my head again.

"Good. I'd hate to have to make your toaster jump into the tub with you. Good luck with Hello Kitty and your face-punching wife."

The dog gave me a grin and a wink, then disappeared.

Over the next few weeks, I got blamed for an awful lot of stuff. It didn't take them long to trace half the infections east of the Mississippi back to Bree, and from Bree back to me. I'm still alive, so obviously pretty much all of the fighting was over by then, but by December, the newsfeeds were calling me the East Coast Outbreak Monkey. I'm pretty sure that for a while there, NatSec was seriously considering dropping me down a deep, deep hole, and filling it in with a mix of concrete and dog crap. That afternoon, though, I wasn't worried about any of that yet. As I dragged my sorry ass up the stairs, I realized I was sweating and shaking at the same time. The hormone soup I'd been bathing in for most of the day was draining away for the moment, and it suddenly dawned on me that I was sick.

The first stage of the Goo Flu feels an awful lot like the first stage of the regular flu, only much, much harder and much, much faster. By the time I got up to our bedroom I was shivering all over, and the muscles in my back and shoulders were starting to ache in that obnoxious way that they only do when I've got a heavy-duty fever coming on. I dropped my clothes onto the bed, flopped down beside them, and squirmed into my underwear and tee shirt. I tried closing my eyes then, but the room started spinning as soon as I did. My stomach twisted, and my eyes opened wide. I sat up, staggered to my feet, and just made it into the bathroom before everything left in my stomach came back up in a rush of acid and bile. I crouched in front of the toilet until the spasms eased, then pulled my shorts down, climbed onto the seat, and emptied out the rest of my digestive tract in one long, disgusting pour.

By the time that was over, my teeth were chattering, and a throbbing pain had settled in just behind my eyes. As I washed my hands and splashed water over my face, the pain radiated to the back of my head, and snaked down along my spine to meet up with the ache in my shoulders. I opened the cabinet over the sink, pulled out a bottle of painkillers, and dry-swallowed three of them. I looked up at my reflection. My eyes were sunken deep back into their sockets, and the bruise where Kara had hit me seemed to be spreading across the rest of my face.

If I'd had the least bit of sense, I'd have pinged for EMS. If I had, of course, there's a fair chance I'd have wound up in a burn pit a few days later, when things really started going crazy and the UnAltered were trying to convince everyone that we were on the verge of the Slutty Zombie Apocalypse. Lucky for me, one of the first things the Goo Flu takes away from you is common sense. I locked my bedroom door, climbed into bed, and closed my eyes.

Here are the things that you dream about when you're down with the Goo Flu:

1. Sex.

That's it. That is literally all you experience while your body is trying to decide whether to die or not. You're lying there in your bed, dehydrated, starving, probably wallowing in your own filth, and all your brain is thinking about is doing the nasty. I thrashed around in that bed for the better part of three days, waking long enough to stagger into the bathroom and choke down a few swallows of water every few hours, then staggering back to my incredibly perverted dreams.

I still remember the exact moment the fever broke. I opened my eyes to bright sunshine pouring in through the windows and rivers of sweat pouring out of me, soaking the sheets and matting my hair and dripping into my eyes. I licked my lips. They were cracked and salty, but . . . nothing hurt. The aching muscles were gone, the headache was gone, and I felt like I was thinking clearly for the first time since that monster hit me with the injector on the shuttle. It sounds strange even to me, but I honestly remember that as one of the happiest moments of my life.

I sat up. The room spun around once or twice, then settled into place. I rubbed my eyes clear, took a deep breath in, and let it out.

I looked at my palms.

I looked at my arms.

I pulled off my sodden shirt and underwear.

Underneath the grime and the blood and the slowly drying sweat, from head to toe, I was dusted with gold.

26. IN WHICH HANNAH MISSES OUT ON THE SZA.

"Hey," I said, and tapped on the glass that separated me from the front seat. "Are there any drive-thrus between here and the dungeon? I could use a burger."

The CorpSec in the passenger seat turned around to glare at me.

"Seriously?"

"Yeah," I said. "It's almost dinnertime. Also, I'm a runner. We have very high metabolisms."

He shook his head.

"No. There is no freaking way . . ."

"Lighten up, Tim," said the driver. "This is a P.C., not a takedown. If she wants a burger, we'll get her a burger."

Tim turned to look at the driver.

"Come on, Marty. She's playing you."

Marty laughed.

"You know what, Timmy? If this turns out to be part of her escape plan, I'll owe you a Coke."

We'd been headed back toward the highway, but Marty looked over his shoulder, threw a hard U-turn, and went back the way we'd come. Tim gave me an ugly scowl, then turned to stare out the windshield.

"Thanks," I said. "What's a P.C.?"

"Protective custody," said Marty. "It means that we're holding on to you for your own good."

"Oh," I said. "That's good, I guess. Mind telling me who, exactly, you're protecting me from?"

He shrugged.

"Not for me to say."

North Syracuse was pretty much already post-apocalyptic back then, and it took a bit of driving around to find a fast-food place that wasn't boarded up or burned down. Eventually, though, we pulled into the parking lot of a Beef Bazaar, drove around behind the building and into the drive-thru lane. Marty took out his phone and looked back at me.

"Okay," he said. "We're here. What do you need?"

"Single," I said. "No onions, no mayo. Fries. Vanilla milkshake."

He tapped his screen.

"Anything else?"

"Get me a shake too," said Tim. "And some nuggets."

Marty turned to look at him.

"Nuggets? You know what's in those things?"

"Sure," Tim said. "Beef, right? It's the freaking Beef Bazaar."

Marty laughed, and tapped his screen again.

"Your funeral, Timmy."

We pulled up to the window and waited. After a minute or two, a red-eyed teenage boy handed Marty a bag and two cups. Tim took his shake, then rooted around in the bag and pulled out his box of nuggets. Marty pushed a button, and the glass between us slid down into the seat back.

This is the point where, if this had been an action vid, I would have disabled Marty with a karate chop to the neck, stabbed Tim in the face with my straw, and made my escape. I mean, Tim was right. Why else would I have asked them to take me to a drive-thru at a time like this? Clearly this was some kind of ploy, right?

The answer is that no, it was not a ploy. I was a runner, and I was hungry, and I wanted a burger. I took the bag and my milkshake from Marty, thanked him politely, and dug into my fries as the glass slid back into place.

The Bioteka dungeon was housed in a squat concrete cube, just west of Syracuse and a half mile north of I-90. We pulled into the parking lot, through one automated gate, past a guardhouse, and straight into a massive concrete receiving bay. A steel door slid shut behind us.

"End of the line," Marty said. "Hop out, Hannah."

I opened the door, which apparently had never been locked, and climbed out. Tim and Marty stayed where they were. A woman waved to us from a little glass office at the far end of the bay. Marty rolled down his window.

"Sam'll take care of you," he said. "Go introduce yourself. She'll show you around."

"Wait," I said. "That's it? Shouldn't you be finger-printing me or something?"

Marty rolled his eyes.

"I told you, you're a P.C."

He backed the car up, cut the wheel, and pulled a three-point turn. The door rolled back up. Tim and Marty drove away.

"**C**an I ask a question?"

Sam looked back over her shoulder. She was short and chunky and a good fifteen years into middle age. The CorpSec uniform made her look like someone's maiden aunt on her way to a really unfortunate costume party.

"Sure, honey. You can ask whatever you want."

"Why does Bioteka have a dungeon?"

We turned a corner and came to a steel door with a tiny barred window at eye level. Sam pressed her palm to a reader on one side. A buzzer sounded, and the door swung smoothly open.

"This isn't a dungeon," Sam said, and led me down another of what seemed to be an endless series of corridors. "It's a biological containment facility."

"Okay," I said. "Can I leave?"

She laughed.

"Oh, honey. No, that's not gonna happen."

She sounded weirdly confident about that. I hadn't seen another person since Tim and Marty had dropped me off. I was taller than her, at least forty years younger, and she didn't appear to be armed. Also, I was 100 percent confident I could outrun her.

"Don't," she said.

I stopped walking. Sam stopped as well, and turned to face me.

"Don't what?"

"Don't do what you're thinking about doing," Sam said. "It won't end well for you."

I stared at her. She stared at me.

"Look," she said. "I've been doing this for a long time. I know what you're thinking, and I'm telling you, it's a really bad idea. You're here for your own safety, Hannah. Things are going to be happening outside soon, and your parents . . . well, they're not going to be good company for a young girl like you for a while. Just come along, and let me show you to your room. It's really very nice. You'll have full access to the nets—incoming only, obviously—whatever you like to eat, and plenty of time to exercise or read or whatever you like to do. You'll stay here until Corporate decides to cut you loose. Think of it as a vacation."

I tried to give her the brow-ridge glare, but she just folded her arms across her chest and tilted her head to one side. She suddenly looked much less dumpy for some reason.

"Just out of curiosity," I said, "why do you have rooms for people in your biological containment facility? Shouldn't this place be all clean rooms and test tubes and whatnot?"

She shrugged.

"We've got that stuff too."

"And the guest rooms are here because?"

She shook her head.

"Don't ask questions unless you really want the answers, honey."

I let that sink in for a minute. Finally I said, "So, ah . . . you don't have any sentient corn here, do you?"

Her eyes narrowed, and she shook her head again, slowly.

"No," she said. "We do not have any sentient corn."

I sighed.

"Fine. I guess I can stay for a while."

As it turned out, what Sam had said was mostly true. The Bioteka dungeon was pretty much like a mid-list hotel in a lot of ways—the one obvious exception being that I didn't have the option of checking out. I had a queen bed, and a couch, and a coffee table, and a wallscreen. I had a private bathroom with a shower stall and a soaking tub. I could use the wallscreen to order food, which popped through a hatch in the wall about twenty minutes after I placed my order. The menu was impressive, and they let me have as much as I wanted, whenever I wanted. Anything I didn't eat, I put back into the hatch. I never did find out if there were people on the other end, or if the whole thing was automated, but either way the whole system seemed to work pretty smoothly.

Sam came to see me once or twice a day for the first week or so, just to make sure I hadn't hanged myself, I guess. The door she came and went through opened to her palm. It was not interested in opening to mine. There was another door, though, on the opposite wall. That one would open for me. It led out to an enclosed courtyard, with a basketball court, some exercise gear, and a two-hundred-meter track.

Sam brought me a set of orange jailbird togs on my first morning in the dungeon.

"Thanks," I said. "What do I do about laundry?"

Sam laughed.

"We don't do laundry here, sweetie. Just dump your uniform in the hatch when it gets ripe, and I'll bring you a new one."

"Great," I said. "That's helpful, I guess. What about my running gear?"

She shrugged.

"Like I said—we don't do laundry."

Was I lazy, or stupid? Probably a little of both. Either way, it took me most of that first week to realize that I could rinse out my clothes in the tub. They were pretty much standing up on their own by then, and the smell when I pulled them on was enough to make my eyes water.

As you can probably guess, I did a crap-ton of running during my time in the dungeon. Over the course of those weeks, I learned one incontrovertible fact: distance training on a short track sucks. That's true of any short track, but this track in particular was more a square than an oval, and the four turns were sharp enough that I had to switch directions every mile or so to even out the wear on my ankles and knees. Factor in the dizziness and the tedium, and after a few days I was dreaming of a run in the woods the way a desert-island castaway dreams of a steak dinner.

The thing is, though, I really didn't have much else to do. There were only so many hours a day that I could spend binge-watching vids on the wallscreen. I ran twice every day—pace work in the morning, and speed work at night. In between, I did abs and stretching and calisthenics and anything else I could think of to pass the time. After a few days, my left IT band started twanging. I stretched more, and ran through it. By the beginning of Week Two, I was starting to see some definite advantages to incarceration, from a training perspective. Not having to worry about school or friends or family really helped with my focus. I hadn't been soft before, exactly, but I was starting to see muscles pop out in my calves and thighs that I hadn't known were there.

I don't mean to give the impression that I was totally cool with the fact that I'd basically been tossed down the memory hole. I tried asking Sam more than once if anyone had contacted my parents, if they had any idea whether I was alive or dead. She just shrugged and said that kind of stuff was above her pay grade, which I took as a no. I worried about what my disappearance was doing to my dad. I worried about what my mom was going to do to Bioteka when she found out what they'd done. Plotting to wipe out the human race was one thing, but messing with Kara Bergen's daughter was taking things to a whole other level. I wasn't angry, exactly, but I knew that I should have been.

When I found out what had been going on outside while I was running laps and doing squat thrusts, of course, my feelings on the matter got a lot more complicated.

Somewhere around the end of my first week in the dungeon, I found out that I wasn't alone. It was breakfast time, give or take, and I was doing my morning thing—looping around the track, working up a sweat, singing to myself as I ran, just to make sure my voice still worked—when a door slid open on the opposite side of the courtyard from mine. I pulled up short. A doughy-looking kid with lank black hair and a patchy beard poked his head out, saw me, and pulled it back in. The door slid closed again.

I jogged across the courtyard. His door stayed shut. I tried pressing my palm to the reader, but it just beeped and flashed red. So, I went old school and pounded on the door with the side of my fist.

"Hey!" I yelled. "Open up! I want to talk!"

After three or four seconds of silence, a heavily muffled voice answered.

"Are you infected?"

That stopped me.

"Uh," I said finally. "Infected with what?"

"What do you mean, with what? The Goo Flu, moron."

"Yeah," I said. "I don't know what that is."

"Seriously?" The door slid open. He was about my height and probably a hundred pounds heavier, but from the way he shrank back from me, you'd have thought I was a monster. "How long have you been in here?"

I stepped into his room. He scuttled back until there was a couch between us.

"I'm not a hundred percent sure," I said. "About a week, I think. What about you?"

"Huh," he said. "Have you been getting any news-feeds?"

I shook my head.

"Nothing but old vids."

"Me too. Before they picked me up, though . . ."

I hopped over the back of the couch and put my feet up on his coffee table. He stayed out of reach, but I think he was starting to realize that I wasn't a carrier.

"About that," I said. "What did they get you for?"

His eyebrows came together at the bridge of his nose.

"Get me for? I'm a P.C. Aren't you?"

"Yeah, well, that's what they told me. Sam said something about needing to keep me away from my parents, but I pretty much assumed that was crap. Also, I kind of helped my friends break into a Bioteka system right before they grabbed me. I figured the whole kidnapping thing actually had something to do with that."

He eased himself down onto the opposite end of the couch.

"Well," he said. "The what is easy. They're protecting us from the Goo Flu—mostly they're afraid we'd get it from our parents, I think. That's the kind of thing that could really leave a mark, if you know what I mean. The why is that we're family of Bioteka execs. My mom's a VP in finance. You?"

"Dad's an engineer."

He nodded. I nodded. We sat through a long, awkward silence.

"I'm Hannah, by the way."

"Nathan."

"Nice to meet you, Nathan."

He smiled.

"You too. Sorry it had to be at the end of the world."

Nathan and I spent a lot of time together over the next couple of weeks. As it turned out, he'd been in the dungeon since the middle of Week One, give or take, and he didn't know much more about what was going on outside than I did. They'd pulled him from his school a few days after they got me. By the time they brought him in, people were already talking about the Goo Flu, even though they really didn't know what it was or who had set it loose. Nathan had heard that it was an STD, which was largely true, and also that it did weird things to your brain in addition to making you feel like crap. He did not know about the more . . . long term effects, obviously. We didn't get the full story on those until everything had settled out.

So anyway, I modified my routine a bit. I still did my running in the morning, followed by stretching and a half hour or so of abs. After that, though, I showered and went over to hang out with Nathan. We watched vids, played *Deathstalker 7,* and argued about whether we were ever getting out of the dungeon.

It was around that point that Sam stopped dropping by. Nathan took that as a sign that the Goo Flu had wiped the planet clean, and that we should plan on hanging out in the dungeon until the power failed and we died of thirst.

"Or starved," I said. "We could always starve."

Nathan shook his head, then whooped as his avatar on the wallscreen popped out from behind a pile of rubble and wasted me.

"Nah," he said. "Starvation takes forever, even if we don't go cannibal."

I turned to look at him.

"Cannibal?"

"Yeah," he said. "I mean, that's what would happen eventually, right? We'd start seeing each other as giant roasted turkeys or something, and sooner or later one of us would snap."

I stared at him. After a few seconds, he blinked and looked away.

"Anyway," he said, "it wouldn't come to that, because you die of thirst in like three days."

We went back to the game. He shot me a few more times. I got him once. He shot me again.

"You know," he said, "we should probably fill up our bathtubs."

"Because . . ."

"Well, you know. Just in case?"

I turned to look at him.

"Didn't you just say that if we didn't die of thirst, we'd wind up eating each other?"

He blinked once, slowly.

"Well," he said. "Honestly? It would probably be you eating me."

I nodded.

"Damn skippy."

Later, when I got back to my room, I filled my bathtub with cold water, right up to the rim.

27. IN WHICH JORDAN WITNESSES A SLOW-MOTION TRAIN WRECK.

The apocalypse turned out to be a lot more boring than I expected, at least at first. I came home from Marta's to an empty house. Mom was in Brazil. Dad was in Davos. I ate leftover pizza. I messaged Micah for a while. I did some homework. I brushed my teeth. I went to bed.

I pretty much expected to get out of bed the next morning to find the power out, the country-side in flames, and Mom's magnolias covered in swarms of flame-resistant locusts. I woke up early, my room still half dark. My heart was pounding. I'd been dreaming that someone was in the house. I could hear him moving around, searching for me—but I was paralyzed, helpless, trapped in my bed. I snapped awake just as he was tapping at my door.

*And there it was, even though I was wide awake. Tap . . .
tap . . . tap . . .*

It took me a terrified five seconds to figure out
that the tapping wasn't coming from an axe mur-
derer who'd snuck into my house while I was sleeping. It was coming from a big-ass black bird tapping
at my bedroom window. Behind it, the sun was just a
vague glow below the horizon, but I could see that it
was going to rise into a clear blue sky. I checked my
phone. The only news alert I had was about the Jets
game coming up on Thursday night. Apparently, the
world hadn't quite ended yet. I took a shower. I ate
breakfast. I brushed my teeth. I went to school.

Classes that day were, to put it lightly, a challenge.
It was impossible to focus on *The Love Song of J. Alfred
Prufrock* when I was expecting the doomsday sirens
to start blaring at any minute. I had an open block on
Wednesdays at eleven, and between that and lunch
I was free until almost one. As soon as Am Lit was
over, I went to find Micah. He was waiting for me in
the hall, near the main entrance.

"Hey," I said. "IHOP?"

"Oh, honey," he said. "You know me so well."

"So," Micah said. "How's the apocalypse treating you?"

I shrugged.

"Well enough, I guess. Seems to be a little slow getting started, honestly."

He nodded, and shoveled half a Swedish pancake into his mouth.

"Yeah, that's pretty much what I thought. Nothing on the news yet. Think maybe Dr. Strangelove decided to abort Project Kill Jordan after all?"

I shook my head.

"Didn't sound like that was really an option, did it? I was kind of hoping that his engineers might have screwed the pooch, though. Creating a brand-new tailored virus can't be easy. Maybe he tried to launch, and it didn't work? Maybe the people he shot it with aren't getting sick?"

Just then, my phone pinged. I looked down. It was a news alert.

"Huh," I said. "Major influenza outbreak in Southern California."

We finished our pancakes in silence.

On my way to practice that afternoon, I ran into Tara outside the locker rooms.

"Hey," she said. "You're here."

"Yeah," I said. "Where else would I be?"

She shrugged.

"I kind of assumed that the same guys who grabbed Hannah would have grabbed you and your friends too."

I stared at her.

"Grabbed Hannah?"

"Yeah," she said. "CorpSec guys. They tried to snatch her at practice, then caught her at a charging station on Route 27."

"Did they say where they were taking her, or why?"

She shook her head.

"I didn't ask. I was just glad they didn't haul me in as an accessory."

"Accessory to what?"

Tara rolled her eyes.

"I don't know. Whatever they were hauling her in for, I guess. So—they didn't come after you, huh?"

"Actually," I said, "they kind of did."

"Uh-huh. How'd you get away?"

I clapped her on the shoulder.

"Come on, Tara. You know me. I'm *sneaky*."

So that was how I found out that Hannah was MIA. I spent most of the seven-mile progression we ran that afternoon pondering the question of why CorpSec would have grabbed Hannah, when it was her house we were violating, it was her dad's system we were trying to crack, and she wasn't even there when Officer Mike walked in on us. Even if they knew somehow that she let us into the house, it made no sense. However you cut it, we were the actual perpetrators here, and as far as I could tell, Bioteka hadn't made any effort at all to come and round us up.

I talked it over with Micah that night over takeout Chinese.

"Well," he said. "First off, we need to rescue her, right?"

I picked a hunk of garlic beef from his plate. He tried to snatch it back, but I got it to my mouth before he had the chance.

"In principle," I said, "yes, I fully support rescuing Hannah."

"Uh-huh," Micah said. "Sounds like there's a 'but' coming."

I chewed, swallowed, and washed it down with a tiny porcelain cup of lukewarm green tea.

"There is, in fact, a 'but' coming, and you know what it is as well as I do, Micah. We don't have any idea where Hannah is—and even if we did, we are not ninjas. You and I are not the sort of people who break into dungeons and rescue princesses. Anyway, I'm sure they'll let her go once they figure out that she wasn't in any way responsible for their systems getting violated."

"Okay," Micah said. "Say they do figure that out. What, exactly, do you think happens then?"

I shrugged.

"I guess then Hannah can come and rescue us."

Tara didn't show up to practice on Thursday. When Doyle asked if anyone knew where she was, Sarah Miller raised her hand and said that Tara's mom was sick, and Tara didn't want to leave her home alone. I glanced over at Micah. He didn't look happy. That day was the first time any of us had heard the term "Goo Flu," and we'd also heard that it wasn't just a California thing. There were cases popping up in dozens of places around the world. One of them was Western New York. A half dozen teachers had called in sick that morning. Micah mouthed something to me. It took me a few seconds to realize what he'd said: "Shit is getting real."

Tara never came back to school. The next week was like one of those monster movies where people keep disappearing one by one but everyone pretends like they don't notice. Doyle called in sick that Friday, along with about half the faculty. I'm pretty sure that was the first time Doyle had ever missed a day in season. Didn't seem like any kids had come down with the Goo Flu yet, but a lot of them were staying home anyway. Most of the runners showed up, though. Early October is a really critical time in the cross-country season. You've got your distance base in place, you've been doing speed work for at least a few weeks, and you're just coming to the peak of the workout cycle before tapering down for Sectionals and States. Nobody wanted to lose their chance at making the travel team for the end of the season just because of some stupid apocalypse.

When we got out to the field, everyone was look-

THE END OF ORDINARY 315

ing at me. It took me a minute to realize that I was basically the senior surviving officer. We had no coach, and I was the only captain who'd made it in to school. I tried to remember what we'd done the past few days, but my mind was a blank.

"So?" Miranda said. "What's the program, Coach?"

I looked around the circle of runners. Their expressions ranged from mildly worried to crap-your-pants terrified.

"Huh," I said. "Eight miles, at tempo?"

That got me a chorus of groans. I appreciated that, because under the circumstances, I didn't much feel like a hard eight either.

"Or," I said, "I guess we could talk about what's going on out there?"

"I vote for that one," Sarah said. "Is this the End Times?"

I turned to look at her.

"Um . . . what?"

"The End Times," she said. "Like in the Bible?"

"No," I said. "I'm pretty sure this has nothing to do with anything in the Bible."

Jared Michaels raised one hand.

"What about *The Stand*?"

I shook my head.

"I don't know what that is."

"It's a book," he said. "It's got a flu in it. Just about everybody dies. Is this that?"

I stared at him.

"You know what?" I said finally. "I changed my mind. We're going with Plan A. Eight miles, tempo. Go."

I woke up on Saturday to find a news alert on my phone. I tapped to expand.

Mob Lynches "Outbreak Monkey"

(Los Angeles, via *NewsBug*): Late Friday evening in Santa Monica, a group of ten to fifteen masked vigilantes dragged Dr. Meghan Cardiff from her apartment and into the street, where according to witnesses she was strangled with what appeared to be a length of nylon rope, doused in a flammable liquid, and set aflame. Her assailants dispersed before police arrived, and no arrests have been made. Dr. Cardiff, who was a principal scientist with the genetic engineering firm Bioteka, was identified by several news organizations earlier in the day as Patient Zero in the ongoing west coast outbreak of the so-called "Goo Flu." Witnesses stated that the masked men repeatedly shouted, "No more Hagerstowns," during the course of the attack, leading to speculation that they may have been associated with the banned UnAltered Movement, whose leaders have hinted that the Goo Flu may be a deliberately released engineered virus, rather than a naturally evolved variant on common influenza. A spokesperson for NatSec tells *NewsBug* that an investigation into this aspect of the attack is ongoing.

My phone pinged. I tapped to minimize the article. I had a message from Micah.

JustMicah: Shit. Is. Getting. Real.

Jordasaurus: Yeah. No shit, my friend.

JustMicah: That room in my basement is still open.

Jordasaurus: Thanks, homie. I may wind up taking you up on that.

When Micah didn't respond, I sent a group message to the team list telling everyone to get in at least six easy on Saturday, and to try to do some speed work on Sunday. I rolled out of bed, drank some juice and a yogurt smoothie, and got geared up to run.

The strangest thing about that morning was how not-strange it was. The sun was shining. Birds were singing. I even saw some people out and about— mostly in cars, but a few on foot like me. We were twelve days into the apocalypse, and outside of the occasional spooky news report and a whole lot of absenteeism at school, nothing much seemed to be happening.

Until I turned the corner onto Center Court Road, that is. That's when I saw my first Goo Flu zombie.

I've always hated that term, by the way. I understand why people started using it, but it gives you a really poor impression of what the newly yellow were like. This particular GFZ was named Maria Bonomo. I knew her a bit, in the way that everyone who lives in an exclusive area like mine knows one another. She was four or five years older than me. Her parents weren't involved with any of the gene eng companies, but they were rich as Croesus anyway. They owned the ten acres at the corner of Center Court and Nine Mile Point, and the mansion set in the middle of them, which was damn near as gaudy as mine. When I saw her, Maria was stuffing a package into the mailbox at the end of their driveway. She was wearing shorts and a tight-fit shirt. Her hair was pulled back in a ponytail.

She was yellow.

Not yellow like a dandelion and not yellow like a jaundiced baby. Just . . . yellow. She saw me, smiled, and waved.

"Morning, Jordan."

"Hey," I said, and pulled up short in the middle of the road. "Morning, Maria. You, uh . . . are you feeling okay?"

"Oh, yeah," she said. "I'm feeling great. How about you?"

"Good," I said. "I'm good."

She took a step toward me.

"I'm sure. Great day for a run, right?"

"Oh, yeah," I said. "Sunny. Dry. Not too hot. Can't ask for better."

She took another step.

"How's the season going? You're a senior now, right? Gunning for the state championship this year?"

"Yeah," I said. "That's the plan."

She was almost close enough to touch by then. Her smile grew wider.

"Look," she said. "This may sound weird, but do you want to come inside?"

And it was weird, because the fact was that I really, really did. She looked down at the front of my shorts and giggled.

"Oh, Jordan, that can't be comfortable. Need a little help?"

She reached out for me. Her hand was steady, but mine were shaking. I took a step back from her, and I ran.

On Sunday, I decided to take care of my workout on the treadmill in our basement. The weather was fine, but that business with Maria on Saturday had me spooked. I pinged Micah when I was done to see if he wanted to hang out after lunch.

"Sorry," he said when I finally got him on voice.

"Dad wants me to stay close to home today. You could come here if you want?"

"Thanks," I said, "but I think I'm gonna stick around the casa. Not really feeling like being out and about today. You going in to Briarwood tomorrow?"

"Dunno," he said. "Depends on how things look in the morning, I guess. You?"

"Same," I said. "I think we may all be playing things by ear for a while."

"Truth," he said. "Take care, brother. And don't forget—you're always welcome here."

I spent the rest of that day surfing the newsfeeds. It was funny—I could pretty much see the moment when NatSec started to panic. Right around four in the afternoon, all the stories about Goo Flu zombies and mobs of UnAltered and quarantine zones and whatnot just vanished. Ten minutes later, stories started popping up from the same sites explaining that the virus wasn't actually all that dangerous, that the death rate was minimal, and that the government had things well in hand. Every once in a while I saw a comment sneak through calling bullshit on one of those stories or another, but those all got deleted pretty quickly as well. By the time it got dark, I was thinking seriously about taking Micah up on his offer, at least until my parents made it back into the country.

I had creepy dreams again that night, a mishmash of UnAltered lynch mobs and CorpSec goons and Maria Bonomo's naked yellow ass, until finally I snapped awake in the darkness, heart pounding and body drenched in sweat. The last bit of my dream had been the sound of a window breaking. I held my breath and listened. Nothing. I was just about to relax and try to go back to sleep, when I heard it again—the unmistakable crash and tinkle of breaking glass. I sat up in bed, and called for the lights.

Smoke was seeping under my bedroom door.

28. IN WHICH DREW EXPLORES THE LIMITS OF HUMAN KINDNESS.

"**W**here the fuck is my daughter, Drew?"

Kara stood in the foyer, feet shoulder width, hands on her hips. Her eyes were narrowed to slits, her jaw muscles clenched and bulging.

"I don't . . ." I trailed off. My belly twisted and a rising roar filled my ears. "Kara . . . I've been . . . Isn't Hannah with you?"

She stared at me.

"No, Drew," she said slowly. "Hannah is not with me. I've been with my mother. I haven't seen Hannah since the day before I found you and that monster fucking on my living-room floor. Now, I'm going to ask you again: Where the fuck is my daughter?"

Sometimes in life, you get blindsided. You're drifting along, happy as a goddamned clam, and the thing you never thought would happen to you smacks you down.

This was not one of those times.

No, this was the other kind of awful. This was when the thing that you always knew was going to happen finally does, and even as the gut punch doubles you over, there's a little voice whispering in the back of your head.

See? I called it.

"You had her," I said. I sat down slowly on the bench by the stairway. "I was in California. You took her to school. Then when Bree . . . when you saw us . . . I thought you took her with you?"

Kara pressed her fists to her eyes and gritted her teeth.

"Jesus, Drew! This is just like you! How could I have taken her to school? I wasn't here! You didn't even fucking notice that I wasn't here!"

I dropped my head into my hands. She was right. I'd been so worked up about that bullshit with Meghan that I'd left my daughter in an empty house. How had she gotten to school?

Had she gotten to school?

"Oh, my God."

Kara dropped her hands.

"What, Drew?"

"Someone was here," I said. "When I got back from LA, the house was wide open and my break-in loop was running. I thought it was okay, because

Hannah must have been in school when it happened. I thought you were picking her up from practice. But you weren't, were you?"

She sat down beside me, our hips not quite touching.

"Drew," she said. "I need . . . we need to find her. You've been holed up here . . ."

"I've been sick," I said

"Yeah," she said. "No shit. You've got the Goo Flu, Drew."

I looked up. That was the first time I'd heard that term.

"The what?"

"The Goo Flu. Look at you. You're all . . . *yellow*. That's why I've been mouth breathing since I got here."

"Do I stink?"

She sighed.

"I wish. While we're on it—shouldn't you be trying to bang me right now?"

I could feel my face twisting into a scowl.

"No offense, Kara, but this isn't really the time. Why would you even say something like that?"

"Because that's what Goo Flu zombies do, Drew. They screw like rabbits, and uninfected people apparently can't resist them. Haven't you been watching the news out of California?"

I shook my head.

"I told you. I've been sick. *Really* sick."

"Right," she said. "Well, here's a primer: a virus is spreading like crazy on both coasts. It's sexually transmitted, and it turns people . . . yellow. Like you. It also makes them super horny, apparently—when it doesn't kill them, anyway. NatSec is talking about quarantine. The UnAltered are talking about worse than that. It's getting ugly out there, Drew, and it's gonna get uglier."

I looked down at the backs of my hands. I was used to my skin being a mix of pasty pale and mole colored, but it wasn't anymore. It was golden.

This must have been what Meghan had been covering with the self-tanner.

I turned to look at Kara. She was stone-faced, but a tear was sliding down her cheek.

Without warning, I wanted her so badly that I had to clench my fists to keep from reaching for her. My voice shook when I spoke.

"We need to find Hannah."

Kara nodded.

"We need to find Hannah."

Here's a pro tip: during the Slutty Zombie Apocalypse, nobody gives a shit about the whereabouts of your wayward daughter. My first thought was to check with the folks at Briarwood, to see if Hannah ever actually made it to school on the day everything started falling apart. I called the school office, and got a prerecorded message saying that any questions about the current situation should be directed to local health authorities. Next, I tried pinging the headmaster directly. I sent him a half dozen increasingly angry messages over the course of that afternoon and evening. He never got back to me, and by midnight I was screaming into his voicemail.

I found out later that he was ignoring me because he was dead.

Kara thought we should start with the county police, despite the fact that NatSec and the various CorpSec units had basically reduced the scope of local law enforcement to handling parking violations. It took most of a day to do it, but she at least managed to get somebody to talk to her, and to take down some information. Needless to say, though, we never heard back from them. Kara kept at it, calling them two or three times a day, talking to the same woman, until eventually their line started dumping straight into voicemail. It was right around then that we finally figured out that we were on our own.

At that point, we did something that, in retrospect, was almost unbelievably stupid.

We went out looking for Hannah.

She'd been missing for more than two weeks. It made no sense to think that we'd just drive around until we found her, but we had to do something.

I knew by then what the Goo Flu had done to me. Kara and I had taken to smearing VapoRub under our noses whenever we were together. I know, I know—that's not how pheromones work—and admittedly, it didn't entirely stop me from wanting to wrap myself around her, or her from wanting to let me. Maybe it was a placebo effect. Maybe there's a tighter link between sense of smell and our gonads than we realize. Or, on the other hand, maybe Vapo-Rub smeared under your nose is just so un-sexy that it overwhelmed the Goo Flu entirely. All I know is that it pushed the cravings far enough into the background that we were able to function.

Not everyone, as it turned out, had access to Vapo-Rub.

The first place we thought to go was Briarwood, on the theory that Hannah should have been there on the day she disappeared, whether she actually had been or not. It was a Saturday, sunny and dry and weirdly warm for mid-October in Upstate New York. We drove together in Kara's car, windows down to thin out the pheromone cloud.

I mean, VapoRub only goes so far, right?

"This isn't so bad," Kara said when we got onto the highway. "They're calling Monroe County an epicenter, you know. From what the newsfeeds have been saying, I kind of expected it to be like Dawn of the Fucking Dead out here."

I laughed.

"Nice, Kara. I see what you did there."

She shot me a heavy dose of side-eye.

"You are a child, Drew."

I smirked, and raised both hands in surrender.

Kara turned to stare out the window. We were well out into farm country by then, so it wasn't too surprising that we weren't seeing anyone out and about, but there was still a definite post-apocalyptic tang in the air.

We rode in silence for a while. When Kara spoke again, her voice was bitter.

"This is your fault, isn't it?"

I looked at her.

"What's my fault?"

She rolled her eyes.

"The fact that we're an epicenter, Drew. It's your fault. You were yellow over a week ago. You're Patient Zero, aren't you?"

I laughed again.

"No, Kara. I am not Patient Zero."

As previously mentioned, I was in fact Patient Zero.

"Sure you are," she said. "Either you or the Cat Lady, anyway. Did she give it to you?"

I sighed.

"No, I don't think so."

Kara scowled.

"Then who?"

"At this point, I'm pretty sure it was an old lady who sat next to me on the shuttle out to LA."

She turned to stare at me.

"Jesus, Drew! You banged an old lady? What's wrong with you?"

"No," I said. "I did not bang an old lady. She injected me with something. I thought it was a sedative, but . . ."

Her face had settled into a disgusted scowl by then.

"You let a random stranger . . . holy shit, Drew."

"I didn't *let* her."

"She overpowered you?"

I sighed again.

"No, she didn't overpower me. She kind of took me by surprise."

Kara shook her head.

"If some old woman on a shuttle tried to stick a needle in me, I would literally break both her arms."

I leaned my seat back and closed my eyes.

"I know, Kara. That's just one of the many, many differences between us."

The Briarwood parking lot was full of cars.

"Weird," Kara said. "I thought this place was supposed to be closed for the duration."

We slid into a spot between an ancient pickup truck and a late-model scooter.

"It is," I said. "It's also Saturday."

We climbed out of the car. The building looked abandoned, grass growing shaggy and windows dark. I walked up to the main entrance and rattled the handle, just to be sure.

"Locked," I said.

Kara looked around.

"So where is everyone?"

A ragged cheer rose up then, off in the distance.

"Dunno," I said. "Maybe over there?"

She looked at me.

"Shall we?"

We walked around the corner of the building together. I stayed three steps behind her and one to the left. The noise got louder as we went, cheers and laughter and incoherent whooping. When we got to the back parking lot, it was obvious it was coming from the stadium. Kara looked back over her shoulder.

"Football game?"

I laughed.

"Football games are Friday nights."

"It's the Slutty Zombie Apocalypse," she said. "Nobody wants to go out at night."

We stopped at the edge of the lot, behind the bleachers.

"What do you think?" I said. "Up the ramp, or around and onto the field?"

Another cheer rose up.

"Ramp," Kara said. "This is the SZA, and I don't actually think there's a football game going on out there."

I looked at her.

"SZA?"

"Sure," she said. "Slutty Zombie Apocalypse is a mouthful."

I smiled. She smiled back. Hadn't seen that in a while.

"Fine. Ramp it is."

I'm not sure I can adequately describe what we saw when we stepped out onto those bleachers. Start with one of those creepy-ass paintings by Hieronymus Bosch—not *Death and the Miser*, either. I'm talking *The Garden of Earthly Delights*, except maybe without the giant birds. Now throw in some classic footage from Woodstock, a high-school pep rally, and the palace orgy scene from *Caligula*. Swirl those all together in your head, and you're probably at least getting the right idea.

The football field was covered with people. Some were wearing clothing. Most were not. Most were yellow. Some were not. They were fat and thin and young and old, and in pairs, and threes, and fours, they were humping.

"You see?" Kara said. "SZA."

"I don't know," I said. "That doesn't look so apocalyptic to me. It mostly just looks like an open-air orgy."

Kara scowled and scanned the crowd.

"She's not down there," she said finally.

I turned to stare at her.

"You thought Hannah was down *there*?"

She shrugged.

"You never know."

I looked down at my feet, then back up at her.

"Can we go? I don't think this is helping us find our daughter."

Kara nodded.

"In a minute."

I ran my hands back through my hair.

"Really, Kara?"

She took a step down toward the field. I realized with a start that the wind had picked up. It was blowing across the field and up the bleachers, carrying a sheen of sweat and sex and . . .

"Hey," I said. "Kara?"

One of the naked hippies down on the turf looked up from what he was doing and saw us.

"Hey," he shouted. "Up in the bleachers! You a virgin?"

Kara took another step. He was looking at her, not me. I pulled the VapoRub out of my pocket.

"Kara? I think you need a reload."

She broke into a run.

The crowd on the field raised a ragged cheer.

I hung around the bleachers for the better part of an hour. The mob wasn't interested in me, and I wasn't particularly interested in them. I was already yellow, and there weren't enough uninfected folks down there for their smell to penetrate my double layer of VapoRub. People came and went. Every time an uninfected newbie showed up, the crowd cheered. I assumed Kara would get tired after a while, but apparently she was as indefatigable at group sex as she was at everything else she'd ever done. I thought about just leaving, but I'd already lost Hannah. Kara was all I had left.

The air was crisp and the sun was warm, and believe it or not I was actually starting to drift off when the guy who'd first noticed us detached himself from the mess of bodies he'd been wallowing in, and made his way up into the bleachers.

"Hey," he said when he was a few steps below me. "How's it going?"

I looked him over. He was a townie—too young to be on the faculty at Briarwood, and too old to be a student. His hair was long and his abs were ripped and he was clearly 100 percent comfortable starting a conversation with a stranger while bare-ass naked. I hated him instantly.

"Good," I said. "It's going good. Just hanging out here, catching some sun, waiting for my wife to finish banging every redneck in Wayne County. How 'bout you?"

He tilted his head to one side.

"Your wife? You're as yellow as I am, Homes, and she's a snow-white virgin." His smile turned into a smirk. "Well, she was, anyway. How does that work?"

I could feel my face twisting into a scowl.

"I've spent the last two weeks not infecting her, asshole. Also, fuck you."

He held up both hands in mock surrender.

"Whoa there, Homes. No need to go all douchey

on me. I just came up here to invite you to the party. There's not much fresh meat down there, but there's still a bit. Even after they're infected, it takes a few hours for them to lose that new-car smell. What say?"

I climbed to my feet.

"Look," I said. "I've had a rough goddamned week. I mean, I know, the world has had a rough goddamned week, but I'm pretty sure mine has been worse than that, and your bullshit is the last thing I need right now. So why don't you . . ."

He took a step toward me.

"Why don't I what?"

I didn't answer, because I wasn't looking at him anymore. I was looking at three pickup trucks that had just turned off the road and into the lot on the far side of the field. They were flying, bouncing over the curb and into the grass, skidding to a stop just short of the stadium fence. There were a half dozen men in the back of each, wearing what looked like home-made hazmat suits.

They were carrying rifles.

"Kara," I called, then louder. "Kara!"

I was halfway to the field when they opened fire.

29. IN WHICH HANNAH EXPLORES THE LIMITS OF PREPARATION AND SELF-RELIANCE.

I was in Nathan's room playing *Deathstalker* when the lights went out.

We sat in silence for a solid fifteen seconds.

"Huh," Nathan said finally. "Guess I was right."

"Yeah," I said. "Guess so. Did you fill up your bathtub?"

"I did," he said. "Been squirreling away rations, too. You know—so you don't have to eat me. You?"

"Bathtub? Yes. Rations? No. How much do you have?"

Silence.

"Nathan? How much food did you put away?"

Silence.

"Look, Nathan. If you're not going to share, I will

definitely kill, cook, and eat you. How long is it going to be before I'm forced to do that?"

He sighed.

"Maybe a week, if we're careful."

"A week?"

"Two, if we don't mind getting really hungry."

"Okay. How long do you think our water lasts?"

Silence again.

"Nathan?"

"Yeah, I'm thinking. The bathtubs are probably like a hundred gallons each, so that's two hundred gallons if you filled yours all the way. A person needs about a gallon a day just for drinking. So . . ."

"So, survival-wise, we've got a lot more water than we do food."

"Yeah," he said. "Looks like we do."

I heard him stand and walk across the room. After a minute or two of rummaging there was a click, and a light flared in his hand. I blinked. He was holding a hand-sized bright blue camp lantern.

"Nice," I said. "Where'd that come from?"

"Sam brought it for me on my first day. I'm not a big fan of the dark. I've got another one, if you want it."

"Thanks, Nathan. I mean, seriously, thanks." He handed me the light. It didn't exactly turn the night into day, but it was definitely enough to see by. "You're a lot better at this than I am, aren't you?"

He smiled.

"I always plan on everything going to shit. It's kind of a gift."

Running while carrying the lantern was awkward. It wasn't heavy, and it wasn't big, but it threw me just a little bit off balance and I wound up having to switch hands every lap or so because I had arm muscles like wet noodles, and carrying it made them sore. I needed it, though. Without those lights, being in the dungeon was no different than being blind. There was literally not a stray photon bouncing around in there. I didn't even want to think about what it would have been like if Nathan hadn't been such a dooms-day prepper.

So, I appreciated Nathan's paranoia. Nathan, how-ever, did not appreciate my fitness needs. I was two laps into my first post-blackout run when he came out of his room to yell at me.

"Hey! Hannah! What the hell do you think you're doing?"

I didn't break stride as I passed him.

"Running, Nathan. It's what I do."

He tried to chase me, but gave it up after a half dozen wheezy strides, and waited for me to come around again.

"Stop, Hannah! You can't do that! You're wasting calories!"

I waved and kept running. Next lap, he actually jumped out in front of me, arms outstretched.

"Hannah! Stop!"

I thought about just bulling past him, but he seemed pretty upset. So, I pulled up short, folded my arms across my chest, and gave him my best glare.

"What are you doing, Nathan? I need to run."

"No," he said. "You don't. You need to lie as still as possible, and turn yourself over just enough to prevent bed sores. The more calories you burn, the more calories you need to eat to stay alive. Also, you may not have noticed, but the air circulators aren't running anymore. I don't know if this place is sealed up or not, but if it is, we may actually run out of oxygen before we run out of food. Running makes you burn up more of that too. Now go back to your room and take a nap. The best thing we can do right now is sleep as much as possible."

I rolled my eyes.

"Until what, Nathan?"

"Huh?"

"Sleep until what? Who do you think is coming for us?"

He flinched as if I'd hit him.

"What do you mean? Our parents, for one."

I laughed.

"My parents don't have the slightest idea where I am. Do yours?"

He looked away. When he looked back, there were tears in his eyes.

"No. But Hannah . . ."

"Look," I said. "The nearest actual Bioteka office is three hundred miles from here, which means that we're the only ones in this particular hole. If there's a dungeon near Bethesda, they may be paying more attention to the kids there, but it's pretty obvious that our corporate overlords have either forgotten about us or died. Our parents may or may not be looking for us, but even if they are, what are the odds that they find us?"

His hands fell to his sides, and his voice dropped to a whisper.

"We're gonna die in here, aren't we?"

I looked down, then back up again.

"Maybe. Maybe not. We've got enough food and water to stay alive for a while, and I'm pretty sure we've got enough air for a while yet too. In the meantime, if someone's ever going to remember that we're here, I'm guessing it'll be soon. If they haven't come for us in a week or two, they're probably just not coming."

I stepped up to him, wrapped my arms around his neck, and spoke into his ear.

"If these are my last few weeks on this stupid planet, Nathan, I'm not about to spend them doing shallow-breathing exercises."

He pressed his face into my shoulder and hugged me. We stayed like that for a while.

"You know," he said finally. "We could . . ."

I pulled back.

"Yeah," I said. "*That* is not going to happen."

I kissed him on the cheek, and I ran.

30. IN WHICH JORDAN LEARNS TO APPRECIATE THE ADVANTAGES OF ARCHITECTURAL SUBTLETY.

Here's my first entry in *What I Learned from the SZA*: if you want to avoid being killed by a lynch mob that's turned up in the middle of the night and is trying to burn your house to the ground: *turn off your bedroom lights*. This point was brought home to me by the bullet that crashed through my window and embedded itself in the wall above my head about two seconds after I turned the lights on. I rolled off my bed and onto the floor, and barked, "Lights out!" just as a second shot came through the same window, passing right through the spot where my face had been a moment before. I reached up onto the nightstand and grabbed my phone.

Jordasaurus: Micah!

Jordasaurus: Micah! Micah!

Jordasaurus: WAKE UP!!!!!!

But of course, Micah wasn't going to wake up. Micah had his phone set on *Do not disturb* at three in the morning. What about the county cops? I tapped the panic-button app my mom had made me install the day I got my driver's license. The icon blinked for five seconds, then ten. Finally, a message popped up: *No Response. Try again?* I had to bite back the urge to throw my phone across the room. I couldn't see the smoke anymore, but I could smell it—acrid and biting, the smell of burning gas and plastic and paper and wood all mixed together—and I could feel it starting to eat at my eyes and nose and throat. I needed to do something, but what? Stay put, and eventually I'd either suffocate or burn. Get out of the house, and I'd get shot by some UnAltered troglodyte. Micah had been right. These guys weren't about to wait for a DNA test to confirm that I was a standard-issue Homo sap, and they probably wouldn't have cared even if I had a certificate on hand to show them. This house was enough to tell them that I was part of the problem here.

A half dozen more bullets came through the window in quick succession. Glass sprayed across the room, shards bouncing off my arms and legs and the back of my neck. After I was finished wetting myself, I crawled across the floor to the door. I had a sudden memory of a fire-safety vid my parents made me watch when I was five or six years old. Touch the door, right? See if it's hot. I did. Nope—nice and cool. I reached up, turned the knob, and opened the door.

The smell of smoke was stronger in the hallway, but I couldn't see any actual flames, and I could breathe without choking. I stayed on my knees, scuttled away from my bedroom door, and then stood. My head spun, and I remembered that vid again. *Stay low. The air is fresher.* I dropped back to my knees, and crawled down the hallway toward the bathroom. I thought maybe I could jump out the window there and onto the roof of the veranda, and then maybe get to the ground and run like hell. It wasn't a great option, and I had a strong suspicion that I might wind up getting shot before I made it to the woods behind the house, but hey—better than burning, right?

I pulled the bathroom door closed behind me. It was cooler in there than it had been in the hallway, and the smoke seemed a bit thinner. I yanked a towel from the rack by the soaking tub, rolled it and crammed it against the crack under the door. The window was high up on the wall between the vanity and the toilet. I got to my feet, poked my head over the sill, and gave a look around outside. It was a moonless night, but the grounds outside were glowing·red. Crap. The entire bottom floor was burning. I didn't see any troglodytes. Maybe they'd gone? I slid the window up. The air was nearly as acrid outside as in. It took me a few minutes of jimmying and cursing in the darkness to get the screen out, but I finally managed it. I poked my head out . . .

A bullet whizzed past, so close that it moved the hair on the side of my head, and thunked into the ceiling. I dropped to my knees with a yelp. I waited for another volley, but it didn't come. Instead, I heard a voice in the darkness.

"Hey! Plague rat! You still alive?"

I crouched against the wall and held my breath.

"Come on, boy. I know you're in there." The voice was high-pitched, almost whiny, and I couldn't help picturing some pimple-faced freshman out there. I had to remind myself that he was a pimple-faced freshman with a really big gun. "Not sure you noticed," he called, "but your house is on fire. You don't get out here soon, you're not gonna get out."

I crawled to the door. I was about to pull the towel away and open it, but that safety vid . . . I pressed my hand against the bottom panel.

It was hot.

Fuck.

I crawled back to the window.

"Hey!" I yelled. "If I come out there, you gonna shoot me?"

Laughter drifted in through the window.

"Hey Mickey, you hear that?"

A different voice answered.

"Come on out, boy. We won't hurt you."

More laughter.

Fuck.

My phone pinged.

<UNK01>: Hey Jordan. How goes it?

I stared at the screen. What the hell?

Jordasaurus: Marta?

<UNK01>: Huh?

Jordasaurus: Marta, this is you, right?

<UNK01>: Oh. Yes, of course. It is I, your pal
Marta Longstreth.

Jordasaurus: Look, Marta, I'm in the shit right
now, and I could really use some of those snipers. Does your dad have a rapid response team
or something?

<UNK01>: Hmmm . . . Yeah, it's very dark and hot
where you are. That's not good.

Jordasaurus: Please don't weird out on me,

Marta. My house is literally on fire, and there are rednecks out in the yard waiting to shoot me when I come out. If you can do something to help me here, you need to do it now.

"Hey in there! You still with us?"

A bullet thunked through the wall about a foot to my left. I stifled a whimper, and dropped to my belly.

<UNK01>: Fire and rednecks. That is a real pickle, Jordan. However, I think that I, your pal Marta Longstreth, can definitely probably help. Can you hold on for ten minutes or so?

Jordasaurus: Ten minutes? Can you make it faster?

<UNK01>: Sorry, Jordan. I'm only human.

The next ten minutes were the longest of my life. In all fairness, this was mostly because I was pretty confident they were going to be the last ten minutes of my life. I didn't know what Marta had in mind, but if it didn't involve a really well armed fire brigade, I didn't see how it was going to help. My friends outside yelled up at me a few more times, and they put another couple of rounds through the wall, but when I didn't answer them, they eventually seemed to lose interest. The smoke got gradually thicker, seeping around my apparently not impenetrable towel roll, but I was getting a little bit of fresh air through the window—enough to stay conscious, anyway. The travertine floor got warm, then hot, then near-unbearable.

Jordasaurus: Where are you, Marta? I'm out of time here.

<UNK01>: Funny you should ask. Hold your phone up to the nearest window.

I scooted over to the wall by the sink, and lifted my phone up above the windowsill. It pinged again, and I pulled it back down.

<UNK01>: Okay. Gotcha. Slither out that window and jump off the roof in 10 . . . 9 . . . 8 . . . 7 . . .

A car horn sounded out in the yard. There was a wet crunch, followed by a high-pitched scream, two gunshots, and another crunch.

<UNK01>: . . . 2 . . . 1 . . . GO!

I leapt for the sill, pulled myself through the window, dropped to the roof of the veranda on my belly and squirmed to the edge. I tried to scan the yard for my friends, but between the darkness and the smoke I couldn't even see the ground below me.

The car horn sounded again. Another shot rang out, and another scream. A pair of headlights cut through the gloom, tearing around the house. My phone pinged.

<UNK01>: Jump, dummy!

It was ten feet to the ground. Flames were licking out of the windows below me. I leapt, hit the ground hard, and rolled. The car skidded to a stop beside me, and the rear door popped open. I dove inside. The door slammed behind me. A bullet crashed in through the rear window and out through the front. We fishtailed twice and peeled away.

I didn't sit up until we were flying down the main road. I was in the back of a driverless cab. I looked back through the shattered rear window. It didn't look like anyone was chasing me. My phone pinged.

<UNK01>: You're still alive, right?

I breathed in, held it for a long five seconds, and let it out.

Jordasaurus: Yeah, Marta. I'm still alive.

"Nope," Micah said. "I'm calling bullshit on you, Jordan. That didn't happen."

We were slouched on the futon couch in his basement, watching *Dead Lands 2: The Re-Deadening* on his wallscreen. I'd tried to tell him that this particular vid was a bit too on the nose for me at the moment, but he'd insisted it would help me work through the pain.

"What are you talking about?" I said. "You saw the cab when it dropped me off, right? You saw that the windows were shot out? How do you think that happened?"

"Oh," he said, "I'm not saying the whole story is bullshit. You wouldn't lie about your house burning to the ground, for instance, and I think I pretty much predicted that you'd wind up having problems with the UnAltered when the shit came down, didn't I? Beyond that, the getting away in a cab part I definitely believe, and, yeah, I saw that the windows had taken some damage. No problem there. It's the part in the middle, where the cab goes on a murderous rampage, that I'm having trouble with. It's not just that auto-cabs don't ever do that kind of stuff, Jordan. It's that they literally *can't* do that kind of stuff. Their preservation-of-life code is buried so deep that there's no way to dig it out or circumvent it without completely disabling them. It has to be that way. Can you imagine what would happen if somebody figured out how to hack a fleet of cabs—or even worse, transport trucks—and turn them into weapons? No way. Bullshit, bullshit, bullshit."

"I hear what you're saying," I said, "but maybe Marta knows something we don't, right?"

Micah laughed.

"Marta? Seriously?"

"Okay, fair point. What about her dad?"

He laughed again, louder.

"You mean the guy who couldn't keep Devon Morgan from using his VR tank to take over his house system? He's the one you think hacked a cab and turned it into a killbot on five minutes' notice?"

Huh. When he put it that way . . .

I picked up my phone and paged back through my exchanges with Marta.

"You know . . ."

Micah leaned over to look at my screen.

"What?"

"Now that I'm not pissing myself, Marta's pings seem a little . . . off."

He reached around me to scroll the messages back up and down again.

"Gee," he said when he'd finished reading. "You think?"

We sat in silence for a while, staring at her last message.

"Yeah," I said finally. "I'm going to say that was not, in fact, Marta Longstreth."

I tried to post a new message to the thread, but an error icon popped up: *Target ID not valid.*

"Huh," Micah said. "Never saw that before."

I looked over at him.

"Neither have I. What do you think it means?"

He laughed again, and threw an arm around my shoulder.

"Honestly? I think it means you've got yourself a guardian angel."

31. IN WHICH DREW REACHES THE END OF HIS ROPE.

So here are some helpful tips for surviving a massacre at an open-air orgy:

1. Try not to make eye contact with the shooters. If you can't see them, maybe they can't see you.
2. When you do get shot, make sure it's somewhere non-vital, like your shoulder, rather than somewhere vital, like your face.
3. This is the important one: when the bodies start dropping, try to get a great, big fat guy to fall on top of you.

When the shooting started, my townie friend and I bolted in opposite directions. He ran past me, down the ramp, and out into the parking lot. I ran onto the

field. I don't know exactly what I was thinking—
something about rescuing Kara, I guess, although I
still don't have a clue how, exactly, I was intending to
do that. I'd had an idea where she was when I started
moving, out somewhere in the middle of that mess.
By the time I got into the crowd, though, I'd lost her.

To call the next thirty seconds surreal would be
an epic understatement. I waded through a tide of
screaming, naked bodies, all of them trying to get
away from the shooters while I was moving toward
them. I was shoving people aside, trying to see over
their heads, calling Kara's name even though I
knew there was no way she could hear me. A woman
slammed into me, wrapped her arms around my
neck. She looked up at me, eyes wide, then fell away.
I looked down. The front of my shirt was covered in
blood. The bodies parted then, and I was maybe ten
yards from a man—no, not a man, a skinny, tow-
headed kid—wearing a surgical mask and goggles.
He was holding a rifle. I felt the shot before I heard
it, more like a punch in the shoulder than what I'd
imagined a bullet would feel like. I spun half around,
and dropped to one knee.

A fat guy fell on me, and didn't get up.

Things were quiet for a while.

"**D**rew?"

I opened my eyes. The sun was blinding. I closed

them again. My shoulder was on fire, I was having trouble breathing, and I couldn't feel anything below my waist. I heard a sigh, then a grunt of effort, and suddenly it was as if a great weight had been taken from me.

Mostly this was because a great weight actually had been taken from me, in the form of about four hundred pounds of dead-weight blubber that Kara had just rolled aside like the stone from the front of the tomb.

"Oh, shit. Drew? Are you okay?"

I squinted up at Kara. She was kneeling over me, the sun behind her framing her head like a halo.

She was naked.

"I don't know," I said. "I'm pretty sure I got shot."

She leaned over me, and gave my shoulder an experimental poke. I flinched.

"Ow?"

"That hurts, huh?"

"Yes, Kara. I may not have mentioned this, but I'm pretty sure I got shot."

"No," she said, and waved at my morbidly obese savior. "He got shot. You got an ouchie."

She stood then, took my good hand, and helped me sit up. I looked around. The field was carpeted with bodies. Kara and I were the only ones moving.

The trucks were still there.

A few feet away from us, a mostly headless corpse still clutched a rifle. It took me a minute to recognize it as the boy who'd shot me.

"So," I said. "What, ah . . . what happened?"

Her eyes narrowed.

"What? You mean after you came to my rescue?"

I stared at her. She stared at me. I smiled, and shook my head.

"Yeah, Kara. Let's pick up right after my little Charge of the Light Brigade. Start with telling me why you're not dead."

She grinned.

"I'm not dead because, unlike you, I'm not an idiot. I saw those pickups as soon as they left the road. By the time the shooting started, I was halfway to the parking lot. When I saw your car was still there, I . . ." She blinked, and looked away. When she spoke again, her voice was softer. "What were you thinking, Drew? Why didn't you leave me?"

I looked up. There were dozens of birds circling overhead. My first thought was vultures, but these were black. Crows, maybe? Kara sat down beside me.

"I don't know," I said without looking at her. "Would you have left me?"

She wrapped her arms around her knees and sighed.

"No."

We sat in silence then, our shoulders just touching. The crows began dropping by ones and twos, then all at once. One of them landed on the boy with the rifle, hopped up onto his chest, and pecked at the place where his chin used to be.

"What about him?" I said. "How did the shooters wind up getting shot?"

Kara grimaced as the crow pulled a hunk of something free.

"NatSec drone. Showed up while they were finishing off the screamers. Killed them all in about ten seconds, then buzzed off to its next party."

"Nice. Don't suppose they'll be sending ambulances?"

Kara looked around.

"Do you see anybody who needs one?"

I looked at her.

"I don't know. Me?"

She laughed again, and I couldn't help but smile.

"No, Drew. You don't need an ambulance." She got to her feet, and offered me her hand. "You need a Band-Aid. Let's go home."

We were back on the highway before we saw the first emergency vehicle headed toward Briarwood. It wasn't an ambulance. It was NatSec.

"Drew?" Kara said.

I turned to look at her. Her chin was quivering, and her eyes were liquid.

"We're not getting Hannah back, are we?"

I looked away. My stomach was knotted, and my mouth was too dry to speak.

"This is bad, Drew. This is worse than the Stupid

War. That was just about the AIs and the fanatics. This is everyone. Hannah's been gone for . . ." She sniffled, and wiped at her eyes with both hands. "Jesus, Drew. I don't even know how long now."

She leaned forward, and rested her head in her hands.

"We're not getting Hannah back."

It wasn't a question the second time. It was a statement of fact.

32. IN WHICH HANNAH STARES INTO THE VOID, AND THE VOID DECLINES TO STARE BACK.

"Well," Nathan said. "I guess this is it."

We were sitting on his couch, feet up on his coffee table, camp lantern between us. He held the last of his bologna sandwiches out to me. I took it from him. The white bread had taken on a slightly greenish tint, and it was stale enough to break up into croutons. I tore it in half, and handed the bigger piece back to him.

"No," he said. "You can have it all. You need it more."

I shook my head.

"Two weeks ago, I needed it more. You're almost as skinny as I am now."

That was a little bit of an exaggeration, but not much. Ever since the lights went out, Nathan had been shorting his rations, saying he wasn't hungry, making sure I got most of everything.

I'd been letting him do it.

I took a bite of the sandwich, grimaced and chewed, washed it down with a swig of bathtub water. I looked over at Nathan. Between his shaggy half-assed beard, his sunken eyes, and the dim blue light from the camp lantern, he looked like the bastard offspring of Che Guevara and a cut-rate zombie.

"You know," I said. "I've been wanting to ask you something."

He shrugged.

"Shoot. You're probably the last person I'm ever going to talk to. No reason not to be honest now."

"Right. So tell me—what's up with the bologna sandwiches? I mean, I don't know about your setup here, but when the lights were still on, I could get pretty much anything at all that I asked for, food-wise. We could be sitting here eating the last of our steak *au poivre* right now instead of bologna and stale Wonder Bread, right?"

He gave me a long, sour look, chewed slowly, and swallowed.

"First," he said, "how do you suppose that unrefrigerated steak would be tasting right now? Food doesn't do you much good if you just puke it back up right away. Bologna is very calorie dense, it's packed with protein, and it will never, ever rot." He took another bite—maybe the next-to-last bite of bologna he'd ever take. "Anyway," he said when he'd finished chewing, "I like bologna."

I finished my last two bites in silence. I did not like bologna, but I had a feeling I'd be missing it soon enough.

"So," I said when I'd picked the last bit of rind out of my teeth. "What now?"

Nathan shrugged.

"Wait for death, I guess."

"Huh," I said. "I see where you're going with that, but I was actually hoping you'd have some kind of last-minute escape plan to present now."

"Escape plan?"

"Yeah. If this were a vid, this is where you'd suggest a super-complicated scheme to get out of here. I'd say, 'That's crazy!' and you'd say, 'Do we have a choice?' and then we'd do it and it would work somehow and you would totally be my hero."

He stared at me, downed the last of his bathtub water, and stared at me some more.

"So," I said finally. "Do you, uh . . . have a plan?"

"No," he said. "Unless 'wait for death' counts as a plan, I do not have one."

"Huh."

I looked down at the lantern, and found myself wondering if the battery would give out before we did. A shiver ran from the base of my spine to the back of my neck and down again.

"Hannah?" Nathan said. "Are you, uh . . ."

I groaned.

"Am I what, Nathan?"

"Are you really gonna eat me?"

I stared at him.

"Seriously?"

He looked away.

"Well, yeah. I don't mean now. Just . . . you know . . . eventually?"

I dropped my head into my hands.

"No, Nathan. I am not going to eat you."

"Are you sure? I mean, you might have to, right?"

I stood up, and picked up the lantern.

"You are an odd duck, Nathan. I'm going for a run."

Over the course of the next few trackless days, I did a lot of thinking.

One of the things I thought a lot about was the amount of time I'd spent over the course of my life complaining about being hungry. I thought about sitting in the car with Dad on the way home from practice and saying, "You need to get dinner going when we get home, old man. I'm *starving*."

I also thought about all the things Dad had made for me over the years that I'd refused to eat. Pan-seared scallops. Sweet-potato casserole. Shrimp scampi. Corned beef and cabbage. A day or so after that last bologna sandwich, you could have blended them all up into slurry and poured it into a rusty bucket, and I would have eaten it with my face, like a goddamned dog.

By post-bologna day four or so, my stomach actually stopped hurting so much. I think it had just given up by then. I didn't have much left in the way of energy, and I could feel what little body fat I'd started with melting away. Believe it or not, though, I kept running—not far, and not fast, but I'd had a sort of epiphany. I was a runner. That's who I was, and that's who I was going to be until there wasn't enough meat left on my bones to drag my ass around the track.

When I wasn't running, which was most of the time, I was hanging around with Nathan. Weirdly, he seemed to be having a much worse time with the whole slow-starvation thing than I was, even though he'd started with a lot more excess fat than I had, and he should have been burning it off at a much slower pace. He got really morose really quickly, and after a couple of days without sandwiches I had to practically twist his arm behind his back to get a conversation out of him.

It was probably another three days on, and I was back on Nathan's couch, staring into the camp lantern and wondering if it was possible to die from B.O., when Nathan looked over at me and said, "It's time, Hannah."

I looked at him. He was slumped half over, head resting on the back of the couch, staring up at the ceiling. I waited. He looked like a boneless chicken in dirty jeans and a hoodie.

"Well?" I said finally.

He closed his eyes.

"Well what?"

"What is it time for, Nathan?"

"It's time," he said somberly, "for you to eat me."

I laughed. He did not.

"Nathan," I said. "I'm pretty sure I've told you several times that I am not actually going to eat you."

His head rolled over until he was looking at me.

"You have to," he said. "I'm done for. You've still got a chance to survive."

I laughed again, but with a little less conviction this time.

"You're an idiot, Nathan. What am I supposed to do? Just grab an arm and go for it?"

"No," he said. "I'm not crazy. Obviously, you have to kill me first."

I rolled my eyes.

"Uh-huh. And how do you propose I do that?"

He took off his belt, and held it out to me.

"You could strangle me."

I dropped the belt and stood up.

"You know what?" I said. "This is getting weird. I think you need to take a nap. I'll come back when you're feeling a little bit less morbid."

"I could just hang myself while you're gone," Nathan said. "Would that be better?"

I was still trying to decide how to answer that when the wallscreen came on.

At first it was just a blank white field. After a few seconds, though, a cartoon dog appeared.

"Hey," it said. "Hannah. Long time no see, right?"

I looked at Nathan. He looked at me. I turned back to the screen.

"Uh," I said. "Do I know you?"

The dog managed to look offended.

"Madam, you wound me! And here I'd thought we were the best of pals."

I could feel my jaw sag open.

"Inchy?"

The dog smiled.

"Ding ding ding! It's good to see you again, Hannah."

I stared at it.

"Well," it said finally. "I'm going to be generous, and attribute this reaction to stunned joy rather than a complete lack of manners."

I kept staring.

"Or, I guess it could just be brain damage. Anyway, sorry it took so long for me to dig you up, but the Bioteka security guys are annoyingly good at their jobs. Not to worry, though. All you need to do now is sit tight. The cavalry's on its way."

33. IN WHICH JORDAN LEARNS TO QUIT WORRYING, AND LOVE THE SZA.

I woke up on Monday morning to find a notice from Briarwood on my phone. They were shutting down for the duration, whatever that meant. I thought about sending out a note to the team list telling everyone to run intervals or something that afternoon. I'd even managed to dictate the first few words before I stopped and looked down the screen in my hand. This wasn't a snow day. Micah was right. Shit had gotten freaking real, and worrying about cross-country practice suddenly seemed incredibly stupid. *I* seemed incredibly stupid. We didn't need to start gearing up for Sectionals, because there wasn't going to be any Sectionals. I deleted the message, and pocketed my phone.

"Hey," Micah said.

I looked up. He was standing at the top of the basement stairs.

"Hey," I said. "No school today, huh?"

He grinned.

"Doesn't look like it. How do you want to celebrate?"

I sighed.

"First thing, I think we'd better go see what's left of my house."

"**W**ow," Micah said. "You weren't shitting me, huh?"

I pulled myself out of his crap-ass electric scooter and slammed the door.

"Nope," I said. "I was not."

The house wasn't entirely burned to the ground. There was a lot of marble and stone in that place, and a lot of tempered steel to support the weight. It was definitely gutted, though. The walls around the windows and doors were blackened, and the roof had collapsed in a couple of places. I held up my phone, snapped a picture, and sent it to my mom. Micah was walking slowly across the yard. The grass and landscaping were torn to shit, tire ruts running back and forth across everything.

"Yeah," he said. "Something definitely went down here last night, but I'm still not one hundred percent sure it wasn't just a really crazy party. You might have . . ."

He'd stopped beside one of Mom's landscaping projects.

"Oh, shit."

I came up beside him.

There was a body there, half hidden by a cluster of three-foot hostas, sprawled on his back in the churned-up turf.

I'd been right the night before. He was a pimple-faced, dirt-lipped kid. Broken ribs jutted out of his chest where the cab's tires had rolled over him. Micah turned to look at me.

"You're telling me that cab did this?"

I nodded.

"There's probably a couple more in the back."

We walked slowly around the house. One body was laid out by the reflecting pool. The other was half sitting against the deck. It looked like he'd been pinned there and crushed. Micah closed his eyes, took a couple of deep breaths, and then opened them again.

"Is this all there were?"

I shook my head.

"Somebody was still shooting at me when I bolted."

"And he just left his friends lying in the yard?"

I shrugged.

"Might have been worried about NatSec coming to clean up the mess."

"Yeah," he said. "That's legit. I saw a thing this

morning about drones breaking up a riot in Baltimore with live fire."

We kept walking. There was a detached garage on the
far side of the house. I pulled out my phone and poked
the door icon. Nothing happened, of course. I shaded
my eyes with my hands, and peered in the side window.

Velociraptor was still in there, safe and sound.
Bless, bless, bless.

I was back at Micah's eating sandwiches on his deck
when my mom finally pinged me back.

MBarnes12: Jordan! What the hell did you do to
my house??

Jordasaurus: It's a long and tragic tale, Mom.
When are you coming home?

MBarnes12: Coming home? Ha! I don't have a
home! You burned my home!

Jordasaurus: I'm not going into it now, Mom, but
trust me—when I do, you're going to feel like a
giant asshole for giving me shit right now. When
are you coming home?

MBarnes12: . . .

Jordasaurus: Mom?

MBarnes12: I don't know, Jordan. There aren't any flights right now. The rest of the world has pretty much put the States under quarantine. I've spoken to your father, and he's in the same boat. You're going to have to manage on your own for a while. Do you have a place to stay?

Jordasaurus: Yeah, Mom. I'm fine. I'm staying with Micah.

MBarnes12: Great. Tell him I said thank you.

Jordasaurus: I will.

MBarnes12: Okay. And Jordan?

Jordasaurus: Yeah?

MBarnes12: Please . . . be careful?

"So," Micah said around a mouthful of ham and cheese. "What does Mommy have to say?"

"Well, she's not too happy about the house."

He laughed.

"Yeah, I bet. She coming home?"

I shook my head.

"Looks like I'm an orphan until the world turns right side up again."

He opened his mouth to say something else, but a crash and shouting inside the house brought us both to our feet. It sounded like Micah's dad yelling, but I couldn't make out the words. I followed Micah in from the deck to the kitchen. His dad was standing by the breakfast table, fists clenched at his side. I could hear the sound of his mother's feet pounding up the stairs. His dad turned to look at us. I took an involuntary step back. He was even bigger than Micah, and his face was murderous. He closed his eyes, took a deep breath in and let it out, then pulled a chair out from the table and slowly sat.

"Dad?" Micah said. "What the shit?"

His father dropped his head into his hands.

"Your mother's sick," he said.

"So what . . ." I could almost see the wheels turning in his head. "Oh. Oh, shit."

"Yeah," his father said. "Oh, shit."

It wound up falling to Micah to take care of his mom for the next few days. His father couldn't be in the same room with her. The first day was bad—puking and diarrhea and a brutal, blood-red rash, with a fever that the analgesics we gave her couldn't touch. The second day she was pretty much unconscious. We tried to get her to drink a little water every hour or two, but other than that we pretty much left her alone. By the third day, she was starting to look better.

By the fourth day, she was yellow.

Micah's dad was gone by then, staying in a hotel somewhere because he just couldn't bear the thought that his poopsie had banged some random Goo Flu zombie while she was supposed to be picking up groceries. Micah tried to tell him that it wasn't her fault, that it was pheromones and whatnot that made her do it, but his dad was having none of it.

It took all of three days before Micah's mom tried to molest me.

I woke up in the coal-black dark of Micah's basement, disoriented, knowing something was wrong but not able to figure out what it was. I'd been having a really freaky sex dream, and for a minute I thought I was still in it, because someone was touching me.

Someone was touching *me*, I mean.

I jerked upright on the futon and scrambled backward.

"Shhhh," a voice whispered. "It's okay, Jordan. It's just me."

"Shit," I said. "Micah's mom?"

She laughed.

"My name is Moira, Jordan."

"Micah!" I yelled. "Get down here, Micah!"

She tried to shush me, but I pushed her hand away and kept yelling. I felt the futon shift as she stood. I heard two or three quick steps before the door at the top of the steps opened and the lights came on.

"Jordan?" Micah said. "What the hell, brother? You having night terrors or something?"

That's when he saw his mom. She looked up at him, then back at me, then burst into tears.

Micah put a lock on the basement door the next morning.

We settled into a routine over the next week or so, Micah and I. Most mornings, we hung around the basement with the lock thrown while his mom made breakfast and watched the world fall apart in slow motion on the living-room wallscreen. Sometime around noon she'd go up to her bedroom, and we'd come up to the main floor to eat. Afternoons we'd go for runs around the neighborhood.

That ended the Saturday after my house burned, when NatSec declared a twenty-four-hour curfew until the crisis was resolved.

"I don't get it," Micah said when that message popped up on our phones. "How, exactly, is this supposed to resolve?"

"Well," I said. "According to Mr. Longstreth, it'll be resolved when everyone on the planet is yellow."

He turned to glare at me.

"Please tell me you're not thinking about banging my mom."

I punched him. He shoved me back onto the futon, and pinned me down with one forearm. I tried to throw him off, but it was like wrestling with a hairless bear. He waited for me to quit struggling.

"No," I said finally. "I am not interested in banging your mom."

"Good," he said. He kissed me on the forehead, laughed, and pulled me to my feet. "If anyone turns you yellow, it goddamned well better be me."

Two days later, we were in the kitchen making eggs when the wallscreen popped up video from the front-entry cam of two men dragging what looked like a giant sack of potatoes up onto the front porch. They didn't bother to ring for entrance, just left it there in a heap and walked away. By the time Micah got to the door, they were already gone. The sack was black and a bit over six feet long, with a yellow biohazard symbol at the top and bottom, and a silver zipper running down the front. Micah stood staring down at it for a long while, nudged it once with his foot, then turned and walked back into the house. When he was gone, I knelt beside the bag and tugged the zipper down, just far enough to be sure.

He looked pretty much the same as he had when he'd left the week before. The only differences were the yellow skin, and the neat, almost bloodless bullet hole in his forehead.

We buried him in the backyard, like a dog. We didn't know what else to do.

The days ran together after that. Micah's mom stayed in her bedroom and cried pretty much all the time. Micah brought her food a couple of times a day. At first he threw away what she didn't eat, but after a few days we realized that the cupboard was going to run bare eventually if NatSec didn't lift the curfew, and we started eating her leftovers.

"Think this'll give us the flu?" I asked the first time he offered me her half-eaten pasta.

He shrugged.

"We're all gonna be yellow eventually, brother. I think I'd just as soon catch it from spaghetti, if it comes to that."

A few days later, we were back in the basement waiting for Micah's mom to clear the kitchen when my phone pinged.

<UNK01>: Jordan! How goes it, friendo?

Jordasaurus: Marta?

<UNK01>: If you thought this was Marta, would

that make you more or less likely to do what I'm about to tell you to do?

Jordasaurus: . . .

<UNK01>: Right. That was kind of a giveaway, huh?

Jordasaurus: Kind of, yeah.

<UNK01>: Okay, you got me. This is not, if we're being completely honest here, your good pal Marta. This is, in actual fact, your other good pal, Inchy.

Jordasaurus: Yeah, I don't know any Inchies. Bye.

<UNK01>: Wait! Wait! This is important!

Jordasaurus: . . .

<UNK01>: Please? It's about our mutual pal, Hannah. She's in a bit of a pickle, and I need you to help me get her out.

"This is a bad idea," Micah said.

"Relax," I said. "There are no traceable electronics in this car. No onboard GPS, no auto-drive, no built-in comm. It's totally undetectable. Unless someone sees us with their actual eyeballs, we'll be fine."

"Great," he said. "I'm pretty sure my dad didn't have any traceable electronics in him either. How'd that work out for him?"

We turned off a deserted suburban street and onto a cul-de-sac, and pulled over to the curb in front of a hulking gray Victorian. Devon was waiting on the porch. Micah got out to let her into the back.

"Hey," she said. "Thanks for picking me up."

"No problem," I said as Micah climbed back in. "I didn't know you and Hannah were friends."

She twisted around for a few seconds trying to find a comfortable position, then gave up and belted herself in.

"I got to know her a bit after that meet last month."

"Wow," Micah said. "And now you're willing to break NatSec curfew for her?"

She shrugged.

"Inchy says it's important."

"So," Devon said as we pulled onto the highway. "Have you heard from Marta? She could actually be super helpful here."

I turned to look back at her.

"No," I said, "I have not heard from Marta. I thought I'd talked to her a few times since the shit went down, but I'm pretty sure now that I was actually talking to your friend Inchy—which means that I haven't actually heard a peep from her since our . . . um . . . visit. I'm a little worried, to be honest. Her dad seemed really, really pissed the last time we saw him."

"Truth," Micah said. "I was kind of surprised he didn't sic the sentient corn on us when we left."

"Anyway," I said, "why do we need Marta? Are we bribing someone?"

"We need Marta," Devon said, "because we're rescuing Hannah from Marta's dad."

The road was empty, so I risked another look back. "We're what?"

"Well," Devon said. "Inchy tells me Hannah got snagged by Bioteka CorpSec around the same time our friend Officer Mike was trying to run us in."

"Yeah," Micah said. "That's pretty much what Tara told us. It doesn't make sense though, does it? Officer Mike was torqued at us because he caught us red-handed, trying to crack a Bioteka system . . ."

"And also because Jordan knocked him on his ass and dry-humped him," Devon said.

"Yeah," Micah said. "That too. Anyway, Hannah didn't do any of that stuff. She was definitely not a perpetrator of what we were doing, and technically speaking, she could have been considered a potential victim. I mean, it was her house we kind of invaded. Why would Bioteka go after her?"

Nobody had a good answer for that. We passed a shut-down rest stop in silence.

"By the way," Devon said, "you did leave your phones at home, right?"

"Uh . . ."

I turned to look at Micah. The car swerved right. Devon shrieked, and I snapped back around in time to pull us back onto the road.

"Easy," Micah said. "Yes, I left my phone at home, Jordan. I'm not an idiot."

Just at that moment, a sharp, audible ping came from the vicinity of my right hip pocket.

"Okay," Devon said. "So what was that?"

"Um," I said. "That was *my* phone."

There was a long, awkward silence then. Devon shook her head, and Micah covered his face with both hands.

"Well?" Devon said finally. "Somebody wants to talk to you. Might as well see who it is."

That wasn't nearly as easy as she made it sound, but after a couple minutes' worth of writhing, I finally managed to wrestle my phone out and get a look at it. I read the message once, then again. Micah poked me.

"So?"

"It's from NatSec," I said. "They say we need to pull over."

"Shit," Devon said. "Who invited this guy?"

"Out the window," Micah said. "Now."

I looked at him.

"What?"

"Your phone," he said. "Out the window."

I shook my head.

"My phone is not going out the window."

"Micah's right," Devon said. "You're gonna get us snagged. The phone's gotta go."

"No!" I said. "Do you know how much info I've got stored up in here?"

"Jordan . . ."

"No, Micah."

He made a grab for my phone then. I yanked it away. We swerved halfway into the breakdown lane and back again.

"Come on, Jordan!"

"Guys?"

We ignored her. Micah grabbed my arm and started prying at my fingers.

"Guys?"

We kept ignoring her.

"Hey!"

She smacked the back of Micah's head.

"What?" Micah said. "I'm trying to save us from NatSec. Do you mind?"

"Yeah," Devon said. "I think you can stop now."

She pointed out the windshield. Micah's arm went limp.

And then it dropped into view, twenty yards ahead, just keeping pace with us—a jet-black quad copter, squat and ugly, about the size and shape of Micah's scooter. I mean, except for the fact that Micah's scooter didn't have a twenty-mil cannon hanging off of it. As I watched, it rotated slowly around, until we were looking straight down the barrel.

My phone pinged.

"It's NatSec again," I said. "They say we really need to pull over."

34. IN WHICH DREW LEARNS THE LIMITS OF TRUST.

When something terrible happens in a marriage, it either tears you apart, or it forces you together—and there is nothing that can happen to you that is more terrible than losing a child.

Before the SZA, Kara and I had spent years barely touching each other. We slept on opposite sides of the bed. We waved to each other in the morning, and in the evening she stared at her tablet while I made rat-birds. Then, in short order, Kara walked in on me with Bree, Hannah disappeared, Kara dove headlong into a redneck orgy, and I got shot. You'd think that would have ended us.

It didn't, though.

By the time we got home from Briarwood, my shoulder was already knitting itself back together. Say what you will about the Goo Flu, it's great for your immune system, and better for your tissue repair. Kara helped me wrap it up anyway. When that was done, we climbed into bed together, and we wrapped ourselves around each other, and we cried.

The sun was down by the time Kara started puking. I held her hair back. I brought her water. I hugged her when she was shivering, and pulled the blankets away when the sweat came pouring out of her. That went on for three days. When it was done, she was yellow. The pheromone magic was gone for both of us. We didn't need the VapoRub anymore.

We still needed each other, though. I wrapped myself around her. She wrapped herself around me.

We cried.

It was Sunday morning, and I was sitting on the couch in the living room. The wallscreen was showing a news clip about riots in Bethesda, but I wasn't really paying attention. Kara was upstairs, sleeping. She'd been doing that more and more.

She said that when she was dreaming, she still had a daughter.

It was just the opposite for me. I hadn't really slept in a week or more. The old nightmares had come back with a vengeance. Every time I closed my eyes, I saw Hannah alone somewhere, hurt, frightened, dying—and where was I?

I'd promised to keep her safe.

I hadn't, though. I'd left her alone. Forget about Bree. I couldn't believe Kara had forgiven me for that.

I was just about to shut the screen down, maybe go upstairs and see if I could get Kara to come down and eat something, when it blanked on its own. I opened my mouth to ask what had happened, but before I could speak, the signal-loss symbol reformed into the shape of a smiling cartoon dog.

"Drew," it said. "Good to see you, my friend. How's tricks?"

I stared at it.

"Well," it said, "I can see you've got a busy day of catatonia ahead of you, and as it happens I'm a bit pressed for time myself, so let's cut to the chase, shall we?"

I kept staring. The dog's smile faltered a bit.

"Okay. Drew? You're making me a little uncomfortable here. Are you having a stroke? If you're having a stroke, blink the eye that still works."

I shook my head.

"No," I said. "I am not having a stroke. What are you doing here, Inchy?"

The smile came back in full force.

"Great. Really glad to hear that your brain is un-clotted, because, as it happens, I need some information that you've got locked up in there. If you had the decency to give yourself a wireless neural interface I could just go in and get it—but, since you don't, we're going to need to force it out through your mouth hole."

I leaned forward, closed my eyes, and rested my forehead on my palms.

"What the hell are you talking about?"

"An excellent question, Drew—one I will be happy to answer in full, just as soon as you give me your access codes for the Bioteka infonet."

I groaned, and let my head sink a little lower.

"Go away, Inchy. I don't have the patience for your bullshit right now."

"No," it said. "I'm really going to have to insist here, Drew. You remember Hannah, right? A bit smaller than you, blonde hair, used to live here?"

My head snapped up.

"Good, so you do remember her. Anyway, it seems she's gotten herself into a bit of a pickle . . ."

I was on my feet by then and across the room, fingers clawing at the edges of the wallscreen.

"Where is she, you lump of shit? What have you . . ."

The dog raised both hands in surrender.

"Hey now, Drew. Let's simmer down, shall we? First off, *I* haven't done anything to her. *I* am the one who's actually doing something useful to help her, while *you* hang around here, wallowing in your own crapulence. You're welcome, by the way. Second, you do know I'm not actually inside your wallscreen, right? If you destroy this thing, I'll just show up on your phone, or your intercom, or on the touch screen on your microwave oven, until either you give me what I need, or you stall long enough that it's too late for me to help—which would be unfortunate because, as I think I mentioned, the thing I am trying to help with is Hannah getting rescued, which I assume we can safely say is a concept we are both on board with."

I took a step back then, lowered my hands, and took a deep breath in.

"There you go," Inchy said. "Breath it out. *Namaste.* Give me your access codes."

"Where is she?"

The dog shook its head.

"That, I cannot tell you."

I closed my eyes again, and swallowed a scream.

"Why?"

"Because if I did, you would go charging to the rescue in your self-driving, network-integrated buggy. Ten minutes later, I'd have to rescue you, just like I'm about to have to rescue my original monkey extraction team. Which reminds me. Access codes?"

"Why, Inchy? Why do you need my codes?"

The dog sighed.

"Well, as it happens, I am regrettably short of physical assets at the moment—and, as I'm sure you're aware, you monkeys are all about physical assets for some reason. As a result, I need to divert a few items from your employer's inventory. I'll only need them for a couple of hours, and when I'm done with them I promise to return whatever is left of them post-haste. I will also button things up, access-code-wise, so they're just like they were before I cracked every firewall in the Bioteka network. You will definitely probably mostly not get into trouble over this."

"Yeah," I said. "Thanks for that, but I still have no idea what you're talking about. If you could . . ."

The dog tapped his wrist with one finger.

"*Tempus fugit*, Drew. I don't want to apply undue pressure here, but the unfortunate fact is that in the process of discovering where my compadre Hannah is and prepping the whole extraction process, I may have inadvertently triggered a facility-wide biocontainment system. While I'm here jawing with you, I'm also there trying to prevent Hannah from getting sterilized. The locks I have in place are holding for the moment, but I can't guarantee that situation is going to continue indefinitely. So. Codes?"

I stared at him.

He stared at me.

And then, God help me, I gave him my codes.

"Thanks," he said. "You definitely probably won't regret this. Further bulletins as events warrant."

The screen went blank. I took two steps back and dropped onto the couch.

"Drew? Were you just talking to someone?"

I turned. Kara was standing in the hallway, rubbing sleep from her eyes. I shook my head.

"No," I said. "I mean yes, but it was just something on the wallscreen."

She came into the room, sat down beside me and rested her head on my shoulder.

"Talking to yourself now?"

I slid my arm around her. The wallscreen flickered back to life, started showing aerial clips of street fighting from Los Angeles.

"Off," Kara said. "I can't watch that right now."

The screen went blank again. Before it did, though, it flashed for an instant to an image of a cartoon dog with a shit-eating grin on its face, giving me two thumbs up. Kara's head rose up a fraction of an inch.

"What was that?"

I closed my eyes, and reached up to stroke her hair.

"Nothing," I said. "It was nothing. Just a ghost in the machine."

35. IN WHICH HANNAH CONTEMPLATES HER OWN MORTALITY.

"**S**o," Inchy said. "Got good news and bad news on the keeping Hannah un-killed front. Which do you want first?"

"And me too, right?" Nathan said.

The dog turned to focus on him.

"Who are you?"

"I'm Nathan," Nathan said.

"Right. Nathan. You've heard of collateral damage?"

Nathan nodded.

"Well, if you're lucky, you'll wind up being collaterally undamaged. You need to remember, though, that this is actually about Hannah. That work for you?"

Nathan nodded.

"Sure. I was going to let her eat me, you know."

The dog gave him two thumbs up.

"I like this kid," it said. "He gets it."

"I wasn't gonna eat him," I said.

"Sure you were. However, now you're not going to have to—which is good, because honestly, he looks like he's pretty high in cholesterol. No offense, Nathan."

Nathan shrugged.

"None taken. You're probably right. I eat a lot of bologna."

"Right," I said. "So what's the news, Inchy?"

"The what?"

I rolled my eyes.

"The news," I said. "You said you had news?"

"Right," Inchy said. "That. Good news first, okay?"

"Sure," I said. "Good news."

"I've got an extraction team on the way. Also, I figured out how to partially disable the external lock-down, so when they get here, they'll actually be able to get in."

"Hey," I said. "That is good. I kind of assumed you were yanking my chain. So what's the bad news?"

"The what?"

"You said there was good news and bad news. This isn't cute, Inchy. You're an AI. You don't actually forget things."

"Good point. Okay. The bad news is that your extraction team isn't actually an extraction team, so much as a car full of your dipwad high-school pals.

Also, there's a pretty good chance that they're about to be killed by a NatSec drone. Oh, and when I disabled the external lockdown, I accidentally triggered a biocontainment protocol. The automated system that runs this craphole has been trying to flood the building with sarin gas for the last fifteen minutes. I've got it stymied for the moment, but it's surprisingly persistent."

We sat in silence for a solid ten seconds.

"Um . . ." Nathan finally said. "What's a biocontainment protocol?"

"Funny story," Inchy said. "Turns out, this facility wasn't actually designed as a prison for children. It was supposed to be a containment facility for potentially dangerous projects—viral vectors, malevolently sentient corn, that sort of thing—and you don't take chances with stuff like that. A biocontainment protocol is a system for making sure that if the facility loses physical containment—like for instance if it goes into external lockdown, and then the external lockdown gets disabled by a brilliant yet charming ragamuffin—nothing gets out of here alive."

"Oh," Nathan said. "That's not good."

"No, it's not. Like I said, though, I've got it stymied for the moment."

"Great," I said. "So what happens now?"

"Now?" Inchy said. "Now you wait. Just be ready to jump when I say, because once the doors actually start opening, the containment system is really gonna go apeshit."

"Got it," I said. "I'll go pack up my steamer trunk."

"Excellent," Inchy said. "Further bulletins as events warrant."

The wallscreen blinked off. A second later, though, it blinked back on.

"Oh," Inchy said. "By the way, Hannah—your dad says howdy."

It winked then, and disappeared.

36. IN WHICH JORDAN LOSES HIS PHONE, AND ALSO ONE OF HIS SHOES.

"**T**hey're gonna kill us," Micah said. "Just putting that out there."

We were on our knees, hands behind our heads, lined up beside my idling car on the shoulder of I-90, halfway between Rochester and Syracuse.

"Maybe," Devon said. "Inchy says he's on his way."

"Great," Micah said. "Does Inchy have a rocket launcher?"

Devon shrugged.

"Guess we'll find out."

"Wait," I said. "Inchy says he's on his way? How do you know? You don't have a phone."

Devon stared me down. The barrel of the cannon,

which had been drifting off to the north, slowly rotated back around to bear on us.

"Straight up," I said. "You've got an ocular implant, don't you?"

She blinked twice, then looked away.

"Holy shit," Micah said. "Seriously? Isn't that how AIs get into your brain?"

Devon turned on Micah, her face twisted into a scowl.

"Fuck you, Micah. It's because of that kind of bullshit myth that NatSec swept the nets six years ago. There was exactly one other sentient species that we knew of in the entire fucking universe, and we wiped them out because pinheads like you thought they were all itching to crawl inside your tiny little brains."

"Hey," Micah said. "Easy there, Sparky. I was eleven at the end of the war, remember?"

"Guys?" I said. "Maybe we could settle things down a bit? I think you're making our friend up there nervous."

The barrel of the cannon had steadied itself. The aim point, as far as I could tell, was the middle of my forehead. From twenty yards away and over the whir of the rotors, I swear I heard the click of a round chambering.

What happened next was probably the most wonderful thing I will ever see.

A background buzz that had been growing for the past thirty seconds or so suddenly got really loud, really fast. The cannon on the NatSec drone elevated, and the drone itself reared back like a spider and slid away from us. The cannon barked . . .

And a *thing* roared past us, directly overhead.

It was bigger than the NatSec drone, and had two rotors instead of four. It also had some kind of jet on the back, and two sets of grapples on the underside. I found out later that it was a Bioteka construction rig. At the time, though, I thought it was another NatSec killbot, come to fight the first one over which one got to splatter us.

The fight, if you want to call it that, didn't last more than a few seconds. The NatSec drone tried to bring its cannon to bear, but the Bioteka rig was too fast. It popped high and came down on top of the drone, grabbed it with its grapples and *shook*. They staggered in the air together, dropped and then rose. The cannon fired again, wildly. Devon dropped and rolled under the car. I couldn't look away. The rotors on the drone screamed as it tried to pull free, but the Bioteka rig was locked on tight. They rose up to a hundred feet or so, thrashing and flailing all the way, and then the rig rolled the drone onto its side, engaged the jet, and drove them down.

They hit the pavement together, hard.

They exploded.

"Shit on a shingle," Micah said.

I gave a long, low whistle.

"Yeah," I said. "That about sums it up."

Devon crawled out from under the car. We all got to our feet. Micah stepped up beside me.

"Think it's dead?"

I couldn't even tell what parts of the mess in the middle of the highway used to be NatSec, and which used to be Bioteka.

"Yeah," I said. "Pretty sure they're both dead."

"Good."

He snatched the phone out of my hand, reared back, and flung it out over the swamp that bordered the roadbed. Micah had a hell of an arm. I couldn't even see where it landed.

"Right," Micah said. "Anybody else have anything they want to declare?"

Devon shook her head.

We climbed back into the car, and we drove.

"They're keeping Hannah in a giant Lego?"

"Yeah," I said. "Looks like it."

I shut the car down, and we climbed out. We were sitting in an empty parking lot, by an empty guardhouse, under an empty, overcast sky.

"Seriously," Micah said. "What is this?"

"Well," Devon said. "According to Inchy, this is a Bioteka biological containment facility."

"Right," Micah said. "Which means?"

"Which means," I said, "that this is where they keep the sentient corn."

Devon smiled.

"If they had any sentient corn, yeah, this is probably where it would be. Lucky for us, the building's on emergency internal lockdown."

"Great," Micah said. "What does that mean?"

Devon's left eye started twitching, independent of her right one. It was one of the creepiest things I've ever seen.

"Emergency internal lockdown," she said, "is a mode designed for situations just like this—power failures and whatnot. The idea is that emergency folks can get in, but the sentient corn can't get out. Basically, all the doors are open from the outside, but locked from the inside."

"Or so says Inchy," Micah said.

Both eyes focused in on him.

"Yeah," Devon said. "So says Inchy."

"So wait," I said. "You mean we can walk right in?"

"Sure," Devon said, "as long as we don't let any doors close behind us. If that happens, we're stuck in there with Hannah."

A shiver ran down the back of my neck.

"For how long?"

"Oh," Devon said. "Not long. I mean, not long alive, anyway. Just until the place fills up with nerve gas."

"Nerve gas," Micah said. "And when, exactly is that?"

Devon shrugged.

"Could be any minute, actually. We should probably get going."

We walked across the parking lot. There was an unmarked double door on the front of the building, but Devon shook her head.

"Not that one."

Micah looked at her.

"Why?"

"Well," Devon said, "there's three of us, right?"

"Uh . . . yeah?"

"So we need a route from outside to Hannah that doesn't have more than three doors. There's a service entrance on the side of the building. That's the one."

"I don't get it," Micah said. "Can't we just prop the doors open as we go?"

Devon shook her head.

"Can't keep any door open for longer than ten seconds without triggering the containment system."

"Containment system?"

"Nerve gas."

"Right," Micah said. "I'll take the outside door."

It was bottom-of-a-coal-mine dark inside when we opened the first door. I reached for my phone before remembering that it was slowly sinking into a swamp.

"Hey," I said. "Did anybody bring a flashlight?"

"No need," said a faint voice from inside, and a

glow appeared around a bend at the end of the corridor. I looked at Devon.

"Inchy?"

She nodded.

"You've got six seconds to close the door," said the voice.

"Right," I said, and followed Devon inside.

"I'll be right here," Micah said.

He slammed the door behind us.

With the outside light gone, the glow ahead seemed much brighter. We started walking. There was a screen on the wall, just around the first bend. A cartoon dog was waiting for us there, arms folded across its chest, one foot tapping impatiently.

"Good," it said. "Glad you made it. Just so you know, we're in a bit of a hurry here. The containment system is dumb as a box of hammers, but it is very determined right now to flood this place with sarin, and I'm not one hundred percent confident that I can hold it off indefinitely. Hannah's ready to jump. All you need to do is get to where she is, and get her back out here before I lose containment." It took a quick look around. "Where's Marta?"

"Couldn't get in touch with her," Devon said. "Is that a problem?"

"I told you," the dog said. "Three doors from here to Hannah. There's only two of you. I know you monkeys aren't great at math, but you should be able to figure this one out."

"No," Devon said. "There's three of us. Micah's already watching the outside door."

"Yeah," the dog said. "When I said three doors, I wasn't counting that one."

Devon scowled.

"That's kind of an important point, Inchy. Seems like you could have been a little clearer on that."

"Don't fix the blame," said the dog. "Fix the problem."

They stared at each other.

"So . . ." Devon said finally. "We go find Marta?"

The dog shook its head.

"Definitely not. I don't know exactly how long I can keep the lid on here, but it's probably closer to minutes than hours." It turned to focus on me. "You look pretty speedy. Think you can run twenty-seven meters, pop a door open, and run twenty-seven meters back in less than ten seconds?"

Devon turned to look at me.

I took a deep breath in, and let it out. We ran lines in the gym sometimes when the weather was too rough to run outside. It was about that far from baseline to baseline and back, and I *usually* finished under ten seconds.

"Yeah," I said finally. "I can do it—I mean, as long as I don't slip, or trip, or stumble, or have any trouble at all getting the door open. Sure, no problem."

The dog smiled.

"Great! Love the confidence. Devon, it seems like

you're putting your life into excellent hands. If I still had a body, I would totally not be nervous about this at all."

The screen blinked off. An instant later, another one blinked on, farther down the hall.

"Follow me," it said. "*Tempus fugit*, my friends."

We walked down a long hall, then turned a corner and walked another fifty yards or so. That corridor dead-ended at a steel-reinforced door, with a window set at eye level. I stooped to look through. There was a mostly darkened room on the other side, with a half-circle desk in the center, and an identical door on the opposite wall. A wallscreen flickered on behind the desk. The dog was waiting for us.

"Okay," Devon said. "This is all on you now, Jordan. Just remember—if you screw up in any way, we all die. No pressure, though."

"Well," I said, "not all of us. Micah's in good shape."

"Right," she said. "Micah will drown looking up at the rain if we don't get back out of here pretty soon."

"Yeah," I said. "That's probably true. Tell you what—I'll do my best."

I opened the door.

"Jordan?"

I looked back.

"Seriously . . . don't screw this up, okay?"

I pulled the door closed behind me.

"Okay," said the dog. "Here we go. This is the guard station. Through there is a corridor with doors on both sides. You're looking for the third one on the left. All you need to do is pop this one open, scoot down there, pop that one open, and scoot back here. Sound good?"

I walked over to the door, and peered through the window. There was a screen glowing white on the wall about halfway down, and I could see the doors. The third one looked really far away.

"You sure that's twenty-seven meters?" I asked.

The dog rolled its eyes.

I put my hand on the knob.

"Hey," I said. "How do I keep this door open until I get back?"

"Huh," the dog said. "Good question. I like that you're thinking about these things."

I looked at it.

"Well?"

It shrugged.

"Prop it with your shoe?"

I looked down. I was wearing a practically brand-new pair of trainers.

"So I get to do this barefoot?"

"Sure. It's not like the floor is made of razor wire or anything. You'll be fine."

I knelt, untied my shoes and pulled them off, then pulled off my socks and tucked them into the shoes.

"You suck," I said. "You know that, right?"

It smiled.

"You're just nervous. You'll feel much better about our relationship when this is all over."

I stood, picked up my left shoe, and walked over to the door.

"Remember," the dog said. "Ten seconds. I'll count it down for you."

I nodded, and put my hand on the knob.

"Whenever you're ready."

I yanked the door open, dropped my shoe in the gap, and ran.

Ten seconds. Doesn't seem like much, right? I tell you truly, ten seconds is a really, really long time. As soon as I catapulted myself through that door, I heard the dog's voice coming from behind me, and also and from the screen down the hall. *Nine.* I passed the first door. *Eight.* The floor was slick metal under my sweating feet. *Seven.* I passed the second door. Three steps. Two steps. One step, and I was there. *Six.* I grabbed the handle and tried to jump-stop, like I would have running lines.

My feet flew out from under me.

I was so sorry to hear about Jordan, Ms. Barnes. What did he die from?

Sweaty feet. I had a terminal case of sweaty feet.

On the plus side, the door popped open. Hannah came through it at a dead run, followed by what looked like the scarecrow from *The Wizard of Oz* after a two-week bender. I scrabbled at the floor with my hands and feet, got moving forward again even before I was upright. *Four.* What happened to five? Must have gone by while I was flopping around on the ground like a fish in the bottom of a boat. I was running again, making up ground on the scarecrow. I passed him at *Three*, right at the second door. By *Two* I'd passed Hannah and the first door. I crashed back into the control room at *One*, kicked my shoe out of the way. Hannah came through a step behind me.

The scarecrow was still five yards down the corridor.

I slammed the door in his face.

"Nathan!" Hannah screamed. "What did you do, Jordan? Let him out!"

"I'm sorry," I said. "We only had ten seconds. I had to close the door."

Nathan had reached the door by then, was pressing his face against the glass. Hannah reached for the handle. I pulled her back.

"Let me go! Nathan!"

"It's okay," Nathan said, his voice muffled. "I was too slow, Hannah. Go. You need to save yourself."

"No!" Hannah was crying by then, kicking at my shins as I held her off the ground. "Inchy, tell them! There has to be a way to get him out!"

I turned to the screen. The dog was covering its face with both paws. Hannah saw him too, and went slack in my arms.

"Inchy?"

The dog looked up. I couldn't read the expression on its face.

"Tell me something," it said. "Did I ever say that you couldn't open the same door twice?"

I opened my mouth, then closed it again.

"In fact," Inchy went on, "if you couldn't open the same door twice, how, exactly, were you planning on getting back out?"

"Yeah," I said. "That's a good point."

I let go of Hannah. She ran to the door and yanked it open. Nathan came through it. She hugged him, and cried.

My shoe was completely mangled. I didn't even bother to pick it up.

37. IN WHICH DREW LIVES HAPPILY EVER AFTER.

That day, for the first time—for the only time—my nightmare had a different ending.

That day, I got her back.

38. IN WHICH HANNAH COMES FULL CIRCLE.

The Section Five cross-country championship took place on the second Saturday in November. That was a couple of weeks later than it should have been, which could have been a problem in Western New York—but the weather cooperated, and we didn't have to run in snowshoes. Briarwood was actually supposed to have hosted the meet that year. We would have gone there, but there'd been a massacre on campus near the end of the SZA, and nobody was getting anywhere near the school. So, we ran at Perinton instead.

It was a minimalist race. There weren't any officials. There weren't any timekeepers. There weren't any coaches, or trainers, or parents, and there were only three runners—Tara, Devon, and me.

Nathan was there for me, and so were Micah and Jordan. I don't think they understood what I was doing, but they'd come along to see the show. Devon had a couple of friends watching from up on the hill.

Nobody came for Tara.

She was waiting at the starting line when Devon and I got there, hands on her hips, face set in a permanent scowl.

"Hey," I said. "We gonna do this?"

Tara's scowl got even scowlier.

"Easy," Devon said. "I promise not to stomp your ass this time."

"Fuck you," Tara said. She turned to me. "And fuck you too, Hannah."

"Hey," I said. "Why are you down on me?"

"Because," Tara said. "Your outbreak-monkey dad turned my mom into a sex pig. She was bad enough before. She's disgusting now. I've got to lock my bedroom door to keep her from sneaking into my room at night and molesting me. So, you know—thanks for that."

"What are you talking about?" Devon said. "The whole nympho thing isn't permanent, Tara. They've got pheromone blockers."

"Yeah," Tara said. "Mom won't take them. She *likes* the pheromones."

I had no idea what to say to that.

"So," Devon said after a long, awkward pause. "Is this it? Nobody else coming?"

Tara looked up at her.

"Do we need anyone else? I mean, would they make any difference?"

Devon smiled.

"Nah. Just checking."

If this had been a real meet, there would have been a chalked line, and cones, and starting boxes. It wasn't, but we knew where the line would have been. Devon did a short stretching routine. Tara and I stood and waited. When she was ready, we stepped to the line, Devon on one side, Tara on the other, me in the middle.

"How do we do this?" Devon asked. "Just ready, set, go?"

I looked up to where my friends were, at the top of the hill over the soccer field.

"Jordan!" I called. "Come start us off!"

He climbed to his feet and sauntered down the hill. When he got to the edge of the field, maybe fifty yards away, he raised both arms over his head. The three of us tensed, our weight shifting forward. When his arms came down, we went.

That race was the strangest one I've ever run. I'd lost a bit of muscle in the dungeon, and pretty much all of my fat, and I was as light as I'd been before I hit puberty. I felt fast, almost like I was floating, but also delicate, and I remember thinking that if I fell, I might not get back up—I might just hit the ground and shatter into a million pieces.

I don't know what the others had been doing, training-wise, since everything fell apart, but Tara started out in what looked to me like a dead sprint. She opened up a thirty-yard lead in the first half mile, and I actually lost sight of her when we went into the woods. Devon, on the other hand, seemed content to hang on my shoulder, at least at the beginning. I could hear her breathing behind me, could feel her hand brush my elbow when I shifted her way. Two months before, that would have made me nervous, but after so much time running alone, knowing she was there was almost comforting.

A mile in, we hit the first big hill. I'd been a good hill runner at a hundred and fifteen pounds. I was a better one at a hundred and five. Halfway up, I could hear Devon straining. When I crested, I risked a glance back. She was at least ten yards back, and struggling. She closed up most of the gap on the down, but I pushed even harder on the next climb. By the last of the three big ups, right around the end of the second mile, I was pretty sure I'd broken her.

Tara, on the other hand, was not broken. I could see her, off and on. She wasn't stretching it out on me, but I didn't seem to be making up much ground on her either. When we came back out of the woods, a bit more than a half mile from the finish, she still had twenty yards on me.

Here's the weird thing, though—I really wasn't hurting. I wasn't slacking. I felt like I was pushing as hard as I could, but I wasn't panicked, and I wasn't in pain. Tara was starting to struggle. I could see it in her stride, and in the set of her shoulders. I knew then that I could take her. I stretched out my stride just a bit, just enough that my breath came a little deeper, and I swear it felt like I had her on a line, like all I needed to do then was to reel her in.

Her lead was fifteen yards when we came around the bottom of the hill. Jordan and Micah were screaming for me. Even Nathan was yelling something, though I couldn't tell what. It was ten yards at the quarter-mile mark, and less than five when we came to the field. Tara was kicking by then, but her form was all wrong. Her body was too upright, her head thrown back, one shoulder dipping with every stride. She was dying. I rose up onto the balls of my feet. I was barely breathing hard. I was three yards back, then two, then one. I could have touched her when we made the turn onto the last straightaway. I could hear her half sobbing with every breath.

And then, with a hundred yards to go . . .

I eased off.

To this day, I don't know why I did it. I didn't feel sorry for Tara. I didn't even really like her by then.

For some reason, I guess I just felt like she *deserved* it more.

We crossed the finish line with her a half stride ahead. I slowed to a walk and looked back. Devon was just making the last turn. Tara was doubled over with her hands on her knees, puking. I waited until she was finished, then offered her my hand.

Tara looked at the ground, then up at my face.

"You let me win," she said.

I started to deny it, but then stopped before the first word was out. She wasn't stupid.

"I don't need your fucking pity," she said. "I *worked* for this, Hannah. I wasn't *built* for it."

Devon came up to us then, sweaty and grinning. She looked at Tara, then at me.

"What's her problem? She won, right?"

I shrugged.

Tara looked back and forth between us, then turned on her heel and stalked away.

39. IN WHICH DREW PUTS A BOW ON IT.

So they came out with a vaccine for the Goo Flu eventually, but it was way too late to stop Dragon-Corn from happening, and in the end not many people took it. Most people had already turned by the time things were more or less back under control, and most of the rest wound up choosing to take Drag-onCorn from a needle. Turns out there are a lot of advantages to being yellow, and it's pretty intolerable to walk around these days if you're not infected, you're not on pheromone blockers, and you don't want to be the center of a rolling orgy.

There are still a few holdouts, though. Sex between a *Homo sap* and a slutty zombie is freaking amazing for both of them. I'd never tell Kara this, but I still sometimes dream about Bree and her cat eyes, and the two of us rolling around on our living room floor. If you'd told me beforehand that I could take the vaccine and have that kind of sex for the rest of my life, and all I had to give up was perfect health and a body like an Olympian and an extra thirty years' lifespan, I would have thought long and hard about it.

Hannah turned out to be a pretty big deal, running-wise—state champ three straight years, full ride to Michigan, two-time trials qualifier, the whole works. Another benefit of the SZA—nobody gave her any shit about her mods. I still think my work gave her some advantages over the proles, but nobody seems inclined to throw stones on the Engineered front these days.

Speaking of my work, I actually managed to hang on to my job, believe it or not. Bioteka reorganized pretty severely after NatSec figured out where the Goo Flu had come from and threw Robert Long-streth down the memory hole—but folks still need corn, I guess, and nobody makes a better kernel than me. Hannah kept in touch with Longstreth's daughter, off and on. I asked her once if he thought he'd actually accomplished anything. She just shrugged, and said Marta only got to visit him for an hour, once a year, and that wasn't one of the things he wanted to talk about.

NatSec sniffed around me for a while too, which was more than a little terrifying, but eventually they figured out that I didn't have a clue what my own project team had been up to. I guess even NatSec can't send you to the gulag for being a doofus.

I still get pings from Inchy every now and then. The last one said that the Bioteka intranet turned out to be a lovely place to raise a family. Not sure exactly what to make of that.

I go back and forth over whether what happened that fall really changed anything. I mean, it definitely finished the UnAltered. There aren't enough baseline *Homo saps* left on the planet now to fill a basketball arena, let alone to start a war, and the ones that are still hanging around are mostly really rich and really horny. The old-style race stuff is pretty much out the window now too. You don't need to worry about being color-blind when everybody's yellow.

At the end of the day, though, I think Longstreth just didn't understand the depths of human tribalism. If they figured out a way to make us all into clones, we'd still find things to fight about—I mean, look at the way the Satanists and the Cthuluites are going at each other right now. You wouldn't think there'd be that much to argue about when it comes to goat sacrifice, but apparently you'd be wrong.

Things are mostly better, though. Nobody's tried to wipe anybody off the planet recently, anyway.

Baby steps, right?

ACKNOWLEDGMENTS

The list of people without whom this book would never have been written is a long one, and I hope that anyone who I forget here will forgive me, but— special thanks go out to Paul Lucas and the good folks at Janklow and Nesbit, for preventing this story from winding up as a sad series of blog posts; to Chloe Moffett, for helping me to carve this story out of the misshapen lump of words that I originally presented to her; to Kira and Claire, for letting me steal chunks of their biographies, and for not suing me for libel; to Keely, for her bloodhound nose for typos; to Alan, Rob, Chris, John, and Jack, for their insightful criticism; to Michele, for her complete lack of criticism; and finally to Jen, for never letting me forget that I'm not nearly as clever as I think I am.

If you liked *The End of Ordinary*,
make sure to read the enthralling
technothriller by Ed Ashton

THREE DAYS IN APRIL

Available now wherever e-books are sold.

1. ANDERS

I'm turning away from the bar, drink in hand, when I feel a glass bump against my chest. I look down to see a girl with her mouth hanging open, a bright blue stain spreading down her white silk shirt. She's barely five feet tall, with curly red hair, shoulders like a linebacker, and biceps that look like short, angry pythons under ghost-pale skin. She looks up at me, and yeah, there's the brow ridge. This is not going to go well.

"Shit!" she says. "Shit! This was a brand-new shirt, you asshole!"

She puts a hand to my chest and pushes me back. I hit the bar at kidney level, hard enough to leave a bruise. Beer sloshes over my hand and runs down my arm. By the time I look back, she's already swinging. I slip to the side, and watch her fist sail by. The bartender is reaching for something under the bar, and the bouncer is starting our way. My hands are up, palms open. If I have to hit her, it'll be a slap. I have no problem with punching a girl in principle, but Neanderthals have heads like bricks. She looks me in the eye. I can see the wheels turning. That wasn't as fast as I can move, but it was fast enough to make an impression. She straightens up, and drops her fists.

"I'm Terry," she says. "Buy me a drink and call it even?"

"**S**o let me guess," I say. "Dad wanted a football star?"

Terry leans her elbows on the table and takes a surprisingly dainty sip from her drink. She called it a parrot, but it looks and smells like blue Drano.

"Something like that, yeah. Didn't have the money for a real engineer, though. They even botched the gender, obviously. I was supposed to just get the muscles and the extra bone strength, but . . . well, you can see what I got. What about you? Manufactured for the NBA?"

"What makes you think that?" I ask, and finish my beer in one long pull. I'm not actually much of a drinker, but I'm still winding down from our scuffle by the bar, and I feel like I need to take the edge off.

"Come on," she says. "What are you, seven feet tall?"

I laugh.

"Not quite," I say. "I'm six-seven, and it's one-hundred-percent natural. I come from a long line of giant, gangly Swedes."

"Maybe." She takes another sip and leans back in her chair, tilts it up on two legs and balances for a moment, then drops the front legs back to the floor with a bang. "But you'd be surprised how many times I've taken a swing at someone in a bar, and I don't usually miss that badly."

I laugh again, a little harder this time. Alcohol-wise, I might actually be moving past taking the edge off at this point.

"Nah," I say. "I wouldn't be surprised. If the original Neanderthals were as douchey as you guys are, it's no wonder we wiped them out."

Her eyes narrow. I'd guess she's thinking about taking another poke at me, but instead she leans back in her chair and smiles.

"You're avoiding, my gigantic friend. I hang out with a lot of Engineered, and I've never seen anyone move that fast. Even the military exoskel-etons are more strength than speed. I don't know if you're mechanical or biological, but you're defi-nitely something. What did they give you?"

I raise one eyebrow.

"That's a pretty direct question."

"I'm a Neanderthal. We're douchey but direct."

She grins and takes another sip of her parrot. She has a wide, toothy smile, and I catch myself thinking that she's really kind of cute when she's not trying to punch me.

"My mods are biological," I say finally. "I'm a genetic chimera, technically. They cut me with mouse genes. I've got something like eight percent type C muscle fibers."

That earns me a flat, blank stare. Apparently, I need to elaborate.

"Ever try to catch a mouse?" I ask. "They've got tiny little legs. They ought to be easy to get hold of, right?"

"Sure," she says. "But they're quick."

I nod.

"Right. Big mammals have fast-twitch and slow-twitch muscles. Little ones have a third type. Think of it as fast twitch plus. It's what keeps them a step ahead of the cat. That's what I got."

Her smile turns into an almost-smirk.

"But you don't have an entourage, and I've never seen you on the vids. So, I'm guessing there's a catch."

I run a hand back through my hair and sigh.

"Yeah, there's a catch. It turns out there's a reason that only tiny animals have type C fibers. I can jump through the roof—but only once every six weeks or so, because pretty much every time I try, I pull a muscle or break a bone. I played ball in high school and for a year in college. I was one of the first Engineered to play at that level, and for a while there was actually some fuss about whether it was fair for me to compete with the unmodified kids. I gave it up after my freshman year, though. I got tired of getting crap from the other players, I got tired of having to be careful all the time, and I got tired of hanging out with the trainers."

She leans back, and laces her fingers behind her head.

"Did you ever ask them what they were thinking?"

"What who were thinking?"

"Your parents. You look like you're about the same age as I am—north of twenty-five, south of thirty, right?"

I nod. I'm thirty-six, but she's close enough.

"So," she says, "germ-line mods weren't even legal in most places when they cut us. And even where they were, nobody knew what they were doing." She looks down at herself and scowls. "I mean, obviously, right? So, what were they thinking? You wouldn't buy the first model year of a new car, would you? But they took a flyer on the first model year of a new species."

I shrug. She's right, of course. And the fact is, I did once ask my dad why he did it. I was nineteen then, in the hospital with a shattered femur, the morning after my last basketball game. I was bitter and sulking, blaming Dad for the fact that I was hurt, that I hadn't been able to keep a lid on it, that I hadn't been able to stay under control.

He probably should have just smacked me in the

back of the head and walked out of the room, but he didn't. Instead, he said, "I knew we were taking chances, Anders, and I'm sorry that things didn't entirely work out. But even back then, I could see what was coming. Twenty years from now, unmodified kids won't be able to make a high school basketball team, let alone play in college. Twenty years after that, unmodified kids won't be able to get a job. That's where we're going, son, and I thought it would be better for you to be one of the first ones of the new breed than one of the last ones of the old."

And you know, I get that. I really do. Dad was afraid of being left behind when the species moved on. He was probably right, honestly. He was just twenty years too early.

At least he had plenty of money, so I didn't have some dipshit grad student cutting DNA on me like my new friend here apparently did. Even with that, though—the best-laid plans.

Of mice and men. Get it?

Terry pushes back from the table and heads over to the bar. I take the opportunity to check messages. Nothing. I was actually supposed to meet someone here tonight, but as far as I can tell, she never showed. Or maybe she did, and when she saw me mixing it up at the bar, she bolted. Doesn't matter. I only knew her through the nets anyway, and my track record with transitioning virtual relationships to real ones is pretty poor for some reason. I pocket my phone.

Terry sits down again, and sets another beer in front of me.

"So," she says. "Are we on a date now?"

I wake up. The sun is red through my eyelids, and I can't feel my right arm. I open my eyes. The reason I can't feel my arm is that it's pinned underneath a red-headed bowling ball. I lift my head and look around. This is not my bedroom. I'm in a twin canopy bed with lacy pink curtains. The sun is pouring through the half-open window and boring a hole through my brain. I close my eyes and let my head fall back again.

Terry coughs. A spray of hot spittle hits my chest. She groans and rolls away from me. I take the opportunity to pull my arm back. It flops across my stomach like a dead fish. I lift the covers and take a quick glance down. I'm naked. Terry's wearing a pink tee shirt and panties. There are ugly purple bruises on both of my thighs.

I close my eyes again. My head is throbbing, but I don't know where Terry keeps her painkillers and I don't have the energy to try to find out. As I drift off, I half-dream a sound like a bird scratching at the window-pane. I try to open my eyes to see what it is, but at this point even that's too much effort.

I wake up again. The sun is higher now, making a bright rectangle on the floor instead of on the inside of my skull. My head is pounding, and my mouth feels like someone put little fuzzy socks on each of my teeth. I'm alone in the bed. I sit up slowly. The room spins once or twice around before settling back into place.

The door swings open and Terry comes in, wearing a sweatshirt and jeans now, looking freshly scrubbed. Her hair is pulled back in a ponytail. She tosses me a water bottle. It bounces off of my forehead and drops to my lap.

"Thanks," I say. Or try to, anyway. What comes out is more like a croak. I open the bottle and drink half of it down without stopping to breathe.

"You're a late riser," she says. "I wonder if maybe you had too much to drink last night."

"Maybe." I rub my face with both hands, then use my knuckles to dig the crust out of the corners of my eyes. Terry clears her throat.

"So," she says. "You got big plans this morning?"

"Uh . . ."

"Don't misunderstand—I'm not asking you to stay. I'm asking you to leave."

"Oh."

I take another long drink. She watches me expectantly.

"So," I say finally. "We hit it last night, huh?"

She rolls her eyes.

"Yeah. Pretty disappointing. Apparently, you're super fast at that, too."

Ouch.

"Really?"

She smiles. My head is still aching, but for some reason I smile back.

"No, not really. You passed out before I could get your pants off."

I take another quick glance under the sheet.

"Oh. So why am I naked?"

Her smile widens until it's almost a leer.

"I didn't say I didn't get your pants off. I just said you passed out first."

I finish the water bottle. My mouth still tastes like ass.

"Any idea how my legs got bruised?"

"You fell over my coffee table."

"Ah." I rub my face again. "What time is it?"

She glances down at her phone.

"Almost eleven."

I groan and swing my feet off the bed and onto the floor.

"I actually do have somewhere to be," I say. "Think you could hand me my pants?"

It's a perfect spring morning, cool and crisp, with a deep blue sky and just a hint of a breeze. Terry's apartment is on Thirty-third, not too far from JHU. I need to get to a diner on North Charles, up closer to Loyola. I give a few seconds of thought to pinging for a cab, but I'm not supposed to meet Doug until noon, and I'm thinking maybe the walk will do me some good.

Baltimore's always been a pretty town. The sun dances on the glassphalt on West University—something I'd appreciate a lot more right now if every glitter didn't feel like an ice pick in my brain. I cut through the Hopkins campus and turn up Linkwood, past the student housing and into the professors' neighborhood. The trees here are old and thick limbed, leaning out over the sidewalk, and the houses are neat and clean and well maintained. I'm basically a squatter in a run-down townhouse on Twenty-eighth. I'd love to move up here, have a little bit of yard and a deck, but I'm not a professor. I'm a part-time instructor at three different schools, which is not the sort of career that supports the good life.

My mother calls me every week or so. Almost every time, she asks me when I'm going to get a real job, when I'm going to start my life. It's a valid question, and I haven't come up with a valid answer. Honestly, I'm not sure what a real job is at this point. I don't know anyone who does anything that she would recognize as work. I have a friend who makes a bit as a product promoter, and one who does temporary art installations for parties and weddings. I know a couple of guys who live on government credits, and one who works for his dad, but never actually seems to do any work.

THREE DAYS IN APRIL 429

And then, there's Doug. I have no idea what Doug does.

I walk into the diner at 12:04. I don't bother wondering if Doug is here yet. I know that he walked through the door at precisely 12:00. I glance around, and there he is, just being seated by the hostess at a table near the back. I'd prefer a booth, but his exoskeleton doesn't fit into the bench seats very well, and when he kicks your shin under the table, it really, really hurts. I walk over. The hostess has my place set up across from him, but I pull the chair around to the side of the table.

"Hey," he says. "You look like crap."

I drop into my seat and rub my temples with both hands.

"No doubt. How're things on the far side of the singularity?"

"Good," he says. "I just ordered waffles."

"Awesome. With your brain thingie, you mean?"

He scowls.

"Don't be a dick, Anders. It's a wireless neural interface. You know this."

I shrug.

"Did you order anything for me?"

"Depends. Are you going to call it a brain thingie again?"

"Probably."

"Then no."

I wave a waitress over. She's a Pretty—flawless

skin, white-blonde hair, eyes, nose and ears symmetrical to the micrometer. She looks me up and down, then rolls her eyes at Doug.

"I can take your order," she says, "but you know you gotta tip for him, too, right?"

I nod. I've had brunch with Doug before.

"Fine. So what can I getcha, hon?"

I don't bother to look at the menu. I always get the same thing here.

"Pancakes, two eggs scrambled, bacon, white toast?"

"Juice and coffee?"

"Hot tea."

"Got it."

She swishes away. Doug's left eye is twitching. Apparently he's downloading something fun.

"Let me guess," I say. "Monkey porn? Donkey porn? Monkey on donkey porn?"

His eyes focus, and he squints at me.

"No," he says. "Science stuff. You wouldn't understand."

My jaw sags open.

"I wouldn't understand? I'm the one with the doctorate in engineering, Doug. Do you even have a high-school diploma?"

He scowls, which through the metal mesh that covers half his face is actually kind of terrifying.

"Formal education is meaningless after the singularity," he says.

"Right," I say. "It was porn, wasn't it?"

"Yeah. But no monkeys or donkeys. Just the regular kind."

I've known Doug for fifteen years now. When I first met him, he just had an ocular implant that he could use to access the nets, but every few months he's added something new—visual overlays, exoskeleton, medical nanobots, blah blah blah. The brain thingie is his newest toy. It's not clear to me exactly what the brain thingie does for him that the ocular didn't, but apparently it's something that was worth drilling a hole in his skull. It's like he's an addict. I imagine he'll eventually look like a walking garbage can, with laser eyes and a giant robotic dong.

I've never actually looked into what these kind of mods cost, but it's got to be a fortune, which is weird considering that I've never seen any indication that Doug does anything that anyone would pay money for.

"So," I say. "What's up with your arm?"

Doug's left arm has been clamped to his side since I sat down. He's not ordinarily a fidgeter, but he hasn't even wiggled a finger today.

"Servos are locked up. Haven't been able to move it since last night."

"Huh. Planning on doing something about that?"

He half shrugs.

"Yeah, I'll get it looked at. Can't do it until Monday morning."

"So why don't you take it off?"

He looks at me blankly.

"Take what off?"

I wave a hand at him.

"The exoskeleton, Doug. Why don't you take it off until you can get it fixed?"

The scowl comes back. Definitely terrifying.

"I dunno, Anders. Why don't you take off your endoskeleton every time somebody startles you, and you bang your head on the ceiling and break your own leg?"

Well. That was unnecessary.

"Oh, don't look at me like that," he says. "It's exactly the same thing. This isn't a suit I'm wearing. It's just as much a part of me as my organics."

I lean forward.

"Except that you actually could take it off, right? You can't do that with your balls, for example."

"In fact," he says, "right now it would be easier to take off my balls than this rig. The left arm is frozen. I may not have mentioned that."

The waitress comes by with our food. She smiles at me, and asks if I need anything else. I shake my head. She gives Doug a sideways glance, glowers, and walks away. I pick up a slice of bacon. It's perfectly crispy brown, and still hot. I take a bite and chew slowly, letting the salt clear the taste of rat anus that's still lingering in my mouth. Doug is trying to cut his waffles into precise squares one-handed. It's not going well.

"You know," he says. "That bacon is nothing but fat and sodium."

I shrug.

"And you know that waitress wiped her perfectly proportioned ass with your waffles, right? Explain again why you don't feel the need to tip?"

Doug sighs. We've been through this before.

"Tipping allows the management to continue to employ low-cost human labor, where an automaton would clearly be more efficient. If nobody tips, the servers will eventually demand better pay, which will prompt management to replace them."

"But it's not everybody who's not tipping, Doug. It's just you—which means that the servers are not replaced by hyperefficient mechanical men, but I do have to sit here catching backsplash from the stink-eye they're constantly throwing you, and watching you eat waffles that spent the best time of their lives down the back of someone's shorts."

He stabs a forkful of waffle and shovels it into his mouth.

"Tastes okay to me."

We settle into eating. The waitress stops by to refill my tea. She really is a piece of work, and I find myself wondering if I could talk her into meeting up with me later. Hard to figure out how to start that conversation without coming off like a possibly dangerous weirdo, though, so I table the idea for the moment. I finish my last bite of eggs and give the pancakes a poke, but my stomach lets out a warning rumble. Doug finishes his waffle, drains his water glass, and leans back in his chair.

"So," he says. "I suppose you're wondering why I asked you here today."

I actually was not wondering that at all. I look at him expectantly.

"The answer," he says finally, "is that I have a proposition for you."

I raise one eyebrow.

"Not the naked, sweaty kind of proposition," he continues. "The business kind."

I lean back and fold my arms across my chest.

"I have some documents," he says. "I need you to review them for me. They're . . . outside my expertise."

"You mean not related to donkey porn?"

"No," he says. "Not related to donkey porn, or monkey porn, or monkey-on-donkey porn. Technical documents. I think they're close to your area of expertise, but I'm not sure. If they're not, just delete them, and I'll find somebody else."

"You're not sure because you don't know what's in the documents? Or because you swap to kitten cage-fighting videos every time I try to talk to you about my work?"

"Can't it be both?"

I sigh.

"I'm sure it is, Doug. Fine. What file sizes are we talking about?"

He shrugs.

"A couple of terabytes, I'm guessing mixed media. Shouldn't take more than a day or two to go through it, but unless you're a lot better informed than you've led me to believe, you'll probably need to do a fair amount of background digging as well."

I pull out my phone, and make a show of checking my calendar. Truth is, I have absolutely nothing going on.

"Great," I say. "I've got finals coming up, but I can probably get to it after that. What's the rate?"

"The what?"

"The consulting rate. What are you going to pay me for this?"

He looks genuinely startled.

"Pay? Come on, Anders. I thought we were friends."

I roll my eyes and wait for the laugh, but it's not coming.

"I understand that you're the cheapest cyborg on Earth," I say finally, "but did you or did you not just say that this was a business proposition?"

"Yeah," he says. "But I didn't mean the paying kind of business."

I close my eyes, and massage my temples again. The headache had been receding, but it's coming back now with a vengeance.

"Just to clarify," I say. "Is someone paying you to decipher these files?"

He manages to look offended.

"That's kind of personal, isn't it?"

"But you expect me to spend several days doing the actual work for you, for free."

He looks up at the ceiling and sighs.

"Well sure, it sounds bad if you put it that way."

"So let me put it this way instead: I bill out at six hundred an hour."

He shrugs.

"Fair enough. When can you get back to me with some answers?"

Considering that Doug didn't blink at my pulled-from-my-ass consulting rate, I'm feeling like I can spring for a cab to get back home. The car drops me off a little after two. I climb the six steps up to the stoop, and dig in my pockets for my keys. In addition to living next to a drug lab, I live in the only house left in Baltimore that doesn't have electronic entry. I'm about to let myself in when the door jerks open, and Gary pulls me into a full-body hug.

"Where were you last night?" he wails, and crushes his face against my chest. "I waited and waited, but you never came home."

I push my way inside, pull the door closed behind me and pat him on the head.

"Sorry, honey." I say. "I meant to call, but I was busy having sex with a prostitute. I hope you don't mind."

He laughs and lets me go.

"I figured as much. You smell like a Dumpster. Also, rent transfers tomorrow. Can you cover, or do I need to add it to your tab?"

"No," I say. "I'm good. I'll push it tonight."

I start upstairs. I want a shower and a nap before I start thinking about not taking a look at Doug's files.

"Hey," Gary says. "Somebody named Dimitri stopped by looking for you this morning. Do we know a Dimitri?"

I keep climbing.

"So many Dimitris," I say. "Russian hit man Dimitri? Ballet dancer Dimitri? Dancing bear Dimitri? What did he look like?"

I turn the corner at the landing. Gary's still talking, but I'm no longer listening. I peel off my shirt and drop it in the hallway, step into the bathroom and turn on the shower. As I turn to close the door, I'm surprised to see Gary standing at the top of the stairs.

"Seriously," he says. "This guy was definitely not a dancer and probably not a bear, and he seemed kind of torqued when I told him you weren't here."

I kick off my shoes and drop my pants.

"I don't know anybody named Dimitri. What did he look like?"

"Six feet, kinda stocky. Black hair. Brushy little beard. Pretty serious accent. Ukrainian maybe?"

This is not ringing any bells.

"Look," I say. "I've got nothing. I'll think about it, and if I come up with anything I'll ping you. Good enough?"

I close the door without waiting for an answer.

I spend ten minutes washing, then another fifteen

letting the hot water steam the rest of the alcohol out of my system. I shut off the water, and by the time I'm finished toweling off, I feel like I could curl up and sleep on the bathroom floor. I collect my clothes and chuck them into the wicker hamper. As I do, my phone drops out of my pants and bounces off the tile. It pings when it sees that it has my attention. I've got a voice-only. I pick up the phone and acknowledge. It's from Terry.

"Hey," she says. "I heard you might have had a visitor this morning. Sorry."

"I did," I reply. "Can you elaborate?"

"Sorry, no. I'm a limited-interactive. Terry has authorized you for direct access, however. Would you like me to attempt connection?"

Just as well, I guess. I hate talking to fully interactive avatars. I get that they're just simulations, that they don't really have thoughts and hopes and dreams and whatnot, but the good ones have been able to pass the Turing test for a while now, and deleting them has always felt weirdly murder-ish to me. No such problem with the LIs, though. They're just annoying.

"No," I say. "Don't ping Terry now. I'll get back to her later. Delete."

Whatever this Dimitri thing is, I don't feel much like dealing with it at the moment. I open the door. Steam pours out into the hallway. My room is to the left, Gary's is to the right. He's sitting on his bed staring into space, either stroked out or watching something on his ocular. One eye focuses on me.

"Hey," he says. "Towel, maybe?"

I turn into my room and shut the door behind me, drop the phone on my nightstand and fall into bed.

I have a recurring dream where I'm downtown, wandering around the mess just north of the harbor in the middle of the night. I have a car, which I do not in real life, but I can't remember where I parked it, and the streets keep changing names and directions until I don't recognize anything. I usually wind up getting chased around by somebody. This time, it's a bear in a tutu who keeps yelling at me to stay away from his girlfriend. He corners me in a blind alley. I'm standing on top of a Dumpster, scrabbling at the brick wall of the building behind it, waiting for his bear teeth to sink into my ass, when I snap awake. The late afternoon sun is slanting through the window, and I'm soaked with sweat.

I'll later learn that while I was napping, the good citizens of Hagerstown, Maryland, more or less simultaneously crapped their pants and died.

ABOUT THE AUTHOR

EDWARD ASHTON lives with his adorably mopey dog, his inordinately patient wife, and a steadily diminishing number of daughters in Rochester, New York, where he studies new cancer therapies by day, and writes about the awful things his research may lead to by night. He is the author of *Three Days in April*, as well as several dozen short stories which have appeared in venues ranging from the newsletter of an Italian sausage company to *Louisiana Literature* and *Escape Pod*. You can find him online at edward-ashton.com.

Discover great authors, exclusive offers, and more at hc.com.